THE SEAT OF POWER

Books by James D. Horan

FICTION

King's Rebel

Seek Out and Destroy

The Shadow Catcher

The Seat of Power

NONFICTION

Action Tonight: The Story of the Destroyer O'Bannon

Desperate Men

Desperate Women

The Pinkerton Story (with Howard Swiggett)

Confederate Agent

Pictorial History of the Wild West (with Paul Sann)

Mathew Brady: Historian with a Camera

Across the Cimarron

The Wild Bunch

The D.A.'s Man

The Mob's Man

The Great American West

C.S.S. Shenandoah: The Memoirs of Lieutenant Commanding
   James I. Waddell

The Desperate Years

THE SEAT OF POWER

by James D. Horan

CROWN PUBLISHERS, INC.
NEW YORK

This story never happened; its people never lived. Only the city, cold, ruthless, beautiful, is real. And Harlem's shortcut fuse.

bW

For Gertrude—now more than ever

CONTENTS

. . . and therefore as Chief Executive of the State of New York, I hereby direct you to conduct a free and impartial investigation of all crime and official corruption in the County of New York, State of New York, and I hereby further direct you to allow nothing to impede or distract you from investigating any individual, groups, corporations or associations occupying a corrupt seat of power in your community.

EXECUTIVE ORDER NUMBER 75
(signed) *Desmond Russell*
Governor, State of New York

It would not be an exaggeration to say that the American people, in the vast majority, are shocked by the refusal of the New York officials to expose the political criminals who have been involved with gangsters. The Soviet Union has fought hard against the maklak and the bribe taker. Unlike the American public, Soviet citizens have always condemned bribery or contribution to bribery. The closer the Peoples of the Soviet Union approach Communism, the higher will be the wave of resentment against predatory people of any kind. The citizens of New York must end their self-complacency, or such criminals and public officials will continue to commit their misdeeds for a long time.

—From a front-page editorial in *Pravda*.

BOOK ONE

THE INFORMER

[1]

ANYONE WITH A dime can call a newspaper. For the tenth part of a dollar, as the barkers used to say, you can praise, damn, criticize, smile with, cry over, even share your final thoughts before slipping into eternity. It's slightly terrifying to realize that there are not many places left in the world where for a dime you can sneer at your head of state, curse your Congress for a pack of pinheads, solemnly advise the UN—the world if need be.

One night I asked a man why he had called. After a pause he said: "You're a newspaper, aren't you? I called because you're there."

I guess that sums it up: we're always there, the Big Listener, bored maybe, but always listening. And, brother, in this town listening is a big part of living.

Believe it or not, there are cycles in telephone calls. If you know a newspaperman or a New York cop, check this: on a full moon the calls increase. There are the "ray people," who beg us to investigate the origin of the unbearable rays that are turning their brains to mush, their feet to red-hot coals. They usually insist their tormentors are J. Edgar Hoover, the FBI, the Secret Service, or the White House. Then there's the shrill middle-aged woman who demands the name of the editorial writer who obviously is a card-carrying member of the Communist Party; the man or woman contemplating suicide. This is the kind really on the brink; one wrong word and they can be pushed over.

Then there are the offbeat calls, like the frantic Staten Island zoo-keeper who phoned late one Sunday night to say he needed a rare serum

3

for a child who had just been bitten by a coral snake. It took countless calls to help the police locate the curator—he was out playing bridge—in time to stave off the creeping paralysis before it stopped that young heart.

For a change of pace there's the three-hundred-pounder who claims she was raped by "men of color," and insists on whispering all the intimate details.

In between there are the normal callers who want to know what happened to the crossword puzzle, accidentally dropped by a harassed news editor; the indignant fan who discovered the pro football score pied; the chairman of the local heart drive who would like to have a photographer assigned to the dinner-dance—it's always the biggest, the most important.

A bored deskman or copyboy listens and gives the proper replies; the callers are never insulted, brushed off, or ignored. Cranks or crackpots, they still represent the mysterious outside, the vague army of faceless readers who apparently gobble up newspapers from the weather report under the masthead to the last classified ad.

There's another reason: this call may be the big one that every newspaper hopes to get. The authentic tipster, the informer, the cold, calculating man or woman ready to betray wife, husband, lover, partner, colleague, friend, and enemy. The motivations are commonplace, and as old as man: hate, revenge, money. Sometimes love.

I look for hate and love. The greedy make me suspicious, I've found them to play both ends against the middle. While you're paying them they're bargaining with the very people they intend to sell out. A sudden, even soul-shaking desire for revenge can evaporate overnight. After the booze has worn off and the false courage has dissipated, the injured informer begins to wonder if it's really worth the trouble. On the second trip you can feel him beginning to hedge. ("Actually, I didn't really hear him say he paid the commissioner the dough. Actually, the guy who works in accounting told me . . .")

Actually. Actually. You sigh and toss the notes into the waste-paper basket.

No, I'll take hate; the kind that is almost tangible, like molten venom. This kind hones the ax lovingly with one desire—to destroy. Their voices have tumbled the highest justices, sent national leaders to jail, swayed elections, destroyed political hopes, saved the innocent from prison, exposed fantastic frauds, even changed history . . . all because a man in a newspaper office picked up a telephone.

As I did one winter's day in my cubbyhole west of Financial and east of Drama, in the office of the New York *Blade-Leader*, New York's fourth big afternoon. Looking back, I can't help but feel that a deadly, capricious fate was responsible, for if that phone had rung five minutes later I would have been gone. As it was, I had my coat on, my desk was locked, and I was on my way out when it went off. To hell with it, I thought. I was in the midst of an investigation and was late for an appointment in the Municipal Building—but something made me pause, something that turned me around and pointed me back to my desk.

"I would like to speak to Malloy—Duke Malloy."

I never forgot that hard, cold voice. A few years before—with my help—it had led to the biggest shake-up in the history of the New York City Police Department.

Action Jackson, indispensable member of Harlem's numbers mob. Trusted by the East Side syndicate. I could almost see the impassive gambler's face and the unconscious, nervous habit he had of arching his neck.

I always try to sound casual in guessing their identities; it throws even the best offguard, and you have an immediate advantage.

"How are you, Action? It's been a long time."

"Jeez! You recognized me, kid."

"I'd recognize your voice in a minute. The last time you called it was to break a date."

He chuckled. "I didn't know how far I could trust you, kid. I thought maybe you might bring the law along with you that night."

"I told you I never betray an informant."

"I figgered you newspaper guys will do anything for a story."

"You've seen too many late shows, Action." I tried to sound hurt, to corral all the advantage I could. I knew Jackson wanted something, and eventually there would be some horse trading.

"What the hell, you got enough headlines to last you a month," he said. "Your goddam stories cost a couple of captains their jobs and you even shook up the man in the Hall! And didn't you get some kind of award? I bet the phony paper even gave you a raise."

"Well," I said, "it's all water under the bridge."

"Look, kid, you want another one?" I could hear the mouth come closer to the receiver.

"How big?"

"So big I don't know if that phony sheet of yours can handle it."

"This paper has handled a few big ones in its day," I said. "A little bigger than that tinhorn numbers racket you work for."

There was an edge to his voice. "Maybe you're not interested."

I stopped playing games: Action Jackson was no fool.

"I'm interested. When do you want to meet?"

"This afternoon at four. Where do you want to make it?"

"The Automat across from the Library. Where we met the last time."

"Christ! You can find more creep joints!"

"You want to meet in a bar where some snoop is leaning in your J&B?"

"Okay. Okay. Four o'clock in your creep joint."

There was a click; he was never one for amenities.

Well, I met Action Jackson that wintry afternoon in the Automat across from the Fifth Avenue Library. A lot of awards, citations, honors have told how well we served our community, yes, even our country. As for me, I don't think I want any more of what goes with that service: the battered hulk of what had once been a man hanging from a meathook in the hard white glare of the searchlights of the Emergency Squad; that terrible hour of decision in the strange place called Torytown on the ridge of a Jersey mountain, an hour and a half from Times Square; the frightened man who kept asking bitterly if I was ready to give him protection for the rest of his life, as the woman who had just killed for him gently comforted him; the man who they said was the absolute lord of the underworld in this country, crawling from table to table while impassive assassins picked him off inch by inch; the frightened kid in a southern fishing camp looking down at that terrible diary and saying over and over he couldn't believe that the man he always called Uncle was the most evil man in the country; to say nothing of a striking, aristocratic woman with gray in her hair and iron in her bones who left us out on the longest limb in the world. . . .

If all that goes with serving our community, I'd say it's one hell of a price.

And unforgettable as those moments were, they're wiped out completely by the memory of a savage, howling mob roaming through the streets of Harlem, inflamed by a madman, and, like all mobs, blind to kin, color, or cause. Its chant of "Kill Whitey . . . kill Whitey . . ." echoed for months in the Kremlin, Whitehall, and Washington, while angry and bewildered Americans searched their souls for the reason why.

One brief call. But it was the stone tossed; the ripples followed. . . .

Yet something fine and decent also emerged for me out of those terrible months—the friendship of three men, who could not be more unrelated in personal philosophy, background, ambitions.

A hard-jawed cop whose honesty has made him a legend among the thieves in the ranks of what has been laughingly described as "New York's Finest"; a young prosecutor who I once wagered could be seduced by the cheapest of magistrate's jobs; and a frail man who believed, perhaps naïvely, that American newspapers, big and small, should serve their communities, fairly, objectively, and above all with courage.

It is in tribute to them that I am writing this story when the facts are still clear and not blurred by myth, legend, and natural distortion of time.

Let's begin when the paper was blank, the day I met Action Jackson.

[2]

I HAVE ALWAYS liked the impersonal air of the Automat. Authentic New Yorker–*Homo Manhattaniens* use it not only for a rapid-transit dining room but also as a meeting and conference room. The one across from City Hall invariably sports a few fat politicians shaping the destiny of the city, while the Times Square branch crawls with bookmakers and press agents. One thing the Automat supplies that other restaurants do not is anonymity. Eisenhower, Truman, or LBJ weaving through the noontime crowd with loaded trays probably would have one devil of a time finding a table.

I brought my coffee to one of the tables in the rear, all but deserted at that hour. I didn't have to wait long. Promptly at four Action was there, carefully folding his coat over a vacant chair. I hid a smile; he was careful to expose the Finchley label. He was wearing an English tab and at least a five-dollar tie.

"I hope you have a few hours, kid."

"I have all night if you're interesting."

He stared at me for a long moment, then said softly: "I think you'll find it interesting. I'll be back in a minute."

As I watched him walk to the coffee spout, I felt a quickening, a brief eagerness. I was beginning to believe that Jackson might be ready to deliver something big. Back at the table he sipped at the coffee, arched his neck as if his collar were too tight in his telltale sign of nervous tension, and studied me.

"Those were good stories you did a few years ago on those government houses. The D.A. got anything on 'em?"

He was referring to a series I had done on a government bonding

8

group. They resigned when the story broke, and the deal never came off.

He made a circle with his spoon. "What would they have cleaned?"

"If the deal had come through? Two hundred, perhaps three hundred thousand in fees . . . maybe more."

"Chicken feed," Action said softly.

"Not bad for a few hours' work." I moved cautiously. "You have anything better?"

Action stared at a man carrying a tray who was hovering near our table. The cold blue eyes unsettled him enough so he moved to a far-off table.

"Let me ask you something, kid," he said. "Who would you say is the boss—the top boss in the whole country?"

"Of course you're referring to the rackets," I asked.

"What the hell do you think I'm talking about—politics? They do their own stealing."

"Well, Vito Gennaro," I said. "The Department of Justice has said it, Treasury, the local cops. You name it."

He leaned forward. "But they haven't been able to get anything on him, right?"

"The last time he did time was more than twenty years ago. He knows one more conviction makes him a three-time loser. Then it's life."

He twisted the tiny cover of the saltshaker loose, then tightened it and put it back on the revolving tray.

"I'm going to deliver Gennaro to you, kid," he said softly. "Runners, drops, comptrollers, banks, and cops."

I could feel my lips go dry.

He looked up. "Interested?"

"I'd be lying if I said I wasn't. But square with me, Action—what ax are you grinding this time?"

The words were rough and cold as a saw going through ice.

"I want Gennaro busted—all the way."

"You planning to take over?"

"Before he's busted I'll be out of here."

"You didn't answer my question."

"The answer is No. I want no part of his action. Let it go for grabs."

"What about the syndicate? They'll be back in action the next day."

For the first time he smiled. "Kid, there won't be any syndicate after you get through with them."

I fought back the mounting excitement and tried to horse-trade.
"Why?"

"Do you have to know?"

"You weren't exactly aboveboard the last time."

"Last time it was business. Let's say it's personal this time."

I took a long chance. "I'm sorry, Action. I have to know the whole
story or it's no deal."

He brooded for a moment, toying with his spoon.

"I don't know what the hell's the difference, but if you insist."
He added harshly, "This isn't part of the record, kid."

"It's a deal. Let me get some coffee."

I didn't particularly want any coffee but I did want Jackson to
settle down, and besides, that short walk to the coffee spout gave me a
chance to collect my thoughts.

When I returned, Action went into his story immediately. He
spoke low, deliberately.

"Last time we had a drink I told you my score, a few heists when I
was a kid, no strong-arm stuff, mostly gambling. I've been in policy
since the Dutchman took over in the thirties. In fact, it was Bernie
Rosenkrantz, Schultz's guy, who put me on as a runner." He took a
sip. "I had a knack for getting the guys to hustle, so they gave me a
drop. This was good for fifty a week, which was a hell of a lot better
than the WPA.

"After I got out of the army I went back in numbers. During the
war some of the shines who got Section 8's or 4F's had moved in and
taken over—"

"Who was in charge before the war?"

He waved his hand. "The wops on the East Side. East Harlem.
Trigger Mike and some of the others. All Moustache Petes. After the
war the young Turks started to take over. Remember Valachi?"

"The big-time stoolie on TV?"

"The same. The Feds put some heat on the mobs for a while after
that, but nobody can do anything about them; they're big business, like
U.S. Steel. They're here to stay."

"They went back into action after Valachi?"

He gave me a look of contempt. "They never got out of action.
Maybe a little quieter but they are there—every minute of your goddam
life, and don't forget it."

"Okay. Get back to Harlem."

"Easy, kid. I'm with you." He pushed aside the cold cup of coffee.
"After the old Dons retired, the Wop really took over—"

"The Wop. You mean Vito Gennaro?"

He sighed. "There's only one wop in the U.S., kid—Vito Gennaro. Junk. Broads. Business. Numbers. Bookies. You name it. He's the boss."

"Go on."

"The Wop had some of his guys toss a few shines in the river, and they got the message. They stepped down. Some we kept on as runners and comptrollers."

I held up a hand. "We?"

"Yeah." He gave me an impassive look. "We. I was called over to see the Wop. He gave me a big hello and broke out the J&B. I told him to cut the carny and get down to the nuts of it. I told him he needed me more than I needed him. He agreed, and we sat down to talk. He told me there had been a meeting in some tank town in the Middle West and he was now top man. He said he had the cops and the politicians who counted in his vest pocket."

I said quickly, "Did he say which politicians?"

"Let's not get ahead of the story, kid," he said. "Let's take it chapter and verse. Okay?"

"Fine," I said. "Go ahead."

He arched his neck, moved a saltshaker to one side, and continued:

"He said he knew I was the best man in numbers on the West Side and he wanted me to organize the operation. I was to locate the drops, pick the comptrollers, contact the cops, and pay them—" He waved his hand. "You know, put the whole thing on a business basis." He shrugged. "That's one thing about shines in the rackets; they can't organize. They get a few bucks, begin drinking Scotch and milk so they can make believe they're on Madison Avenue, put up a high yella, and that's the end of the racket until they're broke. . . ."

"And you took over?" I gently prompted.

"I took over the West Side." He added wryly, "For the East Side. I put things on a business basis. It took me more than five years, but the way I have it now—well, J. P. Morgan would approve." He carefully moved the saltshaker and the mustard jar in line.

I didn't interrupt or prompt; I knew what was coming—Jackson's motive for coming to see me.

"Now let's get to the ax I'm grinding," he said, and his voice was taut and bitter. "I come from a hick town named Lisa in Missouri. It's about fifty miles north of St. Louis. My old lady had a rundown farm. She died when I was five. I never knew my old man. There was only me and my sister, Jo. She was a good kid. I ran away when I was fifteen and bummed around the country before the war. Whenever I needed a few bucks, I would wire her. She would always send me what she could. Then when I came to New York I just never wrote any more. One day I got a letter from Jo. I almost fell over. I hadn't heard from her in almost twenty years. It seems she married a lush whose liver finally fell apart. They had a daughter, who, from what she wrote, must have been a wild kid. That's why she wrote me; the kid had left home and was in New York. She wanted me to look her up and keep an eye on her."

"Where did you find her—in the Village?"

"No. In a fleabag on Forty-second Street. Ten minutes after she got off the bus in the Port Authority, a guy had picked her up. He was ready to set her up when Tilley and I got there—"

"Tilley?"

"My comptroller. A big shine I trust with my life. Tilley worked the bum over, and I brought her home with me and got the landlady to fix her up with a nice room. The wife of a bookie I know runs a small insurance place, and we got her a job as a file clerk. I even sent her to a secretarial school at night." The hand tightened around the shakers. "You know there are some dames that are born with something wrong with them, and there's not a thing you can do about it. This kid lived in a dream world. She swallowed every phony tale a guy told her. Once a guy picked her up in a bus and told her he was a movie producer and was going to put her in a movie. It took me a week to find her—in a riding academy off Times Square. The bum didn't have a nickel. After Tilley and I worked him over, he admitted he was a lush worker from Detroit! Twice I sent her back to Missouri. Each time she got off the bus and wound up in Times Square."

He took out an expensive wallet, searched through it for a moment, then threw a snapshot on the table. It was a fuzzy picture of a young girl with a thin, sober-looking woman. The girl was smiling and looked attractive even through the blur.

"That's Jo and the kid," he said. He slid the picture back into the wallet. "The last time I really told her off—once more and I would take her back to Missouri myself. She went back to the job and to school." He carefully examined his highly lacquered, manicured nails. "Don't get me wrong, kid; she was no virgin-sturgeon. But she was Jo's kid. . . ."

There was silence a minute, as silent as it ever gets in the Automat. Then he continued:

"Everything was going along all right until the night Frank the Sheik delivered some holdover numbers. I don't know if you remember your policy, kid, but holdovers are the adding-machine tapes—the ribbons—and the day's play. They send the ribbons and the slips back the day after, if some of the players insist they played the winning number.

You have to show them the slips and the tapes to convince them they are wrong."

"I know about the holdovers, Action," I said, "but Frank the Sheik's new to me."

"He drives the ribbon car for Gennaro. He was a pimp upstate and served two to five on a Fed rap before he came to New York. I think his old man knew Gennaro in Italy." He twisted his head slowly from side to side, and his voice became cold and bitter. "He's a con merchant with women. The son of a bitch wouldn't pass up a snake. He's a pimp for the East Side. Every time they want a dame for a circus, they call him." He abruptly stood up. "I'm going to get some coffee. Want any?"

"Okay. Get me a cup."

I watched Jackson weave in and out the thickening crowd—a man obviously under a strain. His face was tight, his lips thin when he sat down. He stirred the coffee, sipped it.

"Two weeks after he met her that night he brought over the holdovers, she took a powder. I didn't know it then, but she was shacking up with Frank the Sheik. Tilley sent out word, but this time there was no sign of her. I guess the reason was the shines are not allowed to cross Fifth Avenue, at least the numbers guys. That's strictly Wop territory. That's why they have the Sheik or one of the other Italians drive the ribbon and money cars over to the West Side.

"I didn't hear from the kid for about a month. Then one night about eleven o'clock I got a call from Harlem Hospital. She was over there with two black eyes, her teeth knocked out, and her stomach kicked to mush. She lasted three days. The doctors said her spleen had been busted by the kicks. Then Tilley heard the story from one of the young wops. It seemed the Sheik tried to set her up in a joint. When she tried to leave, he belted her. She lasted a week, and then they staged a circus with her and some whores for the East Side. She tried to run out, and the Sheik gave it to her but good. He said she made him look like a fool in front of the Dons." He sipped the coffee and then pushed the cup to one side. "Gennaro was at that party. The bastard!"

He stared down at his hands. "I waited until the Sheik came over. It took a few weeks. I guess he wanted to test the wind." The thin lips curled. "He got the wind. I was behind the door with a jack handle. I cracked his skull. Tilley was in the john and came running out. He said I had the Sheik on the floor and was coming down with the handle with both hands when he caught me. He said none of the guys in the drop would touch me." He stared at me. "Do you know, kid, I never knew what happened after that bastard came in? I never knew . . ."

"Did you kill him?" I asked.

"No. He spent three weeks in the hospital. For a while they thought they'd have to put a plate in his head."

"What about Gennaro?"

"A few days after I belted the Sheik I got a call from the East Side to come over and see the Wop. I wanted to take a heater, but Tilley talked me out of it. This was one time a shine crossed the Avenue. Tilley was packing a shiv nine feet long, and told the two punks who met us at the front door that if I wasn't down in an hour he was coming back with half of Harlem.

"Well, I saw the Wop. He didn't act mad. He just said it was one of those things. He claimed he didn't know the girl was my niece. He said he was very sorry but he also couldn't afford to have any fights in the organization. He said that if he heard me or the Sheik tangled again, he would take care of us. He said he knew how valuable I was, but no matter how valuable I was the organization was all-important . . ."

"In other words he will have you killed if you try to touch the Sheik again?"

He gave me a startled look. "What the hell do you think he was talking about?"

"Was that all he said?"

He shook his head, and his eyes, normally cold, almost glittered with hate.

"No, it wasn't. He took out a roll and counted off five C notes. He gave them to me and said I should give them to the girl's mother for her trouble." He spat the words through clenched teeth. "For her trouble! That lousy wop bastard!" He leaned close to me. "I took the money and walked out. I told Tilley to blow and I walked all that afternoon. The first church I came to, I went in and stuffed the bills into the poor box. Then I went back to the drop and back to business. From the moment he handed me that dough, I swore to get Gennaro. It goes without saying, that includes the Sheik."

Slowly, savagely, he rolled a napkin into a tight ball.

"I want Gennaro busted. Drop, collectors, the bank. You said it: with any kind of a case he'll be a three-time loser. That's life under the Baumes law. But there's another thing: publicity. For his grandchildren's sake he avoids it like poison. That time down in Washington before the committee on TV almost killed him. He'll go nuts in stir thinking of those kids and all that dough going down the drain." He rolled the paper across the table and watched it fall to the floor. "In six months he'll be in psycho."

"And the Sheik?"

"I paid a stoolie two C's for the name of the parole officer the Sheik's paying. I know the company that has him listed as a salesman. I also know he carries a rod in a shoulder holster when he delivers the ribbon and the money to our drop. That should make him a good candidate for a long stretch up the river. A parolee carrying a rod!" The blue eyes studied me. "That's one bum I want you to make something of in your stories. That parole officer is an old nervous guy; if somebody puts the screws on him he'll blow the whistle on the Sheik. Just make sure he gets a lot of publicity, and the mob will throw him to the wolves. They don't want anyone around who attracts publicity. That only means trouble."

The cold-blooded plan made me uneasy. "Gennaro has an enormous amount of political pull. Maybe he can get himself off."

He shrugged. "I give you Gennaro, kid; you put him away."

"How can I guarantee you a judge will send him away?"

"The word's been out for months the politicos don't want any trouble this year. Even the cops on the pad have been saying that. You put enough heat on Gennaro, and the old Dons will trade him in fast. We're not stupid uptown. Everybody knows D.C. is depending on McShane's boys."

The name caught me off guard. "McShane? Big Jim McShane?"

Jackson looked around quickly.

"Take it a little easy, will you? What's the matter, you want the whole place to know—"

"Okay," I said. "Okay. You just shook me up a bit. I thought you said Jim McShane."

A veil dropped over his eyes. He nodded slowly.

"I said McShane, kid. You know I did."

I tried to remain impassive but I'm not so good at that Indian stuff; if I'm surprised I show it. After all, Jackson was talking about the man who, it was said—and I never doubted it—could get the President of the United States on the phone. Just what did Action Jackson have to do with someone this powerful?

But Jackson wasn't biting. He looked blank. "Look, kid, I go as high as Gennaro."

"Is McShane in this setup?"

"I give you Gennaro and you take it from there."

"Just say Yes or No—is McShane in Gennaro's setup?"

He arched his neck and peered over my shoulder.

"Remember, kid, we haven't made a deal . . ."

"Let's say Gennaro is busted and gets five to ten."

He shook his head vigorously. "Oh, no, kid, no five to ten— Gennaro's a three-time loser. After the jury comes in, they throw away the key—"

"When he knows that they have thrown away the key will he talk?"

"That's one thing I like about you, Duke," he said with a sudden grin. "You're always trying. How the hell can I tell you if Gennaro will blow the whistle?"

"Give me an educated guess."

He leaned forward slightly. "Wait a minute. Hold the phone. What I want to make sure of, kid, do you get my pitch on Gennaro and the Sheik?"

"You want blood, right?"

"All they got," he said. "Every goddam ounce."

"The setup will be the same as last time, Action?"

He nodded. "I give you all the dope and you blow the stories— just like the last time. You tip the cops before your paper comes out, and they knock off the banks and the drops. The cops are heroes," he said wryly. "They'll really hate your guts for turning off their graft, but your newspaper will get the headlines."

"For your own information, Action," I pointed out quietly, "this stuff doesn't sell an extra paper. Believe it or not, it's our job."

He shrugged. "Personally, I couldn't care less. I just have a big hate that has to be taken care of. How it's done I don't care." He toyed with the mustard jar, then said softly, "You interested, kid?"

I hesitated only for a moment—but that was enough for Jackson.

Carefully he slid the jar back and started to rise. "It's been nice seeing you. One of these days—"

I held him back in his chair. "Where are you going?"

"Don't stall, kid," he said, his eyes cold and flat as a snake's. "What's the word?"

"Of course I'm interested," I said, "but I don't own the paper. Before we go into a project this big, I have to have the green light from downstairs."

"Who's the guy with the green light?" he asked.

"The publisher. He makes the decisions on the big ones."

Jackson said blandly, "So you go down and see this joker and have him switch on the green light."

"That may be tough. He died last month."

The thin lips barely moved. "Come on, kid, give me some real answers."

"A new publisher will be here very shortly, surely before Christmas. The rumor factory has a man named Julian Savage taking over—"

"Savage? Where does he come from?"

"From a Midwest paper. He's supposed to be the son-in-law of the owner."

"He doesn't sound like much," Jackson said glumly. "Relatives are usually foul balls in a big job."

"I'm inclined to agree with you," I said. "But old man Dolbar is as tough as Gennaro when it comes to losing money, so perhaps he might see something in Savage."

"So when Savage comes around you just ask him if he's interested," Jackson said. "Hell, he wants headlines to sell your crummy sheet, doesn't he?"

He was starting to get under my skin, but I bit my tongue. I realized that Jackson was obviously under a tremendous strain and had taken all kinds of risks even seeing me. And besides, my instinct told me he really had something big.

"I haven't the slightest idea what this man wants to do with the paper," I said. "He may be the type of publisher who doesn't want to rock the boat. Maybe he plays local politics. Perhaps he's a bug on typography. Or he may regard the editorial department as a necessary evil and worship advertising. Who knows?"

Jackson stared at the rapidly filling room. After a long moment he said: "Let's leave it this way, kid: I'll give you ten days. If your green-light man doesn't make the scene by that time, we'll forget it. Okay?"

"Where can I call you?"

A thin smile. "You might try me at the Waldorf Towers. The President could use a little advice these days. Tilley and I figger we can help out . . ."

"Okay, comedian," I said. "You call me."

He reached over and gathered up the two-hundred-dollar Finchley.

"One thing you left out, Action," I said, trying to sound casual. "What's that?"

"Do you have proof?"

He slid into his coat, arched his neck, then bent down to whisper in my ear.

"Kid, I have everything but movies. If we make a deal I'll guarantee the noise you make will shake up this goddam city like it has never been shaken. And that includes a couple of big jokers down in Washington."

He straightened, gave me an amused look, then joined the stream of men and women disappearing out the revolving door.

Now that he was gone, my mind raced back to McShane. Big Jim McShane. I was so engrossed I put two dimes in the coffee slot until a man tapped me on the shoulder and pointed to the sign—two nickels. Back at the table I never drank the coffee. I just stirred and remembered: Big Jim McShane and the kid in the Brooklyn Supreme Court.

It went back more than ten years and involved a paragraph I had written about a political Flatbush hack McShane was grooming to be the new district leader. The machine was playing up this character's wartime record on the orders of McShane, and by the time it got to the desk of the political writers he was a guerrilla leader who had set out personally to avenge the Bataan Death March.

My part started with an innocent call one Saturday night just before I had finished my weekend political column. The caller was a kid who worked in Brooklyn Supreme Court, and was indignant as hell. The hack's war story was a phony; far from being a guerrilla, he was a member of the company band. I verified it with Washington and used the story. The *News* picked it up for a tongue-in-cheek story for page three, and that ended it.

I never knew what happened until months later. McShane found out who tipped me the story, then went to work on the kid. First the word was quietly spread about in his department that he was a municipal informer, so no one would talk to him. A month later he was up on charges of irregular time slips—they docked him for fifteen minutes. Then a notorious drunk in his office was jumped over him for a promotion.

He was made to work one day in every long holiday weekend; he had to file a special slip for every item of petty cash—I found the last time this was done was twenty years before—and through a simple technicality he lost his seniority, a death blow to any municipal employee.

In six months this promising young municipal employee quit the city and left town.

Big Jim McShane really milked his revenge out of that one.

Typically, he never sent me a note of protest over my item or questioned its accuracy. It was correct, and he simply went to work on this kid in his own way.

From that day I knew that no matter how many Presidents he called by first name, McShane was vicious.

And now from the very depths Action Jackson had confirmed it.

[3]

Two days after I had met Action Jackson, Julian Savage appeared.
That was on Monday. By Wednesday we knew he was around. We
had a new advertising director, a new promotion head. On Friday the
word was, he had hired an outside typographical expert to revamp our
page one and install new type fonts, which was welcome news for
Editorial; we had been using type that was outmoded in Lincoln's day.

As the days passed the building buzzed with his activities; he
seemed to have his finger in almost every department. A virtual blizzard
of memos fell on the heads of all departments. The ones I read indicated
he was intelligent, curious, and impatient with incompetence. From
what I heard, when he sat down to discuss a subject he had a firm grasp
of details.

I had discussed Jackson's proposal with our managing editor,
Turner Elliott, who agreed I should write Savage a detailed memo.
Several times I sat down to write one, but curiously, for a man to whom
writing comes easily, I found it difficult without knowing the man I
was addressing it to.

Oh, I knew the facts, all right. He was the son-in-law of old Sam
Dolbar, who for years had been quietly buying up newspaper properties
around the country until he was a miniature Hearst and Scripps-
Howard.

Dolbar had been sniffing around New York City for a long time,
and the *Blade-Leader* was his grand entrance into big-city journalism.
The paper had been in the hands of the Miller family for almost a

19

hundred years; they had ignored the paper but disliked losing money. Dolbar managed to buy up some of the family's control, then successfully won a minority stockholder's suit. It was a break for the newspaper, for with the rising union wages, the increased costs of paper and ink, and the Miller family apathy, the *Blade-Leader* would have sunk out of sight within a few years. Dolbar had made it a practice never to interfere with the editorial operation of any paper he purchased —after he had installed the new publisher. But not really knowing the new publisher dried me up. I simply could not write to a stranger.

One day, it was Christmas week as I recall, Elliott called me over to his desk.

"I think you're going to like Savage, Duke. He looks like a crusader."

"Not all crusaders are likable, Mr, Elliott."

"How right you are," he said. "When I broke in on a western paper, we had the damnedest sin-chasing prosecutor you ever saw. I covered him a few years later entering the state pen. He had extorted money from roadhouses on the threat of prosecution. He was a fine-looking man—always reminded me of Harding."

"I'm foolish enough to believe we haven't been doing our crusading for headlines."

"That makes two of us, Duke. And from what I know of this new man downstairs, there may be three of us." Then he added: "When I was in his office this morning I saw a bundle of your clips on his desk. He liked that construction series you did on the state two years ago, said he hoped you had more like that. I told him you had one on the fire you'd like to discuss with him. He said he would call you."

A few days later Betty, his secretary, called and said I was to come down at three. When I walked into the office I knew changes had been made. Julian Savage's predecessor had been a good newspaperman and a fine publisher, but he belonged to the Edwardian Age. His office had been dark-paneled, the chairs stuffy and cumbersome, the few prints on the walls etchings of a cathedral and London in the eighties. Now it was newly painted, bright and cheerful with Herald Square in watercolor and a fine crayon of the Battery. The dull green carpet that had always reminded me of army tenting had been replaced by burnt orange wall to wall. Conspicuous behind his desk was a framed page one of the New York *World*.

Julian Savage was a slight, quiet man with questioning brown eyes. He appeared frail and good natured, yet I had the sense of inner toughness.

He stood up, and I was surprised to see he was no more than five eight and weighed almost nothing at all. The hands toying with the Blaisdell pencil were slender as a woman's. Like myself, he was in his mid-forties. He leaned over and offered his hand. It was lost in my big paw but there was strength in it.

"It's about time we said hello, Duke," he said, smiling.

"I'm always available, Mr. Savage."

"Look," he said softly, "I'm not going to have every copyboy in the shop calling me by my first name, but in our case suppose you make it Julian and I'll make it Duke." He grinned. "After all, we're going to the same party this afternoon."

This was a surprise. The D.A.'s Christmas party.

He held up the plain white card. "Last week I went to the swearing in of the new U.S. Attorney and the night before last had a drinking bout with that hack who's Attorney General. Do you know why?"

"Knowing both parties it certainly wasn't for their sparkling conversation," I said.

"Those idiots haven't read a book or seen a play since they went to college. I want to cultivate people like them for one reason only. They represent exclusive news to me. News that our competitors won't have." He opened a drawer and took out several envelopes of clips from our reference room. "I've read everything that's been written on Flaherty. He's had quite a career as prosecutor."

"He's been around," I said cautiously.

He eyed me for a moment. "I gather you don't believe everything you read in the papers, Duke."

"Reporters have been known to become somewhat enthusiastic over a favorite son. . . . I know I have myself on occasion."

"I notice from the clips you haven't thrown him any accolades."

"A few years ago I did an exposé on a building syndicate that was robbing the city on welfare cases——"

"I read it."

"I taped a telephone call from a crooked real-estate agent to a Fifth Avenue lawyer who represented the syndicate. I thought it should have been presented to the Grand Jury. Flaherty didn't. As a result, the Grand Jury indicted two little agents on misdemeanors, a few minor clerks in the Buildings Department were shifted around or kicked out, but no one really big was grabbed. I didn't think too much about it until almost a year later when a lawyer on that tape was named by the National Committee as the head of a fund-raising group for the campaign."

"Could be a coincidence."

I said bluntly, "There are no coincidences in politics."

"If you had such a good thing on this lawyer, why didn't you press it?"

"I wanted to, but your predecessor told me not to."

Savage stared down at the clips for a moment. "In other words my predecessor didn't have the guts."

"You said it—not me. Criticizing publishers isn't in my contract."

He opened a folder. "Speaking of contracts, yours comes up next month."

I took a deep breath. "I'm not sure I'm going to sign it."

He looked genuinely startled. "Oh? That's a surprise. May I ask why?"

"I've been with the paper twenty years. You remember what Hemingway said, 'If you stay in this business over three years you've been seduced.' I have some money saved and I thought I'd try my hand at some writing. I had a number of short stories published after the war."

" 'Capt'n Sam.' I could almost smell the jungle. It was Guadalcanal, wasn't it?"

"The Tenaru. I covered the campaign."

He slid my folder aside. "Well, let's leave that for the moment, Duke. I hope I can persuade you to stay on. After all, it's not every new publisher who finds the best investigative reporter in New York on his own staff."

"One of the best."

"Oh, there are others around, I know. But thanks to you this paper has brought about grand-jury investigations, produced presentments, changed laws, and really helped the community."

There was a lift in his voice and just the tinge of color in his cheeks.

"I may sound corny, Duke, but my hope is to make the *Blade-Leader* a newspaper for the people. I don't think it's enough for us to print the hard news. I believe we have to seek out the truth, illuminate evil and tyranny, even the petty kind, and make our community a better place to live in." He smiled at the clichés.

"A wonderful ambition, Julian . . ."

"Remember what Lippmann called the *World* the day it folded? 'Sword of the Press.' That's why I would like you to stick around, Duke."

I guess after twenty years the great phrases, the call to arms, just don't stir the blood as they once did. But I said I'd think it over.

He carefully pulled back the small white thread of the Blaisdell and unraveled the paper from the lead point. "I see that you have used a tape recorder quite extensively in your investigations."

"Fifteen years ago I did an interview with a politician who gave me chapter and verse on how his boss was juggling some city contracts. After it was printed he denied everything. It was his word against mine. Someone got to the Millers, and we printed a retraction. From that day on, I used a tape recorder in every investigation I have ever done."

"Is that how you nailed the supervisor in that hospital exposé you did a few years ago?"

"I received a tip he was selling hospital supplies to the highest bidder," I said. "I posed as a fast-buck guy from Connecticut who was opening a kids' camp and wanted some supplies. I taped three calls in which he gave me a price. He denied everything to the D.A. in Connecticut. He fell apart when they played the tapes."

"But I thought the Supreme Court outlawed taped phone conversations."

I explained, "The court in the Lopez decision says that if one party—that's me—agrees to allow his voice to be recorded, it is legal evidence."

He fanned out some clippings like a hand of cards.

"Highway exposé, hospitals, shylock racket, city asphalt kickback, parking-lot payoff, state payroll padding—the *Blade-Leader* can do a lot of boasting, Duke."

"This is a big city—there's a lot more to do. Take the subway situation, for example. Buy a token and run the gauntlet of muggers, rapists, and homicidal maniacs."

"How right you are, there's a lot to do and I want to do it." He picked up a clip. "I notice when you go into an investigation you more or less play a role." He glanced at the story. "In this parking-lot exposé you worked in a parking lot."

"For a week. I parked one hundred and fifty cars a day, seven days a week, ten hours a day. Not a scraped fender . . ." Frankly, any discussion of my work embarrassed me. It was finished, written. Now get on to something new.

"And that led to how they were paying off the fellow in the license bureau?"

"The boss of this lot was a matinee drinker. When he saw I could take over the lot so he could have his drinking time he got very chummy. One night he started to talk about payoffs. I was carrying a tape recorder, and the playback made very interesting dialogue."

"What do you do with the material when you have finished an investigation, Duke?"

"Any law-enforcement agency will work with a newspaper who gives them good information. Federal, state, the D.A.'s in any borough will make a deal. They get the case, we get the exclusive rights to all news, along with the knowledge we have done a public service."

The light blinked on the phone. He picked it up, listened for a moment, and sighed.

"I forgot I have a date to see this advertising joker," he said. "I'm trying to get the Cummings department store account. He was in my class, and maybe the old school ties will swing it." He glanced at the card. "What the devil time is this party?"

"Six to eight."

"Suppose I meet you downstairs at five-thirty? We can walk over."

I can recall how I walked back to my desk, slightly amused at the high-flown phrases and the stars in his eyes. Well, give him two months. The Mayor will court him over a confidential lunch at Gracie Mansion. The Majority Leader will gravely ask his opinion about an important bill. A judge will tip him to an important decision. Perhaps even the Governor will join him for a quiet drink and make a big show of telling him the real inside, which any alert Albany reporter would know. The advertisers will have him on their committees, and before long the edge of that bright, newly-honed sword will be dulled before it has had a chance to swing once in anger.

[4]

THE CHRISTMAS PARTY of Quinn Flaherty, District Attorney for the County of New York for the past twelve years, was the most exclusive in town. A politician who received an invitation considered it one notch below canonization; it was acknowledged as official confirmation of his standing as a public servant, that he had not been caught taking the Tammany oath, as the boys called it: right hand raised and left hand outstretched behind the back.

The party was also welcomed by political writers and sages who used it to predict with considerable accuracy the latest appointments or dismissals of the kingmakers just by checking cozy twosomes in secluded corners. I always felt that more important political deals were consummated at Flaherty's parties than at any other gathering of leading politicians. This year's party would be interesting; Flaherty's veteran head of his Racket Bureau had died, and I had heard he was considering appointing Johnny De Lorenzo, one of his young stars, to the post.

At first I found this hard to believe; De Lorenzo had gained some well-deserved fame by uncovering a huge interstate gambling conspiracy and battling doggedly through the courts to win long-term convictions. But Johnny was comparatively young, and while he came from one of the most respectable Italian families in New York City, studded with famous judges and lawyers, I couldn't see where Flaherty needed support from the Italian community. Then came the rumors that Bob Hoff, Flaherty's old friend and party press agent, was getting a leave of absence from his job as Deputy Commissioner of State Public Works to rejoin Flaherty, and the pieces slipped into place.

The Racket Bureau in the New York County District Attorney's office has always been a political time bomb. The man sitting on it never knows what day he will get a call from an informer in the Tombs, from a disgruntled city worker, a political foe with an ax to grind—willing to give information that could lead anywhere politically.

Flaherty needed an honest man for his Racket chief, but he also had to have one who wouldn't tip over any rocks. Not this year, when the man in the White House was going to run again. With the bad goof in the Middle East and the shocking deal involving his secretary and the five-million-dollar oil lease, the party just couldn't stand another major scandal.

I explained all this to Julian as we walked across City Hall Park and bucked the winds of Foley Square.

"Why should Hoff appear on the scene now?"

"With the presidential election coming up," I told him, "the word I get is that Washington wants things nice and quiet in the city. They don't want any scandal. Nothing to disturb the electorate. It's going to be tough enough getting the vote out for the man in the White House this time. The administration is going to depend heavily on New York."

"And to keep things nice and quiet?"

"Flaherty has been D.A. longer than FDR was President. He's had it; he wants out. He hopes the next step will be right into the Court of Appeals."

"Has he been promised this?"

"There's no proof, if that's what you mean. But the same unimpeachable source tells me he will get the appointment if he doesn't rock the boat. You saw what happened to the rent scandal that was brewing last month. Flaherty indicted a few ratty landlords, then got the Mayor to appoint a four-man board to conduct a year's investigation. Their report will come out after Election Day."

"So Hoff will be there to backstop him?"

"Exactly. When you meet him, Julian, don't sell him short. He looks like he's falling asleep on his feet—up in Albany where Flaherty got him a job after Hoff split up with his wife the boys still call him Sleepy Bob—but Hoff knows more about New York City politics and has the locations of more buried bodies than all the legislative correspondents put together."

Savage shook his head.

"I still don't see how he fits in with young De Lorenzo, Duke."

"If Hoff shows up today at Flaherty's party, it means the return of the prodigal," I explained. "With Hoff back on the D.A.'s payroll, Flaherty can put a five-year-old child in the Rackets job. Hoff won't let anyone in the office make any wrong moves."

"But Flaherty wouldn't abdicate completely . . ."

"You haven't been reading your own paper, boss," I said cheerfully. "We had a piece on page one last week that Flaherty's been appointed by the President as one of the five U.S. representatives to that big UN conference on narcotics in Geneva. He's going to be over there for some time."

He seemed genuinely embarrassed. "I do remember now—it was a White House announcement on Thursday. You mean to tell me Flaherty and Hoff are that close. How did they meet?"

"In the late thirties I think it was. Hoff was covering the U.S. Attorney's office, Eastern District, and writing a political roundup for the Saturday paper. Flaherty was a young assistant in those days. As I heard the story, Flaherty was assigned to a minor dope smuggling case but, unknown to anyone it seems, the narcotics agent on the case had taken a roll of film showing the junk being passed over to the mob. Flaherty managed to get the film and gave it to Hoff. Naturally, his paper went to town on it, and in return for the exclusive, Hoff built up Flaherty. They began sharing the same bottle and the same dames, and before you knew it they were blood brothers."

"I remember Flaherty in that Senate crime investigation," Savage said.

"It was Hoff who maneuvered him onto the staff as an assistant."

"And didn't the regular counsel have a heart attack shortly before the hearings started?"

"The regular counsel was a hotshot Chicago lawyer. Two days before the hearings opened he had a gallbladder attack. Everyone in the pressroom swore Hoff was responsible. Flaherty took over and did a fantastic job. Before the proceedings were finished, he was a household word."

Savage nodded. "I remember those hearings; they were absolutely incredible. I couldn't leave the TV set."

I asked if he was in the newspaper business at the time.

The answer came without hesitation: "I was sales manager for my family's toy company in Detroit . . . and doing my best to get Sam Dolbar's daughter to the altar."

"Of course. Savage toys. I remember buying one for a niece. They're damn expensive."

"Before I turned the business over to my younger brother, Savage toys were the best in the country," he said quietly. "Of course, there was the usual cost—a bad ulcer. But I try to watch my step—bland diet and all."

"Running a newspaper can be a rough business, especially when you're in the driver's seat.'

He patted me lightly on the shoulder. "I think I'll survive, Duke."

It isn't hard to remember Flaherty as he looked that day: double-breasted blue suit and dark silk tie, holding himself a bit aloof, as though to make sure the herd knew who he was as he weaves slowly in and out the crowd. One hand holds a highball, which he never touches, and he smiles. That smile is his most distinguishing feature. It is fixed, serene, and he shares it equally with everyone. But as I know from experience, he can be looking straight at you and be four hundred miles away.

"Handsome man," Savage said.

"Don't let his smile get you off center," I told him.

I led the way through the crowd. As always, the Christmas party was held in the ninth-floor conference room with the big oak table loaded down with buffet, and a small bar off to one side. A quick glance around the room confirmed the fact that this was more than the usual political gathering.

I recalled how one political boss had put it: "It's the beginning of our Holy Week," he said. "Now we mend our fences, do our penance, and look like altar boys on Easter morning for the voters. This year they're never wrong—from Mr. Jones's parking ticket that the old son of a bitch more than deserves, to Ramasas Jones, the shine who wants to get into the Post Office. They're all votes, and this year being the Year of the Drought, so to speak, because that chucklehead in Washington has been anything but the genius we thought he'd be, we need every one of them."

As I looked at the round red faces, all closely shaven and smelling of the best aftershave, the phony loud greetings and quick darting glances to make sure they registered with anyone who's important, I remembered I had heard that the boys gathered at Flaherty's East Side penthouse after every Christmas party. I would have traded my soul for a taped recording of tonight's postmortems.

I pressed my way forward exchanging greetings, but got as many cold, bitter looks as smiles.

"Some of the people look as if they would gladly cut your throat," Savage whispered.

"The day it's any different I'll turn in my police card."

I touched Flaherty's arm, and he turned. Although his smile broadened in pleasant surprise, I was positive he already knew I had arrived with my publisher. Flunkeys at the elevator door passed the word the moment certain guests arrived.

"Duke! How good of you to come," he said in his soft, mild voice. He smiled tentatively at Savage.

I introduced my publisher to the District Attorney.

"Pleased to meet you, Mr. Savage. I've been meaning to give you a call. That's a fine paper you're putting out."

The implication that the former publisher had put out an inferior product wasn't lost on Savage. I stole a look at him and liked what I saw; there was no acknowledgment of the phony praise.

The magic smile swung to me. "I've known Duke for a long time, Mr. Savage. He's one of the best."

"We consider him that," Savage said, "and we all think his department is one of the most important, not only to the paper but to the city. That's why from now on he gets free rein."

I had all I could do to maintain a poker face. This was the first I knew I never had free rein.

I thought I detected Flaherty's smile strain slightly. "Uncovering those people in the building racket was a public service," he said carefully.

Savage shrugged. "Well, it was good but it could have been better. All your office really wound up with were some minor real-estate agents and Building Department clerks." He took a sip of Scotch. "I would have liked to see someone really important get indicted, Mr. Flaherty. As I was telling Duke last night, I don't see how a thing like that could have operated without the connivance of some higher-ups, either in the city government or among the real-estate people."

Flaherty remained unruffled. "We must be guided by the rules of evidence, Mr. Savage. My staff didn't think we even had a prima facie case against some of them, so we did the next best thing and turned our evidence over to the Building Department for department trials."

"And by latest count, Chief, the department has kicked out two inspectors and transferred ten on the material you sent over."

We all turned. Bob Hoff hadn't changed much since I had last seen him. He was still thin as a split rail, with a long, bony face, and dark brooding eyes that were hooded like a perched hawk's.

He held out his hand. I took it and introduced him to Savage. A waiter came by and we all had refills. I saw Hoff take a fast double.

"I didn't know they had moved that much, Bob," Flaherty said with a great show of pleased earnestness. But I had made a mental note that Flaherty seemed mighty anxious to record what his office had done.

"I checked with Commissioner Aymes—the city's investigator," he explained for Savage, who nodded.

"Oh, then you're officially back on the D.A.'s payroll?" I asked.

"A release was sent out for the A.M.'s," Hoff said. "Actually, it's only a leave of absence from the state."

"Then you'll be handling public relations for the D.A.'s office?" Savage said innocently.

"Well, it's more than just public relations, Mr. Savage," Flaherty said, a faint note of impatience edging into his voice. "Bob will take over the very important post of community relations—"

"Community relations in the D.A.'s office?" Savage said wonderingly.

Flaherty, who had quickly stifled his momentary surge of irritation, was all charm as he launched into a logical and explicit explanation of what the Bureau of Community Relations did for the city and why it was so important. He was impressive when he talked, and smart as a fox chasing coon. He turned slightly to the passing Commissioner of Deeds, who stopped to listen, and before many minutes passed we were surrounded by a crowd of attentive listeners who wanted to make sure Quinn Flaherty knew how interested they were in the problems of his office.

Savage caught my eye and gave me a faint smile. This boy wasn't being fooled; he knew he was getting the treatment from an expert. But one thing I did notice during all the ostensibly earnest discussion: Bob Hoff was studying me and my publisher very carefully.

I was about to nudge Savage to move on when I got a whiff of expensive perfume; it had to be costly to penetrate all the cigar and cigarette smoke.

"Connie, this is Duke Malloy. If you ever want to rent an apartment, don't mention his name."

I had never particularly liked Johnny De Lorenzo, Flaherty's bright young star. I always thought he looked too much like a big St. Bernard, ready to sit up, panting with pleasure when Flaherty was around. But then again, maybe it was because he was young, fresh, and vigorous, with every morning a new day to conquer.

The girl with him was the Southampton type: cool, assured, and dressed in a plain but expensive black dress with a single strand of pearls topped off by clear, green eyes, hair the color of new honey, and a catching smile.

An elderly man, gray-haired, expensively groomed, accompanied them. The starched collar, the silk tie, and the pearl stickpin brought the word "hotel" to my mind, even before Johnny introduced his fiancée, Connie Ryder, and her father, Colton Ryder—and I remembered the *Life* cover that showed him in his penthouse office looking over the city and his billion-dollar projects.

I could feel something stir inside me: Colton Ryder, Quinn Flaherty? An ambitious District Attorney plus money and influence. It had to add up to something.

"Before I look for an apartment I'll call Mr. Malloy," Connie said with a smile.

"I'll guarantee satisfaction," I said.

"He will, too," said Johnny. "I told Connie perhaps you could give her league dinner a plug."

"Be happy to. When is it?"

"In a few weeks at the Astor," she said. "We're going to have Senator Henderson."

"You're lucky. He has a tight schedule these days."

Marvelous dimples showed when she smiled. "Oh, I know he'll come. I appointed his daughter my assistant on the committee."

"We might even assign a photographer, Duke," Julian said.

"Marvelous!" she said.

"She's getting to be quite the politician, Colton," Flaherty said.

"If phone calls are the key to political success, I can assure you, gentlemen, my daughter will end up in the White House," Ryder said.

"We'll certainly make use of you girls," Flaherty said with great seriousness. "It's going to be quite a campaign."

I tried to make the question casual: "Do you intend to be active in it?"

"Come off it, Duke," Hoff said quickly, "you know a D.A. can't electioneer."

Flaherty, still smiling, elaborately dropped his arm across my shoulder.

"This boy is always looking for a story, Mr. Savage."

"When he stops I'll fire him," was Savage's firm reply.

"Speaking of stories," I said, peering about, "I don't see Jim Mc-Shane here."

"Oh, he'll be here, even though he's not keen on cocktail parties." Flaherty turned to Hoff. "I think this is one of the few he attends, isn't it, Bob?"

"This and the Legislative Correspondents' Dinner. He's a tee-totaler, you know."

"He doesn't drink, he doesn't swear, and he always remembers Mother's Day," I said. "Just a Jim-dandy fellow."

Flaherty gave me a frosty smile. "Personally, I think he's just that, Duke."

"Come off it, Flaherty. McShane's a politician first and always. As I'm sure some of you gentlemen may recall, he was the one who pulled the President through in New York four years ago, and Washington hasn't forgotten it. Remember when the Mayor started feeling his oats three years ago and announced he was the party leader? Two days later the White House announced that McShane was distributing the city's patronage. And it's been like this ever since. The Mayor was glad to have gotten away with his marbles." Then, out of perversity, I asked Johnny what he thought of McShane.

Johnny frowned a bit. "I don't know much about the man, except that he's an active politician in our community."

"For God's sake, Johnny—"

Ryder broke in, "Well, what would you call him, Mr. Malloy?"

"Boss politician. Kingmaker. A cold, ruthless individual who believes the end justifies the means. I have reason to know."

"Why, Duke," Hoff said, "I'm surprised at you. You make him sound unique. Every city has one or more. It's part of our political system."

I said: "I've always considered the party boss a flaw in the democratic system. Besides, his type is anachronistic. The Hagues, the Pendergasts—and the McShanes, all political dinosaurs."

Colton Ryder shrugged. "Yet, as Mr. Hoff just pointed out, it's our political make-up. There must be a kingmaker, as you put it. In business we call him chairman of the board. In your years of experience, Mr. Malloy, you must have met many—"

"Sometimes I think too many."

"Perhaps. But honestly, haven't you found something in these people that others just don't seem to possess? A certain charm, intangibles which perhaps we can't fathom?"

"The most evil men in history often have been the most attractive," I said. "You don't hear of many humpbacked villains."

"I must agree with both you and Duke, Mr. Ryder."

We all turned to Julian, who surprisingly was not smiling but grim.

"I agree with you, Mr. Ryder. These people possess certain intangibles, designs, demeanor which can attract us, even rivet our attention."

"And sometimes mystify us?" Ryder asked.

"With prestige there is always mystery, Mr. Ryder," Julian said softly. "But with that mystery, the intangibles which perhaps we cannot understand, I have found there is also a cold-bloodedness, a ruthlessness, a single evil determination that, thank God, most of us do not have."

"And is that the way McShane shapes up with you, Duke?" Ryder asked with a smile.

"I base my conclusions on outside evidence," I said. "I have only met McShane a few times personally."

"But you fellows have met in print?"

"Let's say that Mr. McShane has had occasion not to forget my name."

He chuckled. "I think I know what you mean. But seriously, I have heard some fine things about McShane. Really fine things."

"I guess we don't travel in the same circles, Mr. Ryder."

"Perhaps," he said in almost an amused way. "Perhaps, Mr. Malloy."

"Well, I don't think you can condemn a man simply because he's in politics, Duke," Johnny started to say somewhat pompously. "I never met the man, but—"

"You're going to meet him now, Johnny," Flaherty said, staring over our heads. We turned as the entire room moved like a great eddy toward the elevator door. Then a complete phalanx of glasses, unlit cigars, jowls, flashing teeth and broad smiles moved slowly in our direction. It reached us, split apart, and Big Jim McShane was walking forward, his hand outstretched to Flaherty.

"I hope I'm not too late, Quinn," he said in a deep voice that had just the touch of a rasp.

"Not at all, Jim, not at all," said Flaherty, as he pumped McShane's hand. Then, with one arm across McShane's shoulder, he carefully turned to face us.

"Ladies and gentlemen, Jim McShane."

I was immediately conscious of the eyes: winter-sky gray, and just as cold. He was smiling, but his eyes were searching and hard. Although I knew he was in his sixties, McShane looked like a healthy fifty. The handball sessions at the New York Athletic Club—according to the best information his partners were always national and local celebrities —had trimmed away any fat. He was immaculately groomed, from manicured nails to the custom-made suit.

Yet the acquired polish somehow failed to cover the toughness earned the hard way—on the piers he once ruled with shape-up whistle and longshoreman's hook.

"A wonderful turnout, Quinn," McShane said.

With hearty joviality, Flaherty introduced his guests. "Mr. Colton Ryder."

McShane and Ryder locked eyes. Their grasp was firm and businesslike. I felt they could sit down, divide up the city between them, and be finished by dinner.

Flaherty gently took Connie by the elbow.

"And his daughter, Connie."

"I have a daughter your age, Connie," he said. "You're both very beautiful."

Connie's smile did not hide the fact she seemed a bit flustered.

"And my assistant, Johnny De Lorenzo."

McShane said quickly, "De Lorenzo and Sons Produce. Right?"

"That's right, sir."

"A fine company," McShane said. "One of the city's best. I knew your father. One of the finest men on the West Side."

Color came to Johnny's face as he acknowledged the compliment.

Flaherty turned to Hoff. "And Bob Hoff, our new Director of Community Relations."

"Just come down from Albany, didn't you, Bob? Deputy Commissioner of Public Works, wasn't it?"

"That's right."

"Going to give Quinn a hand?"

"Yes, sir," Hoff said eagerly.

McShane stared at him. "I hear the boys are doing a lot of partying upstate."

Hoff flushed. "Well, you know—during the session . . ."

McShane said shortly, "I wouldn't know. I don't drink."

I thought: In other words, I know you're a lush and I'll be looking over your shoulder.

Flaherty said, somewhat hurriedly, "And this is Duke Malloy of the *Blade-Leader,* Jim."

The warm smile returned, but the eyes were still cold and searching.

"Oh, I know Duke. I hope you read his stuff, Quinn. He's the best in town. How are you, Duke?"

His voice was almost conspiratorial, his grip firm.

"Fine, Jim," I said, and the sound of my voice brought me up short. It had the same phony air of joviality that had amused me in Flaherty. Quickly I introduced Julian.

"You have a fine paper, Mr. Savage. One the city can be proud of."

He touched each one of us; the new Ryder Building was already the talk of the town; he wanted to see Connie for lunch one day to discuss "politicking," as he put it, for her group in the forthcoming election; Hoff's opinion of the upstate vote and the Albany climate was sought after; and Flaherty was gravely asked what he thought the legislature should do to curb rising narcotics addiction among the young. He also wanted Johnny's ideas on how the subways could be better policed. "The city must be made safe for our womenfolk," he said seriously.

I realized we were all trying to impress this man who listened so intently to our opinions, chuckled at our quips. He had an excellent sense of timing. When one had finished he would look over our shoulders, nod and smile.

"Denny, how are you?"

A commissioner or a deputy would brush past to grab his hand. "Did the boy connect down in D.C?"

A beaming smile was his answer. "Your letter opened all the doors, Jim. He's in Commerce now. A million thanks, Jim."

The gratitude was waved aside.

Our little island was the party's center of attraction. Men stood on its fringe, faces tense and expectant, waiting for the opportunity to get a nod and a quick handshake; the more fortunate even got the chance to reminisce briefly over some shared political adventure.

Suddenly McShane glanced at his wristwatch. "Lord, the time flies. Much as I hate to leave, Quinn, I do have a dinner date uptown at the AC."

"Of course, Jim," Flaherty said. "Do you have a car?"

"New Yorkers don't use cars, you know that," McShane said with a grin. "Cabs and subways."

Ryder said, "My car is waiting downstairs, Mr. McShane. And Connie, Johnny, and I have another party to catch uptown. Can we give you a lift?"

"Not if it takes you one block out of the way."

"We have to pass the Club," Ryder said promptly. "Connie, Johnny . . ."

Connie gave her father a puzzled look. "A party uptown, Father?"

"The real-estate board's shindig, dear," Ryder said smoothly. "I mentioned it at lunch."

Connie said nothing, nor did McShane. I wondered why Ryder was so anxious to get McShane alone; he had to lie—the real-estate board's Christmas party was tomorrow . . .

The firm, manicured hand reached out. "Duke, it was good to see you. Mr. Savage, keep up the good work. Quinn, a wonderful party. It's really the only opportunity I get to meet some of the old-timers."

We shook hands. The warm smile touched us; the cold eyes studied us briefly; then he was moving toward the elevator, past hurdles of out-stretched hands and pats on the back.

"Truthfully now, Duke," Flaherty said, "he didn't seem such an ogre, did he?"

"Truthfully he did not. But give me a little more time, or some privacy."

"He's a terrific guy," he said seriously. "There's something about him—"

What was that something, I thought, that even had me off center for a moment? No question about it, there was something about the man that attracted other men and, judging from Connie, women. But what would it really be like to come up against him in a life-and-death struggle? I recalled those hard eyes, and mentally shuddered.

"The guy's a powerhouse," Hoff was saying. "A real powerhouse. Up in Albany they run when he whistles."

"He calls the turns in Washington, too, these days, Bob," Flaherty said.

"He certainly does, Chief."

"By the way, what was Ryder doing here?" I asked Hoff.

I thought I detected a slight defensive note as Flaherty answered.

"Colton Ryder and I were classmates. In fact, Johnny and Connie met at our Christmas party two years ago. He just came down to say hello."

Hello to whom I wondered. Big Jim McShane?

Hoff broke in. "They're wonderful kids," he intoned.

"Is his daughter really in politics?" I asked.

Flaherty nodded. "She adores politics. She started that League of Young Women Voters last year, and it's catching on. She's a regular doorbell ringer."

I tried to slide in the next question. "I hear you're making Johnny your next Rackets chief."

Hoff needed no prodding from his boss; he stepped in fast.

"There will be an announcement this week about the new appointment, Duke. I'll send it over."

"Hell, it's been in the *World-Telly* and the *Journal-American* City Hall Saturday roundups."

"Want to talk off the record?" he asked me.

"You know I never talk off the record, Bob. Say it on the record or don't say it."

Hoff gave me a cold look, hesitated, then took another double from the passing waiter.

"If that's the way you feel, you'll just have to wait for the release."

Belting that booze in Albany hasn't sweetened your disposition, my friend, I felt like saying, but skipped it.

"What would you say if it was Johnny, Duke?" Flaherty asked cautiously.

"I'd say he's young for the job."

Julian asked me how old he was.

Hoff answered, "Twenty-seven next summer."

"Which means you've been gathering material for a biog for his release," I said.

Hoff snarled, "For Christ's sake, get off my back, Malloy."

"My, aren't we getting touchy?" I said, and with a mental thumb tested the edge of the knife I was going to slide into this drunk's guts, but before I could say anything Flaherty held up his glass in mock dismay.

"Gentlemen! Where's your Christmas spirit?"

But the quick look he gave Hoff held a warning. A waiter passed, and Hoff put his half empty glass on the tray.

"I guess you don't think twenty-seven is too young for the job, Mr. Flaherty?" Julian asked.

"No, I don't," Flaherty said emphatically. "Johnny's been in the Racket Bureau for the last few years and he's done a fine job. He's a wonderful boy—"

"I wouldn't want a wonderful boy tangling with Vito Gennaro or some other hood who was at an Apalachin cookout," I said.

Flaherty said coldly, "If Gennaro gets out of line in this town, I'll take care of him."

"Fine. I'll remember that."

"Weren't the men all seasoned who had this post before?" Julian asked.

"I don't think age has anything to do with appointing a man to a responsible post, whether it's in city or federal government." He smiled his infectious smile. "Or journalism."

And on that note Flaherty decided it was time to change topics.

"Do you plan any innovations in the paper, Mr. Savage?"

Savage smiled. "Do you want to talk off the record or on the record, Mr. Flaherty?"

Flaherty threw back his head and roared.

"Touché, Mr. Savage, *touché."*

"How did I do, Duke?" Julian asked when Flaherty drifted off.

"Excellent. I'm glad you didn't let his smile get you off center."

"He's personable, there's no doubt about it. Has he ever given us a break on a story?"

"I've gotten one or two things out of his assistants, but now that Hoff's back they won't talk to their own mothers. Hoff doesn't want a thing going out of here without his okay."

He looked thoughtful. "Suppose a paper gave Flaherty a lead or information that would eventually lead to an indictment?" Before I could answer he added quickly, "For example, you gave him all you had on the real-estate racket, didn't you?"

"I told you how that fizzled."

"But suppose it hadn't."

"You mean if there had been indictments?"

"Yes. Let's say on the basis of information we had given him, his office built a fairly big criminal case."

"The deal I made was that we get the exclusive story. This is nothing unusual. It works this way with any prosecutor's office."

"As a result the grand jury investigates, and if there are any results the D.A.'s office publicly commends us. Does that go along with it, too?"

"The D.A.'s office would have to really hate us not to give the paper credit."

He smiled. "Be patient with me, Duke. When I don't know the whole picture I ask questions."

"That's the only way to get anywhere in this business."

He speared a ragged-looking triangle of white bread and tired ham from a passing waiter's tray and studied it with disgust.

"Let's go to my place for something to eat. The old man probably will be out. Okay with you?"

"Fine."

As we stepped into the elevator, someone brushed past, almost knocking me over. A woman anxiously begged my pardon, and a man grunted in my ear with a powerful whiskey smell. I looked into the flushed face and glazed eyes of the Commissioner of Ethics and City Affairs. He was leaning against the elevator, arms braced on the wooden bar that ran around the sides of the car.

He had the deep red face and the owlish look of the heavy drinker. The woman beside him was in her late thirties or early forties. She was smartly dressed in a clinging black dress and mink stole and had a patrician poise that not even this drunken lout could disturb.

"Hello, Commissioner. How are you?"

He gave me an airy wave of his hand. "Fine, Malloy, fine." He spread his arms still further on the wooden rail for support. "How the hell is that scandal sheet you work on?"

"Oh, Cliff," the woman whispered.

"I'm only saying hello, dear," he said with drunken earnestness. "Really, this is my old friend Duke Malloy of the *Blade-Leader,* the worst paper in New York." He tried to keep a straight face but he was too taken with his own humor. He slapped his leg. "Honest, it's the worst paper in New York, and Duke will tell you so. Right, Duke?"

She turned to me with an imploring look. "I'm Lydia Aymes," she said, "and I have seen your by-line many times."

"This is my publisher, Julian Savage," I said.

Aymes dismissed Julian with a brief look. "Hiya."

Mrs. Aymes said hurriedly: "I'm particularly fond of your book reviewer, Mr. Savage. I enjoyed his column last week. He—"

"Hey, Duke, when are you guys going to give Ethics and Affairs a write-up?" Aymes said, poking me. "We make all the news for you guys. Want anybody kicked out? Just let me know."

His wife's eyes were pleading, so I tolerated that beefy arm in the dirty polo coat.

"Oh, I'll give you a good piece one of these days," I said.

"Good boy," he growled drunkenly. "Look, why don't you come over to the Municipal Building some time and see what we do for the city?"

I promised, and he hugged me.

"Did you hear the one about the two hebes who died and came up before St. Peter?" he said. "Did you hear that one?"

He didn't wait, but leaned over and told me, his hot, whiskey breath filling my ear. I could hear his wife and Julian loudly discussing books so they wouldn't have to hear the obscene, viciously anti-Semitic ending.

At long last the elevator reached the ground floor.

"Can we give you folks a lift?" Julian asked.

She smiled. "Thank you. But we—"

"We have a car," Aymes said brusquely. Then with that loud, businesslike air that drunks always seem to adopt when saying good night, he said, "Duke, you pop over to 412; I'll tell you what's going on over in the Hall, Okay?"

"Okay, Commissioner."

His wife smiled apologetically, and entered the revolving door. With a last wave Aymes vanished behind the flashing glass.

"That's Commissioner Aymes, I take it," Julian said in an amused voice.

"Commissioner of Ethics and City Affairs. A lush if you ever saw one."

"How long has he been around?"

"At least eight years in this job. He was in the Borough President's office, then the Comptroller's."

"How does he hold down his position?"

"He has a rabbi real high up. I have never been able to find out just who it is. The bum is good for any hatchet job the Hall wants."

"His wife seems a real lady."

"True. This is the first time I've met her."

"You're not married, are you, Duke?"

"I guess I'm the original one that got away."

"My wife died a little over a year ago," he said shortly. "In a way I'm glad I got this job. I can bring as much homework as I want"—he gave a short laugh—"it's either that or play gin with the old man."

"Is that Mr. Dolbar?"

"Samuel Dolbar of Hester Street. Do you know he began by lending money to merchants on the East Side after the Bank of U.S. flopped in 1933?"

"Yes, it was in an article last year."

"From lending money to newspaper tycoon," he said musingly. "Quite a jump."

Savage lived in a cooperative just off Seventy-eighth and Park. The first thing I saw as we entered the long corridor of the apartment was a suit of armor and an old-fashioned grandfather's clock.

"My wife was an antique buff," he explained. "After she died, I got rid of all the stuff but I kept this—it's genuine fourteenth century." He shrugged, and laughed almost self-consciously. "I know it's a monstrosity, but I guess when someone you really cared for is gone, you hang on even to their monstrosities."

We walked down the corridor that opened into a dining room and library. While these rooms appeared immaculate and cold, the next room, a combination bedroom and study, did not: the desk was piled high with papers, clippings, memos. There were two telephones; one, I knew, was a tie line direct to the office. There were more books and a pile of British and out-of-town newspapers. On the first shelf of the bookcase was a framed picture of a woman about thirty, with a pixie-like face, framed by dark, curly hair.

"My wife, Dona," he said. "She's gone more than a year now. It was in childbirth . . . imagine that, a woman dying these days giving birth to a child? One minute we're in the cab and I'm telling her everything's all right, and a few hours later she's dead." He took my coat. "What will it be—rye or Scotch?"

"Rye on the rocks."

He disappeared, and I examined his library. There were a number of biographies, colonial histories, and a shelf of current novels. The book on his desk was Ireland's recollections of Pulitzer. As I flipped through it, I noted passages underlined; they were principally in the chapters dealing with the *World*'s famous exposés.

I was still glancing through the book when he returned with our drinks.

"Have you ever read it?" he asked.

"Years ago. You've undoubtedly read Chapin's autobiography."

"The *World*'s city editor who killed somebody?"

"His wife. His book gives a good flavor of the *World*."

"Don't think I'm a nut on the subject," he said half apologetically.

"It's just that I have always admired the *World* as one of America's great newspapers, and I want to know as much as possible how Pulitzer pulled that off."

"It's a different era, you know. I don't have to tell you that you face problems Pulitzer never dreamed of."

There was an edge to his voice as he handed me my drink. "That's what my father-in-law keeps telling me. But I'll be damned if I agree. My father-in-law . . . well, he doesn't really care about the editorial content of his papers; he's a businessman. His idea is to let the local people take care of things. Actually, it's because of my wife I'm here."

"Oh?"

"After we were married he insisted I join the organization. Frankly, he didn't have to twist my arm. Who the hell wants to make a life's work out of guessing what kind of toys the kids will go for next Christmas? He put me in the business end for a few years, but I always had a yen for the editorial side. He brushed me off, but Dona kept after him. He couldn't say no to anything she wanted, so when he bought the *Leader* I took over as publisher."

"That was when you were in Los Angeles?"

"Los Angeles, Detroit, and the Newark *Register.*" He gave me a wry smile. "I guess you can say I came to New York gradually. But I learned along the way. That's why I feel so deeply that the *Blade-Leader* should be a real public-service newspaper. I may be wrong, but I think the people realize when you're fighting their battles."

He fumbled among the papers on his desk and came up with a large brown envelope that I knew came from our reference room.

"Take this policy exposé you did four years ago. Why the hell didn't they keep the series on page one? Why did they take it all inside on the jump page after the first break?"

"The Miller family didn't like too much crime on page one," I explained. "The publisher always leaned toward international news, like that Southeast Asia business."

Savage leaned forward, his body tense.

"Granted they were history-making stories. But for God's sake, if you don't treat your own crusades as if they were important how can you get the reader interested and angry and indignant?"

"To hear a publisher talk like that is an occasion for another drink."

Savage splashed some Scotch in his glass on ice, but it wasn't the whiskey that was putting a flush in his cheeks.

"Beginning Monday morning," he said briskly, "I want you to start looking for something big that the paper can target in on—crime, official corruption, injustices to the little guy." He stopped. "Wait a minute. Didn't Turner Elliott tell me you had something cooking?"

"Yes, I have. Something that could be big."

His face lighted up. "Fine. Let's have it."

He saw me hesitate. "Duke, if there's something on your mind, let's talk it out. If we start out with secrets, we'll never get anywhere."

"I would like to level with you, Julian."

"Fire away."

"You say you want to make the paper an instrument for the good of the people of this community. Only—"

"Only what?" he asked quickly.

"You have no idea what pressures are put on the publisher of a New York newspaper."

"Suppose you tell me what you have in mind, Duke."

"It's an open secret that Dolbar Newspaper Enterprises intend to go into television."

"That's true. It was in *Variety* last month."

"Do you realize what pressure—let's call it legal pressure—could be put on your father-in-law: license examinations, court moves, until you were sick of the whole proposition or the competition has time to take over."

"I can handle that sort of pressure. Remember, I'm boss here—not my father-in-law."

"There would be other pressures—perhaps more subtle."

"Like what?"

"An old friend who is chairman of some wonderful charitable committee gets on the phone and wants to know why you are being so foolish . . . she wishes you would get off somebody's back."

He gave me a calm, impassive look. "I believe I can handle do-gooders."

"Suppose a union official calls. He might owe a favor to somebody—"

Abruptly he held up his hand, like an angry traffic cop.

"Let me say once and for all time: nobody intimidates me. Friends. Politicians. Businessmen. Does that answer your doubts?"

"I guess it does."

He settled back in his chair.

"Now I'd like to ask you a few questions, Duke."

"Turn about is fair play."

"How would you describe yourself?"

"My philosophy?"

"I'll get to know your philosophy," he said with a grin. "Let's start professionally."

"Well, in every city room I guess there's a digger."

"Are you a digger?" he asked quickly.

"I suppose I am."

"What do you dig for?"

"There's only one thing to dig for in this business—facts."

"I guess the next question is, why do you dig for facts? Is it for news?"

"It comes under the general heading of news. But I like to think it's gathering together a certain amount of facts that rights an injustice. Suppose a Brooklyn mechanic is jailed for a minor offense. He comes to us and claims the court was wrong. We dig, and the facts show he was right. Together we fight City Hall, and win. That's what I like to do."

"Suppose you don't win?"

"You can't always win fighting City Hall."

He smiled. "Why fight if the odds are against you?"

"Because if you fight long enough, hard enough, and often enough, the word gets around among the readers. One thing I have found out is, don't underestimate them. They may be a bus driver, a waitress, or a stockbroker. You can't fool them all the time with comics and gimmicks. They know after a while who really is on their side."

He leaned forward. "So you're a crusader."

"I hate the word."

"Why?"

"Because sometimes crusaders believe they're gods. They can do no wrong. They adopt their own phony phrases, and innocent people get hurt."

"That's true," he said slowly.

"I hope that when I get on a tangent I become aware of it," I said. "I hope I never get drunk on the great phrases and the glib speeches, and never forget there are people with opinions which I don't have to like or believe in but which I must respect."

"Was any pressure ever put on you to end a series or an exposé?"

"The housing survey," I said. "The more I dug into it, the more I realized there was an enormous cancer in this city. Harlem."

"Who put the pressure on you?"

"The Miller family owns a lot of New York City real estate."

He sipped at his drink. "You say there might be something crooked in Harlem housing?"

"It's a ghetto, and where there's a ghetto in the largest city in the world you can be sure there are injustices and corruption. They go hand in hand with poverty."

"What do you think you might find?"

"Somewhere in this city there's a syndicate that controls these slum buildings. Apparently the backers are so powerful they can defy the city. No city department ever shut down the buildings; the violations have been going unchallenged for years—"

"Didn't I read there were some rent strikes a few years ago?"

"That was a desperation move on the part of some of the tenants. I recall one of the tenants telling me they had no heat all that winter. If you recall, it was the coldest on record."

He was nodding now and there was a glow in his face.

"Is that what you had in mind—what Elliott meant?"

"Not exactly. But I think it's part of the whole picture. In with the housing and rats, there's crime—organized crime, also a partner of poverty. And this is what I want to tell you about."

He poured a drink for each of us, and I sat back and told him the whole story of my meeting with Action Jackson. When I finished he was leaning forward, intent as a coiled spring.

"God, that sounds very big."

"Don't have too many great expectations," I warned. "Informers have a way of exaggerating or changing their minds."

"Something tells me you don't doubt this man Jackson."

"Frankly, I don't."

"But there is one thing," he said. "How does this policy business and police corruption tie in with the housing racket?"

"When I was on housing," I said, "I came up with a pattern that indicated the building situation is linked with the rackets. How, I don't know."

"Let's find out."

"Fine with me."

"Don't you have to wait for Jackson to call you?"

"That's the way we left it."

"Then, why don't you do this: continue on housing until he calls. Perhaps by that time you will have developed something. Does that make sense?"

"It does for me."

"Excellent," he said, slamming one hand down on the table. "That's just excellent. I think we have something started. Perhaps we—"

Somewhere a door closed, and Savage broke off. He listened for a moment, then gathered his notes and put them into a drawer. A bit of the light in his eyes seemed to have faded.

"That's my father-in-law," he said.

We both waited, tensely, as footsteps approached.

Then a small old man with a tanned bald head came into the room.

For a moment he stood in the doorway, smiling. I noticed his eyes were like a ferret's, small, dark, and cold. He wore an old brown suit complete with a vest and the gold watch chain that had been featured on the *Time* cover. Standing there, old Sam Dolbar reminded me of a foxy moneylender standing on the Quai Saint-Michel in a Childe Hassam painting.

He walked, or rather bounced, in. His voice was high pitched without the heavy East Side accent that I expected.

"Good evening, gentlemen . . . good evening."

"Good evening, Dad," said Julian. "I'd like to have you meet Duke Malloy; he's on the *Blade-Leader*'s staff."

"He doesn't look like advertising, son."

"Editorial, Mr. Dolbar," I said.

"Editorial!" he exclaimed. "The headache department!"

"Oh, come on, Dad, you don't mean that," Julian said with a trace of impatience in his voice. "If you don't have a good Editorial Department, you just don't have a newspaper."

The old man gave me a slight smile. "Julian likes to argue about newspapers. Me, I just read the P. and L."

"Okay," Savage said resignedly. Then he gave his father-in-law a look of mock fierceness. "Tonight I'm going to take it out of your hide."

The old man rubbed his hands. "So tonight's for blood! Good, that's the way I like it." He turned to me. "You play gin, young man?"

"I'm a crapshooter at heart, Mr. Dolbar."

The old man gave Julian a look of disgust. "See, that's Editorial for you."

He said it so drolly we both had to laugh, but I sensed I was being given the word; so I shook hands with the old man, and Julian walked me to the elevator.

"He's the best gin player I have ever known," he whispered, "but tonight I think I'm going to take him." As we waited for the elevator he said, "Check out some of those things and see what looks good; then come down and we'll talk about them. Okay?"

We shook hands, and he walked back down the long carpeted hall with a determined air. Later, he told me he did take the old man that night, for the first time in months.

[5]

FILES, STATISTICS, corporation papers, and records of violations I had accumulated in my investigation of housing in Harlem had told me a great deal, but the first time I felt the real impact of the ghetto that is Harlem was when I interviewed a family in Spanish Harlem.

I started to explain to the father that I was checking on a list of rat-bite victims when he cut me off and walked into the bedroom of this squalid railroad flat and returned with a little black-haired child of about five. Her upper lip was swollen with what looked like an angry dark red boil.

Through his teen-age interpreter the man told me the child had awakened him with her screams. He ran into the bedroom and snapped on the light. A huge Norwegian water rat leaped from the child's face. Fortunately, his kick caught the rat in mid-air and stunned it. He literally kicked it to death. He went to one side of the kitchen, took a cardboard box from beneath the stove, and held it out to me.

My stomach turned; inside was an enormous gray rat, its head stomped to a pulp. I shuddered at the twisted mouth and the terrifying fangs.

The father explained he had called the Health Department and was told to save the rat.

"This guy on the phone says to save the rat," the boy-interpreter said, "but how the hell long does he want us to keep it? It's beginning to stink."

"What about this little girl?" I asked.

46

There was a rapid exchange in Spanish, then the boy said:

"They took the kid over to Harlem Hospital yesterday and they gave her a shot. They gotta go back today."

"Are you bothered with rats?"

The boy looked at me as if I were an idiot.

"Man," he said, "everybody's got rats up here. The guy across the hall killed four last week."

I asked why he hadn't complained to the landlord.

"That bastard! He's got a girl in an office as big as a telephone booth on Twenty-third Street." He mimicked: " 'I'm sorry, mister, but Mr. Moneybags ain't in. He'll be here Thursday.' " He added bitterly, "There ain't no Thursday in his calendar."

"What about the Health Department?"

"They tell us to take the kid to the clinic."

"Did you call the Building Department?"

He suddenly became cautious, suspicious. "Look, we don't want any trouble—we just want to be rid of the rats."

After that, all I got from him were shrugs and evasive answers. It was the same with a few other tenants. Only one blurted out: "Why don't you go into that store downstairs?"

"The candy store?"

He gave me a contemptuous look. "Mister, you ain't been in Harlem long, have you? Up here they don't sell candy in candy stores."

I told all this to Julian the next day. "Did you get a look at the store?" he asked.

"It was a typical Harlem numbers drop—a few fly-specked ads, dusty pencil boxes, and a few rubber balls."

"Numbers are big in the city, aren't they, Duke?"

"Policy arrests make up twenty-three percent of the city's arrests. Vito Gennaro, the man Jackson wants to give us—he's *capo* of the Cosa Nostra."

"The Cosa Nostra? A domestic branch of the Mafia?"

"Sort of . . . there are syndicates throughout the country based on family ties, blood relationship, marriages, and so on. Vito's the boss."

"And you think there's some connection between all these elements?"

"Bound to be," I said. And then at his insistence I explained how I had planned to go about digging into the housing situation.

What I had done was first update my files of the Building Department's list of old-law tenements—tenements built before 1902—that had standing violations. Then, in another department I had checked the list of owners. After that came a Health Department list of all reported rat-bite victims in the Harlem area for one year. Now I was in the process of checking every violation, the length of time it had remained uncorrected, how many complaints had been filed by the tenants, who the owners of the building were, what their excuse was, the rat condition, and so on.

"How many corporations did you come up with?"

"There are about seventy that own these rattraps. Some obviously are holding companies and dummy corporations."

"What did that boy mean when he said one company had an office as big as a telephone booth?"

"That's either a dummy corporation office or just a drop where they shrug off the tenants' complaints. That's where our story is: Who really owns these places and how do they get away with it?"

"Well, Duke, take as long as you want—but find the answer."

"I hope to."

"By the way, what are you doing the twenty-ninth?"

"Who knows. Rats and crummy flats have been fouling up my social calendar lately."

"Well, you're invited to a cocktail party given by Connie Ryder, some kind of auction for her League of Young Women Voters. Suppose you give her a call and write a piece for tomorrow. Tell the city desk it's my must and should run in all editions. Ask them to send a photographer." He picked up a sheaf of heavily lined paper. Circulation figures. "Well, here's the scoreboard."

"Are we going up or down?"

"We gained a few thousand in Jersey and Long Island with our new suburbia sections. I grabbed off that Fifth Avenue account; it's really the first class advertising we ever had in this paper." An unmistakable note of triumph edged into his voice. "That shook up his gin game the other night."

I went out, wondering about the personal duel that went on every night in the quiet of that sprawling Park Avenue apartment.

Her voice was cool, but friendly. "If this is the man who was once my favorite reporter, I don't want to talk to him."

"Not even if he apologizes and promises you a top head tomorrow on our society page?"

"I don't know what a top head is, but the society page sounds fine. I accept your apology."

"Okay. Now where's the dance?"

"At the Astor on the twenty-ninth. And—wait a minute, Duke. Are you free for a quick drink at about eight at Pasquale's?"

"Pasquale's—behind Criminal Courts?"

"Johnny's working late, and I'm supposed to meet him around eight-thirty. Suppose I buy you a drink and give you all the details."

It wasn't until I hung up that I realized I had accepted with a great deal of enthusiasm and a full knowledge that I had already promised a dancer by the name of Gwen that I would take her to an early dinner and drop her off at the theatre.

Within whistling distance of every courthouse in America, whether New York City or Medicine Run, Montana, there's a Pasquale's. It has a bar and four or five booths, where adjournments are agreed upon, tickets taken care of, the neighborhood cop in illegal shirtsleeves sits in the rear booth and writes up his daily reports; the staple of the house is spaghetti and meatballs, and the chef is the owner's father-in-law or cousin who comes to the doorway of his domain of steam and copper pots to survey his guests with a brief, impassive look before wiping his face with a towel and disappearing behind the swinging door.

Pasquale's has been in back of the Criminal Courts Building as long as I can recall, and the Associated Press man who has been covering the building long before Tom Dewey's days claims it was there when he first arrived.

In the summer it's dim and cool, in the winter, dim and warm. There is always the same smell of newly baked pasta.

Connie waved from the middle booth when I came in. Apparently she had just arrived; her cheeks were rosy from the cold and her eyes sparkling.

"I'm glad you could make it," she said. "Pasquale's making me a stinger. What will you have?"

I turned and beckoned to Pasquale, who nodded.

"I think if I had anything other than Canadian on the rocks, Pasquale would snap."

"Have you been coming here that long?"

"The first week I was on the paper I covered a murder trial in the building. I had my first drink here."

"That was right after the war, wasn't it?"

"The winter of '46 . . . that winter, as Merle Miller called it."

"I read your piece on Guadalcanal in an anthology Daddy got from a book club last year." She reached over and lightly touched my arm. "I almost cried when you told how they led that blind corporal to the beach."

"Want to know something? I cried too when I wrote it." And then I realized, almost wonderingly, that I had never told that to anyone before.

Her hand tightened slightly on my arm.

"What's Johnny working on?" I asked.

"He said they have to put together—" she stopped, and the dimples showed. "You better ask him, Duke."

I guessed it before she had finished. "Bob Hoff usually makes his releases for the A.M.'s," I said. "So it will probably be in the *Times* and *Trib.* Congratulations." I lifted her left hand. "No ring yet?"

She gave me a quizzical look. "Soon . . ."

"You hope?"

"I hope."

"Did you like seeing him get the Rackets job?"

She frowned slightly. "You didn't, did you?"

"Not to give you a short answer, Connie—no."

"You make being young a crime."

That hurt, and to mask how much I took a swallow of the smooth Canadian before I answered.

"Being young in that job *can* be a crime," I said, "not against Johnny but against the people he's there to protect." She started to say something, but I held up a hand. "It's not enough to be honest. You have to be smart and tough and sometimes ruthless."

"But Johnny's been in the Rackets Bureau two years, Duke."

"Johnny has been one of ten assistants," I pointed out. "And in reality the Rackets Bureau has been a nothing bureau the last few years. Flaherty has made a lot of noise with it, but compared to what it was years ago it's a joke."

She sipped at her drink thoughtfully. "Johnny says he's going to make it what it was in Dewey's and Hogan's day. He plans to—" She stopped and stared at me over her glass. "You don't believe him, do you?"

I shook my head.

She put down her glass and leaned across the table. "Duke, give him a chance."

Looking into that face, I couldn't help assuring her I would do everything possible to keep her Johnny afloat, and after collecting some facts and a release on her dinner dance I said good night. I was on my way out when Johnny came in.

"Hey, Duke," he said with a lot of boy-scout backslapping. "Come over and have a drink. I've got something for you!"

"I'll read it in the *Times,* kid," I said. My return slap on the back was like the one a coach gives some substitute coming off the field, while he keeps both eyes on the important pay-off play.

[6]

THE WEEK of the ninth was a momentous one: New York's Governor Desmond Russell announced his presidential candidacy, Big Jim McShane once again showed how ruthless he could be where votes and his machine were concerned, and I received the second phone call that eventually was to completely alter our lives.

The week began, not with the phone call, but with Governor Russell's announcement that he was entering the presidential race. The press conference at the Mid-Towners Club was a blistering one; he tore apart the administration's program on everything from taxes to civil rights and really leaped on the oil-lease scandal. Russell, a young and handsome Wall Streeter who appeared to be a political natural, had an excellent record as governor. He gained national fame when he entered the bloody milk strike, and in famous no-sleep-round-the-clock negotiations settled it just when it threatened to affect the nation's youngsters.

All the old pros who covered Russell's press conference were impressed with his candor, forthrightness, and savage delight in ripping apart the ruthless attempt by the White House to cover up the oil-lease scandal. He had new material, including some headline documents, and ended by denouncing the party as tinged with scandal.

The tremendous publicity Russell received, along with thoughtful editorials in what were thought to be friendly newspapers, apparently infected the lower echelon, because two days after Russell opened his headquarters at the Biltmore with another fanfare a West Side lawyer

who had been active in the party, as a liberal, announced he intended
to run for councilman in the primaries against the regular McShane-
elected candidate. The announcement caused a brief flurry, but compared to the mayoralty and citywide contests, it was only a minor
offshoot. I predicted to Julian that this lawyer had placed himself facing a buzz saw. The *Times* had a piece, and the *World-Telegram*'s City
Hall column made it the lead paragraph.

Despite his pompous public statements that anyone has the right
to run for what office he pleases and in the end it will be the electorate
who will decide, etc.—I knew McShane would never take this.

All that week I made it a point to attend the varied clambakes,
soup-and-fish and phony testimonials to departing commissioners, commissioners who were observing their silver anniversaries in city service
—I gag on the phrase—newly appointed commissioners, and just plain
fund-raising dinners in the guise of honoring a noble Jesuit, a wise rabbi,
or a vigorous minister. In the cocktail time before dinner, I circulated
with a glass of ginger ale, renewing old friendships, making promises,
even subtle threats, taking many notes about topics I never had any
intention of using. It was nights and days of old-time placer mining; you
washed pan after pan of political mud to come up with a few nuggets.

One nugget was the name of a former actress who had been questioned by our drunken friend in the elevator, the Commissioner of Ethics and City Affairs. I have found that getting someone out of bed at
1:00 A.M. and putting the questions to them bluntly, even roughly, usually produced stuttering truth.

Yes, she admitted, Commissioner Aymes had questioned her about
her ten-year affair with the West Side lawyer.

Savage whistled when I showed him my story. "That's real dirty
pool."

"In a way," I said, "I'm glad I found this out."

"Any particular reason?"

"It confirms my suspicions that McShane's a dangerous man. Ten
years ago I knew he was deadly, but now he's twice as deadly because
he has twice the power. And when Action Jackson brought up his
name . . ."

"It sounds like a personal vendetta," he said.

"It is—as of now." And I told him the story of the kid clerk in
Brooklyn Supreme Court.

"It's hard to reconcile the man you describe with that charming,
magnetic personality we met at Flaherty's cocktail party, Duke."

"Please believe me, they're the same man."

"Why should he go to such lengths to smear this young lawyer on
the West Side?"

" 'Absolute power corrupts absolutely,' " I quoted. "McShane could never let this joker get away with defiance; it might be contagious to the West Side leaders. And at a time when the man in the White House might find Governor Russell a tough match in November."

"McShane doesn't do the dirty work himself, does he?"

"Of course not. He has a hatchet man. Commissioner Aymes."

Savage lifted his eyebrows. "The drunk in the elevator?"

"The very same. Two years ago the Mayor appointed Aymes because McShane told him to. He belongs to McShane's Tamayanka Club. He does what hatchet work there is to do, and after Election Day he'll be made a magistrate. That will be good for ten years."

He threw the story back to me with an air of disgust.

"What do you think this lawyer will do?"

"Before the week is out he will announce that he is withdrawing; McShane will welcome him back in the fold. Ethics and Affairs will forget the whole thing, and anyone else who has thoughts of making a break from the party lines will think twice."

Savage leaned back in his chair, put the tips of his fingers together, and touched his lips.

"Suppose the attorney didn't have this woman in his background —suppose he was clean? What could they do?"

"Nothing so violent as shooting him in City Hall Park," I said. "But if he held a city job, they might find some charges to lodge against him. They might find a thief in his department and indict him—just pointing out that he works for the lawyer in the press release. They could harass him legally on his petition, buy, bribe, or threaten one of his supporters. . . . Oh, they have ways, Julian, they have many ways."

He gave me a tired smile. "I have a lot to learn, Duke."

I never knew how much, and at what cost.

As I recall, it was a few days later—actually, the day after Connie Ryder's cocktail party. I was studying the weird records of the Sugar Hill Financing Company that owned most of the old-law tenements in West Harlem. I had spent all day tracking down the corporation. Apparently the parent company had at least ten holding companies with officers and offices that just did not exist. I had the name of each company on a piece of paper spread out across my desk and my city map tacked up on the wall.

I had become so interested I sent a boy out for a sandwich and coffee and had just unwrapped the sandwich when the phone rang.

"Duke? Jackson. What's the word?"

"It's a deal."

"You'll go the distance, kid?"

"As far as you can run."

"When do you want to make a meet?"

"This afternoon. The same place."

He groaned. "Okay. Okay. I'll see you in that espresso joint with handles."

Jackson was there promptly at four. This time there was no wasting time over coffee. After a few minutes we left and crossed Fifth Avenue to Bryant Park, deserted and cold looking in the winter afternoon. I followed him to a bench near the archway in the rear of the Library. The only other person nearby was an old lady who kept cooing to herself as she fed a flock of pigeons with pieces of bread.

I tried to appear casual but I was jittery with anticipation. Long ago I discovered I possessed a powerful intuition, and at this moment it was operating at full strength: this could be a big one.

Jackson was tense; it showed in the set of his shoulders, the arch of his neck, the tightness of his face.

He took out a notebook and one or two folded city maps.

"Don't take notes," he said in a low voice; "it makes me nervous. I have everything written out in this book: names, telephone numbers, addresses. This is an Esso map of Manhattan, the Bronx, Westchester, and Jersey. Each red ring has a letter inside. Check the letter with the book. For example, *A* is the big-day drop on West 138th Street."

"You mean they have a night operation?"

"Come on, kid, don't be dumb! You know they get a big play with the night workers."

That was one mistake I vowed never to make again. Never to ask an edgy man a silly or obvious question is commonplace strategy, but anticipation can make a man stupid.

"Sorry. Go on."

"All you have to do is check the letter on the map and look in the notebook for the corresponding letter to get the collector's name, phone number, and code number." He said wearily: "Don't ask it—every collector turns in his plays with a code number on the envelope. This is included in the bag that's sent over to the East Side. They have a master list over there and they check every night. If they find a certain guy is falling behind, I get a call asking how come."

"Gennaro's got quite an operation going."

"You're damn' right he has," Jackson said. "But on the other hand, that's what's going to make it easy. It's all in the notebook and on the maps."

"What about the cops on the pad?"

"In the back of the book there's a list of the cops. We know some of them only by their first names or nicknames. . . . But there's something even better than names."

"What's that?"

"Badge numbers. For two months now I've taken down the shields of every creep in blue that I have paid."

"What do you think you pay out, Action?" I asked cautiously.

He shrugged. "Five G's a week. Christmas and New Year's it's more . . . you know, the single-O guys come in and ask a pound."

The simple arithmetic made me whistle. "That's big money."

"That's only what I pay out," he said. "You have to include what comes off the top."

"You mean what Gennaro pays?"

"Nobody, Gennaro or not, could operate a syndicate this big only with the help of crooked cops," was his flat reply. "The Vagrancy and Vice Court has a turnstile on it now. How do you think they're turned out like that? And how about the big cops that gave Gennaro trouble? You've got to have a lot of pull to take care of a gold star that big."

"I have news for you—Tom Murphy's back at headquarters."

"He's only been back since the new Police Commissioner came in. I'll take all the money you have that they'll both be out before next Christmas."

"Who says so?"

He nudged a piece of stale bread toward a jittery pigeon.

"I said so. When the presidential election comes around, you'd be surprised how many people want to do favors for the guy who controls the most votes in town." He gave me an amused look. "You know, for a guy who's supposed to be so smart you're awfully dumb today. What's the matter? Got a dame on your mind?"

"Okay, okay," I said, and slid the notebook and maps inside my coat. I was suddenly anxious to get away and pore over them in private.

"Let me go over these for a few days and I'll—"

"You can do all the looking you need in a few hours, Duke," he said roughly. "I'll meet you tomorrow morning on this bench, and you tell me where we go from here. This is my game and I'm calling all the plays."

"What's your hurry . . . you waited this long?"

I could see the malice in his tight face and in the way the white-knuckled ball of a fist hit his knee with measured strokes.

"I got a big hate," he said, "a great big hate. I want it taken care of and then I want to blow fast."

Abruptly he stood up. "Make it ten o'clock on the nose. Don't keep me waiting."

"One last question, Action—is Gennaro or his mob in real estate?"

He eyed me narrowly.

"That wop's in a lot of things, but real estate"—he shook his head —"that's a new one, kid. Sorry, I don't have anything on that. See you tomorrow morning."

He strode out of the Forty-second Street exit. Two young punks walking toward him shoulder to shoulder hesitated, then parted quickly as he forged between them.

[7]

THE BENCH WAS as good a place as any to examine Jackson's material. There were few stragglers. Those who moved through the park walked with a determined, home-bound stride. The old lady had finished feeding her pigeons and gone her way. I carefully unfolded the map of Manhattan. It was dotted with small red circles, a letter in each one. The circles stretched from the Wall Street district to the tip of the island. The notebook started off with the listing "Manhattan." Then under this, in small block letters, were the addresses that corresponded to the letters on the map. With the addresses were one, two, or three names, some only last names, nicknames of the collectors, incongruously complete names, including middle initials, and in the rare cases when there was no name there was a terse, vivid description: "a little guy with curly hair who makes love to Jack Daniels all day." Most names had phone numbers.

In the last several pages of the notebook, under the block letters P.D., were printed the names of policemen, sergeants, lieutenants. Each one had a red circle and a letter inside. Obviously this identified the particular drop paying him. Some were not named; instead Jackson had listed their badge numbers.

I counted them swiftly; there were easily more than fifty. But on the last few pages was the real Klondike of graft; Jackson had listed B.M. for "bagman." These were the important links between the syndicate and the organized ring of corruption in the Police Department.

There were only three, all sergeants. Jackson had twisted the

57

knife deep on these pages; after each name he had printed the cop's precinct number and home number. In addition he had added the important information of what days of the month each sergeant appeared at the drop to collect the graft for his inspector.

The last name was the big one—Jackson had simply printed "Downtown," and alongside it the name "Peters" and the approximate time he appeared at the main drop to collect the biggest part of the graft for the mysterious protectors "downtown"—police headquarters.

The Westchester and Bronx maps were similar. On the New Jersey map Gennaro's drops went across the state from Hoboken to Camden, and instead of cops he had the names of local politicians.

But the main nugget was missing—Gennaro's main bank in East Harlem, the heart of his entire policy organization. I flipped through the notebook and finally found the tiny slip paper-clipped to the inside cover. The carefully printed letters stared out at me: 420 PITTMAN PLACE. . . .In my mind I walked up Third Avenue, past the new development on East 139th Street and the flock of old-law tenements they were tearing down for another project, but I couldn't place it . . . probably only a block long and off the main avenues.

I carefully clipped it back to the cover and put the book and maps inside my jacket pocket. It made a comfortable but uneasy bulge.

The winter light was fading; the sun had set, and although stains of rose-pink and gold were spreading across the West Side to touch the Sixth Avenue rooftops, the afterglow had not penetrated the lavender twilight in the park.

If all that Jackson claimed was true, I had in my pocket the big exposé Julian Savage wanted. I could almost see the gleam in his eyes. How this would shake up the little man with the old-fashioned watch chain and a big contempt for the headache makers in editorial!

It also became clear that while Jackson had given me a phenomenal set of facts, they had to be proved, and true to my own set of ethics I had to see them in operation for myself before I would write one word.

But first I had to tell Julian Savage his big one had arrived. The phone buzzed for only a few seconds before he answered.

"Duke? What's up?"

I quickly sketched what had happened.

"Come up right away," he said.

Julian met me at the door and ushered me into that same cluttered room. I waved away his offer of a drink, took some coffee instead, and settled back while he read the notebook and listened to my report on my meet with Jackson. I spread the map out on the floor and explained the red circles.

"Do you realize what we have here!" he exclaimed.

"I think I have a hint."

"It could be an enormous scandal. Enormous!"

The time had come to calm him down, face facts. "Remember the exposé we did on policy some years ago?"

"I think so. Nothing much ever came of it, as I recall."

"It was partly our fault. We rushed into print too fast."

"But didn't one story tell how the police raided a large number of policy drops and made arrests?"

"That's true," I said. "But the publisher, on the insistence of the Legal Department, decided to print the articles without the names and addresses of the specific locations. The day the first article appeared, we handed the real list over to the cops. By the time the first edition came out they had made some raids and nabbed a few runners and comptrollers."

"But obviously the ring couldn't operate without the connivance of the police. What did they do about it?"

"It's the same old story, Julian. After the raids the commissioner came out with a big statement transferring a whole division and some inspectors. The reporters at police headquarters called it the biggest shake-up in the history of the Police Department. This was the ninety-eighth time they said this. In fact, if you get together all the stories about police transfers that have been printed over the years, they'll all read alike."

"It's only for public consumption, then?"

"The public takes it all with a grain of salt."

He smiled. "I gather, then, you are not ready to turn this information over to the police."

I put down the glass. "Definitely no. What I want to try and do is prove it myself."

"How? By playing the numbers at these spots?" he asked.

"No. That would be breaking the law and letting ourselves open for criticism. What I would like to do is go along with Jackson, see everything for myself, and get as much down on tape as possible."

He looked concerned. "You mean on the miniphone and the other taping devices you showed me? Won't that be terribly dangerous, Duke?"

"It's only dangerous if you are caught—and I don't intend to get caught. From what I know of the people who work in the policy drops, they are not especially dangerous; it's the bosses who are."

"I'd rather give this over to the police than risk your getting hurt."

"It would be a waste of time to give it to the cops in this shape. They will be forced to do their own investigation, and it will be news to me if one cop turns in another for taking money." I got up to intensify what I was saying. "Look at it this way. Either we can have a brief flash in the pan, slam-bang series, or we can really have something important to give—not to the cops—but to Flaherty's office for a possible grand jury investigation."

He may be a good gin player but he's not much of a poker player, I thought, as the quick glow of interest showed in his face.

"In that way the paper will really be doing that important public service you talked about," I went on quickly. "We will present fully documented evidence of official corruption that cannot be ignored."

"But as you yourself said, Flaherty doesn't want any scandal."

"Actually, we have no choice. If we uncover evidence of a criminal conspiracy, we must eventually go to the D.A.'s office. But it's a break for us with Flaherty going to Geneva."

"You mean with Johnny De Lorenzo taking over the Racket Bureau when he's away?"

"Johnny has never worked on a deal with a newspaper before but he's young and ambitious."

"But can he be trusted, Duke?"

"You and I have to gamble on the answer to that question, Julian. I don't know if De Lorenzo is so honest he would rock the boat in his own office. Frankly, if the chips were down he might be bought with a cheap magistrate's job. I just don't know."

"Then we're really playing against odds?"

"Yes, but how do we know the odds won't be with us? As I said, I don't know anything about De Lorenzo, except that he's young and comes from a fine family."

"The most unprincipled rogues have come from fine families, Duke," he said with a wry smile.

"We may be worrying about bridges that haven't even been built yet."

"That may be true," he said in a soft but firm voice. "Maybe it's my way—but I like to have things set in place, even tentatively. Now what about Hoff? You said he was really masterminding the D.A.'s office. Although I'm frank to say, I just can't understand the importance you place on him. To me he looks like a"—he waved his glass, seeking out the right word—"an irritable gnome."

"So did Louie Howe," I reminded him. "If you read all the New Deal memoirs, he was the man behind FDR both in Albany and in Washington. If he had lived, who knows how his thinking might have affected us today."

"That party was the first time you'd seen him in two years?"

"The first time to speak to. Of course, I've seen him in Albany to say hello." I added: "The boys at the Hall say his wife left him and he's brought a red-haired secretary down with him."

"For a moment there I thought you two were going to tangle," Savage said with a grin.

"I don't like press agents in city or state jobs—no matter what title their boss gives them. They have only one real job, and that is to give us the news they want to see in print and to keep us from getting the news they don't want to see in print."

"And that's Hoff's job in the D.A.'s office?"

"That, and keeping an eye on Johnny De Lorenzo. But there was one thing different I noticed about Hoff: he's become a hard drinker. You can see it in his face and the way he was polishing off those doubles."

"But that's paradoxical, Duke," Savage cried. "On one hand you say he's a lush and on the other you say he's running one of the most important offices in the city."

"I guess it's unfortunate that in our business there are drunks that have talent. I once knew a city editor who disappeared one week out of every eight. Once I had to bail him out of Bellevue after a cop found him directing traffic in the altogether. But sober he was the greatest; he ran his city desk like Patton ran his tanks. On the other hand, I knew another city editor who never took a drink. He was a loudmouthed bully who shouted everyone down to hide his own incompetence. He was always cursing reporters, passing the buck, and never had an idea in his head.

"I guess that's the way it is in politics. The boys would rather let Hoff disappear for a few weekends and know that when the chips are down they have a pro on the job.

"I'll play Hoff close to the vest. I've done a little checking around with that redheaded secretary he brought down from Albany. I don't think the D.A.'s office will see too much of Hoff."

"When someone tells me they don't make good reporters any more, I'll give them your name, Duke."

"I told you this might be my last; I want to make it a good one. By the way, how was the cocktail party?"

"Very nice. Miss Ryder asked me to be sure and thank you for that story. She seemed disappointed you couldn't come."

"I hope you gave her appropriate excuses."

"I told her you were out molding public opinion," he said with a grin. "She asked if the opinion was blonde or brunette."

"It will be a neglected blonde," I said, "who will be slightly annoyed if I don't see her this evening."

"Something serious, Duke?"

"It was when we first met two years ago, but now I think we both accept it for what it is."

"Well, about this policy business . . . I'll go along with you if there are no risks involved. As I told you, I want exposés and big ones, but not if it means you risk your neck. If there is the slightest possibility . . ."

"I'm beyond the age of wanting to play cops and robbers for a by-line, Julian," I told him. "I simply want to prove as best I can what Jackson is giving us. No matter what his motives, I believe we owe it to him."

He slapped the table lightly, as if his mind had been made up.

"Very well. Go ahead. But you must give me your word of honor, Duke, that at the slightest hint of any danger—"

"—I'll run like the coward I am."

[8]

I'VE KNOWN Gwen Erickson for more than two years. We met at a cocktail party, one of many such parties during the winter thrown to celebrate everything from the debut of a starlet to launching a new salami. This one was a press party to introduce a luxurious hotel. I was wandering through the beautiful sample suite when we collided at the doorway. I gave her the complete guided tour, returned her to the watering spot, and tried to rescue a few canapés. Gwen has a fantastic appetite and told me quite frankly she was starving. A two-inch thick sirloin at the Pen and Pencil remedied that.

Gwen is thirty but looks years younger. Her father was a ship's captain who died in a torpedoing when she was an infant, her mother a superb cook. The thick blonde hair, blue eyes, and coloring came from her Swedish father, but she inherited her love of the theatre from her mother, who died several years ago. Gwen is a cheerful, optimistic soul. She's never defeated or crushed, even though plays and parts have escaped her. She always managed to survive on unemployment insurance and a spot in Macy's hardware department. Finally she clicked in a small off-Broadway drama about the French resistance and got some fine notices. Two other mild successes followed, then the big one a few months ago. Hollywood bought it, and Gwen's agent has gone all out to include her in the package.

In the beginning I told Gwen I loved her, and she said that was nice but let's wait awhile. Then I got busy, and it was her turn to confess that maybe she was in love with me. Her success in the off-Broadway show made her change her mind, and she was again brightly, intensely in love with the theatre. This's the way it has been going on for the past few years. I think down deep we both feel we will eventually get married, but we're in no rush, which is slightly ridiculous at my age, and Gwen, for all her beauty, isn't getting any younger.

The first feverish physical intensity has worn off—not that we both don't enjoy it; in fact, for me Gwen has forever killed the legend of cold Swedes—but we have found that intimacy of emotions is just as important. We share as many weekends and vacations as possible. Gwen is bored with Europe, so for the past two summers we explored New England from Maine to the Cape, and last Christmas we spent in Wisconsin with her sister, who is just as beautiful as Gwen, although she has a small army of kids and helps her husband on a dairy farm.

There is one thing that Gwen and I do not have in common and that is the newspaper business. She loathes Broadway columnists and insists I should leave the business and devote all my time to writing. When I point out to her a writer can spend months, even years, only to have the work rejected, she points out that's the way she had to move up and why can't I do the same thing.

There's no use telling her that such moves should be made in the hard, white light of the twenties, not the mellow glow of the mid-forties.

Anyway, we both need each other, although of late I have sensed a restlessness in her I never noticed before . . . moments of dreamy-eyed vagueness . . . more fights with Bunny, her fairy director . . . more than usual distaste for what I am doing.

Despite this, Gwen is still my favorite sounding board. She has a shrewd insight and often has put her finger on a vital flaw I have overlooked either because of closeness or personal involvement. Cold objectivity is not one of my characteristics; as Gwen once said, I'm the type that starts civil wars.

Her place was on East Fifty-seventh Street, a stone's throw from the Plaza. I gave the usual one-two-three buzz, which was answered promptly.

She was standing in the midst of her impeccable big single room. She had on slacks and that deep-blue turtleneck sweater that never failed to take my breath away. Every time I see Gwen I have the feeling she just came in from a two-mile walk in a Vermont woods. She's a damned attractive woman, and I have never found out why she went for me.

"As Jackson would say, you have enough health for three broads," I said after kissing her.

The blue eyes widened. "Who's Jackson, Duke?"

"A gangster friend of mine."

"You have the damnedest friends," she said. "What does he do, murder people?"

"You know the fifty cents you gave your doorman to play that number last summer just before we left?"

"The one I had in a dream—seven, seven, seven?"

"Right. Well, Jackson is in that kind of a racket. Numbers, Bonito, or whatever you want to call it."

She went over to the small bar and poured me a drink.

"And what do you have to do with Mr. Jackson?" She turned slowly and, without waiting for my answer, said, "Another exposé?"

"It could be a big one. Cops, politicians, the works."

She turned back to the bar. "Oh, God." She splashed whiskey angrily into the glass.

"It's my job."

She handed me the glass. "Your job! Exposing those horrible men in that parking lot, then government loans, bail bonds! And policy, some crooks padding a city payroll. You should leave all this and write —not stories that are forgotten in a few days but something important!" She walked across the room and picked up a battered *Collier's*. It was the one containing a story I had written that had made the Foley collection that year.

"I reread this the other night and showed it to Bunny. Fairy or not, he's a damn good judge of writing, and he says you're a fool to continue to write those nothing stories."

She mixed herself a drink, studied me over the rim of her glass; then, in her impulsive way, she leaned over and kissed me. "I'm sorry." She took me by the hand and led me to the sofa. "Tell me about it."

"How much time do you have?"

"About an hour. Tell you what, bring in your drink and while I make us some scrambled eggs, you talk."

"It's a deal." I followed her into the tiny kitchen, which was nothing more than a stove, a sink, and a few shelves, and sat at the breakfast bar. Here Gwen and I had finished many a party and welcomed many a dawn. As she broke the eggs, and prepared toast and bacon, I started to tell her about policy—New York's favorite game in which any man, woman, or child can dream for a penny or a dollar.

"Well, it's a big racket," I started off, "probably one of the biggest in the country. I once read a report put together by a foundation that estimated the annual gross at more than five billion."

Gwen stopped whipping the eggs and milk. "You're kidding."

"I wish I were."

She set the bacon strips on paper napkins and buttered the toast. "But if it's illegal, how does it make that much money?"

"Take your doorman and multiply him by hundreds of thousands. In factories, offices, on street corners, anybody that has a penny can bet."

"But how does it work? How do you win?"

"Well, it goes like this. You can pick any three-digit number from 000 to 999. If your number comes out, you get 600 to 1. If you want to hedge your bet, you can box it, like this." On a napkin I made a box and inside it the combination 165. "By boxing this number you bet on a number of combinations, 165, 156, 615, 651, 561, and 516. But if you hit you get only 100 to 1."

She placed the eggs and bacon before me, poured boiling water into the cup of instant coffee, glanced at her watch, and slid down opposite me.

"But why don't the police stop it?"

"Very simple. Too many cops are being paid."

She gave me a vexed look. "Every time you talk about policemen, Duke, you act as if everyone in the whole city is crooked. I just don't believe that."

"I never said there aren't honest cops. It would be a hell of a city if there were twenty-four thousand thieves guarding our lives and property."

"I don't like it when you sound so cynical. You'll get like those old actors. So sophisticated. So smart. So annoyed with the world."

"Well, then we'll be a great pair," I said. "You can be an old actress and I can be an old newspaperman. We can both be so smart, so sophisticated, and so annoyed with the world."

She went to a dresser and got a towel. Again I felt the restlessness, the air of uncertainty.

"I don't know if I want to be an old actress." She shuddered. "What an empty life."

"I thought you were going to outdo Bergman."

"That was last year before Fancy Living." She turned to me. "You know something I found out?"

"What's that?"

"The kicks are not in getting the big part but in fighting for it. Yesterday I went over to tinware in Macy's and saw all the kids I used to work with. It made me blue all day." She paused at the door of the bathroom. "Duke, dear, do you really think it's important that cops are being paid by gangsters and little people like my doorman spend fifty cents on a number?"

Before I could answer, the door slammed and I heard the hiss of the shower. I poured another drink, settled down in the sofa, as the old doubts began to stir. . . .

She came out, a flash of exciting white skin that the big towel didn't hide, and ducked behind the small wooden screen near the closet.

"I guess I should mind my own business," she said softly.

"But it is your business, Gwen."

A zipper stopped midway. "Oh? What have I got to do with your thugs?"

"Remember that documentary we saw on television last month— the one about the young boy who got hooked on dope?"

I could see her shudder. "It was horrible."

"Well, who do you think brought in the drugs that hooked that kid?"

She came from behind the screen, still zipping. "Racketeers, I suppose you're going to say."

"Correct. And where do you think they got the money?"

"I wouldn't know, darling. You're the expert."

"Gambling, mainly policy. Your little doorman's fifty cents, plus some crooked cops, some tinhorn politicians, and you."

"Me?"

"You and a lot more like you in this city who ask the same thing: Is the enforcement of law really important? While you—"

She glanced at her watch and whooped. She raced across the room, picked up her coat and purse.

"I'm sorry, darling," she said breathlessly, "but Bunny will kill me if I'm late."

The thought of Bunny putting on one of his girlish tantrums made me grin.

"You can continue your good-government lecture when I get back."

When you get back, Gwen my love, only an idiot would think of good government.

She blew me a kiss and clattered downstairs. I watched her hail a cab and disappear in the thickening theatre traffic.

With Gwen gone I made more coffee, then spread the maps on the floor. There, in the comfort of Gwen's apartment, I think for the first time I got the real impact of Vito Gennaro's vast policy empire.

I finished my coffee, turned off the lights, and stretched out on the couch. Outside, the wind was up; the traffic had dwindled. Strange, I thought as I dozed off, the greater the city, the greater the scandal. While New York boasts of its magnificence . . .

I was awakened by the click when Gwen snapped off the light in the bathroom. She hesitated for a moment, then started across the room in her long, flowing white nylon gown. She looked like a moth gliding across the room seeking the light. I kicked back the covers and said her name, and she came to me with a heady scent and a whispering passion.

[9]

TWENTY YEARS AGO, after that first disaster as an investigative reporter, I rented a tape recorder, purely for my own protection. As a result of my story on that corrupt city official, a reader had sent me an anonymous tip that a Times Square druggist was selling black-market vaccine overseas; more frightening, the vaccine was watered down. The druggist was the greediest man I had ever met; his greed dulled his common sense. I told him I had recently come in from Berlin and mentioned a soldier's name, and within fifteen minutes I had been admitted to his back office.

I promised to return the next day. That night I sought advice from Ben Parsons in our Legal Department.

"Rent a miniphone and get the conversations on tape," he advised me. "That way you'll have something to give the U.S. Attorney's office, and we'll have something to shut up a lawyer if he screams libel."

The next day I rented a miniphone. It was small and compact, not much bigger than a cigarette case, and strapped around my waist just under my belt. The microphone, no bigger than a button, I scotch-taped to my neck, just under my tie. The electronics dealer assured me the powerful mike would pick up conversations many feet away. When I wanted to record, all I had to do was to click the tiny handle I could feel through my shirt. The tape lasted an hour and a half.

It was amazingly simple. The horrible druggist dickered with me for over an hour for two thousand dollars' worth of vaccine. A stupid man, he was easily flattered; it didn't take much to wheedle out of him how he paid a young clerk in a pharmaceutical warehouse to steal the vaccine.

On the basis of the recordings the U.S. Attorney's office assigned the FBI to the case. The druggist was arrested along with the clerk. Both insisted they were innocent until my recordings were played. The druggist broke and implicated the clerk, who in turn accused the druggist. The ring stretched from Germany to some of the occupied countries. The Food and Drug Administration got into the act, to pass stronger regulations to control the drug. The recordings went from the government to the State Educational Board in Albany, who stripped the druggist of his license after he was sentenced to a year. Later reports from the State Department revealed shocking cases of victims of the cut drug.

After that, I had no trouble persuading the *Blade-Leader*'s management to buy electronic equipment. Before long I was using the latest types, miniphones weighing only a few ounces, recorders in attaché cases, one in the form of a hearing aid, and an invaluable machine that records a telephone conversation by simply attaching a small suction cup to any receiver.

In the beginning I was ragged in the city room. To one rewriteman who seriously argued that I was doing a cop's job, I pointed out that the newspaper's job still was to root out corruption and injustice, and the only way to do that was to obtain evidence that would force politically motivated officials or hacks to act. Newspapers have no power of subpoena, only the hard white light of public print, but often to get the facts published a reporter found electronics more useful than his police card to get past his own Legal Department.

By now my arguments have been confirmed by other newspapers throughout the country who have established departments of investigative reporters using tape recorders to gather evidence. Their Pulitzer prizes, their congressional hearings, their new laws, are my briefs.

Before I left to meet Jackson, I strapped on a small, powerful recorder. I didn't know where we were going, but I wanted to be ready if he agreed to take me uptown. I decided not to tell him about the tape for two reasons: the knowledge I had the recorder might make him cautious and uneasy; more important, I was sure he would refuse to let me accompany him.

I clicked on the machine and recorded: "This is Duke Malloy, Tuesday, eight-thirty. The headline in the *Times* is on the race clash closing the Detroit schools and the WOR program *Morning Tips to Housewives* is at this moment featuring a new type of diet aid called 'Low-Sweet.' I am about to leave my residence, 214A East Thirty-eighth Street, to meet a man named Jackson, who has promised to bring me to one or more policy drops he operates in West Harlem as a member of the Vito Gennaro syndicate. The conversations that will follow will be what I believe to be pertinent to a series of stories my paper, the New York *Blade-Leader,* proposes to publish following the conclusion of my investigation. I have fully advised my publisher, Mr. Julian Savage, and our chief counsel, Mr. Benjamin Parsons, of my actions. This machine will be next turned on by me when I am in the company of Jackson. It is now eight-forty."

This was a procedure I adopted each time I used a tape. First, identify the day and the hour by current headlines or radio talk, and give the reasons for the use of the tape.

I took one last look around my cluttered two rooms that I had since just after the war, switched off the radio, and went out, still unable to shake off the vague apprehension that clung to me since the night I first met Jackson.

I found him leaning against the wall, his coat collar up around his ears, watching the same old lady feeding the pigeons. He had an unmistakable look of disgust on his face.

"Why don't they stop these old nuts from feeding these damn' pigeons. I read in *Reader's Digest* where they bring all kinds of disease," he said. "Well, what's the word, kid? I want to know how far will you go."

"As far as possible," I said defensively. "I want to get Gennaro and the cops and the whole thing, but it can't be done just by writing a series on what you gave me."

"Why not? I even gave you the cops' shield numbers, the locations of drops."

"I want to see it in operation."

He was indignant. "Don't you believe me? Why the hell would I lie to you?"

"Come on, Jackson, let's not be stupid. You know I have to see it for myself before I write a line. This is too important, too big. Why blow something this good by a slipshod operation?"

This seemed to mollify him. "I told you it was big. I never bother with any small-time crap." He studied the cooing pigeons glumly. "How are we going to move?"

"Very simple. I'll just tag along with you. I'm just a guy from Jersey."

He considered that. "None of the uptown boys know any of the Jersey guys. It's a separate operation."

"I won't stay long, maybe an hour or so, just to get an idea of what's going on."

"I could pass the word you're on vacation in the city." He snapped his fingers. "Wait a minute! The A.G.'s office in Jersey knocked off one of Gennaro's drops in Camden last week."

I made a mental note to contact the Attorney General's office in New Jersey. Apparently it was one office Gennaro couldn't buy.

Jackson began to warm up to my role. "I'll have one of the runners from Jersey bring in his car. You'll drive me up to the uptown drop, and we'll park in the garage near the candy store."

"Why a Jersey car?"

He explained patiently: "You're supposed to be from Jersey, right? After you come in I'll send one of my flunkies to get a pack of cigarettes from the glove compartment. Because those bums don't trust their own mother, they'll check the cache and find the Jersey ribbons."

I knew what a ribbon was—the adding-machine tape used in the policy racket—but cache was new to me. I said as much.

"I forgot to tell you about that. One of Gennaro's friends in Brooklyn sent him a guy who can do more mechanical tricks than a monkey with coconuts. He equipped every one of our cars both here and in Jersey with a cache . . . a hiding place for the ribbon."

"You mean he just made a place in the trunk or the seats?"

"Hell, no. He fixed it so it's like a secret drawer."

I was truly puzzled. "How does it work, Action?"

"When I get the car from Jersey I'll show you," he said impatiently. "Well, we can't do anything without the car for the setup."

"How long will it take to get it?"

"About two days. Suppose we make a meet Thursday morning. Make it uptown. Somewhere on the West Side near the Drive."

On impulse I said, "There's a small place named Hamilton Park on Eighty-second just off the Drive. Meet me there about nine, okay?"

"Okay," he said in his abrupt way. "I'll see you then."

Thursday morning was diamond clear when I emerged from the subway exit and walked down the long sloping street from Broadway to the Drive. I walked slowly, savoring every old brownstone, ash can, elderly housewife glumly walking the dog, dim-smelling areaway. I knew there were two sewer plates, one for home base, one for second. Then I saw the small park, and beyond it the icy-gray Hudson, the winter-stark Palisades, and the graceful span of the Washington Bridge, its toy cars moving at a snail's pace. There was little wind and the air was almost painfully cold, and so clear I could see a deckhand on the passing tug hurrying below with a steaming pot of coffee.

I kicked a stone, and it bounced off the battered drinking fountain. It's funny, I thought, to go back to a place where you grew up. You almost expect to see yourself in shapeless slacks and the proud old sweatshirt with Newman High in block letters, carefully taking lay-up shots at the netless rim, recovering fast off the backboard, and pushing the ball up again with just enough english to make the shot fancy but true. And you expect to see that boy, bored after a while, slump down against the wall of the handball court and glumly eye the deserted playground, and you feel like telling him not to be bored but to appreciate what he has because they're his greatest years and no matter how hard he tries he will never be able to go back.

And then you close your eyes and try to believe it's you slumped down in the handball court, feeling the warm heat from the sunbaked wall coming through the old sweatshirt. But then who is this guy with the touch of gray at the temples standing by the fountain? Why, this is Duke Malloy, of course. Don't you remember Duke Malloy? He used to come out here and play basketball morning, noon, and night until he was the best damned basketball player in the whole school—in fact, on the whole West Side. He was so damned good they gave him a choice of scholarships, but he chose the one to Missouri because that's where he heard they had the best journalism school, so he went there because he wanted to be a writer and a newspaperman more than anything else in his life.

That's Duke, Mary Malloy's son. You mean the schoolteacher with the old-fashioned bun and the big brown eyes? The very one. What ever became of her? Don't you remember when Duke went off to war and his name was in all the papers because he was crazy enough to go ashore with the marines on Tarawa and Guadalcanal? She died in that old brownstone right down the block. And after Duke came back from Woodlawn, he went right back to the war. He said he was going to write the damnedest novel about it, but somehow he got sidetracked and later he could almost taste the envy when he read Dick Tregaskis and John Hersey who were with him and who had the guts to sit down and write it all.

And after the war what happened to old Duke? Oh, he came back and finally did write some fine short stories, but he got hung up on the *Blade* where the dough was good, the life was easy, and boredom was never a problem. So that's the story.

You come back to an old place, stand in the cold sunshine, see a kid in an old sweatshirt lazily throwing up a few, and you see ghosts. . . .

I looked up when I heard the car door slam, and Jackson was walking toward me, hands thrust into his coat pockets, collar up about his ears. Automatically I touched the tiny recorder under my belt. It had about four hours of life in it.

He shook his head as he looked around my postage stamp of a park.

"You certainly got a collection of creep meeting places, kid."

"I once knew somebody who hung around here. You all set?"

"As set as I'll ever be." He added morosely, "I hope we don't goof on this one, kid."

"Look, I worked in a parking lot, in a hospital, and on a tow truck," I told him. "I met every wreck hustler on the island, and they never doubted me. If I can con them, why can't I con some of your bums."

He shrugged. "I guess so." He looked at me wonderingly. "I read those stories you wrote about the tow-truck racket. You know, someday, kid, somebody's going to kick your brains in."

"Just make sure it won't be in a Harlem spot, Jackson," I said fervently. "I'm the biggest coward in ten states."

He grinned. "Don't worry, they'll never get on to you. Just keep your mouth shut and don't ask questions." He looked at me admiringly and threw me the keys. "You drive, Jersey."

I had decked myself out to play the part: tan suede jacket, black slacks, highly polished shoes. I don't know why, but I have yet to see a gambler or a policy racketeer without highly polished shoes.

As we approached the car I could see the Jersey plates. It was a new Cadillac, which certainly fit my role. Like their polished shoes, gamblers or guys who work in numbers must drive Cadillacs.

Jackson carefully looked about the neighborhood. There was only a woman shepherding two small children across the street. In a moment they disappeared around the corner.

"I'm going to show you the cache," he said hurriedly. "Turn on the radio, then the defroster and fan." I followed his instructions as he climbed into the back seat. His hand slid back the plastic covering near the rear window and uncovered a small brass button.

"Watch the panel near the radio."

As I turned I was amazed to find what appeared to be part of the dashboard click open.

Inside was a small bundle of adding-machine tapes, the sacred ribbon of the policy racket. So this Cadillac was a legitimate ribbon car for some part of the Jersey operation.

Jackson pushed the button twice and the compartment closed. He smoothed the plastic back into place and slid into the front seat.

"Who thought up that?"

"Some con named Louie who came out of the Connecticut State pen last winter. They got him in touch with Gennaro, and the next thing I know we have to turn in the ribbon cars, one at a time. When I went over to see Gennaro, he showed me the first one. Even the cops haven't caught on yet."

"And you're going to make sure one of your boys checks this compartment?"

"As I told you, kid, these guys are born suspicious. This is just added insurance. The guy who checks the cache will pass the word that you're a Jersey collector. They're like old women. Talk, talk, talk."

We drove up the West Side Highway, turned off 125th, and went up Lenox Avenue. No matter how many times I visit Harlem, it never ceases to disturb me that a city as large and beautiful as New York could allow this cancer to exist. Not only does it exist; it grows with each passing year. I have a strong stomach, but there have been hallways that made me taste bile for a day. The sight of this teeming, God-for-saken place never fails to infuriate me. This is something I tried to point out to Gwen about corruption; it can begin with a few greedy landlords who make fortunes on helpless human beings who never let a bed grow cold—with four shifts, how could they?

"Christ! How the hell can they live like this?" Jackson murmured as we screeched to a stop to avoid a cursing five-year-old.

"Put on a black skin and find out," I told him.

"Balls," he snarled. "I got collectors who make two C's a week. They still live like slobs!"

"You wear that black suit and go down to Park Avenue with a handful of money and try to rent an apartment."

"Most of 'em are baboons, black baboons," he said, "no matter where you put 'em."

Thus Professor Jackson's lecture on the Dignity of Man as it pertains to the Bill of Rights, Section One, Part Five.

At Jackson's directions I swung into West 138th Street and came to a stop in front of a shabby garage just off Amsterdam. The heavy grease-smeared doors were covered with chalked four-letter words and old political posters. Jackson reached over and blew two sharp blasts on the horn.

"They'll be out in a minute. Christ, look at this street! This creep street! Christ, how I hate it!"

There were tenements on both sides. People were sitting on nearly every stoop, savoring the cold sunshine. Refuse from overturned ash cans littered the streets. A scrawny, half-starved mongrel savagely tore apart a paper bag and gobbled down its contents. Midway down the block several small boys were jumping in and out of a car that had been stripped down to its rims. Two drunken derelicts lurched past, and the boys rolled an ash can in front of one, who clumsily tried to dodge, then fell in a heap while his companion raised a half empty bottle menacingly to the boys, who shrieked curses from behind the junked car. The bum got to his feet and, holding on to his companion, both carefully descended a flight of basement stairs and disappeared.

Leaning against a stoop a few doors from the garage, a dark-skinned man in an old overcoat waved to Jackson.

"The invisible man couldn't walk down this street without being spotted," Jackson pointed out with satisfaction.

"How do they tip you off?"

"Notice every guy on the stoops has a rolled paper? They just touch their hats with it and everything closes down like it was the Fourth of July." His wave took in the whole busy block. "I have 'em all on the payroll, from kids to grandmothers. Last winter one old dame spotted a guy on the next block who didn't look kosher. We shut down while the East Side checked him out. He was one of Murphy's heroes from downtown."

"Didn't you say Murphy is honest?"

"He's a straight arrow cop," Jackson said, and added with feeling: "The son of a bitch! If I . . . Here they come." The overhead garage door was rising to reveal a thin, morose-looking man in greasy overalls that hung from his shoulders like a scarecrow's coat. Jackson gave him a perfunctory wave, and we drove into the gloomy cavern tainted with the sweetish smell of gasoline and oil.

"Pull over by that Buick," Jackson said. "That's our ribbon car."

"That one got a cache in it?"

"I told you they all have." He lowered his voice as the man in overalls came up. "Say nothing and saw wood, kid."

"What's this heap doing here?" the morose-looking man said in a monotone.

"We got business, Louie. Come on, kid." On the street he explained, "Act like he's dirt. He expects it. Treat him nice and he'll get suspicious."

"That's Louie?"

"He's the guy Gennaro calls the genius. He makes the caches in the cars. He's got a shop back of the garage with a lot of electrical stuff." He gave a short laugh. "He even installed a hi-fi set for a magistrate."

"Wait a minute! Do you know the name—"

"Cool it, kid. Don't you think I've been trying for the judge's name? Sure I know it's important, but you just don't go around asking for judges' names—you know that! I'll wind up in the river."

"Where's your place?"

"The store next to the corner. Now, you got it straight? Anybody ask you questions, just shrug." He arched his neck. "This is only good for maybe today and tomorrow, kid. You know that?"

"If it's as wide open as you say—"

"Don't worry about it being open." He waved. "Hiya, Johnny."

A smiling, dark-faced man sitting on a rail tapping his knee with a paper rolled with a rubber band flashed a smile. A woman called out from a hallway; the game in the ruined car erupted into a fight and a girl's voice began wailing, then snapped off as someone played with a radio dial.

"Baboons!" Jackson exclaimed.

Suddenly there was a shout at one end of the block. I turned to see several young Negroes turning the corner. There was an eerie robot air about them as they marched down the street, eyes unwavering, backs arrow-shaft straight. They were neatly dressed in drill trousers and dark blue overcoats. But they all wore the same funny hat, small, red, and shaped like an upside-down flowerpot. Long tassels of blood-red silk dangled from each one as they passed. In size, shape, and dress they could have come from the same mold. The street seemed suddenly silent, hushed. The young boys stared out at them through a shattered window of the old car, eyes big and round. After they had turned a corner, the block rushed back to life; the boys began slamming the battered hood with a stick; a woman came out of a doorway and shouted a command at one of them. A janitor dragged out a heavy ash can and cried hello to one of the lookouts on the porch.

"Who were the guys with the hats?" I asked Jackson.

"They call themselves the Young Liberators. They work with the Prophet. The bastard's going to cause trouble up here someday."

"Who's the Prophet?"

Jackson waved impatiently. "Some nut. Here it is."

The store was large, with two big display windows. Their contents were incredibly old, a few sunbaked boxes of cigarettes, a badly fly-specked school notebook, sagging strips of tattered colored tissue paper, and a bent cardboard figure of a girl in a bathing suit begging the customers to buy a special brand of ice cream. One foot had been torn off. Curtains served as backdrops for both windows. Obviously the store hadn't been used for years.

Jackson started to open the door. "Hey, just a minute . . . Oh, boss! Hey, boss, where you been?"

Inside, several men, black and white, sat around a table playing cards. To the left was a candy counter with bits of moldy candy.

Behind the counter was a short, round-faced man with skin the color of polished ebony. He was wearing a checkered flannel shirt, a stained fedora, and had a pencil stuck behind his ear. The guard at the door turned out to be a slender mulatto in his late teens.

The Negroes and white men at the table turned, stared at me briefly, then went back to playing cards. The round, dark face impassively watched us approach the counter.

"Hiya, Action. We just got the night numbers."

"Good play?" Jackson asked.

He grunted. "Why not? It's payday." He held up a yellow pad, and as both he and Jackson bent over to examine it I casually moved my hand inside my jacket as if to scratch myself, and turned on the recorder.

"Not bad for a beginning," Jackson said, and half turned to me. "This is Duke from Jersey. We got business later. Duke, this is Tilley." He swung around to the table. "And these jerks are just a lot of bums."

The announcement was greeted with tentative smiles. One or two mumbled hello; the rest nodded and turned away. Tilley smiled briefly and said, "Make yourself at home, Duke. . . . Johnny, get off your ass and give the man that chair."

Johnny, grinning, flipped his chair over to me and I sat down.

"How many PD's got paid off today?" Jackson asked.

"Those new jokers that just got on the job," Tilley said angrily. "They came in for a pound note five minutes after the last number yesterday."

"The bums got a stopwatch," one man at the table said.

"Did the East Side call?" Jackson asked.

Tilley shook his head. "I took care of three stand-ins. They each got an SS." He gave me a smile. "You got stand-ins in Jersey, Duke?"

For a moment he took me off guard, but I remembered Jackson's warning and mumbled, "Sometimes yes, sometimes no."

Jackson gave me an approving look.

"Did you get the shield numbers of the cops?" Jackson demanded.

Tilley shook his head. "They came in with the night collectors. I didn't have time."

"The bastards got a stopwatch, Action," the man at the table repeated with outraged indignation. "I swear it!"

"Get their numbers the next time they come in," Jackson said. "The East Side wants the numbers of every cop we pay."

I suddenly realized that Jackson was trying to put things on the record for me. My mouth went dry as I thought of the slow-moving recorder under my shirt.

Jackson eyed the large paper bags Tilley was tying together. "How many night collectors we got now, Tilley?"

"About twelve. That new guy who'll pick up up at the project next week will make thirteen."

He looked questioningly at Jackson, who appeared to be mulling a problem.

"I think we need a few more," Jackson said. "Ask that guy at the project—what is he, superintendent?—if one of the day guys he works with wants to pick up. Maybe two more guys, what do you think?"

"One more's enough. We'll split the project between them. Lots of single-action play over there."

"Okay. You handle it."

The morning passed with Jackson totaling and initialing piles of adding-machine tapes and calling out the totals to Tilley, who rapidly double-counted seemingly endless piles of greenbacks and mountains of small change. They were as efficient as any bank tellers. The cards were now cleared away, and two adding machines were on the table with the cardplayers totaling the night numbers, which were delivered in large paper bags and handed in through the door to Johnny. As each batch was totaled, a man scrawled "night" on the paper bag in black crayon and a number—the code numbers I had in Jackson's black book.

Toward the end of the first hour, Jackson paid off his first policeman of the day. Johnny said in a low tone, "Here's the PD," and opened the door. A uniformed patrolman walked in, and through the half open door I could see a radio car at the curb.

The cop was jovial and white haired. "Hello, boys," he called out. "Looks like a busy day. . . . Hello, Jackson, we missed you the other day." He turned around, gave me a brief look.

"Give him a pound note, Tilley," Jackson said with contempt.

"Come on, Action; I got a partner outside," the cop said.

Jackson stared at him in long silence. "You come from the 53rd D, don't you?"

"Sure. What's that got to do with our pound?" the cop said, his smile fading a bit.

"You're over at the East Side, that's what it means," Jackson snapped, "and this is the West Side. Eighteen blocks to pick up a pound note from me! You want me to call the sergeant down at the 19th Division?"

The cop looked uneasy. "Okay, if you—"

Jackson snapped to Tilley, "Give him a pound."

Tilley took a small roll of bills from his pocket and carefully, deliberately counted out five singles on the counter. The cop hesitated a moment, then picked them up.

"Maybe I can do you guys a favor someday," he said stiffly.

"Do yourself a favor and stay in your own precinct," Jackson said, "or maybe someday the walls will fall in on you."

The cop, in a half whisper, said, "Just look out the walls don't fall in on you someday, wise guy," and went out.

The man at the adding machine said bitterly, "Like the commissioner sent him."

Jackson asked, "Did you get his number?"

"One-Zero-Four-Jay-Six, Manhattan East," Tilley sang out.

Jackson looked up, irritated. "Wait a minute, repeat that."

Tilley repeated the number, and Jackson wrote it down. He looked over at me, and I sensed he was following a natural opening.

"Can you imagine that, Duke, those bums came all the way over from the East Side to put the bite on us!"

"Aren't they on your pad?" I asked.

"Hell, no," Tilley said. "They're freeloaders."

Jackson said with a show of anger, "We pay downtown twice a month, we pay the Sergeants' Club—"

"Sergeants' Club?"

"The precinct sergeants," Tilley told me. "We have to pay every shift in the three precincts we cover."

Jackson clicked off on his fingers: "That's not counting the courts, the lawyers, and bail bondsmen. After you get through paying you got—"

Tilley asked me, "You pay big in Jersey, Duke?"

"Big enough," I said shortly.

"He's got the town knocked up," Jackson said. To Johnny at the door he said: "Get my cigarettes in the glove compartment of that Jersey car in Louie's. . . . Duke, give him the keys, will you?"

I could almost feel the stir of interest in the room as I threw the key case to Johnny. I sensed that Jackson was moving in fast to establish my role; the key case had a small black bottle with the name of a Paterson, New Jersey, nightclub.

Johnny returned in a few minutes with the cigarettes, then went back to his guard duty. I caught a brief look pass between him and Tilley and the men at the table: although Johnny had never uttered a word, through some weird underworld osmosis Jackson's policy hoods knew I was driving a New Jersey policy-racket ribbon car.

At noontime Johnny brought in some hero sandwiches, those huge, unwieldy gastronomical horrors, and a few cans of beer and soda. But Jackson, probably to maintain some kind of status, took me to a nearby barroom where we had a surprisingly good hot-meat sandwich and a beer. This was Tarcey's Bar, he told me, patronized mostly by the policy mob.

"Is this where you hang out?"

He nodded. "There's a phone booth in the back. That's where

Gennaro calls me when he has something personal to talk about."

"Like what?"

"Like anyone who makes a big hit. He wants to make sure they're relieved of their dough by a heist man."

"You mean to say that winners are held up!"

"They leave 'em a C note . . . that's more than the slobs had in the first place," he said indifferently.

"Good God! And they're stupid enough to keep playing even though they know they'll be robbed of their winnings?"

"It's not done every day," he said. "Only in the case of a big hit. What the hell, it's six hundred to one! Besides, you have to know these people, kid. It's not only the money; half the fun is the thrill of winning. You ought to see how they carry on! Everybody buys 'em a drink; everybody's slapping 'em on the back, even old ladies! It's like a big game, and every day's a new session. Anybody can play for a dime." He finished his beer. "Don't look now, but at the end of the bar there's a toy monkey; when the inspector's man can't make it I put the loot for downtown in an envelope behind it."

"There's a set time, isn't there?"

"Four o'clock, the first and fifteenth of every month. Like they were punching a time clock."

"If the inspector's man can't come, how do you get word?"

"I get a call on that back telephone—the one Gennaro uses. Somebody says: 'Charlie can't make it today. Please give the message to Tarzan.' "

" 'Tarzan'?"

Action grinned. "The toy monkey. Hey, Dummy! Come over here and let me rub your back for luck."

Wiping a nearby table was a tiny man not more than four feet high. He had a towel tied around his waist and he was wearing a bright checkered shirt. He was not only a dwarf but a hunchback and deaf and dumb as well. One of the men turned him around and pointed to Jackson. The horrible little man, grinning foolishly, waddled over to the bar, and Jackson reached down and rubbed his back.

"Got to rub the Dummy's back every day."

"Man, why don't you rub his ass? That's better," someone called out.

The men at the table roared, and one reached over and pinched the dwarf's cheek. The little man kicked out violently and ran behind the bar.

Jackson, still grinning, said, "Come on, let's get back before they rob me blind."

The drop was humming when we returned. A steady stream of

collectors from all over West Harlem delivered their bundles of plays in brown paper bags. Tilley was a busy office manager, the cardplayers now clerks. I leaned against the door and made small talk with Johnny, who tried to pump about the operations in Jersey. My monosyllabic replies soon forced him to give up.

Once the wall pay phone rang. No one bothered to look up when Jackson answered, listened, and hung up.

"Seven," he announced. The mob's service, or racetrack contact, had called from the track with the first pari-mutuel number of the first race. Shortly after the second number had been called in, Johnny said, "PD, Action."

"Those bastards from the East Side again?" Jackson exploded.

"No. Peters," Johnny said.

Jackson gave me a quick look. This was Sergeant Peters, the bagman in his notebook. I felt my mouth go dry.

When Johnny opened the door, a stocky cop with sergeant's stripes walked in, swept the room with a glance, not missing me, and walked over to Jackson. Despite the cold, there was no color in his face; the hair under his hat was white. He looked dangerous.

He approached the counter and stared for a moment at Tilley.

"Blow, jig," he said almost tonelessly.

Tilley gave him a look of unconcealed hate and walked into the tiny toilet at the end of the counter. The sergeant said something in a low voice to Jackson, then turned away. He walked straight toward me.

"Who are you?" he asked in a flat, emotionless voice.

My heart began to beat faster; those hard green eyes seemed to pierce right through my jacket to the tape recorder.

"The name's Duke," I said, the words coming out like dry stones.

"Duke what?"

"Duke Mantee," I said lightly, but he never got the connection.

"Where are you from?"

Jackson sauntered over. "He's a friend of mine from Jersey, Peters. Maybe you'll be dealing with him one of these days."

The thin lips said, "Maybe I will and then maybe I won't." He said to Jackson, "I'll see you on the fifteenth."

Action walked him to the door. "Okay, I'll see you on the fifteenth. Regards to the boys."

Jackson and Johnny watched the sergeant ride away in his radio car, then turned to us.

"No playday tomorrow," Jackson said tersely.

"Downtown going to visit us?" one of the adding-machine operators asked.

Jackson nodded. "Two o'clock." He said to Johnny, "Make sure the door is locked so they can bust it open. That'll make them feel better. Joey, you and Tommy be here so they can make some vag arrests. Tilley, get the machines and work over at Tarcey's in the morning. Johnny, tell the collectors no playday tomorrow. I'll tell the East Side."

Tilley said softly, "Someday I'll take that white bastard and turn him inside out."

I prayed that the machine was still running as Tilley explained to me: "He's from the Sergeants' Club I told you about. The meanest son of a bitch in Harlem. He'd turn in his mother for a buck. Last month he broke up a kids' crap game, took all their money, and knocked one kid's teeth out." His voice rose slightly: "Man, I'm telling you! Someday we're going to take these white—"

"Me too, Tilley?" Jackson said lightly. "You going to turn me inside out, too?"

Tilley's anger slowly died, and he gave Jackson a crooked grin. "Man, I'm gonna put stove polish on you when that day comes."

The men at the table grinned, and Johnny kept mincing around the room, rubbing his face with a dirty handkerchief, and whining, "Mastah Jackson, you better give me some of that polish . . . man. I need to get darker. . . . Mistah Tilley say he gonna turn all us white folk inside out."

"Come on, come on," Jackson growled, "let's get this show on the road."

I glanced at my watch; it was just about under three hours since I had switched on the tape.

As the afternoon went on, runners and collectors delivered their work and were checked out. Money was counted and stacked in cardboard shoeboxes. After the hundredth bag had been delivered I stopped counting.

As the piles of currency began mounting, I felt the tension grow in the room. Johnny now carefully scrutinized the visitors and locked the door behind them after they had been admitted. Later, Jackson told me this was the highly dangerous hour for any large policy drop; young junkies, desperate for money for their fix, sometimes selected the drops as targets. Gennaro's thugs usually caught up with them, but to the policy mob they were classified as necessary business risks.

Shortly after five, Jackson snapped a rubber band around the last stack of bills.

"I'm going to buy Duke a drink," he said shortly to Tilley. "We have a little business."

Tilley looked at his watch. "You want me to take care of the Sheik today, Action?"

Jackson spat out the answer, "No. I'll take care of that son of a bitch myself." He added grimly, "Someday, real good."

Tilley gave me a self-conscious smile. "They ain't the best of friends, Duke."

"So I gather."

Outside, Jackson said: "I don't want you around when the ribbon car arrives. The Sheik hates my guts and may just start to ask some questions. We'll sit near the window and you can see him."

"You have a pretty smooth operation."

"Not bad." He gave me a look. "What do you think?"

"What I've seen today—is the same all over?"

"Some are busier. Especially near the projects."

"Was that the Sergeant Peters in the book?"

"The same. He collects for the Sergeants' Club . . . and downtown. He's mean." He shook his head. "I didn't like the way he came over to you. . . . Who the hell is Duke Mantee?"

"That was Humphrey Bogart's role in *Petrified Forest*. You can see it on the late show. I was only trying to get a smile out of him."

"Don't try any humor on that guy. You heard what he said about the fifteenth? That's Sergeants' Day."

"How much do you pay?"

"Six sergeants in the 18th . . . five in the 20th . . . seven in the 25th . . . eighteen, total. A hundred a week for each . . . eighteen hundred a week . . ." He thought for a moment. "Ninety thousand a year. And Peters gets fifty bucks extra each time he picks up the envelopes. And a few other incidentals."

"What did Peters want, Action?"

He whispered, "Murphy is going to pay us a visit tomorrow."

"Just how would Peters, a sergeant up here, know about a raid to be made by the Confidential Squad?"

Jackson shrugged. "I found money buys a lot of people, kid. It's simple; there's a leak in Murphy's squad. Maybe nobody more important than a telephone man or a clerk. Maybe they're not even crooked. Cops get diarrhea of the mouth sometimes. They talk like old women downtown. Maybe this guy wasn't told outright; maybe he got just a hint, a word here, a word there, and with his know-how he put it all together and out came a raid. He's not right all the time, but I'd rather get ten false alarms then one good bust. Murphy and his heroes got big feet!"

"Were you ever hit by Murphy?"

Jackson nodded and said almost admiringly:

"He kicked in the door, tore off the phone, kicked Tilley's big ass down Lenox Avenue, threw every adding machine and typewriter out in the street, personally smashed them to pieces, broke every window in the place, and not only grabbed us for numbers but gave me a summons for keeping a public nuisance and yanked in the super of the building for Fire Department violations."

"I can't figure it out," I said. "There are cops like Murphy and cops like Peters."

"With Peters and his bums it's a way of life," Jackson said philosophically. "They've been doing it since they got on the job. What are you going to do?" As we reached the door of the bar he said in a low voice, "When we sit down I'll talk a lot about take and percentages— okay? You play me by ear. I can't prove it, but I think the bartender stoolies for Gennaro."

In Tarcey's a few patrons called out greetings, but when one made a move to join us Jackson's cold stare discouraged him. We sat at the far end of the bar where we had a clear view of the block and the drop, and engaged in an intense discussion of a fictitious policy operation in New Jersey, its growing expense, and the demands of the collectors for a bigger percentage as the bartender meticulously wiped a section of the bar near us. I told myself that before this investigation was completed, I had better carry an Actors' Equity card besides my police card.

It was a few minutes after six when Jackson said casually, "Well, here's the East Side, Duke, I'll be back in about fifteen minutes." He called to the bartender, "Hit us again, kid."

The East Side's ribbon car was a dark green, late-model Cadillac. The man who got out first was young, slender, handsome. When he turned I could see he was swarthy and had thick, wavy hair. While he waited for the other two men to get out, he carelessly ran a comb through his hair, and then, with an unconscious, almost feminine gesture, gently set a deep wave. A dark-skinned woman walked across the street, and he followed her every step.

Frank the Sheik who wouldn't turn aside a snake.

The two other men were young and tough looking. Both carried large paper bags. They all went inside the drop. I jotted the car's license number on a paper napkin. License-plate numbers are as important in any investigation as the record of toll calls.

It was closer to a half hour when the trio came out and drove away. Jackson soon rejoined me at the end of the bar, to tell me in a whisper that Gennaro was leaving town for a few days.

"The Sheik told Tilley the Wop had a long-distance phone call."

"It could be important. Did they say where from?"

"Down South. He said it sounded like a dame's name. Isn't that just like that bum? Everything means a dame, even the name of a town."

"Will you try to find out, Action? This could—"

"Okay, okay," he said impatiently. "Look, you better blow now, and I'll pick you up tomorrow."

"Same time?"

"No. Make it noon. I got to come here in the morning." He walked me to the street. "I'll take care of the car."

"Will you hit other places tomorrow?"

He looked down the crowded street. "I gave you my word, didn't I, kid?"

"That you did."

"I'll see you in the morning."

I spent all that night transcribing the tape. It was a laborious business of listening to a sentence, then typing, missing a word, rewinding and replaying. There were a few scratchy spots, but the important segments came through clear and vibrant. I played the Sergeant Peters section several times to make sure I got every word. Each time the flat, emotionless voice filled the quiet of my apartment I could see those chilly lime-green eyes and the dead-white face. I wondered if they would change expression in the Grand Jury room. . . .

I watched the dawn edge over the city. It was another clear, bright winter's day: a sanitation truck noisily chumped on its breakfast of refuse; construction workers in drill pants and yellow, mud-stained shoes exhaled the first sweet drag to the cold dawn; taxis impatiently crouched at the lights, buses insolently elbowing their way to the curb, the first shifts of precinct men eyeing their victims parked in no-parking zones.

I waited until seven, then called Savage. He sounded bright, alert, and listened intently as I outlined what I had accomplished.

"It looks like a good start, Duke?"

"But it's only a start," I pointed out. "The one thing we have in the tape is this sergeant warning Jackson about the raid today."

He sounded dubious. "How can you prove it?"

"I'll be up there when Murphy's men hit. What we have on tape, together with my eye-witness report, should interest the police commissioner—"

He broke in, "Oh, I had a call from your friend Hoff yesterday afternoon."

I felt my hand tighten on the phone. "What did he want?"

"He wanted to alert me on a release he was sending over—"

"De Lorenzo's appointment?"

"Right. There will be a small ceremony this afternoon, so I told him we'd send over a photographer. He wanted you to know he made it a P.M. release—just for the *Blade*. He said he remembered you hate to read things in the *Times* and *Trib*."

"Well, how nice. Look, Julian, did the release say anything about De Lorenzo sitting in for Flaherty?"

Savage chuckled. "I was saving that for last. Listen: 'Mr. De Lorenzo will be Acting District Attorney when Mr. Flaherty leaves for Geneva where he will attend the International Conference on World-wide Drug Traffic as representative of the United States. Mr. Flaherty, who was appointed by the President, will leave on the tenth, accompanied by his wife and assistants Martin Solomon, Luther Rundy, and George—' "

I interrupted, "They're all legislative assistants. Well, now we know how things will be."

"Do you think with Flaherty gone we can get De Lorenzo to act, Duke?"

"Let's see what we can get in the next few weeks," I said. "So far, one drop isn't evidence of an organized syndicate. I'll give you a call in the next few days and we'll see what we have."

Like a veteran bachelor I went through breakfast and shaving automatically. Before I had finished the last stroke, I had made up my mind to play the tapes for Jackson and try to persuade him to let me tape one of his calls to Gennaro.

When we met at Hamilton Park I told him we had to go back to my apartment. He eyed me impassively.

"I thought you wanted to start the grand tour today, kid?"

"We have a few hours before the action starts," I said. "I want to play a few records for you."

For a moment I thought he was going to explode, but instead he nodded slowly and settled back in his seat as I drove across midtown. He followed me silently up the elevator and inside my apartment. I heated what coffee remained and poured two cups.

"I didn't play it straight with you yesterday," I said.

He tested the coffee and set it down. "Who told you how to make coffee?" He looked up at me. "What did you do—call the cops?"

"Don't be stupid," I said. "I taped everything that was said in your drop."

"Including me?" he asked softly.

"Including you. And frankly, if you walk out of here and blow the whole thing I won't blame you."

"You have the tape?"

When I nodded he said shortly, "Let's play it."

Those were the longest hours I have ever spent. The voices filled the room: Tilley, the cardplayers, against the rapid clicking of the adding machines, the curses, the laughter, even the far-off flushing of the noisy toilet. It was all there, preserved on the shiny thin wire that wound in and out the portable recorder.

When it was finished Jackson said simply: "I ought to break a chair over your head, you crazy bastard! Suppose one of those cops decided to frisk you?"

"Why should they—you were my insurance," I said to him—bluntly and honestly.

He arched his neck and glared at me. "Something could have happened. Suppose the damn machine made a noise or broke down—"

"Impossible."

"Or one of the guys decided you weren't kosher and called the East Side."

"Did they ever call the East Side over your head, Action?"

He took a sip of coffee, and grimaced.

"I'll heat it up," I said, and went back to the stove. "Look, Action, we just have to use tapes. It will be indisputable evidence."

"Why tapes?" he snapped. "I gave you all the info and I'm taking you around to prove it! What the hell more do you want?"

"I want tape recordings of everything I can get," I said. "What I saw yesterday is only the beginning. If I can get tapes like this in every drop we hit—we'll have the biggest thing in New York." I put a steaming cup before him. "Look, Jackson, you want Gennaro more than anything else in the world, is that right?"

He stared silently at the black coffee.

"And I'll do everything I can to put him there; but remember, we'll need every bit of evidence we can get. Look at yesterday, what did we get?"

His head shot up. "Didn't I prove everything I said?"

"You proved to me that a policy mob was in operation. But under the law you showed one policy drop, two tinhorn cops guilty of taking five dollars, and a sergeant named Peters possibly guilty of departmental violations by being off his beat. There's nothing here to connect Gennaro. It's a numbers drop, that's all!"

He kept staring into the coffee, then slowly poured in some cream. He tasted it, added some sugar, drank half a cup, then gave me a look.

"When this thing blows in your paper those tapes can be Grand Jury evidence. Right?"

"I promise you I will never turn them over to the D.A. unless you give me the okay."

"But I don't get it—why the tapes?"

"They will be evidence backing up our stories. It's up to the D.A. or the cops to prove it in their own way. It's nothing unusual not to reveal the name of an informer—er—confidential source."

"Don't try to spare my feelings, kid. I'm your stoolie. If that ever gets out"—he slowly drew his finger across his throat—"it will be open season on Action Jackson."

"You must have known that in the beginning, Action," I said. "Or else you wouldn't have told me you were going to blow town two days before it broke."

He said wryly: "You got a long memory, kid. I forgot I told you that. Okay, I did figure that eventually they might finger me." He nodded to the recorder. "You really believe that can do in the Wop?"

"I'll give you a guarantee with every tape."

At last, in a very soft voice, he said, "Okay, let's shoot the roll."

I moved in fast while I was ahead.

"Okay. The whole roll," I said. "I want to tape a call from you to Gennaro."

He looked startled. "Why, for Christ's sake?"

"First of all I want to get his voice on tape at the unlisted number over at the East Side. Then I want you and him discussing something to do with the numbers."

He whistled silently.

"He's the mainspring."

"Show me the machine," he said.

I brought out the small gray metal box with the pencil-thin cord and its tiny rubber suction cup. I carefully explained how it worked, then demonstrated by attaching the cup to the phone and dialing the weather bureau. Then I rewound it and played back the tape.

"Okay," he said, "I'll make the call, but not from here."

"Why not?"

He gave me a contemptuous look. "You're not so smart after all, kid. Suppose Gennaro says he wants to call me back, what do I do—give him your number?" He carefully wrapped the wire around the box and put it in his overcoat pocket. "We make the call from uptown. If he wants the number I'll tell him I'm in Tarcey's joint."

Of course! The phone booth in the rear of Tarcey's bar where Gennaro usually called Jackson.

"You don't think there's any danger?"

"Nobody goes back there when I'm on the phone. They know it's East Side business."

"What can you get him to talk about?"

"I'll put in a beef on those cops that came in yesterday and tell him

Peters rates a bonus. Every time that bum tips us off on a Murphy raid, he gets fifty bucks."

"Incidentally, I have to see that raid. Suppose I stay in Tarcey's."

He shook his head violently. "Are you nuts! Murphy will sweep every crumb out of there. After he hits it, he'll know it's a setup! He'll bounce every bum in the cooler."

"Isn't there any spot, on a roof, or from a basement? This stuff I got yesterday won't mean anything unless I can swear I saw Murphy's men raid the drop, which was empty as a result of the visit by Peters I have on tape."

Jackson glared at me. "Jesus Christ! What do you want, a case wrapped in tin foil?"

"I want it so that no one can unwrap it," I said.

He went to the stove and kept grumbling to himself as he poured another cup of coffee.

"Well, maybe if I put you up at Tilley's place," he said grudgingly. "He has a place down the block. I think you can see the action from his window." He glanced at his wristwatch. "We better be moving out." He finished the coffee and made a face. "What did you make this coffee out of—shoe buttons?"

Even though it was half empty, I could feel the undercurrent of electric tension the moment I entered Tarcey's Bar. Three of the adding-machine operators were at the bar talking to the bartender when we entered. The jukebox was blaring a wild jungle tune, and the bartender was nervously polishing some glasses. The adding-machine operators, who looked high, shouted a boisterous welcome.

"You pass the word?" Jackson asked Tilley, who slid out of a booth.

"Everybody knows it's no playday. The whole Avenue's playing up at 145th Street." He turned to me. "Hiya, Jersey."

"Duke wants to see the action, Tilley, so take him up to your place. Okay?"

"Sure, why not?" Tilley said. "How about a drink?"

Jackson looked at his watch. "Okay, order me one. I'll be back in a few minutes; I want to call the East Side."

"Big business with the East Side," Tilley murmured. "Gennaro blows all gaskets when it's no playday. He figgers he buys one cop, he buys 'em all."

"You can't buy everybody," I said with a suffering air. "You think maybe you can, but you can't."

"That's a fact," Tilley said soberly, "that's a fact. The last time

Murphy busted us I told Jackson, from now on we get hospitalization."

I grinned at the recollection of Jackson's description of Murphy booting Tilley's big rear down Lenox Avenue.

After we ordered a drink, Tilley asked, "How long have you been in the Jersey action, Duke?"

"Too long, Tilley, too long."

"I went to Jersey once to visit a cousin," he said with a trace of bitterness. "They got Harlems everywhere."

"You married, Tilley?" I asked, more to change the subject.

He nodded. "Two kids, boy 'n' a girl. I'm gonna move 'em out of here when they get the project finished on Seventh Avenue. I got a guy in McShane's club who's working on it."

I tried to sound casual. "McShane? He's the big man in this town, isn't he?"

Tilley gave me a startled look.

"Are you kidding, man? He's the—here's Action."

Jackson hung up his overcoat above the booth and slid in. His only sign of nervousness was his habitual arching of his neck; he moved it from side to side as though the collar he wore was unbearable.

"East Side give you a hard time?" Tilley asked.

"No more than usual."

"The Wop mad about no playday?"

Jackson said evenly: "The Wop's always mad when dough don't come in. Look, you better take Duke up to your place and tell those guys at the bar to blow. I don't want any short hands tomorrow."

"Business as usual tomorrow?"

"Of course," Jackson said shortly as he downed his drink. To me he said, "I'll see you tomorrow about the same time."

As Tilley squeezed out and went to give the orders to the men at the bar, Jackson whispered: "Got it. I'll pick you up at the park at seven."

The tension I had sensed in the bar was even more evident outside. One of the adding-machine men walked rapidly down the street, half lifted his hand, and men lounging on the stoops vanished in basements and doorways. Even the wrecked car was abandoned, but I had the eerie feeling that hundreds of eyes were watching as I followed Tilley across the street.

"In here," he said, and walked up a stoop and pushed open a scarred, battered front door. The smell inside the hall almost gagged me—foul, acrid, unbelievable.

"The bums use it for a toilet," Tilley said shortly as he mounted the stairs. "And the junkies for their shooting gallery. What a joint!"

There was only a single naked bulb hanging from the ceiling.

On the second floor he knocked twice and called, "Lola, it's me." There was a rattling of chains and locks before the door was opened by a pretty colored girl, obviously pregnant.

"Hello, honey," she said. "I didn't know you were bringing company."

"Come on in," she said as Tilley locked and chained the door. "I have the coffee by the front window."

As we walked through a typical railroad-flat bedroom, Tilley moved the bed and felt what appeared to be a newly plastered hole near the molding.

"It will be hard by tonight."

His wife bit her lower lip. "I hope so. The children are just frightened to death, and so am I."

Tilley grunted at me. "Rats. They bit both our kids last winter. One kid, the youngest, had nightmares for weeks. They come through the walls every month at a different place. Last time I stuffed in about a dollar's worth of steel wool, and plastered it. The next day they came through again. I swear they had a meal." He slammed back the bed. "God, how I hate this place!"

"No word from the club?" she asked.

"They told me we'd get in by summer," he said, with a false note of cheerfulness.

The kitchen was the largest and obviously most lived-in room; there was a TV set in one corner, with a pile of magazines, a knitting bag, a worn sofa, and a few chairs near the lowered venetian blinds. A small table held a coffeepot and cups. The oven, door open, was on.

From the kitchen we went to the front room, or parlor, which overlooked the street. This room was cold and almost bare. The windows had paper stuffed aorund the edges of the sill.

"This is our summer place," Tilley said. "Everyone in Harlem calls their front room their summer place because the bastards don't send up enough heat and the room is too far from the kitchen stove." He kicked at the rusty radiator. "There hasn't been any heat in this thing since 1959. The pipe's been busted that long. Here you can see the drop." He opened the venetian blind and pointed to the store, then to a tenement at the far corner.

"One of the guys is up on the roof of 471," he said. "That's halfway up the block. When he spots 'em coming, he signals to the guy up on our roof and he'll come down and tell me."

"In other words the lookouts moved from the street to the roof."

"That's about it. How about some coffee?"

We sat in our jackets, drinking coffee for about a half hour, making small talk: the bazaar of the United Baptist Church of West Harlem; the PTA of P.S. 108; the story of a young boy named Petey, aged fifteen, who died of an overdose; the woman who keeps throwing her garbage down the airshaft, and the landlord who can't be found to fix the toilet on the floor above, which floods every week.

"Man, I called that landlord fifty times," Tilley said. "I just can't find him. When the man comes with his hand out for the rent, I grab him and say, 'Where's the man?' but, hell, he don't know from nothin'."

"Can't you bring the owner to court?" I asked.

Mrs. Tilley said, surprised, "Sugar Hill?"

It was all I could do not to spill my coffee.

"They're the owners?"

They both looked at me in surprise, and Tilley said, "Hell, they own everything on this block." There was a pounding on the door. He jumped up.

"Here they come!"

We joined him at the blind and peered down at the empty street. In a few minutes an unmarked police car spun around the corner, roared down the street, and came to a stop in front of the candy store. Men with axes, crowbars, and sledges jumped out, and in almost one motion a sledge crashed in the door. It flew open and the raiders poured in.

"Benny, Joe, and Tommy's in there," Tilley said. "They'll rough 'em up and then take 'em downtown on a vag charge."

"Is that serious?" I asked.

"Like spitting on the sidewalk. They'll be out working tomorrow." He nudged me, "There's Murphy."

A square, rugged-looking man in a black overcoat and gray hat stepped out of another car, walked inside the door, and emerged almost immediately. He stared up and down the block, studied the roofs, then returned to the car, which left.

"Murphy knows when it's a setup," Tilley said, chuckling. "He knows he's been had."

"What does he do about it?"

"What can he do? Shift a few guys, move in another few, and just hope he can pin his leak down." He added emphatically, "Man, I wouldn't be his leak if they found me out. Will that Murphy burn him!" He spread the slats of the blind. "Here's the boys."

The raiders emerged with three of Jackson's men and pushed them none too gently into the car. Then they turned and almost methodically smashed the windows of the front door, shattered the big pane of glass, and reduced to junk an adding machine one of them tossed into the street.

"That adding machine ain't worked for a year—Jackson was going to throw it out anyway," Tilley crowed gleefully. "Man, these cops are as bad as firemen!"

The sledges and crowbars were tossed into the back of the car, and it left. The street seemed to hold its breath for a few minutes; then the lookouts emerged to take their same positions on the stoops; the band of young boys began jumping in and out of the wrecked car; and a colored man in an army coat began sweeping up the shattered glass.

"I gotta call the glazier and the carpenter," Tilley said.

"I have the list for the A&P," his wife said. "You can pick up the stew meat." To me she added, "I hope you can stay?"

They both seemed genuinely disappointed when I refused, but insisted that before I went back to "Jersey"—to every New Yorker it's a major journey—I would have dinner with them.

The winter dusk had settled in the dirty street and the lights were on by the time we started for the subway. Once I casually asked about Sugar Hill Financing Company, but all that Tilley could tell me was that it seemed to be accepted in some areas in Harlem that Sugar Hill— "Sugar Daddy," as they called the company—owned their crumbling tenements. It was also accepted that it was virtually impossible to reach anyone of authority in the company who would authorize repairs. I sensed a sort of reluctance on Tilley's part to discuss the company.

"Sugar Daddy can be real mean," he said vaguely. "You squawk too much and they'll kick you out."

"That's impossible."

"Nothing's impossible if you got connections downtown," was his reply. "Look at the Wop . . . see what I mean?"

I saw what he meant.

It was a four-block walk to the subway; the A&P was across the street on Seventh Avenue. As we came up, a crowd of about two hundred men and women were gathered in the street in front of the supermarket's parking lot.

"What's going on?" I asked.

"The Prophet's holding one of his meetings. Ain't you heard of the Prophet over in Jersey, Duke?"

"Can't say I have. Wait a minute, isn't he the one who was arrested a few years ago in Philadelphia?"

"Philadelphia? Man, he's been arrested in more places than any guy in Harlem. 'Member last summer in Baltimore? Man, they bounced their clubs off that nigger's skull!"

Now I remembered. The Prophet, an obscure black demagogue who seemed to be getting more and more publicity—and more followers—in the last few years both in the South and in the North as a result of his hate-white program. A few years before he received national publicity when he was beaten in Philadelphia for leading a riot at a new school site. Later, in a press conference at his hospital bed, he prophesied that the local chief of police and Public Safety Commissioner would die violently within twenty-four hours for what they had done. Four hours later the police chief and the Public Safety Commissioner were killed and more than a dozen policemen seriously injured when a boiler exploded in the Philadelphia police headquarters where the chief and commissioner were holding a high-level conference. The Prophet, whose real name was Isaiah Redmond, was immediately arrested and held for investigation, but a Grand Jury attributed the cause of the explosion to an overheated boiler. After that, the Prophet's membership skyrocketed.

"Let's listen to him for a few minutes," I said.

"No white man's talk, Duke."

There were four mounted cops, a sergeant, and two patrolmen standing on the fringes of the crowd.

"It looks like the cops expect trouble."

There was an edge of bitterness in Tilley's reply. "There's a lot of trouble in Harlem. Last week the cops killed those two colored kids in a car. They said they caught 'em snatching a lady's pocketbook. Maybe. Why the hell they take 'em in a cop's car eight blocks away? Why the hell they don't take 'em to the precinct and book 'em? A woman said she seen the cops beating one kid. The cops said they pulled a knife. But nobody ever saw the knife. The poor kids were junkies. They needed a fix. Okay. They snatched this woman's pocketbook. They do this to Lola, I kick their teeth in. But I wouldn't kill 'em." He turned to me. "The cops in Jersey break nigger heads, Duke?"

"I guess there's trouble everywhere on this score, Tilley."

"Someday the cops up here will hurt a colored guy once too often. Then things will blow up." He added admiringly, "Man, that Prophet can talk!"

Standing on a makeshift wooden platform was the strangest man I had ever seen. A long, pointed face, black as a coal shovel, topped by long white hair gave him the look of an angry black eagle in shabby clothes. His head was perched on a neck so thin I was sure a good sneeze would snap it off. His voice wiped the smile from my face; it was deep, rich, and full of savage music. It soared over the heads of the listeners and smashed me across the face. White man. White man. God-damned white man.

"The white man doesn't want you to be good citizens," the voice cried. "They hate you! Hate you! Hate you! He wants you to get drunk and act like pigs so he can take you to his precinct and put the club to you. The white man taught you to hate. He taught you to hate yourself. Some of you hate your hair so much you put lye on it to make it straight."

He gripped the wooden railing and peered down at the crowd for a moment in silence. Standing in a row, shoulder to shoulder in front of the platform, were several tough-looking young Negroes in red fez hats, like Shriners. Young Liberators, Tilley had called them yesterday. In that sudden silence all that could be heard was the shouts of boys playing stickball down the street and the heavy, lumbering noise of a Seventh Avenue bus.

Then the deep voice said slowly, "You know what hell is, Mister?" The thin bony arm and the arrow-straight finger pointed. "You down there! He paused, and when no one answered, bent lower. "I'll tell you what hell is, brethren. Hell is when you're dumb! Hell is when you have the white man's foot on your neck. Hell is when you have what the white man calls justice! His justice! The devil's justice! There are twenty million dark men in this country!" He straightened and threw his hands in the air. "Dark men, are you going to leave the white man's foot on your neck?"

The crowd roared, "No . . . No!"

"Dark men, you gonna be his slave?"

"No! No!"

"Dark men, you gonna let these crooked cops beat your heads in?"

"No! No!"

The coal-black face twisted with hate.

"Dark men, you ready for the Night of the Black Fire?"

The crowd flung back its answer.

"Yeah, Prophet! Yeah!"

"Black Fire that will burn up the white man, make him ashes under our feet!"

He was screaming now, his bony hands waving in the air. Threads of spittle hung from his lips.

Beyond the crowd the mounted cops exchanged uneasy glances. One bent down and said something to a sergeant, who leaned into a police car. A patrolman picked up the microphone.

It happened very quickly.

A rock sailed through the air, and the big window of the A&P crumpled with a loud crash. More rocks followed; some toughs leaped on the back of a parked car and began bouncing it up and down. The mounted cops swung their horses about, and the crowd began retreating. Then one horse screamed in pain and flailed the air with its front hoofs. The mounted cops slashed down with a billy, and I could see a man clutch a bloody face. A woman clawed at the cop's reins; another cop grabbed her coat. The cheap fur collar came away in his hands, and the woman plunged into the crowd, which closed on the cop, fists and shoes working. Sirens wailed in the distance.

"I got to get you out of here, white boy," Tilley said, "before you get a broken head."

White boy. In that moment I was the enemy.

He pushed me into a hallway. Men were shouting and pounding down the stairs. I followed Tilley through the door at the rear of the hall into a yard, knee-deep with filth and festering garbage. We squeezed through a broken fence and into a back door of another tenement. Dark faces. The sweet smell of marijuana. Harlem's teatime. Tilley pushed them aside.

"They're shootin' up," he said as we walked down the front steps onto Eighth Avenue. "I'll walk you over to St. Nicholas. You better get a cab."

The cold street was almost deserted. Lights showed through torn shades. Black faces stared out at us from a candy store. More sirens wailed across the rooftops.

"What is this Night of Black Fire, Tilley?"

Tilley seemed taciturn, almost sullen. He was walking fast, as if he wanted to get rid of me.

"The Prophet keeps talkin' about it. He says it's the night Harlem's gonna blow up."

"You think it ever will, Tilley?"

He threw me an angry look.

"Somethin's gotta give up here. How would you like to run in and find a rat hangin' on your kid's face? When your mother comes over, how would you like to sleep in the summer room in an overcoat with the cold freezin' your balls off? How would you like that?"

I said I wouldn't.

"Whitey's got us in a jail up here," he said in an angry voice. "A great big jail where there ain't no bars—only stinking tenements, high rents, no jobs, and time, lots of time. Man, it's just like prison." A big black fist pounded an open palm. "Time. A lot of hours to do nothin'. Sit and look out the window. Sit on the stoop. Get drunk. Take junk. Listen to Whitey sob in his beer over you. Then when he's done sobbin' he just locks the door of our cage and goes back to his goddam nice comfortable world." He took a deep breath and exhaled noisily. "Man, I want to break out of this place! I want to break out of this place so bad I can taste it!"

"Listening to that madman isn't going to help, Tilley."

"Dammit," he cried, "I know that! All Harlem knows that! But who else is there to listen to? I don't mean those guys with the letters after their name! I mean the guys who move! The guys who do something! Sure the Prophet's a nut, but he's the only son of a bitch who gets things done!"

"You mean a madman is the only one who gets things done up here?"

"Man, you are so right," Tilley said, shaking his head. "Listen to this—last week he said he was gonna burn down a tenement on Seventh Avenue if the city didn't take it over and give the people heat. City Hall didn't want any house burned down, so the city took it over and the people got heat. He's nuts but he moves!"

"Did they ever find the landlord?"

"They fined him a hundred bucks. It wasn't even in the papers. The bastard went over to the club and put a fix in."

He walked in silence for a few minutes.

"Is that McShane's club?"

"Tamayanka, over on Fifth Avenue near the Rivington Houses. I just wish that bastard would put in a fix so I can get in that project! Man, just think of goin' to sleep at night and not worryin' about rats!"

A cab with a lighted hood came around the corner, and Tilley whistled shrilly. The cab swung into the curb.

"You comin' up tomorrow, Duke?"

"I'll be here. Jackson and I have a little business to work out."

"I'll see ya . . ."

He waved and walked off. It was almost seven o'clock. I forgot the Prophet, his weird Night of the Black Fire, and Tilley's anger, in the eagerness to know what Jackson had got on his taped call to Gennaro.

[10]

THE SMALL PARK was windswept and filled with moaning ghosts. The streetlight wavered in the chill wind, and somewhere down the dark street a horn sounded impatiently and a waspish woman's voice answered angrily. I could visualize the bickering as the gears ground into second, third, and the car sped down the drive.

I wondered what I would say if a passing radio car stopped to ask my business—waiting for a policy racketeer with a recording that could set off a time bomb in their own department?

But no radio cars passed, and I just walked up and down the block. When Jackson finally drove up, I slid into the front seat before he had put on his emergency.

"Kinda in a hurry, aren't you, kid?"

"Let's forget the kidding, Action. What did you get?"

He lighted a cigarette, inhaled, exhaled, and seemed to take an eternity before replying. In the tiny ruby glow his face was tired and tense.

"I got something so good I'm scared, Duke," he said finally.

"Did he talk about cops—"

"For Christ's sake! Stop havin' a baby."

"I'm just anxious."

"Okay. So am I," he grunted. "I got him talking about the East Side cops, and he okayed a bonus for Peters. But the main thing is, he was in a hurry so he told me to call Ricky tonight at his house and tell him—"

"Ricky Strasser! His lawyer?"

"There must be something big going on out of town or he wouldn't have told Bernie to call Ricky and tell him I was going to call with a beef—"

"Wait a minute," I said, exasperated. "Who is Bernie?"

"Bernie Levin. He's a kind of office manager over at the East Side. He used to be head of a department in a bank, but the horses got him. He's been with Gennaro for years." He sniffed. "He's a nice guy but a jerk."

I wanted to go over it step by step to make sure I had it all down in my mind.

"So when you called and put in a beef about the cops shaking you down, Gennaro told you to call Strasser; but first he had his office manager contact Strasser so he would expect your call."

Jackson turned to me and spoke slowly and emphatically, as if explaining to a child, using his cigarette as a pointer.

"He told me to speak to Strasser directly. But he also told Bernie to get in touch with Strasser and get a number where I can call him. I think it's the number of some dame's apartment. From what I—"

The impatience almost bubbled out of me. "And Bernie will give you the number when you call?"

"Right."

"And it will be of some girl's apartment where he's shacking up?"

"My, are we smart—"

"When do you call Bernie?"

He glanced at the luminous dial of his watch. "In an hour and a half—eight thirty."

"And you'll call Strasser right after that?"

"That's the idea."

"You got the recording?"

He patted his overcoat pocket. "I have everything okay. I did exactly as you told me . . . wet the suction cup, click the—"

"Let's go to my place," I said. "I need a drink."

He turned on the ignition. "Come to think of it, so do I."

Coming from Jackson, the cold, emotionless gambler, that was quite an admission.

Although I could scarcely contain my impatience, I sat sipping a drink while I pumped everything Jackson knew about Bernie Levin and Ricky Strasser. Levin, it developed, had been arrested shortly after World War II on an embezzlement charge. He had done some accounting work for Gennaro, who, Jackson insisted, fixed it so Levin received a suspended sentence and was put on parole for two years.

"The bum never reported to Worth Street once," he said. "His parole officer got fifty bucks a week, and just put down that Bernie was working in a paint store on Third Avenue."

"And after that he teamed up with Gennaro?"

"Gennaro put him on full time, and now he's in charge of all the paper work for the syndicate," Jackson said. "He's a hell of a man with figures but he's a real jerk. He still plays the horses and he's got some dame in Flatbush he's keeping."

"Is he married?"

"Got two kids—one is married and the other is going to NYU." He added wryly, "He told me the kid's taking accounting."

"Where does he live?"

"I think he said Brooklyn."

I found the Brooklyn telephone book and quickly scanned the "L's": "Bernard Levin, 435 Harrison Street" . . . another name for the Grand Jury.

"You want his dame's name, too?" Jackson asked.

"Definitely."

"I remember it because it sounded so stupid," he said with a grin. "Stella Schwartz. She runs a bail-bonding outfit on Schermerhorn Street, right outside the Kings County Court."

The same phone book produced "S. Schwartz, Bail Bonds, 2367 Schermerhorn Street."

"Her old man died about ten years ago, and she runs the business."

"You think she knows anything?"

"Are you kidding? She gets all the policy business from Bernie. The bum gets ten percent of every bond she writes. That's why I say he's a jerk."

"How does that make him a jerk?"

"Can you imagine what the Wop would do to him if he ever found out? And instead of keeping it a secret, he told me and Tilley last summer."

"Speaking of Tilley—he tells me his tenement is owned by the Sugar Hill Financing Company."

"Sugar Daddy owns most of Harlem. So what?"

"Nothing," I said. "Come on, let's play your recording."

He took off his jacket and a heavy sweater, opened his shirt, and took out the metal box. Then from a zippered inside pocket of his coat he removed the tiny coil of wire and the suction cup.

For a long moment we both stared at the oblong, gray metal box. Then I slowly rewound it and snapped it on.

Here is the Q and A of a transcript I made later that night:*

VOICE (*unknown*): Hello.

JACKSON: Let me talk to Gennaro. This is Jackson.

VOICE (*unknown*): The Wop's on another phone. I'll get him.

JACKSON: Okay.

  (*Pause: five seconds*)

GENNARO: Hello . . . what do you want?

JACKSON: We had a no play today, Boss.

GENNARO: Yeah . . . yeah . . . I know. Did they show?

JACKSON: Murphy came up, but they just busted in the doors and windows and took in Tommy, Benny, and Joey on a vag charge.

GENNARO (*Italian translated*): He should die in a trolley car.

JACKSON: You owe Peters fifty bucks.

GENNARO: He's a good man. The bum's always on time.

JACKSON: Yeah, this is the third time he tipped us this year.

GENNARO: Yeah, he's got a good pipeline downtown. . . . Maybe this time I give him a C note. Okay?

JACKSON: Okay with me.

GENNARO: Look, I gotta go. I'l be out of town, two, maybe three days. You listen to Bernie. Okay?

JACKSON: Look, Boss, I got a beef. Those East Side cops are shaking us down again.

GENNARO (*Italian translated*): Mother- ——— bastards.

JACKSON: Every day they come in with the hands out after the first number.

GENNARO: You get their badge numbers?

JACKSON: Sure. Tilley's got about fifteen . . . a pound note each—

GENNARO: A pound! You crazy? Tell 'em to screw their captain. What's the matter with these bums? . . . Wait a minute. (*Pause . . . Gennaro's voice resumes.*) Look, Action, I gotta blow—

JACKSON: Look, Boss, we have to—

GENNARO: Okay . . . okay, you talk to Ricky. . . . Okay? Tell him I said—

JACKSON: Ricky?

GENNARO: Yeah, yeah, you stupid today? Ricky—Ricky Strasser.

JACKSON: At his office?

GENNARO: For Christ's sake, listen! Bernie will call him and get a number where you can call him tonight. . . . (*Off phone, Gennaro shouts,* Hey, Bernie . . . Bernie . . . *low voices are indistinguishable.*)

GENNARO: Okay, you call Bernie tonight and get the number, okay?

* All transcripts were subsequently turned over to the Extraordinary Grand Jury.

JACKSON: Wait a minute, Boss. What do you want me to tell him?
GENNARO (*shouting*): Tell him? What do you mean, tell him? Tell him I want him to call downtown and to get those lousy cops off my back! That's what I want you to tell him. Tell him if they don't, I shut off the juice! That's what!
JACKSON: Okay, I'll—
GENNARO: You tell him good! You tell him Gennaro said so!
JACKSON: Okay, tonight.
(*Conversation is ended by Gennaro slamming down the phone.*)

After the rough, almost metallic voice broke off, the silence in the room was deafening. Jackson tested his collar with his finger and looked at me.

"Now you got my heart and my balls, kid."

I clicked off the machine and poured another drink.

"You know what we have to do now?"

He said blandly, "Sure, call up Gennaro and tell him I'm stoolin' for a newspaper and just taped his call—"

"Let's cut the comedy, Action. We have to tape your call to Ricky Strasser."

He laughed shortly and shook his head. "Jesus Christ, I love you guys! You know how many people we're going to hang tonight?" He checked them off on his fingers: "Gennaro, his stooge, Bernie; Bernie's dame, Ricky Strasser, and we must not forget Ricky's girl, right?"

"I'm going to get everyone possible," I said, "even the doorman at the apartment where Ricky is right now." I leaned forward and tapped him on the chest to emphasize my point. "And each one is going to help put Gennaro where you want him, right?"

"I know what you want, kid, but it's getting tougher every day." He stared at me for a long moment. "You know something?" He looked at the tape recorder. "After I left you I started to get scared."

The thought came to me suddenly, and my stomach went ice cold.

"Give it to me straight—did anything happen in the bar?"

"Tarcey's?"

I knew he was stalling.

"Look, Action, play it straight. We've gone too far—"

"Maybe I'm just getting jumpy, but after I got through talking with Gennaro I pulled off the wire"—he demonstrated—"and started to wind it around the box when I happened to look out the door."

His hand, palm out, made a diagonal slash in the air. "A little off the side where the booth is, is a door leading to the alley where Tarcey puts his ash cans. The Dummy usually takes care of that—"

"The Dummy! Did he see you?"

Action shrugged. "The door was closing when I looked up. I just caught a glimpse of that crazy checkered shirt he wears." He shrugged again. "Maybe he was just opening the door so he could move some of the cans. Tarcey's always yelling how he piles the cans up against the door."

But the thought shouted in my mind: How much did the Dummy see?

"Anyway, I had my arm up so nobody could see the wire while I was talking," Jackson continued, "and the box was under the phone box, so even if that crazy Dummy looked at the phone booth he couldn't spot it."

Jackson said almost angrily: "Look, that's the last time in Tarcey's. Anything could have happened—the Dummy, the cops could have knocked off the place—Christ, I was stupid to do it!"

I hastened to mollify him. "Okay, we made our score in Tarcey's, Action. Now let's get to Strasser."

"Not from here," he said emphatically. "Ricky's a jerk in a lot of ways, but he don't have policy comptrollers calling him every night."

"He won't object if you called from a phone booth?"

"Of course not—that's the way he would want it."

"There's a million phones in the lower level of Grand Central," I said. "Let's go over there."

Jackson had been a gambler most of his life, and almost instinctively avoided any show of emotion; but, despite his indifference, I knew he was disturbed by the incident in Tarcey's Bar. He turned down three phone booths for one at the end of the terminal, and before he would let me take the recorder from my pocket, he insisted on walking to the farthest corridor and peering down its length.

Only then did he squeeze in the booth, looking bunched up and uncomfortable in his overcoat and fedora.

"Okay," he said harshly, "let's get this one over with. What do you want to get on the tape?"

"You'll have to play it naturally," I began, but he cut me off.

"Okay, okay. I know what I'm doing. But this is a big one, and tonight I'm going for broke."

"Anything he says is important," I pointed out. "Have him make the point he will do something about the cops. You don't know his girl's name?"

Jackson gave me an indignant look. "For Christ's sake—" he began, but I shut him off.

"Only asking." I wet the suction cup and stuck it on the receiver, then snapped it on. "You're on your own."

He put in change, lots of change—it was a long call, probably the longest I have ever suffered through. I could hear Jackson's muffled voice once slightly raised as if protesting. Then at last he hung up and opened the door. His face was tense, and even in the dim lights I could see the sheen of perspiration.

"We got a break," he said. "He was high."

I snapped off the machine and replaced the phone recorder wire with the tiny plug-in mike.

"It is now eight forty-five in the evening," I whispered into it. "Mr. Jackson has just completed a call to Samuel Strasser, alias Ricky Strasser, attorney for Vito Gennaro, at ST 4-6676. The call was made from the third booth in the lower level, Lexington Avenue side, Grand Central Station. The number is WA 6-4320." I peered out the booth and saw at the far end a United Cigar booth attendant closing for the night. "At this moment, at the end of this corridor leading into the lower level, a United Cigar booth is closing. The attendant, a man in his sixties, wearing a gray shirt and pants, is pulling down clay-colored blinds over his booth. A man, obviously a commuter, is running past the booth, but stops and says something to him. He then hands the man something, and rushes on. This is for the purpose of identification made by Duke Malloy of the New York *Blade-Leader*."

I snapped off the machine, wound up the cord, and put the recorder in my pocket.

"I don't know about you," Jackson said as he arched his neck, "but I need a drink."

So did I.

In a booth in a bar off Third Avenue, Jackson filled me in. "As soon as he started talking I knew he was a little loaded, so I hit him hard. He tried to brush me off, but I kept saying Gennaro wanted action in a hurry. Finally he talked business." He gave me a wry look. "The dame's name is Vickie." He held up a hand as I started to interrupt. "He called out her name a few times when he wanted a pencil. I guess she was in the john."

I downed the drink. "Let's go to my place and hear it."

Jackson shook his head. "Brother, I need another one."

I made no attempt to hide my impatience while he nursed the second one.

"Take it easy, kid," he said. "I don't do this every night and I'm an old man."

When he finally finished, I started to slide out of the booth, but Jackson reached over and stopped me.

"Wait a minute, kid," he said softly, "I told you a little while ago I was going for broke tonight, right?"

I nodded, wondering.

"There's one more thing I can do; call Bernie and sort of report to him. This will make him feel important and he'll talk."

"Will he be there this late?"

"He'll have to be at the bank while Gennaro's away. There's night numbers to check. Let's go."

We went back to the same booth, only this time the call was longer, almost a half hour. When he opened the door Jackson was grinning.

"The damn' fool talked his head off. Let's get to your place."

A chilling sleet was beginning to fall when we got out on Forty-second Street. It was hell getting a cab, but Jackson spoke their language—two dollars thrown inside the cab window almost civilized the sullen, bitter driver, who started to tell us the woes cabdrivers face on such a night.

"Cut the crap," Jackson snapped. "You guys are out for every buck you can get tonight."

The driver stared into his mirror, and shrugged.

We drove in silence down a glistening Park Avenue and across Thirty-eighth Street. I noticed his number and memorized it: 1776. It was quite a vintage year.

I have lived many places in Manhattan, East Side, West Side, the Village, before it became the mecca for queers and junkies; Third Avenue before the invasion of big business; the upper West Side, until it became down at the heel, and finally East Thirty-eighth Street between Third and Lexington avenues, the second floor of what was once an old town house. The only other occupant is a small free-lance artists cooperative that is closed by five.

The account executive who leased the apartment before me was a fanatic on antiques and spent most of his time tearing out the old woodwork and scraping the original by hand. By the time he left to take over a Hollywood office, he had rebuilt the old fireplace. I guess some of the passion for the Victorian age took hold of me by osmosis, and for several weekends Gwen and I sanded down the living-room floor to the beautiful broad oak wood, which we shellacked. From time to time I have bought a few things—one a genuine artist's proof of a Charlie Russell—not with a collector's eye but purely because I liked them.

It's a small, dark red stone building, tight up against two tall ones, which always makes me think of that horrible cliché, "snug as a bug." It's owned by an estate, and my monthly bill is paid to some lawyer's office. The one time I had to call was for some minor repairs. Down through the years we have reached an understanding: you don't bother me and I won't bother you.

The fireplace never fails as a conversation piece, and Jackson was no exception.

"Hey, you really going to light that?" he asked as I bent down and removed the screen.

"Of course. Haven't you ever seen a fireplace before?"

He gave me a scornful look. "Kid, I was born on a farm!"

I poured a drink, and he took a deep swallow.

"Okay. Let's hear what we got."

I rewound the tape, snapped it on, and sat back. (Sounds of coins interspersed throughout, sounds of dialing number, several long buzzes, then a woman's voice, identified by Jackson as Vickie.)

VICKIE: Hello.

JACKSON: This is Mr. Jackson. Is Mr. Strasser there?

VICKIE: Is he expecting your call?

JACKSON: Yes, he is.

VICKIE: Hold the phone, please. (*Sound of clicking heels on hardwood floors; voices, indistinguishable; then a man's voice, identified by Jackson as Strasser's.*)

STRASSER: Hello, Jackson?

JACKSON: Yeah, this is Jackson, Ricky.

STRASSER: Bernie said you were going to call. . . . Yeah, he said so.

JACKSON: The Wop told Bernie to call you.

STRASSER: Yeah, I know . . . Bernie said this. Look, maybe we can talk tomorrow. . . . I got a client . . . you know.

JACKSON: Look, Ricky, you can take care of that dame on your own time. Gennaro wants you to get those cops off my back. Understand?

STRASSER: Wait a minute—who the hell are you to—

JACKSON: Okay. You don't want to listen. You want me to call the Wop and tell him you gave me the brush?

STRASSER: Who said that. . . . Wait a minute—

JACKSON: Okay. Now you listen. The cops from the East Side are coming over too often. They cost us money. You know Gennaro about money; he went nuts when I told him. Real crazy nuts—

STRASSER: Yeah, I know how he is. Maybe I can do something.

JACKSON: No maybe about it. You do something and do it fast.

STRASSER: I'll see Harris, maybe in the morning . . .

JACKSON: See who?

STRASSER: I'll see a guy downtown.

JACKSON: You mean down at headquarters?

STRASSER: Where else? Wall Street?

JACKSON: These same two guys keep coming over to the drop. I told them I was going to beef, but they keep coming. Then other cops started in last month.

STRASSER: How many cops?

JACKSON: About eight. But eight this month, there will be twenty next month if you don't stop it. Gennaro said he will turn off the juice if they keep it up.

STRASSER: Gennaro can't turn off that juice, no more than you can stop breathing. Don't be stupid.

JACKSON: I got some badge numbers. You want 'em?

STRASSER: What for?

JACKSON: To give your friend downtown so he can pass the word to the captain to tell them to lay off.

STRASSER: Well, maybe . . . (*Voice away from the phone*) Hey, Vickie . . . Vickie . . . Where the hell's that dame? . . . Vickie, get me a pencil. . . . Hurry up. (*Back to the phone*) Wait a minute, Jackson, I'm getting a pencil. (*Pause*)

JACKSON: Murphy paid us a visit. No playday.

STRASSER: That creep! I got your boys off on the 896. (*A drunken laugh*) We had the right judge.

JACKSON: Can't you get to Murphy, Ricky?

STRASSER: You can't talk to him. Very unreasonable man.

JACKSON: Why don't you try, Ricky? Maybe it needs some class.

STRASSER: My man downtown says it's impossible. He won't take a penny. (*Off the phone:* Thanks, kid . . . yeah, put some more ice in it. *Back to the phone*) Okay, what's the numbers?

JACKSON: H-23456 and B-14567—those are the two yesterday. They ride a Mickey Mouse. Then there's C-23456, B-34567, T-45634.

STRASSER: Wait a minute, you're going too fast.

JACKSON: Sorry. (*Pause*) C-45678, C-43256, and a cop named Shorty from the 22–A Division and his partner, Frank, a big guy with a broken nose, about forty-five, I would say. I got some more back at the drop—

STRASSER: That's enough. Just to let them know to lay off. Is that all?

JACKSON: Yeah, I'm sorry I had to bother you, but Gennaro said you had to take care of the cops. He said you were the only one who could get them off my back.

STRASSER (*off phone, sound of ice in glass:* Thanks kid. *Back to phone*) Yeah, well you tell the Wop I took care of it, okay?"

JACKSON: Okay, now get back to your client.

STRASSER (*high giggle*): What we need is some action, hey, Action?

JACKSON: Yeah. I'll see you.

STRASSER (*still giggling*): Okay . . . okay.

(*Click*)

There was a short pause; then came my voice with the identifying note.

"Will this hang him?" Jackson asked.

"He will have a lot of explaining to do before the Grievance Committee of the Bar Association," I said. "Before we go any further let's find out who his girl is. What's that phone number?"

He repeated it.

I call the night city editor and had him do a fast check through the phone company for the subscriber; it turned out to be Victoria Simms, 230 East Eighty-ninth Street. I then had the desk transfer me to the *Blade-Leader's* reference room, where I ordered a bored clerk to look up all clips and pictures on Miss Simms.

"There are three pictures and about five clips," he reported after a few minutes.

"Send them up to the city desk," I ordered, "and tell them to give them to one of the night photographers to drop off at my house as soon as possible." Of course I got a call back from the night city desk man, who was full of curiosity but got no satisfaction. He promised to send them within the hour. He was as good as his word, and after I had sent off the photographer with a stiff drink for the weather, I opened the envelope.

Victoria Simms turned out to be a long-limbed beauty in a skin-tight dress, big black eyes, and a teasing pout.

"Not bad," Jackson murmured.

I turned the picture over for the caption and date stamped on the back.

"That was eight years ago," I said. I read: " 'Vickie Simms, featured vocalist of the Ray Neuman Trio, now playing at the Greyhound Club, East Fifty-first Street. Miss Simms comes to the Greyhound Club direct from Las Vegas.' "

"Big time for Ricky," Jackson said.

"Big time, nuts. If this dame was in Las Vegas, it was only to play the slot machines. Though I'm no record collector, I certainly know the top singers, and I never heard of the Ray Neuman Trio. Probably a small group that never got anywhere. Let's look at the clips."

The clippings were mostly from the amusement pages of the *Blade-Leader, Journal-American, World-Telegram,* and *Trib.* The most informative one was from an out-of-town paper—apparently a payoff interview for one of the paper's benefits. There were the usual press agent's exaggerations about her appearances in big clubs from Detroit's Black Orchid to the Copa, but it had one legitimate clue—her birthplace: Torytown, New Jersey.

"That town rings a bell somewhere," I said. "Let's check the clips again."

The material included some clips on Torytown from the early days of the war, and I began to recall the story: Torytown was a small northern New Jersey mountain town that sprang into the national news right after the draft, when state policemen had to bring in a draft clerk to register the men in the community. He had tried to go in himself, but someone had shot his tires full of holes. I remembered the pictures in *Life*, the taciturn men in overalls and flannel shirts, lined up in front of the indignant clerk. The citizens of Torytown lived high in the Bearfort Mountains and just never got to town except in the winter for a few months' work at the tool factory. The state police claimed they were the best poachers in the state.

Life had made quite a spread with early woodcuts of the village and shots their photographers took with the state cops. The town, it seemed, was founded by a group of Hessians, Tories, and Indians after the Revolution.

And all this an hour and a half from Times Square.

"Sounds like Li'l Abner," was Jackson's comment when I told him. "Ricky Strasser and Daisy Mae!"

"Now we know who Vickie is," I said. "She could be another witness for the Grand Jury. Let's listen to Bernie."

Again there was the dialing and the buzzing of the number. A guttural voice answered.

VOICE (*identified as a guard*): Hello.
JACKSON: This is Jackson; let me talk to Bernie. (*Pause: five seconds. Low voices in the background, click of typewriters and adding machine.*)
BERNIE: Action?
JACKSON: Yeah. How are you?
BERNIE: Fine. Did you talk to Ricky?
JACKSON: Just now. I thought I'd give you a report so you can pass it on to the Wop.
BERNIE: Sure. Go ahead.
JACKSON: Ricky said he was going to see a guy named Harris downtown tomorrow morning maybe. Hey, is that Louie Harris who used to work out of the 29th?
BERNIE: Are you nuts? That's Fletcher Barrist—

I snapped off the voice.

"Inspector Barrist!" I said, "the head of the Police Commissioner's

Special Investigative Squad! The way Strasser was talking it sounded like 'Harris.' "

"That's why I asked him to repeat it," Jackson said calmly. "I know every thief downtown, and there's no Harris among them. It sounded that way because he was high." He gestured with his drink. "Play the rest."

"Wait a minute. Barrist is one of the big men in the department. There's never been any hint of scandal about him."

"Who's Barrist's rabbi?" Jackson said smugly.

"I don't know the politics of the department well enough to know that. Who is?"

"Big Jim McShane," Jackson said. "Any time McShane wants anything downtown, he doesn't call the commissioner—he calls Barrist. That's been the word for years. The commissioner knows it, and so does City Hall. Ask any cop downtown who's on the sergeant's, lieutenant's, or captain's list what's the best way to get the job and they'll tell you—Get close to Barrist and he'll call McShane."

"I asked you before if you thought McShane had any part of Gennaro's rackets, Action," I said, "and you brushed me off."

Jackson finished his drink. "I told you I didn't have any evidence that McShane is in with Gennaro."

"What have you heard?" I persisted.

"Anybody in the rackets will tell you McShane and Gennaro use the same pot," he said calmly, "but it's only a lot of bums telling stories. Incidentally, kid, remember, I'm not in the market for McShane. You are!"

"What's the matter—does he scare you?"

"Frankly, yes," was his reply. "From what I understand, he plays rough."

"Hell, he's only a politician."

Jackson stared into the fire for a moment. "Politicians have a funny way of picking up a phone and letting someone do their dirty work. They pay off with favors, and sometimes to guys like Gennaro favors mean more than money. Even to Gennaro who has the first buck he stole!"

"Why?"

"Because favors mean power. You pull strings like the guy in the puppet show, and people dance. Like the time McShane got together with Gennaro, Barrist, the judge—"

"What!"

"Okay, okay," he said wearily. "I didn't tell you this before because I have only Bernie's word for it." He looked aggrieved at my eager expression, then continued: "Gennaro was helping some committee in this church where his grandchildren go, and they were giving a big building-fund dinner. So they tried to get some big shots, but only a few would come because it was only a small church and big shots don't bother with small fry. Gennaro, Bernie said, called McShane and told him he needed some big shots. This was in the afternoon. Well, the next morning Gennaro got a call from someone and began laughing and slapping the table. It seemed the pastor of the church called Gennaro's son and told him they got calls from McShane, two judges, a couple of commissioners, and Barrist, saying they would go on the dais. Bernie said he forgot about it, but a few weeks later the Wop came in with a picture of himself and the judges, commissioners, McShane, and Barrist on the dais. As I remember it, the Wop told Bernie he didn't want to embarrass the big shots by asking them to pose with him, so he had the guy who took the picture at the dinner take one when they were eating and nobody was watching."

I could only stare at him.

"Where do you think that picture is now?"

"Who knows?"

I leaned forward. "Look, Action, that picture could be a tremendous piece of evidence. It could rock the city. It—"

He stared at me impassively. "I told you before, kid, you're single-O on McShane. I got two guys in mind—Gennaro and the Sheik."

"Good God, you can't ignore such shocking implications just because it involves McShane!" I cried. "Sure, Gennaro and the Sheik are our target, but McShane overshadowed them ten seconds ago!"

He stood up and silently poured himself another drink; then he held the glass to the firelight and took a sip before he turned to me.

"I had a feeling when you first pulled this tape-recorder bit on me, kid, that I was getting in too deep. Now I know it. Look, we lay off McShane as far as I'm concerned or we scratch the whole race. Now do we understand each other?"

"Why the hell are you so frightened of McShane?" I shouted, "when you're not of Gennaro? McShane's a politician; Gennaro's a racket boss—a killer."

He inquired softly, "Whoever said I wasn't afraid of Gennaro? Just who the hell said that? Me?" He shook his head. "Oh, no, kid, not me. Me? Every time I think of of what I'm doing I have to change my underwear." He leaned forward and poked his finger in my chest. "Do you have any idea of what that Wop would do to me if he even knew I was here with you? And God knows what he would do if he knew the half of what I've done to him now." He slipped back on the sofa. "That's okay—I'll take the long chance to get that bastard." He added earnestly, sincerely, "But me, I don't have that kind of hate for McShane, kid. I don't care if he robs the people of this city blind and corrupts every cop and judge in the country. If the people are stupid enough to stand for it, they should be robbed. Let them get mad and get somebody with enough guts to put McShane in jail."

"But that's what I want to do." By this time I was boiling, and began pacing up and down before the sofa. "Don't you see, that's exactly what I could do—get the people angry enough to force them to indict McShane and put him away. We must—"

He looked at me blandly. "If you tangle with McShane, he'll cut you, your newspaper, and your publisher down to size."

"That will be the day," I said angrily.

He grinned. "Don't say I didn't warn you."

"Okay, you warned me," I said. "Now, as I understand it, you don't want anything to do with McShane. Is that right?"

"Correct," he said sharply. "And you have to be straight arrow with me all the way."

"Will you try to find out where that picture is?"

"No."

"Will you get me the names of the judge or anyone else who was on the dais?"

"No."

The smile was gone from his face now as it tightened in that gambler's mask. I decided to make one more try.

"At least the name of the photographer?"

"No."

I felt I had gone as far as I could go.

"Okay. Back to Bernie."

I rewound the tape a few inches and snapped on the recorder.

BERNIE: Are you nuts? That's Fletcher Barrist in the commissioner's office. He's our boy. Didn't you know that?

JACKSON: You East Side guys don't tell us nothing.

BERNIE (*laughing*): Sure. Barrist is on the pad for two G's a week. You know Peters?

JACKSON: The sarge?

BERNIE: Yeah. The guy who tips you off. He's Barrist's bagman. You know we pay the first and the fifteenth.

JACKSON: Yeah, I know that (*laugh*). I pay.

BERNIE: You pay from your end, but Gennaro pays Peters on the fifteenth.

JACKSON: The same day I do.

BERNIE: I don't like the guy. I give it to him in an envelope. You know the bastard counts it out? Once I asked him what I could do about a ticket my nephew got. You know what he said?

JACKSON: What?

BERNIE: Pay it. A bum, that's what he is. So you had a day off, what did you do?

JACKSON: My favorite indoor sport on the West Side.

BERNIE (*laugh*): I know what you mean. I'm going to get a little tonight.

JACKSON: Bernie! You're a cheater.

BERNIE: A little now and then. But I got to go over to Seventy-ninth Street, Brooklyn, to get it. Long haul for a piece at my age. Hey, you still got Tilley?

JACKSON: Tilley? Sure. He takes the collectors.

BERNIE (*laugh*): You got shines; I got wops. Well, look, I'll tell Gennaro, okay?

JACKSON: Yeah. Tell him Ricky said he will call this guy Harris—

BERNIE: Barrist. Barrist. Where did you ever get Harris?"

JACKSON: Okay, Barrist. Tell him Strasser said he will talk to Barrist and I gave him the badge numbers. You know, so he'll give them to the precinct.

BERNIE: Yeah. Yeah. We pay any more cops, the Wop'll have a heart attack.

JACKSON: What do you think he puts out a month, Bernie?

BERNIE: The way I figger—you pay about thirty-six hundred on the first and fifteenth, right?

JACKSON: Right. On the nose every month.

BERNIE: That's seventy-two hundred a month, and we pay Barrist two—that's over nine; say another C note for cops over here—

JACKSON: About ten, then.

BERNIE: Maybe a little more. But don't worry. I got everything down.

JACKSON: What the hell, you don't put down you paid cops!

BERNIE: Don't be a jerk! It's grease and oil! (*laugh*) Enough grease and oil for the Fifth Avenue bus company!

JACKSON (*laugh*): I know what you mean. Well, look, Bernie, I'll see you. Okay?

BERNIE: Okay, Action. When you come over I'll buy you a drink. So long.

JACKSON: So long, Bernie.

  (*Click*)

I could only whistle softly. "Tell me about Bernie."

"Strictly a schlemiel." He gestured to the recorder. "That should give you an idea."

"You really can't blame him. He was talking to you. He didn't—"

I could have bitten my tongue, but Jackson only gave me a wry smile.

"You mean he didn't know he was talking to a stoolie? Go ahead and say it."

"I didn't mean that. I meant he was talking with confidence with somcone in the same syndicate."

Jackson said, "He's still a schlemiel. I wouldn't talk that way to my own brother.

"Gennaro was free with the words."

Jackson frowned. "You know, kid, you got something there. Usually he just grunts and only says a word here and there, with maybe a few Eye-talian words. Like Bernie says, this trip must be damn' important."

"Gennaro was at Apalachin—in fact, he called it and the one in Atlantic City," I pointed out. "Maybe he's called another meeting of the mob?"

Jackson shook his head. "I don't think so." He looked at me. "That's one I'll find out for you, kid. Anything that has to do with Gennaro—you get."

There was a wild slap of sleet against the window, and the pane rattled. Automatically we both got up and looked out. The ice-slicked streets glittered in the swaying streetlight. Long icicles hung from the evergreens in the small courtyard of the apartment house across the street.

"I'll have to skate over to Grand Central," Jackson said. "I better be going."

"Don't be ridiculous," I said. "You can stay here. The studio couch opens up."

He hesitated. "I don't want to put you out."

"Where *do* you live, Action?"

"I have a furnished flat on West Ninetieth Street," he said. "It's run by an old Italian lady who thinks she's my mother." He looked self-conscious for a moment. "I better phone her before she has the cops out for me. Okay to use the phone?"

"Help yourself. It's on the desk."

Jackson dialed a number, waited a few moments, then said: "Mrs. Zuccartelli? This is Eddie Jackson. Yeah, Eddie. Look, I'll be staying with a friend because of the weather. I just wanted to let you know. Yeah, it's bad out. No calls, Mrs. Zuccartelli? Fine. I'll see you tomorrow. Take care of yourself now. Good night."

He hung up and grinned. "She's had me and two other old guys for years. If we don't show up she gets worried. A couple of times a year she goes down to Bellevue and bails out one old guy." He looked up at the Charlie Russell. "What is this, a cowboy picture?"

"Sort of," I said. "It's by Charlie Russell, a great western artist. You know how much the original of that cost?"

"A grand?"

"Thirty thousand."

He whistled in awe and continued around the room. He picked up my mother's picture on the desk.

"That's my mother. She was a schoolteacher here on the West Side."

"Nice-looking old—nice-looking woman, kid."

"When she retired they gave her a banquet at the Astor. Corning, the poet, was the toastmaster. He was one of her pupils."

"I don't know anything about poetry," he said simply, "but they must have thought a lot of her." He walked back to the sofa. "I can barely remember my old lady," he said slowly. "It always seemed she was chopping wood."

"Well, then your sister really raised you."

He nodded. "Jo was the only mother I knew. And, brother, did she have a time raising me!"

The wind flung a handful of sleet at the window, and the flames wavered delicately in the fireplace.

"I pulled that gas station heist in town—"

"The one you told me about?"

"My partner, a kid down the road, got scared and took off. The owner clobbered me with a tire iron. The local cops belted me around, and I got a year's probation. I was out of the can two days when I took off for St. Louis."

"Did you tell your sister?"

He shook his head. "I left her five bucks on the kitchen table. She knew I couldn't stay." He took a sip of his drink. "I hustled pool in St. Louis, then went to Chicago, L.A., Pittsburgh—anywhere I could make a fast buck. In New York I worked as a bookie runner in the garment center. That's where I got to know some of the mob guys who brought me into numbers. The cops were on the take even then. They—"

The phone ring was so sudden we both jumped. I picked it up, half expecting to hear the voice of our night city desk man, but it was Gwen.

"Why, hello stranger," she said. "Snowbound?"

"I was just looking into the fire and thinking of you," I said.

"You're a cheerful liar, but I love to hear it anyhow. What are you doing?"

I hesitated only for a second, but her voice went cold.

"You probably have some important business. I won't keep you."

"Get off your high horse," I told her. "I do have someone here, but he isn't female. Remember Jackson—"

She gasped. "The man you told me—"

"The same," I said. I handed the phone to Jackson.

"Just say hello. It's a young lady who doubts my word."

Action gingerly took the phone. "You really want me to talk to her?" he whispered.

"Of course, why not?"

He shrugged and said, "Hiya, honey. My name is Jackson. What's yours? . . . Okay, Gwen. Look, we haven't any dames here—just business. Okay? . . . He chuckled. "I know how it is. Nice talking to you. Here's Duke." He handed back the phone, and winked.

Her voice was full of apologies. "I'm really sorry, Duke. I was only kidding."

"The hell you were," I said. "You were jealous, and I'm glad."

"Are you really, Duke?"

I could picture her in those tight blue lounging pajamas that didn't leave much to the imagination, and my mouth suddenly became dry.

"I am—really. When can I see you?"

"How about coming over for breakfast?"

"Wonderful. When?"

"Tomorrow morning. I'll have—"

"Swedish pancakes! Can I bring my friend?"

The lilt went out of her voice. "Please—no, Duke . . ."

"Is it something special?"

She hesitated, then said softly, "Very special."

"You can't tell me now?"

"I think it's too important to discuss over the phone. I'll see you in the morning, darling."

"You must have been nuts asking me along," Jackson said when I rejoined him.

"Why not? It's only breakfast, not a sex orgy."

"Even talking to her wasn't good," he said. "You know, I can't put my finger on it, but something tells me a lot of people are going to be hurt before this is over."

"The way I have it figured, Action, they'll be people who knew what they were doing and who knew the consequences if they were caught."

"It doesn't always happen that way," he said. "When politicians go down, they take a lot of people with them. It's like playing snap-the-whip, and the leader falls off a cliff. Boom, boom, boom! Down they go, one by one."

"What politicians? You haven't given me any?"

He gave me a crooked smile. "Always tryin', heh, kid?"

"I know. I'm single-O. But I don't get the angle with my girl."

"Some of the tar from the brush might rub off on her," he said sternly. "Kid, you've been around a long time—you know how those lousy bastards operate. They can be deadly!" He pointed to the fire. "Come on, fireman, throw on some wood. . . ."

Weeks, months later, I was to remember Jackson warning that a lot of people would be hurt before we had finished. . . . A lot of people.

I learned a great deal about Action Jackson that night.

His early life was almost a stereotyped version of the small-time racketeer who can be found by the thousands in the files of the probation department of any large American city. However, there was one exception; Jackson was a gambler and a criminal only because he wanted to be. There was no whining excuse about lack of love or luck in his formative years.

"The way I see it now, I would have been in some kind of a hassle even if my mother and father lived until they were seventy," he said. "It's not that I hate work. Hell, I can work at that damn drop fifteen hours a day—it's just—" He held up his hands, palms out. "You're the smart guy, kid. Tell me why."

Rebellious of authority? Probably. He was frank in saying he could never stand a boss, but was just as frank to admit that Gennaro was his boss.

"Maybe it's the way I look at it. The Wop is my boss but then again he isn't. If I pull out, the whole West Side would collapse; the collectors would be stuck with their work; the runners would be up a tree; the stand-ins wouldn't know what to do—and the cops!" He slapped his leg. "Can you imagine those thieves if their juice was shut off? So the way I figger it, I'm like an executive and not a flunky. Up in Harlem I'm a big man. You know everybody up on the West Side—kids and old women even come around to me to settle family fights."

When I pointed out that these people would probably be out of work when the raids came, he shook his head.

"Don't you believe it," he said. "Policy will never leave Harlem as long as the people up there remain poor. Even if Gennaro is busted right down to the last drop, it will start up again. And I know who's going to take over."

"Who?"

"Tilley. Before this thing blows up and I scram out of town, I'm going to give him the whole setup."

"But doesn't Tilley know it himself?"

He shook his head vigorously. "Tilley hasn't been out of 135th Street. There is only one guy the Wop trusts to make a tour, and that's me. But beginning tomorrow I'm going to change things."

"How can you?"

"I'm going to start Tilley moving around the other drops. I'll tell him the Wop said okay. And you're going with him."

Even the amount of whiskey I had consumed didn't dull my surprise.

"Me? Why?"

"You're starting to make me nervous with your cracks about McShane. I want my part in this finished. If you go along with Tilley you can see how the rest of the syndicate works."

"But if Gennaro only trusts you—"

"Last year I had an ingrown toenail. My toe swelled up like a balloon, and I had to go over to Harlem Hospital. They wanted to remove the nail, but I stalled them. Gennaro knows that. Every time I talk about it he shouts for me to shut up. How do you like that? The guy's been yanked in for murder twice—he choked one guy to death—but he can't stand having anybody talk about a doctor cutting off a toenail. He says it makes him sick."

"What has that got to do with Tilley?"

"Gennaro knows Tilley. I'll just tell him my toe is acting up again and Tilley has to make the rounds."

"Suppose someone calls the East Side and tells Gennaro Tilley is going around with a strange guy?"

"You're just a guy I know from Jersey. Look, when I tell Gennaro something he doesn't ask questions. I promised you would be around when I paid off, didn't I?"

"You did."

"So you'll be there when I give the dough to Peters for Barrist. Then that will wrap me up. Right?"

"I suppose so," I said slowly, desperately trying to add up the loose ends. "Will Peters let me be there?"

"Don't be a jerk," Jackson said promptly. "You'll be in the john and I'll wear the machine. You can't ask for any more, kid—you just can't."

"I'll think of something."

"Don't strain yourself, because I'm not going to do any more."

The gambler's mask had slipped back over his face, and rather than antagonize him I returned to the early days and listened until the combination of the age-old hypnotism of an open fire, the warmth in the room, the sounds of the savage lashing of the storm, and the liquor drove us to bed.

We woke to find that the sleet had changed to an icy rain to turn the city into a quagmire of slush. I decided it wasn't worth the attempt to try to get a cab; so, like hundreds of others, I became a broad jumper, leaping across the rivulets of slush and water along Park Avenue to Grand Central, to join the most ill-tempered people in the world, New Yorkers on a cold, rainy morning in a subway.

By the time I arrived at Gwen's, I was just another member of that foul-tempered group.

"My, you look cheerful," she said as she stood in the doorway.

"I'm wet and stomped on, so no wisecracks." But I had to add, "And you're a dream."

And she was, in a suit the shade of Scotch thistle that brought out the color in her eyes; her long, thick blonde hair hung in a simple Alice-in-Wonderland style. Added to that Swedish complexion and figure, I wasn't mad any more.

I kissed her, and for a moment she clung to me.

"Oh, Duke . . ."

"What's the big surprise?" I closed the door. Either you're pregnant or you're going to marry somebody else."

She smiled. "Neither. Hang up your coat and have some coffee. I have the batter all ready." As she moved to the stove she called out, "How's your Mr. Jackson?"

"He's going to pick me up later. What did you think of him?"

The batter made a sizzling sound as it hit the hot pan. "All right, I guess. What have you been doing?"

"The policy thing I told you about. The exposé."

"You didn't call once this week."

"To tell you the truth, Gwen, I've been up almost every night transcribing the recordings—"

She turned. "Recordings?"

"We made some tape recordings. Pretty powerful stuff." I walked over and kissed her on the back of the neck. "I know—so what?"

She flipped over the pancake. "It's not that—it's—well let's talk later. . . . You like them brown?"

"Both sides. How's the show?"

"Lousy. I had another run-in with Bunny."

"Is that queen bothering you again?"

"He came in, in a foul mood. One of the kids said he had an argument with his friend."

"If I ever write a play, remind me never to hire a fairy as a director."

She flipped over a pancake with an angry gesture. "You'll never write a play while you're changing the world, dear."

"It's my job, honey."

She put the pancakes on two plates, and we sat down at the breakfast bar to sprinkle them with sugar, smear them with jam, and roll them up Swedish style. They were delicious. After all these months I knew my Swede: when she was ready she would talk, and not before; so during the meal we discussed the weather, Bunny, the kid in the chorus who had a screen test, and what *Variety* had to say about Tennessee Williams' new play.

Finally she tapped out a cigarette, and I knew it was time to talk. "What's the occasion, dear?"

The ice-blue eyes settled on me. "I got a call from my agent yesterday. She spoke to Twentieth Century. . . ."

I cursed myself for a fool for not guessing what was on her mind. Actually, that call from the coast had always become a sort of legend between us, more a dream we felt down deep would never come true. . . .

She took a deep puff, and exhaled. "I have the part if I want it."

Even though from the moment she had started talking I suspected this was the news, the harsh reality startled me. I found myself saying, "Congratulations. It's been a long time coming."

She nodded. "Yes, a long time, Duke. Even longer than you realize."

"When do you leave?"

"They'll notify my agent when they start shooting."

"Will you keep the apartment?"

She shook her head. "It's a three-picture deal. My agent also has some TV work lined up."

Actually, I shouldn't have been surprised, but I was—devastated, I guess, would be the better word. Yet, why? I always knew this was the way it had to be; Gwen wanted that shot on the coast more than anything. I had always played it that way, and really I should be happy for her now, not tasting ashes in my mouth. It came to me with such a suddenness that it was startling; I didn't want Gwen to go. When I looked up she was studying me.

"It sounds like you're really saying good-bye."

She tapped the ash in the tray. "I have a few days to make up my mind."

I could only stare at her. "You mean you're not sure?"

She carried the plates to the sink, and I followed her. "I know it sounds foolish, but when I heard her telling me I had the part all I could think of was you." She turned and faced me. "I guess I realized you mean more to me than I thought." Two tears welled up in the corners of her eyes and slowly, almost mechanically, rolled down her cheeks. I touched each one wonderingly.

"The last time you were here, Duke," she said softly, "you asked me to marry you. Were you really serious?"

"I'm the one who asked you two years—"

"And I said No, and I meant it," she said emphatically. "But lately I'm getting tired of this—" The wave of her hand took in the whole, tidy apartment. "I watch every damn' moron program until the time to go to the theatre; then when I come home I watch the oldest movies in the world. Even the show has become a bore." She gave me a weary smile. "The truth is, Bunny is right; I'm goofing off."

I held her by both arms. "What brought this on?"

She shrugged. "Maybe it was the call from my sister, with everything else piled on."

"The one in Wisconsin with all the kids?"

"She's having another one. God, she sounded happy! After I hung up I cried for an hour." Two more tears trickled down that marble-smooth skin. "I kept asking myself just what am I doing here? Do you know that every woman in my family had six kids before they were thirty? I'm thirty-one and all I have—"

"—is a top spot in a sold-out Broadway musical, and an offer from Hollywood."

"I know all that!" she cried. "But maybe it's not enough. Maybe after ten years of tank towns, off Broadway, agents and more agents, phony promises, and guys with a thousand hands—I'm tired! Maybe I'm just a big Swede who wants a husband, kids, and a home! Maybe I've had it, Duke, then what?"

"Then maybe we should get married."

She tore a section of paper towel and wiped her eyes.

"I thought about it most of the night," she said, "and I have come to the conclusion I really love you, Duke, but I don't know about you. . . ."

"How many times do I have to say it?"

She took a deep breath. "I'll marry you, Duke—tomorrow if you say so—on one condition—"

Automatically I blurted out, "If I get out of this business."

"That's it exactly. I think you're wasting your whole life and your talent on these idiotic stories—"

"That's only one woman's opinion, dear."

"Yes, but it happens to be the woman you say you love. Do you love me enough, Duke, to give it up?"

"Will you turn down Hollywood?"

There was no hesitation. "I'll call my agent this morning—if you call your editor and resign."

I held out my arms and she came to me.

"It's as simple as that?"

She whispered, "It's as simple as that." She pushed back and looked up at me. "Who's hesitating now?"

She was right, and it startled me.

"Six weeks' severance pay won't buy you pancake flour."

She slid out of my arms and went to a desk, opened a drawer and removed a small black book which she waved at me. "There's $15,750 in my account. The play's good for at least six months more, and I get $650 a week.

"So you work and I stay home. . . ."

"You stay home and write," she corrected me. "Which you always claimed was the hardest work in the world." She came back to my arms. "Please, Duke, say Yes. You can write from morning until night."

"I love people who say that. Have you ever written a letter?"

"Have you ever stood on a stage and said the same lines a thousand times, Duke?" she asked, "and two days after the opening go down and collect your unemployment? Who are you kidding?"

"I *have* been thinking about leaving the paper," I said. "I even told the publisher."

"Duke, you didn't."

"I told him I might not sign the contract again."

Her face fell. "Oh, 'might' . . ."

"Look, Gwen, I have twenty years in this business! Before I leave it I have to think about it. Sure, I want to write. But once I cut the strings, it's for good."

"What is it in that crazy business?" she said in a wondering voice. "You die of ulcers or heart attacks. You work crazy hours. You meet the most horrible people. And all to line the ash can."

The bell didn't ring, it clanged, and what was there a moment before shattered like fragile glass.

I could barely hear her muffled whisper. "There's your Mr. Jackson."

"I'll call you tonight. We'll go over to Guido's."

Not lifting her head, she was saying, "It always has been like this, Duke."

"No, we'll talk more about it tonight."

"Let's not answer, Duke."

I thought of Tilley and that tour. We would be hitting the uptown places and the Bronx and maybe Queens. This, as Jackson said, would really wrap it up, with the meeting with the downtown payoff man the only thing left. . . .

I gently pulled her back so she looked up at me.

"Look, it's only going to be a few more weeks. This is a real big one. I have to finish it out. Jackson has gone out on the limb, and my publisher . . ."

She smiled and for a minute seemed like herself again.

"Okay. We'll talk at Guido's." When the bell rang again she called, "Right away, Mr. Jackson," as she got my coat. Then the hat, then her lips, so warm and delicious that I almost shouted to Jackson to stop ringing that damned bell.

"He's an impatient little man," she murmured as we walked to the door.

"He probably has an impatient hackie," I said. "I'll call you about five."

She kissed me again. "I'll be waiting, dear."

The door closed, and I was standing in the self-service elevator listening to the soft, slithering noise of its descent and wondering why I had hesitated with that soft, sweet-smelling hair on my chest; why I had hesitated when suddenly I had what I wanted. I didn't have a hate like Jackson or an unfulfilled dream like Savage.

Minutes after I got into the cab, Jackson was whispering that Tilley had a message from Bernie; Sergeant Peters had called the East Side—Barrist needed some money—two thousand dollars, in a hurry. Jackson was to pay it right after the collectors left at seven o'clock.

I never did phone Gwen. . . .

My copy of the official transcript will show how well our meeting with Peters came off. Jackson wore the recorder, and I was in the small toilet at the end of the counter. I could hear the muffled voice, but the angle of the crack in the door prevented me from seeing Peters. At first we debated about my hiding there; Peters, cold, calculating, and suspicious, might try the door, but Jackson feet the sergeant had never done it before; besides, this was an unusual request and he would be in a hurry. As it turned out, Jackson was right.

(*Sound of door opening, closing.*)

JACKSON: Hiya, Sarge.

PETERS: You got it?

JACKSON: Right here in the bag. Two G's, Bernie said.

(*Sound of paper*)

JACKSON: You going to count it?

PETERS: Don't I always?

JACKSON: I always wanted to ask you—every time I give you some dough you count it. Don't you trust us?

PETERS: I wouldn't trust you or any of your bums across the street.

JACKSON: Thanks.

PETERS: Don't mention it.

(*Sound of paper*)

JACKSON: What's up with Barrist?

PETERS: Why don't you ask him?

JACKSON: Strasser does our talking. Not me. What has he got—dame trouble?

PETERS: You got a big mouth, Jackson. Shut it!

(*Sound of paper*)

JACKSON: I'll see you on the fifteenth.

PETERS: You always do.

(*Sound of steps, door opening, closing.*)

"That lousy bum," Jackson said as I came out. "Mean as a snake."

"What does he do now?"

"What the hell do you think he docs? He brings it to Barrist."

"Where?"

"How would I know?"

"Look, you have to tell Bernie, don't you?"

He gave me a disgusted look. "I guess so. Come on with your damn' machine."

We taped the call to the East Side from Grand Central, and as usual Bernie was talkative.

JACKSON: Hello, Bernie. I paid the bum.

BERNIE: Good, I'll tell the Wop.

JACKSON: I asked him what's up with Barrist, and he almost spit in my face.

BERNIE: What did you ask him?

JACKSON: I was only kiddin'—I just asked him if Barrist had girlie trouble.

BERNIE: Nah, he hasn't got any dames. He's a nine-to-five guy. The bum lives high. He's got a place in Florida that Rickey says will knock your eye out. Like a millionaire, he lives. We take the chances, and these bums live like J. P. Morgan.

JACKSON: I like to see it. Where in Florida?

BERNIE: The place where you see all the old society dames in the news. What the hell's the name of it again? Oh, St. Petersburg. Yeah, that's it.

His kid goes to college down there. Wait a minute! Yeah, that's it—his kid. Ricky said Barrist's kid racked up a car and he's sending his old lady the dough to pay the other guy so the kid won't lose his license. Or something like that. Imagine sending your kid two grand after he racks up your car! I'd kick his ass all over Brooklyn. Right?

JACKSON: Right. What does Peters do, go downtown now?

BERNIE: No, I think they meet at Weldon's on East Third Street—that's where all the police brass hangs out. Well, look, the Wop comes back tomorrow—

JACKSON: Yeah. Where the hell did he go?

BERNIE: Some place down in North Carolina. He says he has to see a cousin.

JACKSON: The Wop going down to North Carolina to see a cousin? Ain't kosher, Bernie.

BERNIE: You are so right. That's what I told myself. (*The voice moves into the phone.*) I think it's a meeting of the boys. That's what I think, Action. You know?

JACKSON: Yeah, maybe. Well, look, I'll be seein' you.

BERNIE: Yeah, come over and get that drink. Okay?

JACKSON: Right. I will.

(*Click*)

I looked up Weldon's Restaurant and found it on Third Street and First Avenue. While Jackson glumly leaned against the wall I taped a call to the restaurant:

RESTAURANT: Hello.

MALLOY: Hello. I wonder if you could tell me if Inspector Barrist is there?

RESTAURANT: He is. Do you want me to call him to the phone?

MALLOY: No, I'm on my way down to join him now. But I want to know if there are two gentlemen with him—one a white-haired man?

RESTAURANT: Oh, Sergeant Peters? Yes, he's here with the inspector. And there's another gentleman in a blue suit—

MALLOY: Rather thin with black hair?

RESTAURANT: Yes. But if you want me to call—

MALLOY: No, thanks a lot. I was supposed to pick them up, and this will save me a trip across town. Thanks again.

RESTAURANT: You're quite welcome.

(*Click*)

"Bernie's right," I said as I came out of the phone booth. "Barrist, Peters, and Ricky are there."

Jackson said impatiently, "You satisfied now? Or do you want to go down and join them?"

"Come off it, Action."

He was plainly irritable and, for the first time since we began, jumpy.

"What are you so nervous about?"

"Believe me, I love every minute of this." He shook his head. "I must be stupid or crazy. Maybe both."

"Come on, let's eat," I said. Then I remembered. "What time is it?"

"Eight-thirty," he said sullenly. "With you I don't even eat on time anymore."

"I'll be with you in a minute," I said and returned to the phone booth. I dialed Gwen's number, but there was no answer. For a moment I cursed Jackson, Gennaro, and everyone else, and then, most heartily, myself, because I had forgotten.

Jackson and I had dinner, which was miserable. He was grumpy and moody and only nodded when I said I would see him in the morning for the first tour with Tilley.

When I got home I finally reached Gwen, but if I expected that she would be cool and hurt I was mistaken. She was jovial and said she understood.

I would have felt much better if she had been angry.

[11]

FOR THE NEXT two weeks I toured Vito Gennaro's policy syndicate from Harlem's West Side to the West Bronx and its foul nests of crumbling tenements, in some instances wore than deepest Harlem; Queens and the drops in the cellars or in the three-story apartments; Brooklyn and St. Marks Place, where the teen-age gangs were so arrogant three of Gennaro's muscle men had to kiss them with a baseball bat to teach them manners; then down to the Wall Street section where most of the action was handled by softly lighted bars complete with the businessmen's lunch and the commuters' fast bar. I even got to meet the collector on West 149th Street Jackson had described in his original notes as "making love to Jack Daniels all day." The description was apt.

After the first few days the tour became commonplace. I felt like a newly appointed sales manager making a tour of his territory. I wore the recorder every day and made transcriptions every night. We would start out at ten in the morning and report back to Jackson at eight. Usually Jackson and I would have dinner, discuss what I had found, or else he would fill me in with additional details. Then I would go home and make transcriptions until I fell into bed, completely weary and heartily sick of policy, Gennaro, and Jackson.

I tried to call Gwen, but after a few times gave up, promising myself I would get to her as soon as I had finished. Despite the drudgery and the stop-and-go monotony, I found myself becoming more jubilant as the piles of transcripts mounted.

I was confident that the voices coming from the gray metal recorder—harsh, tinny, foul, drunken—were establishing the cold, undeniable fact that a tremendous criminal syndicate was operating day and night with complete immunity, certainly with police protection, and possibly with political protection, throughout the city.

Tilley was a marvelous guide, and accepted Jackson's infected-foot story and the possibility I might be joining the Jersey end of the syndicate. But Tilley was no fool, and I had to be on constant guard; his most adroit questions came when they were least expected; I am sure this bland, roly-poly man got to know more about me than I ever intended to let him know.

One morning we didn't leave the drop; when he picked me up, Tilley said simply there had been trouble in the neighborhood.

"A raid?"

He shook his head. "Remember the Prophet?"

"The one by the big A&P?"

"Yeah. Well, he was holding another meeting. There was a PD there with two cops. Then the Prophet started talking about how the white landlords were squeezing the colored man and then he brought up a woman with a little baby who had been bitten by a rat that morning. He started to hold up that kid and the crowd began yelling." He swerved sharply and amicably cursed a cabdriver.

"That wasn't too bad; he done that before. Then he started on the cops and how they were always on the pad and how brutal they were, always clubbing the colored guy in the precinct. Well, that wasn't too bad either because the Prophet was always yelling those things. But then two kids started mixing it up in the crowd and the cops waded in." He shook his head. "Man, that was the wrong thing to do. Real wrong."

"They hit the cops?"

"One cop got an ash can somebody flipped off a roof, and they worked over the other one. They took their guns and their clubs and they were turning over the PD when the other cops came. There was a lot of hate in that crowd, and it didn't do the cops any good." He chuckled. "There's plenty of busted heads in Harlem today, but there's a lot of cops that don't feel good either."

"That Prophet can make a lot of trouble."

His answer was simple. "If things weren't bad, that Prophet couldn't make any trouble."

But Jackson thought differently, when I mentioned it to him later. "These shines up here are ready to blow," he said, "and that crazy bastard will light the fuse. Since last summer he's been talking about how the cops and the landlords are making the shines suffer. He wants to make up a march and go to City Hall."

"Tilley said a big part of Harlem is listening to him."

He cocked an eye at me. "Kid, if I was a shine and living in some dump up here I would listen to him too." He lowered his voice. "It's something to think about when they knock off these places. . . . I don't want to be around when it blows."

Tilley and I made it a habit to walk to the subway after we had reported to Jackson in the evening, and inevitably we passed the Prophet.

He was a superb demagogue, a fanatic, and obviously mad. But he was also a crowd pleaser, and that magnificent voice held its listeners. As Jackson had said, crooked police, brutal police, greedy landlords were nightly subjects that somehow never failed to produce an angry growl from the crowd. Once a tenement fire had wiped out an entire family, and that night the crowd was so big and ugly Tilley drove me to a subway stop out of Harlem. The next day the A.M.'s had an action picture of a wild melee in which several cops had been mauled.

Moving about Harlem and talking with its people—the grass roots, not the elite—I realized the Prophet was only a product of bad housing, the incredible horde of rats, ignorance, poverty, unemployment—the ingredients of the ghetto. The Prophet had been born the day the first crooked real-estate syndicate took over the decaying old-law tenements, gave the apartments a coat of cheap paint and raised the rent; the day the police and the policy racket joined hands; the early-morning hour the first rat crawled into the bedclothes of a crib . . .

Yet, I told myself, what about those in the city who were far more guilty than the syndicate real-estate owners, the racketeers, the crooked cops—what about those men who used their power to make sure the boat was never rocked, the community was never shaken from its lethargy, lest their profits be endangered.

Men like Colton Ryder; to stay in power, to maintain profits, to continue their way of life, they make pacts with the devil or the Jim McShanes.

As the weeks passed, I could feel the tension growing in the city, and I no longer scoffed at Tilley's offers to walk me to the subway. The Prophet was at his spot nightly, and his crowds were larger and uglier.

Finally I felt I had gathered as much evidence as a newspaper could use within its restrictions; I had transcriptions of numerous recordings, of Gennaro, Bernie, Ricky Strasser, collectors, in drops, on street corners, in bars, standing alone with my own eyewitness accounts of police payoffs. There was more work to be done, mostly statistical, of correlating arrests and dismissals from records in police headquarters and from the Chief Magistrate's Court. This, I felt, could be done within a few weeks. The number of dismissals, I was sure, would be shocking. Jackson already had given me the name of a crooked judge, Magistrate Lou Janus, a typical clubhouse attorney. Significantly, he had belonged to McShane's clubhouse before his appointment to the bench. This was the magistrate to whom Gennaro had given the hi-fi set and had had it installed by Louie, the mob's technician.

I spent my final evening with Jackson going over the material for the last time; all we needed was pictures. I was tempted to try it, but decided not to. I didn't mention it to Jackson. He was apprehensive and touchy enough, and I needed him as calm as possible for what was to come.

"What's the next move now?" he asked over coffee in my apartment.

"Tomorrow I go in and talk to my publisher."

"He's the boss?"

"He makes the decisions."

He frowned. "Don't you have anything to say, kid?"

"Of course. But he has the last word. He's responsible for everything that gets in the paper. I don't hold the bag if we get hit with a big libel suit. He does."

"Anybody else do any talking?"

"The managing editor. The city editor. The libel lawyers—"

He said harshly, "Where were they when there wasn't anything on those damned tapes?"

I explained with elaborate patience, "Whatever I write must be cleared for libel, and certainly the people who will put it in the paper have to know what we have."

He nodded grudgingly. "Just make sure my name isn't mentioned. The fewer people who know about us, the better I'll like it."

He followed me to the sofa with his cup of coffee. "Well, kid, I guess tomorrow we jump off—"

"I want to check the courts and the arrest records. I told you that."

"Okay," he said impatiently. "That's only the icing on the cake. But by tomorrow night you'll have the word, right?"

"You call me tomorrow night and I will tell you exactly what went on. Is that fair?"

"I want to know exactly that."

"You still going to leave town before anything happens?"

"Definitely. That's why I want to know every step you take."

Now it had come to the point of final departure. I couldn't avoid it. I wouldn't avoid it. I had to play straight with him.

"As I told you, Action, I make certain recommendations to the publisher."

His voice was low and hard. "So what?"

I took a deep breath. "I'm going to recommend that we turn everything over to the D.A.'s office. Transcripts of the tapes, notes, what I saw, names, addresses—the works."

He never blinked. "You said tapes. I'm on those tapes."

I corrected him. "I said 'transcripts of the tapes.' " I tossed one to him. "As you can see, you're just Mr. X."

The stone face studied me; the thin lips barely moved.

"What if they insist on the name?"

"They can insist all they want. I won't give it to them." I pointed to the pile of tapes. "I'm puting these in a safety-deposit vault, and the key will belong to me."

He silently lit a cigarette. "What's the matter with going along with our original plan, kid? You spread the whole works in the paper. That puts the Wop out of business. Like you say, you give it to the cops the night before and they bust the whole works and grab Gennaro in the bank. What's wrong with that?"

"In the beginning it looked like a wonderful newspaper exposé, Action," I said, "but now it looks bigger. Much bigger. This is an enormous criminal conspiracy, and it may go—"

He angrily tapped an ash in the tray. "Give it to me straight, kid. Going to the D.A. is not a new idea. Right?"

"I changed my mind after I listened to the first tape." I poured us another cup of coffee. "Look at it this way. Let's say we turn the info over to Murphy just before we print it and he hits the big bank. You know Murphy's been sold out. I know it. God, I saw it."

Jackson said doggedly: "They'll have him cold. Murphy's been dying to get his hooks on Gennaro."

"Murphy can't do it alone."

He ground out the cigarette, and now there was a tightness in his voice. "You've really put me on the spot! You know that guy Flaherty will—"

"But Flaherty isn't here," I said quickly.

There was a glimmer, a mere glimmer of surprise in Jackson's eyes; then they narrowed again.

"He left two days ago for Geneva to attend the United Nations Narcotic Investigative Committee's conference."

"Who's sitting in for him?"

"A young kid, Johnny De Lorenzo—"

"Yeah. I saw his picture a couple of weeks ago when he was sworn in. He's in charge of Rackets, isn't he?"

"Remember the Midwest gambling-fix case he did two years ago?"

"That doesn't make him any Dewey."

"No, but he got a conviction and pulled it off right through the Court of Appeals. The guy was sent away for a long time," I emphasized, "and he wasn't even a two-time loser."

He gave me a crooked smile. "You got me in a bind, kid. What can I do?"

"I didn't have to tell you. I could have done it anyway."

He shook his head. "I don't think so. You'll play straight-arrow—even with a bum like me." He tasted the coffee and made a face. "It's cold."

I turned the gas on under the pot, and when the coffee was hot I poured him another cup and remained silent, waiting . . .

"So you think this De Lorenzo guy will go all out?" he said finally.

"There's one stumbling block, a gentleman named Bob Hoff." I said. "Actually, he's in control of the office, but even De Lorenzo doesn't know that. There's a deal on to keep things quiet in town."

"You mean because of the election—the big year?"

"That's about it. Hoff was brought down from Albany. After the convention he'll be working with the National Committee."

He frowned. "But if this guy's job is to keep things quiet, he won't want any part of this one—"

"I'm going to give it to him in pieces," I said. "What he will get in the beginning will be only a policy exposé. We'll give them the usual drops in the city and all the stuff out of the county. Hoff will like that—he can turn it over to the other D.A.'s. I'll tell him we want raids by the D.A.'s men and a lot of hoopla."

"Nothing about Gennaro?"

"That's the pièce de résistance. It would be a feather in their caps to grab Gennaro. They can do something the Senate Rackets Committee's been trying to do for years—send him to jail. It will look tremendous in print."

"What will you hold back?"

"The police-brass angle: Ricky Strasser, the fact there is a Barrist, the fact there is a picture somewhere of Gennaro, McShane, and some other politicians eating dinner . . ." I waited.

"No, kid," he said wryly. "I never found the picture. Or the photographer."

"I'll keep pushing if you don't mind."

He waved his cup. "Be my guest. But I'm not interested. What about McShane?"

"We didn't get anything on McShane. Besides, if I ever do I won't tell you." I reminded him, "You told me I was single-O on McShane. Is that correct?"

"You're correct," he said promptly. He pointed to the tapes. "You guarantee me protection downtown on these—no name?"

"When I do give them the transcripts, you will be Mr. X," I said. "However, this is what I want to do right now to wind it up. I want you to make a tape with me giving the complete inside and out of Gennaro's setup. This will include names, addresses, how the syndicate works, who's in it, what the collectors do, where Gennaro works it, and so on."

"But I gave you all that!"

"That's true, but we're going to put it on tape for De Lorenzo. You will be introduced as Mr. X. This tape we will give him, so he won't squawk we're not being one hundred percent cooperative."

" Mr. X?"

"Mr. X."

He shrugged. "At this point what can I lose? If I can't trust you now, I was an idiot to start with. When will you give him the big stuff?"

"When I feel De Lorenzo has taken his office beyond the point of no return—in other words, when even Flaherty will find it hard to back off."

He walked over to me and said slowly: "But let's say Flaherty does find a way to brush you off. Let's say he steps in over the kid's head and tells you and your publisher to go to hell. What then?"

I knew it wouldn't do much good to appeal to Jackson with some vigorous promises, promises to use the power of my paper to break Flaherty and drive him from public office. First, it would have to be an empty promise, and the threats would mean nothing to him. Rather, I instinctively appealed to his gambler's instincts.

"I'm pulling for cards, Action. How do I know what I will get? Everything tells me it's a good night and to go for broke. Can you honestly tell me this whole bit hasn't sounded right so far?"

He said grudgingly, "So far we've had winning hands. But—"

"Forget the 'buts.' I say we go all the way. Flaherty's in Europe. By the time he gets back, his office will be in too deep. Then we'll hit him with Peters, Barrist, Janus, and all the other big stuff."

He walked back to the window. In the quiet the battered old clock I've had for years sounded like a laboring heart. When I looked down, I was surprised to find my fist clenched so tightly the knuckles were white.

Then, tired, resigned, he said, "When will you go down and see them?"

"Right after the meeting with my publisher."

"You'll call me, kid?"

"I'll call you before I go." I joined him at the window, and for a few moments we stared down in silence at an old lady in a long mink coat who was getting out of a limousine under the canopy across the street. The doorman rushed to hold open the heavy glass doors.

"Too bad we can't hook an old dame like that on numbers," he said. Then he turned and said in a harsh, bitter voice: "Why the hell do you have to change everything? You could have blasted the Wop in your paper; the cops could have grabbed him; and you would have had a big story. Now you want to go to that son of a bitch Flaherty, and God knows what will happen!"

"They'll never get your name out of me. I promise you that."

He whispered in a hoarse voice, as though a hand were on his throat, "Do you know what Gennaro would do to me if he ever found out I blew the whistle?"

"I can imagine—"

He said savagely, "Well, imagine it a lot, and double it in spades when you get down there!"

And for the first time I saw stark fear in Jackson's eyes as he grimaced, stretched his neck, and ran his finger inside his collar. Then he did something I had never seen him do before; he took out his handkerchief and wiped his brow. The room wasn't that warm.

The hoarse voice went on: "Two years ago a couple of punks held up a drop on the West Side. They cleaned it out. The Wop found out who was the finger man. They found him in a trunk on the Drive." He shuddered. "Christ, what they did to that kid."

"It will be as before," I said calmly. "Your name won't be in it. Besides, you'll be out of town. . . ."

His look was scornful. "They always find you and they'll always wait. They never give up. They know we belong in their world, and somehow, somewhere we have to talk to somebody in that world. Maybe a hustler, maybe a bookie, or a guy you once served time with. One of them either has a price or wants to return a favor." He grunted. "I'll be a big favor or a big price!"

Jackson glanced at his wristwatch. "I'm gonna be shovin' off, kid. I'll hear from you tomorrow."

At the door he paused. "Just remember the kid in that trunk when you get downtown."

When he had gone I sat for a long time looking into the dying fire. The jubilation at the thought of the tremendous potential contained in these piles of tapes was dispelled by the fear I had seen in Jackson's face. It hadn't been said before, but it was a brutal fact we both knew that Gennaro would certainly want to get the man who helped destroy his empire and threaten to separate him from his beloved grandchildren.

Tomorrow there would be no return, and while the *Blade-Leader* could stand acclaimed there was little doubt that the life of Action Jackson would be precarious indeed. I tried to tell myself that all this was melodrama—the wavering fire, my exhaustion, the night winds, and Jackson himself had filled my mind with shadows—but the truth was undeniable that Jackson, who looked at life with a gambler's realism, expected to be brutally murdered if there was a single leak, even a hint of his name.

I knew and he knew it could happen. A crooked cop could get a whisper, a detective could put some odd pieces together, somewhere along the line a gear would click out of place—just once—and the secret would slip free.

What did he say? "Well, imagine it a lot . . ." and I did, and what I saw in the glowing coals made me wonder if the price for this cause was far beyond not only my means but also that of my publisher and the stout little gin player with the gleaming, tanned skull who, I was sure, didn't give a damn for swords or shields of the press but only how many copies were sold, how cheaply they could come off the press, and how to keep his advertisers happy.

I tried Gwen again but got only the answering service. I left my number, but long after the toothy weather girl had spoken knowingly of snow and winds Gwen hadn't called, so I picked up Kirkhoff's *Benedict Arnold* and once again marched through the icy wilderness with this ill-fated soldier and left Gwen and Jackson and my own growing fears behind in the moan of the night wind.

BOOK TWO

THE MEETING

[12]

IT TOOK MOST of the morning for the four of them to read the transcripts of the recordings and the long report I had made. There were Julian Savage; Turner Elliott, the *Blade*'s managing editor; Joe Bowers, the city editor; and Sam Parson, senior partner of Parson, Elliott, and Grant, the paper's legal advisers. We were all gathered in a semicircle about Savage's desk. He had read the transcripts earlier. A conservative description of his reaction would be wildly enthusiastic. Now we studied the faces of the others as they read; they nodded, grunted, looked up to ask a question, raised eyebrows, and underlined certain passages, especially Parson.

With the exception of Savage, I had worked with them for years: Turner would weigh it carefully, looking at all sides; Bowers would argue against anything Elliott would suggest; while Parson, who wouldn't give a damn about the story, would automatically try the potential libel case in his mind.

Of all three, Turner Elliott was the closest to me and the man for whom I had most respect. He was the only one who wore a coat in the office. Although he had asked me to do so, I could never call him by his first name. He was a thin, gnarled man with the grooved face of a New England farmer. He was in his late sixties and came from a long line of Midwest editors. His grandfather, a friend of Lincoln, had founded one of the big papers in Cincinnati, and his father had been an early director of the Associated Press. He had won the Pulitzer Prize for his story of the Battle of the Argonne in World War I, and his story of the

selection of the Unknown Soldier had been anthologized in many col-
lections. He had stayed in Paris after the war and had known Fitzgerald
and Hemingway.

The usual doubting Thomases were silenced two years ago when
that long and definitive work on F. Scott included three letters from
Fitzgerald to Turner Elliott, included by permission of the author. And
after Hemingway's death he was included in the moving tribute written
by one of Papa's oldest friends for the *Saturday Review*. Looking back
and being truthful with myself, I guess I really liked him more than
anyone else in the office because, like myself, he had done some fiction
in his early days but gradually had slipped into the morass of professional journalism. Turner Elliott was one of the few who hadn't urged
me to get out of the business. Once, while going uptown in a cab, he
had simply said that I was going to have a hell of a time serving two
masters and eventually I would have to quit one or the other.

Bowers, on the other hand, was a blusterer and a bully. He made a
great show of liking Turner, but the old man practically ignored him.
Even his appearance fitted his nature. He was a thin, waspish man with
deep-set eyes usually clouded by the exhaust of the cigarettes he chain-
smoked from the moment he arrived until he left the office. Bowers
had a secret contempt for any newspaperman who wrote outside his
profession; his world was bounded twenty-four hours a day by his city
desk. He thrived on conflict and was the center of a constant glowing
hate, generated by the men with whom he fought. He liked those who
agreed with him; I never did. He disliked me but respected me.

On the other hand, in the dwindling world of professionals, Bowers
was a pro; he was excellent in the handling of a major story, whether it
was a moonshot or a sensational murder. His fierce, almost savage intensity infected reporters and rewritemen until they were literally
churning out words even as they cursed him under their breath. He
instinctively plucked the lead that would make a readable sheet out of
dry-as-dust wire service copy.

He was a detested professional whose horizon was limited to cops,
detectives, politicians, and the American Legion Post where he was
perennial master-at-arms. One of his memorable arguments had been
with the makeup editor on the day Faulkner received the Noble Prize.
Bowers had fought fiercely to kill the text of Faulkner's acceptance
speech to make more room for the story of the robbery of a minor
actress. The decision was finally put to Elliott, who coldly advised
Bowers not to underestimate the intelligence of his readers.

Parsons, old and crotchety, was one of the best libel lawyers in
the city. He and his firm had been with the Miller family and the paper
since its inception. This long association at times prompted him to kill

stories for reasons other than libel. A deeply religious man, he hated all divorce stories, stories dealing with homosexuality, perversion, or rape. Years ago he had killed one of Bowers' big exclusives dealing with a homo, on the grounds the paper would be sued for invasion of privacy. It was now an office legend. However, he honestly hated official corruption, so today he was a friend at court.

Finally they had all read the transcripts and looked up, waiting for Savage.

"I think Duke has done a tremendous job and the paper is on the verge of something great," he said. He nodded to me, "Congratulations."

Respect for a fellow professional and the party line just laid out impressed Bowers. "It's a blockbuster of an exposé," he said. "I'd like to see it in the paper as soon as possible."

"There is no doubt this is fine material, Duke," Elliott said, ignoring Bowers and talking to me more than to Savage. "But there's more work to be done, isn't there?"

"I intend to make a survey of the courts and the city's policy arrests," I said. "I'm sure they will show a shocking rate of dismissals before certain judges."

"You might get a comparison with some other large cities, let's say Detroit or L.A.," he suggested, "and a breakdown of the FBI reports on policy. The policy stuff is good, very good; it definitely shows a powerful criminal syndicate is operating with immunity in the city. But there was one thing in your report, Duke, that could be just as important but you didn't emphasize it . . ."

Trust that old shrewd fox to seek out the heart of the matter . . .

"You're talking about the Sugar Hill Financing Company, Mr. Elliott?"

He nodded, and I could see Bowers hastily flipping through the pages of his copies to find it.

"I agree with you. But at this point all I have from Building and Housing is a breakdown of how many tenements they own and the number of violations."

"And you checked to see if any of these violations have been corrected?"

"Before I went into Harlem I was doing a housing survey at Mr. Savage's suggestion. I was checking that when my informant called, so I went over to policy."

He persisted, "But you did find many of the buildings had never corrected their violations despite the inspector's findings?"

I glanced at my notes. "I think I counted one hundred and fifty uncorrected violations some years old and very dangerous."

"And what about the summonses? Did you trace their history?"

"Building and Housing said it would be a monumental job to correlate all the summonses, so I talked to some of the inspectors."

He leaned forward. "And?"

"Three inspectors told me off the record they were told to lay off, and they surmised the summonses were squashed."

Savage broke in, "And these are the buildings in which some of the policy drops are located?"

"Nearly all, not only in Harlem but in Brooklyn and Queens. Tilley—one of the collectors—told me no one in his building could ever locate the owners to lodge a complaint."

Bowers interrupted, "Did you check them out?"

"They're on West Twenty-ninth Street in a small office. One girl takes the calls," I said. "When I called I said I was a tenant in Tilley's building and wanted to report that my child had been bitten by a rat. The girl told me to report to the Health Department." I added hastily as I saw Bowers' mouth forming the question: "I did a check at the Health Department. A breakdown of reported ratbites shows a big percentage comes from the tenements owned by Sugar Hill Financing Company."

"How do they get away with it?" Savage said wonderingly.

Parsons growled, "Grafters, that's how."

"What do you think, Duke?" Elliott asked.

"I agree with Mr. Parsons. Somebody's paying off—but big."

"Is McShane your target, Duke?"

Elliott's voice was cool and quiet, but if he had shouted he would not have created more reaction. Bowers grunted as if hit by a fist; Parsons' eyebrows raised and he looked first apprehensive, then delighted; while a slow smile settled over Savage's face as if at last the *Blade* was about to fulfill its destiny. I was taken completely by surprise. There was nothing in my memo to indicate that McShane was involved; I had discussed this privately with Savage and, in fact, had included only factual material in my report. Actually, I didn't have a damn thing on McShane outside my suspicions and what Jackson had told me.

"Why, yes, sir. But just out of curiosity, why do you ask that?"

He tapped the report. "You mention Lou Janus, the judge. He's been McShane's man for years." He gave me a weary smile. "I guess I've been around too many years not to have missed the gossip. In the last ten years McShane's been building up to a regular Boss Tweed. Now that he's National Committeeman, City Hall is afraid to buck him and Washington needs him—"

"—This year more than ever," Parsons observed.

Elliott nodded. "He'll do a typical big-city political machine job.

It's nothing new—we always had the Hagues, Pendergasts, and Tammany Hall."

"What a story!" Bowers exploded. "McShane indicted and we did it!"

"He's far from indicted, Joe," Parsons observed mildly.

Bowers slapped the bundle of transcripts and reports.

"It's all right here, Sam. Right here."

"It's not there," Elliott said sharply. "It's going to require a lot more digging and maybe a lucky break somewhere to put it there."

Bowers looked rebuffed but remained silent.

"I have a hunch McShane is in that Sugar Hill setup," I said. "But I don't know how."

Parsons asked if I had checked their incorpation papers.

"The first thing. It led me to several holding companies."

"If we only had the power of subpoena," he said. "That's what you need in this one."

"Now we're coming to why I called you all here," Savage said. "Duke has given me his recommendations, and I go along with them. But I would like all your opinions. Duke, will you give us your ideas?"

Step by step, I outlined my full plan as I had previously described it, only going into more detail on the exclusive rights we would have to the story. Some of it was on the technical side, dealing with the process of nailing down the story as the *Blade-Leader*'s exclusive, once the official action began. As we were an evening newspaper, our first edition arrived on the street at about 10:00 A.M. Policy raids had to be made in the late afternon or evening if we were to get the exclusive, and if they were on a large scale and defendants had to be booked there was always the possibility of a leak from a precinct deskman to a favorite reporter on the opposition who either covered that particular district or was assigned to police headquarters. Naturally, they would not have our intimate facts. I have never believed that newspaper readers gather at the subway kiosks eagerly comparing the stories of various newspapers, nor do they seek out every edition in these days of televised news. It's the content, the presentation, the integrity, the accuracy that count with the readers.

But Bowers, as I knew, was ready to give battle. Even as I spoke I could see the red slowly spreading upward from under his collar.

"No, sir, I won't go for that, Julian," he said, ponderously shaking his head like some thoughtful elder statesman. "There are a million leaks in the D.A.'s office, and on this one we can wind up reading it in the *News* or the *Trib*. They have men covering the building daily. We don't have that luxury of manpower. We send over there only when we have to."

"Well, what do you suggest?" Savage said patiently.

"Get it into the paper," he said fiercely. "The hell with the D.A.'s office!" He glared around at us, accusingly. "They have a budget bigger than the Pentagon. If they can't dig up a scandal like this—they're derelict. Let's print it and tip off the cops a few hours before, as we did on Malloy's last one." He turned to me. "You got arrests, didn't you, last time?"

"Chicken feed," I said. "If we had kept on it for a month more we might have gotten a Grand Jury investigation that would have gone God knows where. It's true we got some cops—but they were cheap chiselers. This time we can get grafters who really count."

Bowers pursed his lips and again shook his head. "Maybe so, but I hate like hell reading it in the other papers"—he waved the transcripts —"after all this work."

"In this case honor and integrity are more valuable than time," Elliott interjected quietly. He leaned slightly forward and spoke to Savage. "We have gone as far as a newspaper can go—there is massive evidence of shocking conditions in our Police Department and perhaps higher up."

"And you think our best bet is to go to Flaherty with it?" Savage asked.

"I think it's our duty."

Sam Parsons roared indignantly, "You're going to Flaherty after Malloy just told you he doesn't know how far the man's political commitments will let him go? That's crazy!"

"Duke also outlined how he intended to make sure he would go all the way," Elliott said evenly.

"That's all iffy," Parsons persisted. "You're going to get his office to a point, then clobber him with the high-police-brass stuff." He threw up his hands. "What the hell guarantee do we have he won't just turn around and tell us it's all a lot of hogwash."

I asked, "With tape recordings?"

"*With* tape recordings. I know they can be admitted into evidence. But that's not a case! He'll need your informer!"

When I hesitated, Bowers said quickly, "Yeah, what about this guy? You going to turn him over to Flaherty?"

"No. I can testify if Flaherty wants an eyewitness. I was there at most of the recordings. I'm on the tape."

"True," said Parsons, "but you're not a policy racketeer. You didn't have personal dealings with Gennaro. You didn't pay off the cops!"

"I was present."

Parsons punched the arm of the chair. "Fine! Excellent! As prosecutor I want you. I need you." He pointed a long and bony finger. "I also need your informer."

"Well, you're not going to get him, Mr. Prosecutor. I've given you a prima facie case. You go out and get more evidence based on my information. I—"

"Sam," Savage said, "we're in the newspaper business—we're not public prosecutors."

Parsons shook his leonine head. "True. But you have evidence I need." He slammed a big hand down. "Not me, sir! The People!"

"You're so right, Sam," Bowers agreed. "It's the People's Case. Flaherty isn't going to go off half cocked. He wants everything."

Elliott, his voice still even, stared at Bowers. "The right of a newspaper to protect the identity of its informant is as old as public print. Some states have laws supporting this; most don't. But some of our people have gone to jail rather than name their sources." He nodded at Sam. "You even defended one before the war."

"It was in the thirties," Sam explained to Savage. "One of our reporters got ten days for refusing to tell the court who gave him certain information."

Bowers smirked. "The—er—reporter went to jail and made a million dollars in Hollywood."

Good God, I thought, is this what he's thinking?

"Believe me, I don't intend to go to jail or even make half a million," I said.

He looked hurt, as though I had misinterpreted his motivations. "Jesus, Duke, I didn't think . . ."

There were little glints of light in Elliott's eyes, and I could see that his patience was wearing thin.

"We're wasting valuable time," he said bluntly, "and I have an edition to attend to." He turned to Savage. "My advice is to assign Duke to turn over his material to Flaherty just as he outlined it here. I don't trust that sanctimonious tinhorn as far as I can throw him. I don't think we should give him any opportunity to let him label it a lot of hogwash as Sam suggested."

Parsons started to say, "I just said—" but Savage waved him silent.

"In my professional opinion," Turner went on, "we have the germ of a scandal that could have shocking repercussions." He turned to me. "As for that informer, Duke, I don't want to know who he is. As far as I'm concerned he has done the job you wanted. Let the staff that Flaherty is boasting always about pick it up from there. But there's one thing, Julian."

"What's that, Turner?"

"If we hook McShane, do we go all the way?"

Savage frowned. "I don't understand—what do you mean, 'all the way'?"

Turner said flatly, "Just what I said—all the way. To send him to jail."

Savage looked as though he hadn't heard correctly. "Of course! That would be the greatest thing this paper has ever accomplished! This would be"—he spread his hands—"of monumental importance to the community!"

Elliott nodded. "I've been around here a long time, Julian, and I like to get things on the record. McShane's a power in this state. Even the White House intends to lean on him this year."

"No politician can muzzle the paper while I'm still here," Savage said sternly. "Does that answer your question?"

But Elliott was not to be flustered. "Does Mr. Dolbar feel the same way, Julian?"

Two tiny red spots showed on Savage's cheekbones, and I wondered if I was about to see an explosion, but he maintained his self-control admirably.

"I run this paper independently with my father-in-law's complete approval," he said stiffly. "Not to repeat myself, does that answer your question?"

Parsons and Bowers looked at Elliott expectantly.

"I have found that a managing editor who is a devil's advocate is far more valuable to both his paper and his publisher than a yes-man, Julian," was Elliott's soft reply.

Savage smiled, and the tension disappeared from the room. "And I thank you for it, Turner."

Elliott nodded and looked at me. "Duke, do you need anyone to give you a hand?"

"I could use two young, aggressive reporters to help me correlate the court records. One in Brooklyn and one in Queens."

Elliott turned to Bowers. "Can we help him?"

As I knew he would, Bowers looked pained. "Well, I'm using those two college kids in Queens and Brooklyn headquarters—"

"That's exactly what I want," I said.

Bowers held up both hands in a gentle protest.

"Now, wait a minute, Duke. These are only kids—"

Elliott asked me if they would be suitable.

"Perfect, Mr. Elliott."

"Assign both those boys to Malloy when you get back to the desk," he said to Bowers. "Anything else, gentlemen?"

Parsons slapped the back of his chair. "By God, I hope not! I have to get back uptown."

Savage said: "Thanks for coming, Sam. Duke, you'll be sure to clear every story with Sam before we use them."

Sam smiled. "Duke and I have gone down to the mat on many a story. We'll get along, heh, Duke?"

"I'm sure we will," I said. But privately I wondered how hard I would have to struggle on that mat this time to get these stories out of his hands and into the paper once they were ready.

Elliott rose. "I think this is one of the best jobs you've ever done, Duke. It has all the earmarks of an important one."

This was not hollow, meaningless. He said it because he meant it, and despite the cynicism that is experience, I felt the glow that only a sincere man can fan to life in the heart of another.

They went out, one by one.

"Now," said Savage, "we're all agreed you're going to Flaherty's office and you will use the strategy you outlined."

"That's correct."

"Of course, I want to be kept informed on every development. If I am not in you can call me at the house." He hesitated. "I'm glad Turner brought up the question of my father-in-law's interference. I just want you to know I intend to go to the limit."

"I didn't think there was any question, Julian."

He carefully made a few doodling signs on a memo pad. "No, he was right to bring it up. He knows about an editor my father-in-law bought off with a pension ten years ago. They were about to nail a local politician to the cross when the party put on the pressure. It was either start hammering or get out of town. The editor was an old man who was ready to take a pension. Sam gave it to him, and the exposé quickly died. The paper turned out to be his first big money-maker."

"And you don't think that if we—"

He broke in harshly: "I told Turner and I'm telling you again—if we get the goods on McShane we're going all the way and nobody—repeat—nobody is going to stop me from printing it! And that's the last word as far as I'm concerned."

I got up. "It's also the last as far as I am concerned. I'll set up the appointment with De Lorenzo as soon as I can."

From the turn of the century to the end of World War I, most of New York's major papers began an exodus from historical Park Row to uptown. By the time the U.S. had perfected its first moonshot, only the *Blade-Leader* remained downtown. We were then located only a beanbag throw from City Hall Park, just off Broadway.

Like every newspaper, we had a small neighborhood restaurant, simply a bar and, beyond a plywood partition, ten tables. The food was inexpensive, the service casual, the drinks sufficient. It had once been a speakeasy; in fact Louie, its owner, had run whiskey from Canada to the Atlantic Highlands during Prohibition. His prized possession was a framed picture, donated by a *Blade* photographer long gone to his reward, showing him in the custody of two federal officers. At lunchtime, Louie's was a bedlam, with printers, pressmen, and editorial harassing the impassive, ancient, and arthritic waiter who, it was rumored, owned three apartment houses in Brooklyn. Louie had only one firm rule: no rock 'n roll could be played on his jukebox. He personally inspected every record; it had to be semiclassical or operatic. After lunch, for endless hours the deserted dining room would be filled with the soaring notes of Verdi, Bach, Brahms, or Beethoven. I have always liked this hour of the day at Louie's. I could think.

I had sat there for hours, going over my notes and the copies of the transcripts. I made a detailed list of assignments that would produce added material, such as the court and arrest survey, but more importantly I carefully plotted my next step to Flaherty's office. I could call De Lorenzo direct at the D.A.'s office, but I knew on home grounds he would almost automatically insist I first talk to Bob Hoff, and for a while I intended to stay clear of Hoff. For my initial talk with De Lorenzo I wanted him away from the building where the stern, almost sterile corridors and offices were impressive reminders of the well ordered life all assistants had to lead if they wanted to remain on the Quinn Flaherty team. No one spoke out of turn; no one spoke off the record; no one issued statements that had not been approved. It was sacrilegious for anyone to even think of speaking to a member of the press without Bob Hoff's hand on his shoulder.

I called De Lorenzo's home number but found it had been changed and now was unlisted. I knew the De Lorenzo family was one of the city's foremost produce dealers, but it would have been a waste of time for a stranger, especially a newspaperman, to try to solicit his phone number by calling their office.

And then I thought of Connie Ryder. Why not? She had pleaded with me to give Johnny a break; this could be it.

I gave my name to the maid, and in a second Connie came on, sounding sincerely delighted.

"Duke! How wonderful. Where are you?" The words came with a rush. "Why don't you come over and join us? We'll be taking a break—"

"Who's we?" I managed to get in.

"Some of the girls from the club; we're working on an election program three days a week."

"Election! Now?"

She laughed. "I told you I was a long-range politician. Can you drop by?"

"I'll be up in a half hour."

Cabs were not so scarce downtown in early afternoon as they are at dinnertime, so I was ushered into the Ryder Park Avenue apartment well within my half hour. As I followed the maid to the library, I could hear typewriters clicking and phones ringing. In the library several card tables were set up. Each one was covered with boxes of index cards, typewriters, and phones. I couldn't help thinking to myself that it looked for all the world like a busy horse room, except that the tables were attended by attractive young girls instead of lynx-eyed bookmakers.

Connie, lovely in a rust-colored suit, took my arm and introduced me to the young things at the tables. "Girls, this is Duke Malloy of the *Blade-Leader* who swears he will give us oodles of publicity."

They all beamed, and they were all indistinguishable from one another, with their expensive clothes, hair styles, figures, and teeth, all brimming with health and all dedicated to Good Government—at least for this afternoon.

A maid wheeled in pots of tea and plates of cookies, and you would have thought the noon whistle had blown on a construction site. Connie filled our cups, slipped some cookies on a plate, and guided me to a spare room off the library.

"What's all this with the girls and telephones?" I asked. "Running a boiler room?"

"I told you we're working on the election."

"Aren't you a bit early? It's not till November."

"That's what we mean to be—early. We're getting up a card on every registered voter in the district. Complete. How many kids? If they need a baby sitter to come to the polls. Why they don't like our party . . . anything and everything." She laughed. "Like Jim Farley said, elections are won by planning, not speeches."

"This should please the organization."

She studied me for a moment in silence. "But I'm starting to dislike the organization, Duke."

I sipped my tea, and with elaborate care set my cup back on the plate. It seemed that perhaps this might be my good day.

"When you say you don't like the organization, Connie, do you mean your party?"

She said tightly, "You know what I mean, Duke—McShane and all he stands for." She angrily broke a cookie in half. "I really enjoy politics, and since we've started this club I've been working at it. Honest I have. Daddy thinks it's a little-girl kick, and I don't try to disillusion him, but I've been really working at it. In the last several months I've visited a tremendous number of families in this district." She said proudly, "I've met a wonderful lot of people."

"What has that got to do with McShane?"

"This is off the record, Duke." She looked up, dismayed. "Why, that's ridiculous! Me talking off the record to you!"

"I talk off the record even to the elevator man. Don't worry, go right ahead."

"Maybe it's just a lot of gossip, but when you keep hearing the same stories over and over, you think that maybe there's something to them."

"Like what?"

She said definitely, "Like McShane and the gangsters. You know it as well as I do."

"I've been hearing it for years, but that doesn't prove anything."

"I guess not, but what I can't understand is that some people shrug it off." She blurted out, "Like my father! He just says, 'Oh, that's politics.' " She tossed her head. "That's not politics, and someday somebody will tell these old graybeards it's not only not politics, it's criminal!"

"Perhaps one of your bright young helpers will be that somebody."

She said bitterly, "We're only a small group. The people listen to us. They laugh. They smile. They accept our small favors. But ask them to help us go against McShane! I had people tell me how he got them coal during the Depression and got their kids in the CCC's—and that was before anyone in our club was born!"

"He can't be here forever."

"I'm not too sure," she said dryly. Then suddenly she leaned over. "But I never asked you what you wanted, Duke."

"Nothing much. Just Johnny's home number."

"Of course." She slid off the couch, and I couldn't help admiring those beautiful legs and the way that suit filled when she bent over. As she neared the desk she hesitated. "Couldn't you get him at the office?"

I decided not to try to kid her; she was nobody's fool. "Frankly, Connie, I didn't call the D.A.'s office. Let's say politics."

She nodded, but I knew this didn't satisfy her. She took a small memorandum book from a desk and flipped through the pages. "They changed it a few weeks ago. Oh, yes, here it is. LO 4-5467. It's not far from the old Jefferson Market Court."

"One of the brownstones?"

"The De Lorenzo's have been there for years. Besides his parents, his sister lives upstairs with her kids." She laughed, "They even make wine in the cellar."

"It sounds like he has a big family."

"Only about two thousand people," she said, deadpan. "They argue all day long about artichokes, carrots, and beans. Tony—that's Johnny's oldest brother—has a big blackboard in the kitchen. His mother listens to the radio at 5:00 A.M. and marks down the government produce prices. It always makes me think of a Saroyan play."

"More like *You Can't Take It with You.* I saw it in the WPA Theatre for fifty cents."

She wrinkled her nose. "You sound older than McShane."

"I'm not really." I stood up. "Is Johnny busy? I haven't seen him since the Christmas party."

"He's downtown every night. He calls me just before I go to bed." She looked at me. "Will you answer one thing?"

"If I can."

"Off the record—why didn't you call Johnny at the office?"

"Truthfully, I didn't want to talk to Bob Hoff. I want to discuss something in private with Johnny."

She made a face. "Johnny doesn't think much of Hoff. One night last week Hoff was drinking and got in an elevator with him. He kept insisting that Johnny join him for a drink, and when Johnny refused he got nasty."

I tried to be casual.

"I've heard Hoff likes his liquor."

She gave me a sharp look, smiled, and opened the door. "No tales out of school," she whispered.

"You should try diplomacy instead of politics," I whispered in return. On the way out I said goodbye to the slender, beautiful young things, who reciprocated with low wolf whistles.

A sad, nostalgic smile was my only possible answer.

[13]

I CALLED JOHNNY DE LORENZO early Sunday afternoon. He sounded slightly puzzled, although I tried my best to be offhand and casual. I simply said I would like to discuss something important that had just come up and could I drop by? When he hesitated, I said it would take only a few minutes and I could be there within the hour, then hung up.

As I suspected, the De Lorenzo residence was an old-fashioned brownstone on West Ninth, just off Sixth. Like the Mews, Patchin Place, and Macdougal Alley, the street was one of the few left that had a character of its own; the stoops had white lacy-iron railings; there were linden trees on both sides of the street, and in front of the house an old-fashion iron hitchup post and a redstone carriage step. The ceilings would be at least fifteen feet high; the lower hall would smell musty in damp weather; and on the second floor, if you probed the wallpaper, you would find the gaspipe hole of the old Baltimore heater. The stairs would be steep and heavily carpeted, the woodwork dark and polished.

But you can get away with just so much old-fashioned charm in our city; someone had swept a broken bottle into the gutter, and across the top step was scrawled in chalk, "Joey is a rat and so is Mary."

The doorbell clanged rather than rang and the door was yanked open by a wild-eyed kid of about ten, with a rocket-launching pad in one hand.

"Mr. De Lorenzo, please."

"You mean my father or my uncle?"

"He means your uncle. Now beat it," Johnny's cheerful voice called out. "How are you, Duke?"

He ushered me inside the dim hall. There was a dusty stone statue of a shepherd's boy playing a pipe and a sad-eyed Madonna in a niche. Off to one side was an old-fashioned roll-top desk cluttered with papers and light tan legal folders. He ushered me into a room that appeared to be a study. The walls were lined with lawbooks and framed photographs of fierce-eyed men in iron derbies and handlebar mustaches. One was in judge's robes.

"The De Lorenzo gallery," Johnny said. "They go back to the Reconstruction Period."

"I didn't realize your family was in New York that long."

"Actually not in New York. We started in the produce business just after the Civil War. We came to New York in 1895.

He pointed to the man in the robes.

"That's my grandfather, the judge," he said. "The Mafia killed him. I mean the real Mafia."

"In New York?"

"Oh, no. New Orleans." He brushed aside some papers. "Since the boss is away, it seems I have a million things to do. Can I get you a drink?"

"No, thanks, Johnny. How long will Flaherty be gone?"

He leaned back in the old-fashioned swivel chair.

"At least several weeks. After the conference he's going to make a stopover to speak to the International Conference of Lawyers in London, then spend a few days with his mother's family in Ireland. He's crazy if he doesn't take advantage of the trip. The guy's been working day and night." He suddenly leaned forward. "Hey. How did you get my phone number? Did Hoff give it to you?"

"No, Connie. I dropped by her place yesterday. She's quite a girl."

"Yes, but she shouldn't give out my number. The boss wanted me to have it changed when I got the new job."

"Why?"

"For obvious reasons, I would say. I would have every ward heeler in the county calling me."

"Does Flaherty really keep politics out of his office, Johnny?" I said innocently.

He elaborately stacked several folders in a pile. "It's not like the old days when the district leaders would barge right in and tell the D.A. what to do."

"That went out with Boss Tweed," I said softly. "They do it differently now."

He slowly turned in his chair and faced me. "As far as I'm concerned, the boss has, and is, keeping politics out of our office. Okay?"

"Okay. Now let me tell you why I'm here. By the way, I know you're not supposed to talk to us without Hoff, but I—"

The words were like chips of ice: "Suppose you let me worry about Bob Hoff."

"I just wanted to get across that I don't want Hoff in this any more than I have to."

The muscles along his jawline bunched, and I thought he was about to snap out a reply but he just nodded.

This was slightly unexpected and puzzling, but I thought it might be a natural resentment of the meeting in the elevator Connie had described.

"The *Blade-Leader* is going to give your office Vito Gennaro and his policy operation, wrapped up and tied in a bow." I tapped my string envelope. "Our lawyers tell us while we might not have an airtight case, we have one hell of a start."

He eyed the envelope. "What's in that?"

"The transcripts of several tape recordings."

"With whom?"

"Gennaro, members of his mob, policy operators, stand-ins, a few cops."

Though he was trying to keep his voice controlled, a note of excitement had edged into his words. Slowly, almost unconsciously, he was moving upright in his chair.

"Who's doing the talking?"

"Sometimes I am—mostly Mr. X."

He leaned over and searched a pack for a cigarette. It was empty, and he crumpled it in annoyance.

"Take one of mine."

"Thanks." He leaned forward and inhaled until the end glowed. Then he leaned back and blew the smoke in the air. In those brief few moments I could hear the gears meshing.

"Who's Mr. X?"

"We can't name him, Johnny. That's got to be the deal."

"A stoolie?"

"Not a professional. After you read the transcript, you'll see he obviously will have to be in the mob."

"Is he going to be around?"

I examined the question cautiously; it was a tricky one. The cops could put out feelers and discover who was missing and put two and two together. The underworld is sensitive the same way.

"I can't answer that now."

He tapped an ash in the ashtray. "I don't have to tell you how badly we want to get Gennaro. Everyone has been trying, from Justice to the Senate committee."

"I think you can with this stuff. Of course you'll have to do some work."

"How many cops with their hands in the till?"

"A few," I said casually, and added, to change the subject, "We got Gennaro's bank."

There was no mistaking the leap of interest in his eyes. "You don't get that every day."

"Street, house, and apartment," I added smugly, "and tapes from the bank."

"With whom?"

"A guy named Bernie, his office manager."

"Bernard Levins! We had a line on him for over a year."

"You never had a tail on him?"

Now it was his turn to want to change the subject.

"We lost him a few times," he said too casually. "We grabbed him on the Expressway a few years ago but he was clean. All we had were rumors."

"So you have been looking into Gennaro's operations?"

"Not I, the office—about three years back. I just happened to come across the file some months ago. I asked the boss, and he said they never got anywhere. It was just a lot of talk, no evidence. Gennaro was big in Jersey, but not in New York." He looked at me. "Did you run across anything on Ricky Strasser?"

"Gennaro's lawyer?" Then, as if I wanted to show him we had touched all bases, I said, "Let's say we're looking into him."

He gave me a thin smile. "What's the deal?"

"The usual. The paper turns over everything to your office. We want to have our people around when you knock off the drops and grab Gennaro. It will be a *Blade-Leader* exclusive, with Flaherty acknowledging our assistance. If there are any indictments, we get first call before Hoff releases it."

"I told you, let me worry about Hoff . . ."

"It's a pleasure, but he's done it before. Just don't see him too soon. Work on it a little bit."

Impatiently he ground out the cigarette. "For Christ's sake—will you forget Hoff! I'm more interested in your tapes. I'll have to hear them some time."

"That's a problem we'll take up when we come to it. We're just giving you a newpaper's investigation. We'll give you the guts of it. You go out and get it your way."

"You've got the information. We haven't."

"We'll turn over the vital information. By the way, who will you use?"

"If it's all you say it is," he emphasized, "and the office goes into it, I guess we'll use the squad. Why?"

"The D.A.'s squad are all city cops."

"We never caught any of them off base yet, Malloy," he said in a thin, strained voice.

"Come off your high horse, Johnny. I know why Captain Rogers resigned."

"Nothing was ever proved," he snapped, "and for God's sake, that was seven years ago!"

"So it's seven years. I'm only trying to make a point. It could happen again."

"Okay. Then we'll use our own investigators."

"Nearly all of them have been with your office for twenty years or more. They grew up with those cops. I think it would be unfair to them, not to say unwise."

"Come on, Malloy, get with it," he said impatiently. "If we don't use our people or the cops on our squad, who would you use?"

I took a cigarette, offered him one, which he automatically accepted.

"Murphy. My informant says he's a straight-arrow cop and is dying to get Gennaro."

De Lorenzo nodded. "Murphy's a good cop, and honest; there's no doubt about that. But for God's sake, he's one man."

"I'm not saying the whole force is crooked; that's ridiculous. But crooks know crooks, whether they're in the Police Department or on the outside. And that goes for honest men. Murphy will never admit it to either you or me, but he knows who the honest cops are downtown."

"You mean, let Murphy pick his men?"

"Exactly."

"And that will satisfy you and your paper?"

"It will. Actually, there's nothing else you can do." I grinned. "Let's face it, Johnny, you'd be happier this way—you don't trust some of these bastards any more than I do."

He flushed slightly. "You never heard me say I didn't trust my own office."

There was no doubt about De Lorenzo's loyalty to Flaherty and the D.A.'s office; it would take a tremendous amount of evidence to shake that. I was glad I was giving it to him piecemeal. A man's loyalty can distort his own convictions and common sense. This was delicate ground, and I decided to tiptoe past it quickly, at least for the present.

I opened the string envelope, and took out Jackson's maps along with the transcripts of the recordings.

"Well, do you want to start?"

He eyed the maps and mound of bond paper. "This desk is too crowded. Let's spread it out on the floor."

We started in the early afternoon. Outside the study door, the De Lorenzos were an active clan: kids were yelling and jumping; there was a deep male voice; several women chattered in English and Italian; and several children raced up and down outside on roller skates. But gradually the house grew quiet. Once there was a chorus of good-byes, and Johnny absentmindedly murmured something about a niece going back to Brooklyn. Neither of us noticed the passing of the hours, the gradual dimming of the lemonish winter sunlight, and the deepening of the shadows until, in surprise, Johnny looked up and turned on a lamp.

"It's almost six o'clock," he said, glancing at his watch. "How about a drink now?"

"Fine with me. Rye on the rocks."

"I'll be back in a minute," he said. He returned shortly with a tray, glasses, ice, and a bottle. He made two healthy ones, and we silently touched glasses.

"What do you think?" I asked.

I had a feeling he had mulled the question while he was getting the drinks and had reached the answer. It came promptly. "No matter what your lawyers told you, you haven't got a prima facie case."

There is a point in any bargaining where you have to show the iron in your makeup, and I guess this was it; I carefully stacked the pile of transcripts and began to slide them into the envelope.

"Okay, then we'll just print it as it is."

Johnny looked genuinely surprised. "What are you doing?"

"I am going back to the office to inform my publisher that in the opinion of the District Attorney there is no legal case here, so we had better print what we have."

He reached over and took out the transcripts.

"You're crazy," he said. "Why do that?"

"Because of the God-damned attitude of your office," I told him. "We got the same thing when we gave you people the parking-lot investigation. Flaherty told us we didn't have a criminal case. For Christ's sake, we're not the D.A.—you are. A newspaper can go only so far, and then the legal professionals who are being paid by the taxpayers must pick up where we amateurs left off!"

He patted me on the arm. "Easy, Duke. I just made an observation."

This was where I wanted him, on the defensive. It's better that way, as any Vermont horse trader will tell you.

"Why make a negative observation? Why not say we amateurs have made a hell of a case that there is a damned big syndicate operating here in this town?"

He held up his glass, and laughed. "Okay, you guys have done a terrific job. But I'm just saying we have our work cut out for us. We have to develop a legal case."

"No misdemeanor . . ."

"Who's talking about misdemeanors? Contriving to form a lottery is a felony, and a damn' hard case to prove."

"Dewey did it with Jimmy Hines," I said. "Hogan did it with that big mob in the sixties."

"That was a million years ago, in a different time. The mobs today are more sophisticated."

You mean they have found it pays to play power politics, I thought.

"These tapes are admissible as evidence. I checked the law myself."

"That's true. But you haven't gone near Gennaro's bank, right?"

"You know how sensitive the areas are around any policy bank," I said. "They usually have the whole neighborhood on the payroll. And my informant says don't try that bit of having the cops pose as Con Edison men breaking up the street. Years ago, Murphy almost grabbed Gennaro with that dodge."

He looked as if he had suddenly remembered something. "When you were up in Harlem, did you come across a nut named the Prophet?"

"I've listened to him a few times up on 138th Street. I think he's dangerous. Why do you ask?"

"The office received several complaints from Harlem merchants that he's a trouble maker. The Police Alien Squad said he's native born and a menace."

"Can't you grab him on anything?"

"We only have complaints. You can't arrest a man on those grounds even though he's a nut."

"Especially if he's a black nut."

"Come on, Duke, the law doesn't look at the color of a man's skin."

"I'm beginning to think that even the law looks twice if the guy's got enough power to make City Hall jump through the hoop."

He frowned. "Since when did the Prophet make the Hall jump?"

"After he made that big speech at St. Maria's Hall."

"You mean when he threatened to burn down that tenement?"

"That's right."

"Hell, the Alien Squad had men tailing him day and night. One move and he would have been flung in jail."

"If another man had made that same threat five, ten years ago, he would have been arrested immediately," I told him. "Why, this crackpot has even advised his followers to carry pistols! Don't tell me he's not against the law!"

He looked uneasy. "These are delicate times, Duke. We have to move carefully on these things. That's why the boss is checking out every complaint we received. If there's anything to them . . ."

"Okay, Johnny," I said. "Let's forget the Prophet and get back to our problem."

"Problem?" He raised his eyebrows. "There's no problem, Duke. We're going into it the minute you leave here."

I tried hard to keep the jubilation out of my voice. Now it had been started, it was on the record; the deadly package was slowly shifting to their lap. I felt strange, almost eerie relief.

"Good. I'm glad to hear that. And we know the deal."

"Give me a break on that. If we use Murphy, then he's the boss. I can't force cops to take reporters on raids; you know that."

"Well, let me work that out with Murphy. We'll have to meet anyway."

"Okay. But you can always get them at the precinct booking."

"We should get a picture of Gennaro at a precinct when the cops are going to break down a door and get him inside his main bank! Come on, Johnny!"

He grinned. "Okay, that's an item to be worked out. Agreed?"

"Agreed. But I hope we don't have any problems on the indictments."

"I hope you don't think I'm going to give you the true bill before the judge opens it."

"Of course not. But we're an evening paper, Johnny. Indictments are opened when court convenes in the morning."

"Isn't that an afternoon paper story then?"

"Sure. For everyone. Don't you think we deserve some credit for our initiative?"

"Of course we'll do anything within the bounds of propriety," he said. "What do you suggest?"

"Only what has been done many times before with other papers.

In our first edition we project, predict, or disclose that according to a spokesman for the District Attorney's office, developments, possibly indictments, in the Gennaro case will take place . . ."

Johnny shrugged. "If the boss okays it, fine. But what's the difference between having a story predicting something when you know in a few hours you'll have the facts?"

"Unless there is hard news breaking during the night," I said, "the first edition of an evening newspaper is traditionally composed of news you might have read in the morning papers. The first edition is also the keystone edition of the day. By the time your judge has opened the indictments, the reporters turn in their facts to a rewriteman, and it is set in type, placed in forms, then in a mat—"

Johnny grinned. "Okay. You win."

"There's also a question of catching trains, planes, buses, for the first edition—"

"Spare me the logistics, Duke. How about the transcripts?"

I slid the copies into an envelope and handed it to him.

"I'm inclined to think you're going to grab Gennaro, Johnny."

"If we don't, it won't be because I didn't try," he said firmly.

He saw me to the door, and I heard a woman's voice come down from above. I looked up and saw an old lady, a twisted towel tied around her white hair, leaning over the bannister.

"Johnny, the lasagna is done. You come and eat before Tony's kids get it. You hear?"

Johnny looked up with a grin. "Okay, Mom, right after I finish up some business—all right?"

"You come soon, eh, Johnny?"

"Okay, Mom."

"I told Tony to let Joey play the accordion," she said, "I like so much the accordion, Johnny."

"Okay, Mom; tell Tony I said it's okay."

"It won't bother you, Johnny? Your business?"

"No, Mom, you tell him to go ahead."

"My mother," he said, affectionately. "Since my father died last year, she lives for these kids." The wild notes of a distant accordion rose, and he added wryly, "That's Joey."

As I walked down the street, I wondered how chic Connie Ryder would fit in this big, warm, noisy family.

I called the office from the busy drugstore on the corner to see if there were any messages. The boy at the desk said that Gwen had called twice and that the night city deskman wanted to talk to me.

"Duke?" he said, "have you run across Bob Hoff in your travels?"

Unconsciously I moved closer to the mouthpiece. Even the wonderful news that Gwen had called faded into the background.

"Hoff? No, what's up?"

"Nothing too important. We got a tip from headquarters that two of the D.A.'s cops are bringing back that bank president and his girl friend, so we just wanted to check the time they're coming in at Kennedy. She's a nice-looking dame and we want to assign a photog."

I remembered the story, the usual high-living banker who robbed his bank to support his beautiful and young blond girl friend and skipped before the arrival of the examiners. It was a routine story, but what was important was my deskman's next remark:

"I called Hoff's apartment last night and tonight, and the day desk has been trying to raise him. What's the matter with that bastard? Drunk?"

I mumbled that I would keep an eye out for him, then hung up and stared at the black mouthpiece until the persistent tapping of an old man on the door of the booth broke off the images running through my head: images of De Lorenzo, looking irritated when I mentioned Hoff, his snapped comments when I again brought up Hoff's name.

It all added up to one thing: Hoff must be on a lost weekend.

[14]

I GOT GWEN on the second try. She had been in the shower when I first called. When I suggested Louie's she just groaned, and I quickly suggested Lacey's on Third Avenue, the one-time perfectly marvelous neighborhood saloon that had been discovered by all the wrong people and turned into a meeting place for nervous producers who drank only seltzer water, directors with ulcers, fairy interior decorators, tourists, and unemployed actors who wore red sport shorts, chinos, sneakers, and who imagined they looked like Errol Flynn. The food was fair; the drinks were overrated, the prices outrageous. You got glamour instead of quality. But I knew Gwen was in no mood for a cab ride to the dark and lonely streets off Foley Square, so I called, got a reservation, and picked her up.

It was one of those nights that nothing goes right: a long wait for a cab, a cold night, and a misplaced reservation. Gwen forced a smile, but I knew we never should have gone to Lacey's. And the simpering bastard who turned around too quickly at the bar and spilled part of his drink on me didn't help matters.

Finally we got a table and were handed a slate with the chalked prices.

"Why the hell can't they at least type a menu? I feel like Lincoln reading his lessons."

"And down in your Louie's I feel like Mary among the Mafia," she said. "The characters that go in there!"

"They've been living in that neighborhood for fifty years, and don't believe that every Italian is a gangster."

"Nor every cop a crook," she said sweetly.

Happily the drinks arrived, and I touched her glass with mine. "Truce?"

She leaned over and squeezed my hand. "I'm sorry, dear; I was being bitchy, wasn't I?"

"What's up, Gwen?"

She moved her glass to make a circle on the scarred pine tabletop—another bit of Lacey's ostentation. "You know, this is the first time you've taken me out in almost a month."

"Gwen, I'm tied to this investigation. It's getting bigger every day."

I checked myself; she had taken a big swallow, and it wasn't because she liked the taste of whiskey; I was waving the red flag.

"Have you thought about what I said last time?" she asked.

"You mean about leaving the paper?"

"Exactly that."

"I thought about it. . . ."

"And?"

"Believe me, dear, I did think about it."

"I know you thought about it, Duke," she said in a low, fierce tone. "But what are you going to do about it?"

I signaled the waiter for refills.

"If you think you're going to get me drunk, Duke, you're crazy," she said. "I don't feel in any mood to drink tonight—I want answers, not liquor."

"Let me tell you briefly what I'm doing—at least listen."

"Oh, God, not tonight. Please not tonight, dear. What you're doing isn't the important question. I want to know what you intend to do. It's up to you, not up to Mr. Savage or Mr. Turner—just you."

"I think it would help if I gave you a brief rundown," I insisted.

She sighed, then nodded wearily. I started with the appetizer, talked through the steak and side dishes, and ended at coffee. From her questions I knew she was listening, even with the half-hearted attention of a captive audience.

When I had finished she said, "You hope to get this man McShane involved in this policy racket. Isn't that right?"

"Yes."

"And what will happen?"

"He'll be indicted. It depends."

"And maybe he won't be indicted. You said he was powerful in New York politics, didn't you?"

"Maybe he won't be—maybe we'll never hook him, but I'm going to give it a whirl."

She leaned across the table. "Duke, did this man ever do anything to you—to you personally, I mean?"

"No."

"So you're out to get something on this man who never did you any wrong."

I suddenly felt very weary. I closed my eyes and rubbed them with my fingertips. "It's not that simple, Gwen," I said patiently. "It takes in a lot of things—what you believe in, what you think, oh, hell . . ."

"I'm trying to understand you," she said tightly. "I want to understand, but all I can see is a grandstand, quixotic gesture. God knows where it will lead you." She sat back abruptly. "And me. What about me?"

The way she said it made me smile at her. She sat there, beautiful and indignant.

"What about you, dear?"

"Those times you asked me to marry you—don't you think I really thought about it? And don't you think I came to one conclusion?"

"That I'm the handsomest man in town and you had better grab me while the grabbing is good."

But Gwen wasn't in any joking mood; her lips were a thin red line, and she was so taut I felt her body would twang if I touched her.

"Can't you figure it out, Duke? I loved you for a long time and I know we could have a wonderful life together. But I want a man who believes I'm more important than a damned policy gangster or a crooked lawyer with an ax to grind, or an illiterate who drives a tow truck and wants to get even with his gang. And all those senseless, useless people who take over your life just because they have gossip or bad news that might send somebody to jail and give your paper a headline."

"Wait a minute, Gwen—"

"You wait a minute," she said in a voice that trembled. "If you knew how many times I waited for you to call, how many times I went without dinner waiting for you, how many times we have had a week-end planned and you called saying you were stuck writing a story? Or seeing some bum—"

I reached out and touched her hand. "Please, Gwen."

She was crying now, the big tears rolling down through the makeup. This really shook me up. Rarely had I seen Gwen cry.

"Don't try and soft-talk me," she said, jerking her hand away. "I don't want to be soft-talked, not tonight, damn you. I want to be first with you. Just once, let me come before that damned paper and those damned investigations!" She slammed her hand down, and the waiter who was passing involuntarily jumped. "Just once."

With a sudden, decisive move, she pushed the chair back and rose from the table. She glared down at me for a moment. When I started to get up she shook her head.

"Stay here, Duke," she said, choking back the tears. "Just stay here. I just want to be alone tonight."

She slung the mink wrap over her shoulder, and wound her way past the tables. If I knew Gwen, she was crying and didn't give a damn who knew it. The couple at the next table resumed their conversation a bit too loudly, as if embarrassed at having overheard the scene. The waiter, who also looked troubled, virtually tiptoed over to me with the check. I had a brandy to give Gwen some time to catch a cab, then paid my check, and left.

Outside, at the newsstand, almost automatically, I reached for the Blue Streak Final of the *Blade-Leader* and the early *News*. They were all leading with the announcement from City Hall that our chowder-head mayor was going to run again; there was a new Senate candidate from upstate, and inside was a picture of Big Jim McShane. A caption told how he would lead the New York delegation to the convention in Asbury Park and play a major role in the national elections.

As I walked down the street with the papers under my arm, I found myself wondering if Gwen was right. God, it must be worth all the effort . . . it must mean something.

[15]

THE NEXT TIME I saw Action Jackson the wheel had made a full turn. We sat at the same table in the same automat where we had met the day he turned the maps and notebooks over to me. He seemed a bit tense as he listened carefully to my account of the meeting I had with De Lorenzo and those with my publishers and editors. He asked only a few perfunctory questions about the latter, but cross-examined me closely about De Lorenzo. When he was finished I asked him what he thought, and he shrugged.

"De Lorenzo will have to move, kid; you put it in his lap. The poor bastard doesn't know what he's in for."

"You mean about McShane?"

"Of course."

"Why? Do you think Flaherty knows McShane is protecting Gennaro?"

"I don't think Flaherty has any proof. I think with him it's a question of see no evil, hear no evil, know no evil."

"What do you think would have happened if he had been there?"

"You would have gotten a perfect stall, kid. Flaherty's not the greatest D.A. in the world, but he's certainly not the dumbest. Why the hell should he go on a fishing expedition to try and hook McShane in an election year? McShane never did anything to him."

"Any D.A. worth his salary should pursue this stuff."

He gave me an amused glance. "What about this guy Hoff?"

"We got a break; Hoff's shacking up with a redhead from the Tax Bureau in Albany. She'll keep him occupied this weekend."

"Sometimes I think, kid, that if you'd drop a dime down the bowl you'd come up with a Tiffany bracelet."

"Let's hope it continues this way."

"I'm a firm believer in protecting your flanks at all times."

He made an invisible circle on the table with a spoon. "When I blow, do you know where I'm going?"

"I haven't got the slightest idea."

"Back to the farm. I already sent a letter to Jo." He gave me a quizzical look. "That's one place they would never look. Action Jackson plowing the west forty!"

"Will you stay there?"

"Are you kiddin'? I'll go nuts. Soon as the heat's off, I think I'll hit Rio or that big city in Chile where the casinos are."

"Do you have money?"

"I got some stashed away." He added emphatically, "And it's none of the Wop's. I never stole a dime. It's just dough I saved since I've been working the street for him."

"Well, bon voyage," I said. "Are you going to be around when we hit them?"

He gave me an incredulous look. "What do you think I've been doing for the last month with you?" His smile was cold, his voice bitter. "But I'm sticking around only long enough to read your stories and see the pictures of the Wop and the Sheik walking into the wagon with cuffs on. A three time loser—-life in the pen. An ordinary con, who won't be able to see those grandchildren of his—he'll go nuts. Christ, how good that will make me feel!"

"You won't come back?"

"What for?"

"Wait a minute. What about Tilley?"

He held up one hand. "That's the last thing on the agenda, my friend. I want you to call me the day before you plan to knock off the drops." He leaned over and said intensely, "And, look, no *ifs* or *buts*. If I'm not there, just leave the message with Mrs. Zuccartelli and say Duke from downtown called. You understand?"

"Now wait a minute, Action, suppose Tilley—"

"Dammit," he said impatiently, "don't worry about Tilley! He won't show the day you knock off the drop. I'll make sure of that. But he'll have the whole setup. When the dust settles, the shines on the Avenue will go back to him. They trust him; even the cops trust him. . . ."

It was cold, realistic, born of a thousand years of experience in his jungle.

"What you're saying is that after Gennaro is knocked out of the box Tilley will take over, and it—"

"And it will be business as usual, but without the syndicate—at least for a while," he said harshly. "Look at it this way: if it's not Tilley it will be someone else. Don't be a boy scout; as long as there are poor people in Harlem with dreams there will always be policy. Hell, kid, it's their orgasm . . . and when you have policy you have crooked cops. And then crooked politicians—that is, if the take is big enough." He tapped me on the shoulder. "It's up to guys like you to make sure it just doesn't get out of control." He glanced at his watch. "Well, kid, I have to shove off."

We shook hands and walked to the street. The home-going crowds were just starting to fill Fifth Avenue, and the light was fading. The afternoon had been crisp and clear; now, with the sun lowering over the Jersey Palisades, it was getting colder. There was no wind. It would be a frosty night with a moon as cold as brass.

For a moment we stood in silence, watching the crowds surge toward us across the avenue like incoming waves of clicking heels, ponderous brogues, and overcoats breaking against the curbs.

When the signal flashed WALK, he slapped me on the back.

"Kid, I'll be seein' you."

"One thing, Action . . ."

He kept his hand on my shoulder as he stood on the curb.

"What's that?"

"If it really came down to it—that the only way we could get Gennaro was by your testimony—would you come back?"

His hand tightened a trifle. "I don't know, kid. That would take a lot of thinking. . . ." He slapped me sharply on the back. "Take it easy and watch your wallet with those cops." He plunged into the outgoing wave. In a moment Jackson was just another dark overcoat on the opposite shore.

Want to know something? I really liked the guy.

Now with Jackson gone I reluctantly moved into the next phase, surveying the court records of gambling arrests and dispositions and deciding whether the facts proved, as Jackson had insisted, that Magistrate Lou Janus really was McShane's boy who took care of the syndicate's key workers. I have always disliked statistics, and the thought of going through months and months of cards appalled me.

I kept in daily touch with the office, not only to advise them of what I was doing but to get that all-important message from De Lorenzo when he wanted to see me. I also told the city desk to keep checking

Hoff. One morning I was switched from the desk to Turner Elliott's extension.

"Duke?"

"Yes, Mr. Elliott."

"I thought you would like to know the Criminal Courts man reported yesterday Hoff was back. He gave the reporters a yarn about being called to Albany, but from the looks of him you were right—he was on a drunk."

"If he's back I guess I can expect a call."

"By the way, you haven't lost sight of that housing angle, have you?"

"No, sir. But I don't think there's much more I can do until after the raids—"

"Just keep it in mind. Good luck."

I had a difficult time getting through to Savage, but Betty, his secretary, explained he was scarcely in the office; something to do with the Cummings store contract. He had bet his father-in-law he was going to land it, and I gathered he hadn't won his bet yet. But I reached him twice at home, and he sounded as enthusiastic as ever.

Bowers assigned his two young men to me, and I sent one to Brooklyn and the other to Queens gambling courts. I gave them the addresses of Gennaro's spots, the time of the month when Jackson said accommodation arrests were made, and the schedule when Janus sat in those boroughs during the past year. I made a sample breakdown chart so they knew what to look for.

For the next few weeks I lived in a small cubbyhole off the main office of the Chief Clerk of the New York County Magistrate's Court, going through the thousands of small white cards that listed the daily dispositions of the gambling cases handed down by the magistrates presiding in the gambling courts.

The chief clerk, a short stout man with the perpetually pursed lips of a hardworking truant officer, had the traditional contempt of the minor municipal officeholder for the helpless citizen who finds himself answerable to the law for the first time. Despite the bored call from the chief magistrate's secretary granting me permission to examine the records, he viewed me with open suspicion although I gave him a vague explanation that my assignment was to show how congested the courts were and how overworked the judges were.

He was an absolute tyrannical ruler over a score of embittered widows, dusty old-maid clerks, and overfed courthouse hacks. His joy was an impressive bank of IBM machines. There was no doubt he and his machines could have been of enormous help to me, but he chose to

handle me by the book; the dubious shake of his head when I asked a
simple question, the shocked disbelief when I requested to stay after
four o'clock. But I didn't have time to argue and make him more of
an enemy than he was; I took the simple and cowardly way out. I bought
him a few drinks in the bar behind the Criminal Courts Building and
once slipped him two tickets to the *Ice Capades,* which I had wheedled
from the Sports Department. I had to get to his level; he was a minor
means to a big end.

He thawed as I knew he would; the records came through faster
and in a breakdown of offenses. As he became friendlier, he became
superior, as if he wanted to return my favors with bits of his secret
knowledge. He pointed out the important runners and collectors who,
from the records, virtually used his court as a turnstile or a license to
operate.

Once when I observed that poor Magistrate Janus seemed bur-
dened with work, he looked startled, then slowly comprehending,
laughed grimly. He said nothing but silently shook his head as if to
marvel at the unexpected naïveté of a man he thought to be sophisticated.

I discovered my two young reporters were a chap from Yale, an
aggressive digger for facts, and a Harvard man who appeared to be too
much of a gentleman to argue with officious court clerks. The Yale man
called only once to advise me he had threatened his clerk with a call to
the chief magistrate's office. I never met the young man, but on the
phone he sounded articulate and uprighteous as a young deacon. I predict great things for him in this business. Harvard never called. He
simply sent in his reports badly typed on copy paper. I had no doubt he
was as bored as I by this tedious task of flipping through countless files
of cards.

Now that my chief clerk had condescended to accept me as his
friend and sounding board, I was expected to be his luncheon host and
four o'clock drinking companion.

I listened to more vicious gossip, more underhandedness, more
trivial politics than I have ever listened to before in my entire life. I
believe for the first time I saw the minor municipal servant as he really
is: frustrated, pathetic, almost sadistically a strict adherent to the laws
of the civic code when dealing with the ordinary citizen, bewildered
or awed by his first contact with the law or the mechanics of city government. But forcing myself to listen, and wearing the foolish, frozen
smile began to have its compensations; each night the chart grew bigger, the stark facts more shocking. The figures on the cardboard began
to reveal that few, if any, of Gennaro's comptrollers or important runners ever paid a heavy fine or spent time on Rikers Island. Ricky Stras-

ser or attorneys representing him handled the majority of the cases. The statistics showed that Ricky or his aides were working from one day to the next, representing gamblers and numbers men. This is perfectly legal, but apparently no one thought to ask how Ricky or any of the other attorneys who represented him managed to appear so quickly at the precinct. And what was responsible for so many courtroom toss-outs—Ricky Strasser's brilliant legal mind or police so incompetent they couldn't make an arrest stick?

My friend, the chief clerk, introduced me to many other clerks at lunch or over a drink. I always stood for a round or two, and as the weeks went by I suppose I gained a reputation as a jovial, free-spending fellow.

This too paid off. One afternoon at the bar a clerk from Buildings was in an ugly mood; a Negro attorney had put in a complaint that he was belligerent and nasty.

"The black bastard went up to the supervisor, and he went to the commissioner . . ."

I sympathized and let him pour out his venom. When my friend, the chief clerk, went to the john, I cautiously asked Buildings if he had ever heard of Sugar Hill.

"The thing Flaherty was looking into last year?" he grunted. "What about it?"

"I have a nephew, a young lawyer, who wants to make a deal with them for an estate."

He gulped down his drink. I silently motioned to the bartender.

"Your nephew got any connections?" He eyed me. "Good ones?"

"Fairly good. Why?"

He shrugged. "I don't know. I only hear they have a big, big rabbi."

"What about Flaherty? What was he looking for?"

He looked uneasy. "He was looking into it, that's all I know."

"Did he subpoena all the records?"

"There were no subpoenas," he said. "He just called up and we sent them."

"In other words, there is no record of the request."

The clerk nodded. "It was a telephone call."

He finished his drink. He knew he had given me what I wanted, and he resented me. After he left, even the chief clerk admitted he was a surly little guy and he hoped they would can him.

That was one productive afternoon. Flaherty once had been interested enough in Sugar Hill Housing to call for the records; that was a year ago. What had happened?

I made some notes and put them in my Sugar Hill folder. That would have to wait; at the moment the court charts were important.

Every evening a messenger delivered a memorandum to my apartment from Yale and Harvard. The picture gradually began to emerge citywide.

I hired an adding machine for accuracy, and my apartment at night sounded like one of Gennaro's busier drops; before long it was apparent even to the unsophisticated that a shocking core of official corruption existed in both the courts and in the Police Department.

The figures showed that Gennaro's runners and collectors paid little or no fines or received light prison terms, except those arrested in the particular periods of the month when Jackson said the syndicate provided so-called accommodation arrests for the police to maintain their quotas. The burden of arraignments and trials were handled by Janus, with Strasser or his lawyers obtaining adjournments to avoid appearing before a strict and uncorruptible judge and to appear before Janus instead. In one week so many adjournments were requested, one outraged judge called a halt and sentenced several to jail. A casual query to my friend the clerk produced the information that this was the week Janus had spent in Bermuda. Another check of the court calendar the following week showed Janus had disposed of 92 percent of the adjourned cases, dismissing the majority for insufficient evidence, fining a few, and sentencing three to brief terms on Rikers Island. All three case records showed obvious discrepancies between the handwriting of the defendants on the original court docket and the admission slip on the island. Two were noted as white when arrested, and colored when they signed in to serve their five days.

Instead of a glow of excitement, I experienced a strange letdown, an almost weary triumph as though I was finally proving something I had known all along.

I didn't realize until much later how I had isolated myself those days and nights; hours didn't mean anything. I was like a man putting together the final tantalizing bits of a jigsaw puzzle. But the completion of this puzzle meant much more to me than simple pride of accomplishment. I know now I was desperately trying to prove something. After I had seen Gwen I wasn't too sure why, but as the figures grew on my makeshift chart I suspected the reason—McShane.

I wanted to get McShane.

[16]

WHENEVER I SMELL fresh paint nowadays, I find myself thinking of the time I walked down the corridor to Hoff's office on the third floor of the Criminal Courts Building. They were painting the walls, and splattered tarpaulins, scaffolds, and opened cans were everywhere.

Hoff's secretary had called me at the office and the call was relayed to me at home. The secretary sounded flustered: Could I come down and see Mr. Hoff immediately? I said I could but I wouldn't. Perhaps later. I resented the frightened girl and the brazen orders. I worked some more on my charts and graphs, and then went downtown.

Hoff's girl was a slender young thing, very pretty and evidently impressed with her boss. When she heard my name she jerked up straight and hurried inside. In a moment she was holding open the door.

Hoff stood behind his desk. He told the girl in a low voice:

"I'm not to be disturbed—except by Mr. Flaherty." He paused, then repeated, "Not by anyone, is that clear, Miss Delafield?"

Miss Delafield nodded and swallowed hard. Hoff eyed me silently as I came in. He gestured to a chair and I took it.

He wasn't in a hurry. He took a cigarette, offered me one, which I declined, lighted his, but I noticed his hand tremble. Whatever was wrong was deep inside. I waited. It was his party.

Slowly and savagely it came. "You son of a bitch," he whispered, "you miserable son of a bitch."

All at once I felt a great surge of triumph. "Say that again," I told him, "and I'll plant a set of knuckles right in your big fat mouth."

"You couldn't talk to me," he said in a low, harsh voice, "you had to go to De Lorenzo."

"You weren't here," I said. "You were drunk and shacking up with that redheaded dame you brought down from Albany—"

It hit home. He looked stunned for a moment but quickly recovered.

"First of all it's none of your damned business what I do or where I go."

"But it might be the taxpayers'. Who the hell are you to goof off so that even a city desk can't get you for three days?"

"Dammit, don't change the subject, Malloy! You know what I'm talking about! Not your goddam city desk but you! You and that jerk De Lorenzo!"

Another score for us: he and De Lorenzo had had it out before.

"I'm sure Johnny's a big boy," I told him deliberately. "I don't think he needs a lush to hold his hand."

For a moment I thought he would fling the heavy old-fashioned paperweight he was clutching, but he slowly gained control of himself and the red in his jowls faded, like an inner dying glow, leaving the skin a heavy dead white.

"Okay," he said thickly as if there was heavy phlegm in his throat. "Okay."

"Is that what you brought me down here for?" I asked him.

"You know why I want to see you," he said. "You broke the rules."

I was sincerely surprised. "Rules? What rules?"

He slammed his fist down on the desk. "The rules of this office!" he shouted. "The rules every reporter knows and obeys."

I felt a surge of anger, so swift it almost suffocated me. Now I had to fight for control.

"Any newspaperman worth his salt that lives by any rules you lay down should turn in his police card," I said slowly, doing my best to keep my voice on an even keel. "Who are you to tell me—or any other newspaperman—who I can talk to? Dammit, Hoff, I represent one of the biggest papers in this town, and when I feel like talking to De Lorenzo or you or your phony boss I'll talk, and neither you nor your damned rules will stop me! Now is that clear?"

I was surprised to find myself shouting. By now I was warming up, I had a lot to tell him—three years' worth—but I guess he saw it coming and decided to cut it off. One thing about Hoff: he was a practical politician who knows it's a waste of time to frontal attack; guerrilla tactics are much better.

Also he had finally recovered his self-composure. I knew I had won an enemy; Hoff would never forgive me for forcing him to let his guard down and catch a glimpse of another part of him—weak, frightened, and secretly ashamed.

I felt sorry for the man, and although I knew that if our positions had been reversed I would have had to fight to the death, I stifled my intense dislike and stood up.

"Anything else on your mind?"

"I think we know each other now, Malloy," he said in a low voice, "and I just want you to know that if I ever get the chance I'll cut your throat. You understand?"

"I never had any doubt of it," I said sincerely.

He bent over a sheaf of papers as if to signal my dismissal.

"Be here at four o'clock," he growled. "De Lorenzo and Inspector Murphy want to see you." He lifted his head sharply. "And this time I'm going to be here."

"That's fine with me," I said, and it was all I could do to refrain from adding—You had better be sober.

Reporters covering established beats in New York's public buildings are a suspicious breed, especially when they catch an alien colleague trespassing on their province. Because they know the motto of most metropolitan city desks is the battle must be the payoff—what gets in the paper counts—they go through exhausting means to find out what the enemy is up to. To avoid putting five suspicious reporters on my trail, I used the building's side entrance when I left. I had a leisurely lunch, window shopped, and was back at De Lorenzo's office promptly at four.

The atmosphere was taut when I entered the room. De Lorenzo was sitting stiffly behind his desk; Hoff was looking glumly out the window; and Inspector Murphy was straight as a bolt in a chair next to De Lorenzo. Murphy never fails to remind me of a Tenderloin bartender. Of medium height, stocky with graying hair, he has a cast-iron face, frosty blue eyes, thick brows, and a courteous, old-fashioned manner. No student who had won a law degree by laboriously attending night school, he was a career policeman, up from the ranks—and he had fought his way up despite the ward heelers he hated and harassed. The Police Department was his whole life, and in a way his weakness. Five police commissioners had depended on him to root out corruption in their department, and Murphy had served them, ruthlessly, quietly.

To describe Murphy as reticent would amuse those who knew him. He never volunteered information; it had to be pried out of him.

He always struck me as a man who would think twice before answering the questions at a marriage ceremony.

When I closed the door he held out his hand and we exchanged greetings. I smiled at De Lorenzo, who looked tired and angry; he barely nodded. A quick glance at his desk showed my reports sticking from a folder, and there were three small yellow cardboard boxes—16 mm. movie reels!

Johnny doodled on the yellow folder, studied the closed door for a moment, then cleared his throat.

"We all know why we're here."

"I'm sorry, Johnny," I said quickly, "but nobody told me."

De Lorenzo looked at Hoff.

"Didn't you tell him?"

"I told him to be here at four to see you and Murphy. He certainly didn't think it was for tea!"

For a moment I thought De Lorenzo would explode, but he just clenched his teeth, and nodded.

"Duke, Inspector Murphy and some of his people have been checking your information." He opened the folder. "In a word, your stuff checks out; in fact, Tom came up with four more spots that probably opened since you were up there."

Hoff broke in. "That's four spots they didn't have. Is that right, Johnny?"

"For God's sake—" De Lorenzo said, exasperated.

Hoff raised his hand. "Just trying to keep the record straight."

"What we also did," Johnny continued, "was pinpoint the bank. It was the same house number and apartment you gave us."

I turned to Murphy. "They didn't spot your men?"

"My men were not observed," he replied almost formally.

"How did you get into the neighborhood?"

"Police procedures," was the prompt reply, and I thought I caught the tiniest twinkle in those cold eyes.

"What about Gennaro? Did you spot him?"

De Lorenzo nodded, and there was a note of triumph in his voice. "We not only spotted him going in; we have pictures of a whole day's observation. We got him with Bernie and at least three enforcers from his shylock racket. . . ."

"Did you put in a wire?" I asked innocently.

"What kind of question is that, Malloy?" Hoff broke in harshly. "You know damn' well we can't under the law."

I ignored him and spoke to De Lorenzo. "The Lopez decision said you can eavesdrop. And with the stuff you people have . . ."

"I can assure you, Duke," he said with a faint smile, "we used everything available—that is, available under the law."

"Of course."

He gave me a suspicious look, then touched the yellow boxes with his pencil. "We have a wonderful record of the play in that big drop on 138th Street and two more uptown." He paused. "How many cops did you say you had?"

I cringed at the thought of what I had to do next, but it had to be done; as far as I was concerned, a man's life was on the line and I had to play this to protect it as best we could. Johnny De Lorenzo was a nice guy; the grim-faced cop sitting across from me was a man of integrity; but the clod in the other chair was on the make in big-time politics, and few men are so dangerous.

I glanced down at the page as if to refresh my memory.

"Before we go any further, I have to inform all of you I have reports here and transcripts of phone calls which I witnessed and some which I didn't but did transcribe, between Gennaro's attorney, Ricky Strasser, in which he describes their fixer at headquarters; Bernie who discusses the fixer . . ."

I had to swallow hard.

"There is also information in these transcripts that indicates Jim McShane might be the political protector of the syndicate."

For a moment no one said a word; then Hoff whispered incredulously, "Good Christ!"

While I had been reading, Murphy slipped on a pair of old-fashioned steel-rimmed glasses and was writing carefully in a small notebook with an old black pen. It was as thick as a man's thumb, and I wondered idly where you could get such an ancient thing repaired.

For a man who had been hit in the face with a stone, Johnny was surprisingly calm.

"Do you intend to leave this material?"

I slipped it back into the envelope and silently put it on his desk.

"We may have to change our sights, Inspector," he said.

Murphy nodded. "I had better inform the commissioner immediately."

"Suppose we come back to that—"

"Suppose we stay on that subject, Duke," Murphy's cold voice said evenly. "It will be of a great interest to the commissioner."

"And to his office," De Lorenzo said.

I slowly opened the string envelope, dreading the explosion I was about to touch off. They watched me curiously. I took a deep breath and glanced down at the page I held.

"I have the full names, first names, last names, physical descriptions, badge numbers of patrolmen both on foot and in radio cars, sergeants and lieutenants and one captain who we have been led to believe is a contact with someone downtown and who tips off"—I nodded to the inspector—"Tom Murphy's activities to the syndicate."

Hoff's chair creaked as he shifted his bulk. He almost shouted at De Lorenzo, "Did you know about this?"

De Lorenzo looked stunned, then flushed deep red with anger.

"You had this, Duke, and you never gave it to me? For God's sake, man, why?"

"My office instructed me to give you this report in sections."

"Why?" De Lorenzo slammed his fist down. "Why? God dammit, why?"

"Frankly, Johnny, it's none of your damn' business. It's our information, and we can give it to you as we see fit. I might ask, why didn't you people find this out?"

"Only because of what Tom Murphy and the commissioner told me last night did I get a hint of what you now say," he cried. "Don't you realize how you could have helped us with this information? How we could have split this up . . ."

Hoff lumbered to his feet, yanked open the door, and walked out without a word.

"I want to tell you something, Malloy," De Lorenzo said in a cold, flat voice as the door clicked shut. "If I can find a statute you and your paper violated, I intend to put it before the Grand Jury."

"I'm all for that," I said. "Maybe we can get a runaway Grand Jury and really find out what's going on in this town."

"I'll do my damnedest to indict you," he snapped.

Inspector Murphy, who was looking at the ceiling as if it held some great secret, cleared his throat softly, and we both turned to him, relieved.

"I was just wondering, Johnny," he said mildly, "what you want to do about the raids."

"I don't know, Inspector," De Lorenzo said disgustedly, "I really don't know—"

"What raids?"

"Your raids," De Lorenzo almost shouted at me. "That's why we called you down. They're set for tomorrow at six. We got wonderful breaks the last couple of weeks."

"Who did you use?" I asked.

Murphy hesitated, but De Lorenzo waved his hands.

"Go ahead and tell him, Inspector. What the hell, it isn't any secret."

"I've been using some young colored boys right out of school."

"The PD school?"

"The school where they learn how to be cops," De Lorenzo said with a flash of irritation. "The department school."

"They're not known," Murphy said. "I've gotten excellent results in the garment center on bookmaking. I sent them up to the drop on West 148th Street."

"The comptroller who makes love to Jack Daniels?"

"The same. They worked there and in a few other spots as collectors. They also went to Queens and Brooklyn."

"What about the movies?"

"That," Murphy said with a frown at De Lorenzo, "is police business."

"We were going all out on this," Johnny said heatedly. "I just had a big battle with Hoff over letting your photographers know where the hits would be. You were going with Tom"—he jumped up, as if he couldn't bear sitting any longer—"and now you spring this on us! Just what the hell's the matter with you people? Dammit, I demand an explanation."

"I'll level with you, Johnny," I said. "We're not sure how far your office would go—"

He spun around. "Are you indicating that I would not pursue this because of some ulterior motive?"

"Present company excluded."

"In other words you mean my boss?"

"Oh, come off it, Johnny. The whole town knows Flaherty plays politics. He wants that judgeship."

"Prove it," he said hoarsely. "Not gossip—proof."

Then I blurted out the thing that had been stalking in the back of my mind, "What about that housing investigation you had last year?"

He looked genuinely surprised. "What about it?"

"Why didn't you push on Sugar Hill Financing? You know the score on their buildings."

He hesitated for just one brief second, but it was enough.

"That's an active investigation. There's a lot more to be done."

"You'll never move in on Sugar Hill Financing, Johnny," I said with an air of knowing much more than I did, "because that's where the bodies are buried."

For a moment I thought he would explode, but he leaned across the desk and held up a big fist.

"Let me tell you something, Malloy," he said in a soft, almost gentle voice. "There are no bodies buried in my office. We're going through with this as far as we can. You say Jim McShane is in it; well, we'll see. But let me tell you right now, neither you nor your paper is going to pressure me into moving against McShane or Sam Jones, a pullman porter on 125th Street, if we don't have any evidence to warrant it. Is that clear?"

"That's fine, Johnny, but just for the record we don't print gossip." I pointed to the three boxes of film. "You should know that by now."

"And I want you to know that neither you, your paper, your publisher, McShane, or even my boss can pressure me into doing something I honestly don't think is right. Now do we understand each other?"

"We do," I said promptly. "Now, what's the score on Sugar Hill Financing?"

"You never give up, do you?"

"When I do I won't be in this business."

"Do you bring information to this office regarding any illegal activities on the part of Sugar Hill Financing?"

"No. But someday I will."

"When that day comes we'll talk about it. Now let's get back to the current investigation." He looked at Murphy. "What do you think about the raids, Inspector?"

I realized Johnny had neatly sidestepped me, but I didn't care; now it would only be natural for Johnny to be a bit more cooperative. Sugar Hill Financing was probably a delicate, exposed nerve in his office. He certainly wasn't in any mood now to touch it. Nor did he want me to.

Murphy stared between us. "I've sent a teletype requesting all borough commanders to be at my office at five tomorrow afternoon. The subject is ostensibly promotions—a subject, I might point out, they are all deeply interested in. They will be kept waiting until six. In the meantime ten of my most trusted men will appear at as many precincts to await my phone calls. I will instruct the precinct commanders to give each man five detectives and uniformed men. The sledges will be in their car. At 5:45—the peak hour for policy operations—my people begin their calls, at two-minute intervals. Each man will be given an assignment to raid a certain premises suspected of operating a lottery, namely, policy—"

"Then your men will not know the entire scope of the operation until they call?"

"This is correct. They prefer it that way." He added grimly, "Fortunately, there are still many honest men in this department."

"Nobody said there weren't, Inspector, or you wouldn't be here," Johnny pointed out.

"I think sometime we should remember that," Murphy said, half in my direction.

"What about the borough commanders waiting in your office?" Johnny said hastily. "What will they be doing?"

"Missing dinner," was Murphy's bland reply.

"There's one thing, Duke. We can't keep these raids quiet just because you're an afternoon newspaper." He added grimly, "Not that I give a damn, but I made an agreement and I intend to live up to it as best as I can."

"I'm sure you do. I realize the news of the raids can't be kept quiet."

"Obviously, the boys covering headquarters will know about it as soon as they take place," Murphy said.

"Of course. Because of the timing I expect to read in the first edition of the *News, Times,* and *Trib* that widespread raids took place throughout the city."

"What, then, will your paper get out of this?" Johnny asked.

"I think I mentioned before," I said, a bit nettled, "that this whole operation isn't going to sell an extra five papers."

"Come off it, Duke. I bet your circulation—"

I turned on him fast. "Do you think the housewives in Scarsdale or Weehawken or the Bronx are going to rush to the newsstand to buy a copy of the *Blade-Leader* because we had the guts and know-how to expose Gennaro's policy mob—something, I might point out, that was really the job of the largest police force in the world and a District Attorney's office that has a budget of—"

"Wait a minute, Malloy," snapped Johnny. "I simply was trying to respect an agreement I had made. But if you think I intend to take any of your slurs against this office—"

Murphy's soft, almost amused voice made us both sit back.

"If we three fight among ourselves, this operation will be a shambles." To me he said: "We're only trying to make sure that your newspaper gets the facts of this operation as soon as possible, Duke. Now, how can that be done?"

"Well," I said, eying Johnny, who slowly slid back in his chair, "we will have reporters and photographers in the areas where the raids will take place. They will not be conspicuous and will not interfere with your officers. No experienced men would do that. I figure the actual raids will be over in a few hours. . . ."

Murphy pursed his lips. "Without complications, that is."

"The precincts will notify headquarters of the arrests, and of course the regular headquarters reporters will have those facts. However, what my paper will have in its first edition will be exclusive pictures of the raids and Gennaro plus eyewitness accounts and the implications and extent of Gennaro's power plus the story of our own participation in the investigation."

"I'm sure Mr. Flaherty will authorize some kind of statement giving you people credit," Johnny said stiffly.

Frankly, I couldn't care less, I wanted to say, but Murphy's frown make me bite my tongue.

The phone rang, and Johnny snapped it up. He listened for a moment, grunted, then slammed the receiver down.

"That was Hoff. He can't get through to the boss until sometime tomorrow afternoon."

"Where did he go?" I asked. "They even have phones in the Kremlin these days."

"There's a two-day recess, and he's left with the Yugoslav delegate for the country." He said roughly, "Dammit, the guy's going sight-seeing. What's wrong with that?"

"Nothing," I said. "I was just wondering out loud where do you go over there to drop out of telephone contact."

"Hoff said they're going to try to raise him."

"What about the raids, Johnny?" Murphy said quietly.

The big hands with the neatly trimmed nails gently tested the yellow pencil. Murphy and I watched, waiting for it to snap, but it didn't.

"We could cancel the raids, couldn't we?"

"You can cancel any raid," Murphy said cautiously.

The pencil slammed down and the big hand covered it. "Jesus Christ, Inspector! I'm not asking about *any* raid; I'm asking about *this* one. It happens to be a damned important one for me and for you!"

"I believe I'm aware of its importance, Johnny," Murphy said calmly.

"Well, then, give me a straight answer," Johnny said, slightly mollified. "God, don't go by the book now at this point on me!"

"The raids can be canceled—"

"But if it's possible you wouldn't postpone them. Is that right?"

"Precisely."

"Why?"

"There are too many people involved, for one thing. Even though nothing will happen and no one, including my own men, will know what was up, word could get around and somebody could put the pieces together—"

"—And as a result they might move the bank."

"The edge would be taken off, Johnny," I said. "It just wouldn't be the same. Maybe Gennaro won't be in the bank next time, and you'll all look like a bunch of horses' asses with a cage load of runners and small fry. Isn't that true, Inspector? If Vito gets a smell of anything unusual, he'll think twice about making an appearance."

Murphy nodded, "If we make the hits as we planned, we know what we're getting." He shrugged. "If we wait—"

"How about your man?" Johnny said to me. "Would he go back?"

"You're kidding, of course."

"No, I'm only trying to get some facts," he snapped. For a long moment he stared down at the pencil he held in one hand. Then for the second time that day Johnny surprised me by the way he spoke.

"I guess," he said slowly, "we better hit them as we planned."

Inspector Murphy closed his small notebook and carefully, almost primly, slid the pen into his upper jacket pocket.

"I'll go back to headquarters and get started."

I am sure that if De Lorenzo had just told him they were to arrest the mayor, Tom Murphy would have reacted in the same fashion. I guess life doesn't hold many surprises for a man who has served the New York City police force nearly all his adult life.

Murphy hesitated. He seemed debating with himself; then he cleared his throat.

"There is one more thing you fellows should know."

"What's that, Inspector?" Johnny said.

"The commissioner called the Mayor and told him he might have to make a major move in Harlem—"

"Wait a minute!" I broke in quickly. "Did he tell City Hall what it was?"

Murphy gave me a hard look.

"No, he didn't. And City Hall knows enough not to ask."

Johnny said impatiently, "Go ahead, Inspector."

"The commissioner asked the Mayor if he could put in operation Plan A."

"Plan A?" Johnny looked puzzled. "What's that?"

"We have certain police procedures ready to put in operation if a race riot of any proportions breaks out in Harlem." Murphy gave me an uncomfortable look. "Now look, Duke, this is all highly confidential."

Johnny waved him to go on.

"Plan A will move most of the fire equipment from lower Manhattan to Midtown, East and West sides, to ring Harlem. The firemen will use the hoses to push back any crowds. Meanwhile, our tactical groups will move in and set up command posts—"

"Good God," I said, "this sounds like setting up a perimeter!"

"It's just about that, if trouble breaks out up there again."

Johnny frowned. "You seem troubled, Inspector."

The chiseled face looked at him impassively.

"I would say that's an understatement."

"But why? Your men are up there all the time busting drops," I said.

"For one thing, I never had a stoolie placed as good in Gennaro's setup as your man is," he said quietly.

"If you had, wouldn't you do it this way?" Johnny pressed.

"There's no other way," was the prompt answer.

"Well then, what's the problem?" I asked.

"The timing," he replied. "It couldn't come at a worse time. Since the last riots the people up there hate cops. And the Prophet and all those extremist groups have been fanning that hate until you can almost taste it." He stared down at his blacksmith's hands with their carefully trimmed nails. "We won't be staging just one raid; there will be simultaneous raids all over Harlem. In fact, our saturation raids could even give the wrong impression. . . ."

"Like what?" Johnny asked.

"Like the police are raiding something else besides policy."

"You mean like those candy-store temples of the Prophet?"

"Every cop in New York knows Harlem is a time bomb," Murphy said stubbornly. "I don't know how it's going to go off—but some day it will."

"What about this Plan A?" Johnny asked. "Is it workable?"

Murphy shrugged. "Ever since the last riots it's been updated every year. Years ago, when they first had trouble in Harlem, the department began to overhaul it every week."

"What the people in this town don't know," I said. "Hasn't it ever occurred to you cops that the public should be made aware of how bad things are in their city?"

Murphy was a cop, first and always. "We have to be prepared for any emergencies."

"Of course you do," I said. "But don't you think the gravity of the situation could be underscored by some sober statements not only from your boss"—I turned to Johnny—"and your boss, so leaders of both sides could meet?"

"We had conferences with the Mayor," Murphy said uneasily.

"Well, what happened?"

"He told the commissioner to be prepared for all emergencies."

I exploded.

"What did the Mayor say when the commissioner called him on this one?" Johnny said.

"He said any large-scale movement of fire vehicles up to Harlem would certainly attract the attention of the press, and their stories might give the city a bad name." Murphy sighed. "He said he wanted to avoid racial trouble at any cost, so the commissioner hasn't put the plan in action. But we will move more men up there."

"Did he point out this was an election year?" I was sorry when I said it. Murphy didn't deserve that cruel cut.

"The department never discusses politics with City Hall," was his unruffled answer.

"Lay off, Malloy," Johnny snapped.

I apologized to Murphy, who gave me a slight nod.

I said to Johnny, more to change the subject, "By the way, before I forget it, I have an agreement with you."

"That's right." He said to Murphy: "It's their story. He and his creeps will have to be there."

"I can't have any reporters or photographers in a police vehicle," Murphy said, sounding like a statute book. "It's a matter of city insurance."

I was about to protest angrily when he said:

"However, Duke, I can let you know where my car will be parked. I can't help it if you follow me." He pulled on his coat and hat. "You have the other addresses and you know the time we'll hit them. Let me warn you of one thing. If any of your people go near those spots, it will go through Harlem like a prairie fire in the wind. Let my men hit first; then go in for your pictures or get them at the precincts."

"Don't worry, Inspector. We'll stay clear."

He paused with his hand on the doorknob. "I would like to let the commissioner know," he gestured to the yellow string envelope on De Lorenzo's desk, "who is identified as Gennaro's contact at headquarters."

"That's up to you, Johnny," I said.

"I think you should tell Inspector Murphy," he said. "He'll know it anyway in a few hours when the commissioner gets copies of your stuff."

"Sergeant Britt Peters," I said, "and Inspector Fletcher Barrist."

The iron face never changed, but the pale blue eyes turned hard as frozen seas.

"I'll inform the commissioner," he said quietly.

After Murphy left, Johnny offered me a cigarette. I had the matches. We both leaned back, inhaled, and watched the smoke rise in the stuffy room.

After a few moments he said, "That really hurt."

"It's true, Johnny," I said. "I even spoke to Peters in the drop. I was in a john when my man told Peters he would see him on the fifteenth."

Johnny pursed his lips in a silent whistle.

"Is all your stuff on cops that good?"

"I would say so."

The smoke ring hung a few inches from his lips. He gently blew it toward me.

"You going to use the cop stuff in your stories of the raids?"

"Why shouldn't we?"

He blew harder, and the smoke ring disintegrated.

"Let's not kid ourselves. You've been around courts long enough to know how tough it is to get anything on cop payoffs."

"You read the transcripts and put the arm on Bernie when you grab him. If he talks—"

"Bernie might talk if you have something to lean on him with," he said musingly. "I never could figure out why Gennaro kept such a weak sister."

"Bernie's the best office manager the mob ever had. He could be chief accountant in United States Steel. Gennaro needs him badly."

"Could be." He peered at me. "Do you have anything on Bernie?"

"The woman he's playing around with. He talks a lot. Maybe she knows something."

"It's in this stuff?"

"Everything."

"Look," he said, "will you lay off the cop corruption in your stories?"

"Why?"

"Give me a few days to make it as strong as I can. After all, it's in your interest as well as this office's."

"But this is news, Johnny. Suppose someone leaks it to the reporters who cover this building regularly?"

He said angrily, "Is it so damn' important to a newspaper that they get a smell of a story before their competitors? Believe me, Duke, if your newspaper really is serving the community and law and order, you will hold back these facts!" He slammed his hand down on the desk. "Now, dammit, will you or will you not cooperate?"

Everything he said was true, and I would be a hypocrite to deny it.

"Okay. We'll hold off for a few days. But I'm warning you, the sand will fly if some other paper breaks this angle."

"Don't worry. No one will know about it."

He played with the long yellow pencil. "What about this stuff on McShane?"

"It's a start, if that's what you mean."

He studied me through the thin veil of smoke as though making up his mind about something.

"McShane isn't exactly a stranger to this office."

My heart skipped a beat.

"Of course he isn't," I said. "He and your boss sleep in the same bed."

"I don't mean that," he said harshly. "I mean we have a file on him."

"For how long?"

"Eight months or so. The boss gave me a complaint to check out."

"And what happened?"

"I turned everything over to the boss." He crushed out his cigarette. "I don't know why I should be telling you this."

"I'll tell you why," I said quickly, "because you wanted to go ahead on McShane and your boss wouldn't let you."

"You're wrong," he said flatly. "Flaherty never told me to lay off."

"Of course he didn't; he's not that much of a fool—he just never told you to go ahead. In other words he stalled you. Isn't that right?"

Johnny got up from behind his desk and walked to the window. Across the way were the barred tiers of the jail.

"Let's get this straight," he said without turning. "If you're out after Flaherty's scalp, count me out."

I joined him at the window. "Let me ask you this, Johnny. If what is in those envelopes convinces you McShane may have his fingers in Gennaro's operations, will you go ahead?"

"I told you before, nobody can put the pressure on me—"

"Don't be naïve," I said patiently. "Flaherty wouldn't be fool enough to put any visible pressure on you. He can foul you up a dozen ways. Hell, he's already done it to you."

"He's my boss," Johnny said doggedly. "He asked for the McShane material. What am I supposed to do—say no?"

"So then it died. And he didn't put any pressure on you."

"Nothing dies in this office," Johnny said in a strained voice. "We have thousands of complaints."

I walked away from the window. "Stop talking like a schoolboy. If that complaint was about the leader of the other party, you would have been before the Grand Jury."

Johnny, like many big men, is quick as a cat when he's mad. "Are you accusing me of being crooked?"

"I don't know, Johnny," I said evenly. "Maybe this is the first time you've been tested."

He stood there for a moment, staring at me. Then he took another cigarette.

"You know, Duke," he said more quietly, "you may have a point."

Then he walked back to his chair and slumped into it.

I got up and put on my coat. "But if you want to know what I think," I said. "I am sure you could pass any test."

And I was sure.

As soon as I reached the office I called Jackson's landlady, Mrs. Zuccartelli. She gave me a lot of immigrant English, but frankly I believe she was putting on an act. When I tried to find out where Jackson was or when he would be home, I couldn't get through to her, but it didn't surprise me that she got my name without too much trouble.

In less than an hour Jackson called, and I gave him a complete rundown on the conference in the D.A.'s office.

"You know the story I told you I would give the Wop?" he said after I had finished.

"You mean about going to have your toe fixed?"

"Right. Get this. Now it's real. I was making instant coffee the other morning, and dropped the jar on my toe. It swelled up like a balloon. I went over to the clinic, and they said I better have the nail removed. It hurts like hell. I've been walking around with an old shoe cut out."

"Then you're really going in to get it done?"

"I got to. I can't walk, and it's driving me nuts. It's only a little job. They give you a needle like when you get a tooth out."

"Novocaine?"

"Yeah, that's it. They said I should stay off it for about a day or two. The doc in the clinic said it will be sore for a long time, but if I don't have it done it will keep coming back."

"Then you'll read all about it."

There was a deep, rich pleasure in his voice. "I'm gonna buy every paper every day for a month. Every time I see that Wop or read about him, I'll get an orgasm."

"What about the East Side?"

He chuckled. "It couldn't be more perfect. After I told Bernie, he called back and said the Wop sent word I was to take it easy and let Tilley handle everything. I told them I wouldn't be back for at least a week. By that time I'll be gone."

"What shall I do—call you again?"

He hesitated. "No, never mind, kid. Let it go like we said. When the dust settles you'll hear from me."

"One more thing—have you made up your mind?"

"About what?"

"If Gennaro can't be put away without your testimony, will you come back?"

He grunted. "Yeah. I thought about it, and this is the way I figure; do you know what Jimmy Braddock said when he became champ?"

"No, but remember you're an old guy."

"He said, 'If I can do this on beans what the hell would I do on steak?' Well, the way I figure, we did this on beans; the D.A. has all the steak, so let's see what he can do. Okay?"

"It has to be if you say so. Incidentally, just for the record, De Lorenzo asked for your name and I told him to drop dead."

"For the record I never had any doubt that you would. Take it easy, kid."

"You too. Keep in touch."

"You'll hear from me."

Next on the schedule was an editorial conference to arrange coverage of the raids and to plan the number of stories, the picture layouts, the staggering of the hours of the reportorial and rewrite staffs so there would be ample manpower.

When Julian Savage received my message he canceled all appointments and summoned us immediately.

As I outlined the conference at the D.A.'s office, I noticed he was suffering from a heavy cold. But nothing dampened his enthusiasm.

"Then it's all set for tomorrow, Duke?"

"The police will begin raids in all five boroughs on the dot of five forty-five."

He looked at Turner Elliott. "I want the main story to double jump—even triple. I want side stories about Gennaro and his background, a good solid piece on policy, how it came to New York in the thirties, the Dutch Schultz business, and so on."

I couldn't help thinking this boy has been doing some homework. Turner Elliott must have had the same idea, because he gave me a quizzical smile.

"There'll probably be a lot of action pictures. How about a full page?"

"Absolutely. Make sure you check with Publication, so they will clear a full page." He turned to me. "Duke, suppose you help Joe make out a schedule for reporters and photographers to cover these other spots —you'll be with Murphy, of course."

"He'll hit the bank," I said. "That's the big one. I'll take that."

"What about the cop angle?" Turner asked. "Will we go into that in the main story?"

"I gave my word to De Lorenzo to lay off the big police scandal for a few days until they see what they have," I said, "I think we owe it to them—"

"I wouldn't trust them with a red-hot stove," Bowers said. "Get it in the paper before we read it in the *Journal* or *Telly*—"

"If Duke made the agreement, we'll honor it," Elliott said.

Savage nodded. "Absolutely."

Bowers sighed disgustedly.

"What about McShane, Duke?" Elliott asked.

"As I told you, I threw the whole thing at them. There's no doubt it shook up De Lorenzo. Incidentally, they can't raise Flaherty in Geneva. He's off with some delegates."

"From what I hear he's quite a swordsman," Bowers said.

Savage turned to me. "Frankly, that's what I hear. But the important thing is, he probably won't be here for the raids. Is that the way you see it, Duke?"

"That's the picture from what Hoff told De Lorenzo."

"I imagine that after the initial raids there will be constant developments," Savage said.

"We must be on page one every day," I said. "If I know these people, they'll be watching, not for the first day when the hard news breaks—but the follow-up. If we relax they'll shrug it off—"

Savage cut me off with an impatient wave of his hand.

"That's exactly what I don't want. Turner, I want daily stories. I want editorials. Picture displays. I want interviews with people of stature in the community. If we can prove one half of what we know to be true, I think the decent people of New York City will raise a howl."

"Don't be too sure, Julian," Elliott said. "It takes a hell of a lot to stir up New Yorkers. They take everything matter-of-factly—and that includes police and official corruption."

The answer was cold and firm. "Then it is up to us to make sure we stir their conscience. If we don't, then we are to blame." He looked around at us. "I don't have to tell you I expect the best job that a fine brand of professionals can deliver."

Elliott said, "Duke, you'll do the main story. We'll take care of the side stories." He said to Bowers: "I'm staying over. I think you should, too."

I have to give Bowers credit; he looked both hurt and puzzled. "What else would I do?"

"I'll be at home all night," Savage said. "Turner, you keep in touch with me." He walked around the desk to put his hand on my shoulder. "Duke, be careful."

"There won't be much after the raids," I said. "After Gennaro is booked, I'll come back to the office and start writing."

Twenty-four hours later I was to remember this all-time bonehead prediction.

When I got home there was a telegram from Gwen. She had left for the coast. At least she had signed it with love.

BOOK THREE

NIGHT OF THE BLACK FIRE

[17]

EARLY THAT afternoon I returned to the office. There was that peculiar sense of electric excitement in the city room that I always found just before a sensational news story broke; the first day of a big trial, an exclusive story, guarded through the night like a precious gem ready to be set in the stone of page one; the important announcement from the White House with the wire-service machines throbbing and humming, waiting to click out its bulletin in a frenzy of bells.

I sat down with Turner Elliott, Joe Bowers and his assistants, and the photo editor, going over the assignment schedule for the last time, double-checking the assignments for each team of reporters and photographers. It was decided that all information would funnel through the city desk and finally to me, along with the wire copy. There would be many side stories, color, background. The head of the Advertising Department had turned over the dummy of his next day's ad schedule to Turner Elliott, who would have clear inside pages, uncluttered with ads.

It looked like a big night.

I made routine calls to Johnny and Murphy, but there was nothing to report.

Murphy's arrangements were going ahead without any last-minute upsets. Johnny reported Flaherty still couldn't be raised. Hoff, he said, was in the office but was drinking and vicious. Betty, Julian's secretary, reported she didn't expect him till later. He had canceled a luncheon and his cold was hanging on.

The afternoon dragged, each hour winding the springs a bit

tighter. Finally the call came from Murphy; I was to meet him on the east corner of Forty-ninth and Third Avenue. He gave me a description of the car and the license number. I already had a photographer waiting, and we quickly moved uptown. The traffic was thick on Third, and moving fast. I spotted the car and we double-parked slightly ahead of it. When it pulled ahead, we followed. I could see Murphy sitting in the rear seat with three well-dressed young Madison Avenue types, who looked as if they were more at home with sales conferences than in splintering doors and arresting policy mobsters. There was no excitement, no sirens; only respectful attention to the staggered lights and the nimble jaywalkers.

Five blocks from the bank, Murphy's car slid over to the curb and he got out. I joined him.

"We hit in ten minutes," he said. "I have two of my men starting now to move up from the cellar and down from the roof."

"I hope they don't queer it."

"They know their business," he said quietly. "When we go in, give us a few minutes. The apartment is 5D, and for God's sake be careful! Please ask your photographer not to take the faces of my men; you'll only ruin their value to me."

The spring wound a bit tighter.

"Do you think Gennaro's in there, Inspector?"

"He was there five minutes ago." And then he added grudgingly, as if reluctant to release the information, "My teams in the building are synchronizing by walkie-talkie. We'll hit at the same time."

"What about the other drops?"

"My people will be hitting drops all over the city—from West Harlem to Bensonhurst." He shook his head. "That West Harlem . . ."

"Good luck," I said.

I waited until his car had disappeared; then we proceeded slowly. The area we entered once had been similar to the Lower East Side of Manhattan many years ago, but lately projects and middle-income apartment houses had replaced the old-law tenements. Gennaro's policy bank was in one of the newer block-long apartment houses. East 148th Street just off Harlem River was quiet when we drove up; Murphy's car was double-parked in front of the building. We pulled up behind him, and I dashed out, followed by my photographer with his camera bouncing over his shoulder and his heavy bag slamming against his knees. Two housewives with bundles and toddlers were in the elevator when we jumped in.

"Hey, photographers!" one cried. "What happened, mister?"

"Mrs. Russo's son was appointed to West Point," I said. "They just made the announcement."

"My, isn't that wonderful," one said.

The other nodded knowingly. "He's a nice boy. Always smiling and holding the door open—"

The photographer just grunted.

There were a few people in the hallway when we got there. The door was hanging on its lower hinge and there was a detective on guard. Some of the people who lived on the floor were staring but that was all. The photographer quickly took some pictures of the door and in we went. In the kitchen seven men were sitting, all with their hands flat on the porcelain table. In the next room were three more men and a frightened middle-aged woman.

"Did you get Bernie?"

"In the kitchen," Murphy said. "He's the one who keeps talking. Don't tell him you're a reporter—he keeps begging us not to give his name to the newspapers." He lowered his voice. "Get what you can in a hurry. I'm sure someone in the building by now has been on the phone with Gennaro's lawyer. I want him out of here as quick as possible."

"What about Frank the Sheik? Did you find a gun on him?"

Inspector Murphy gave me a cold smile. "He tried to throw it under a couch when we hit." He cleared his throat. "You can say he offered some resistance to the arresting officers."

As Murphy said, Bernie was an easy find in the kitchen. He was nervously polishing his glasses and dabbing at his face, which was glistening with a sheen of sweat. He smiled brightly at each member of Inspector Murphy's team who passed through the kitchen, but they ignored him. The other prisoners were young, tough, and seemingly bored. Hired guns. Off to one side, handcuffed to a radiator, was Frank the Sheik. There was a darkening mouse under one eye. He called over to one of the other toughs, but they didn't answer. Even among prisoners no one wants to be associated with a loser, I thought.

I held out a cigarette to Bernie. "Care for one?"

He gave me a grateful look. "Boy, this is going to taste good." He bent down, took the light, and inhaled deeply.

"How long have you been taking care of Gennaro's books?" I asked.

He almost jumped. "Look, mister, I don't know anything about any books. I just happened to come up this afternoon on a tax job. Mr. Gennaro, the man inside, will tell you that. I take care of his books and several other firms on—"

"Come off it, Bernie," I told him. "They have you cold."

He stared at me for a moment, wet his lips, and looked about at the other hoods.

"Look, I have to have a lawyer . . ."

"I'll call Ricky Strasser for you."

His face lighted up. "Would you?"

"What's his number?"

He started to give it to me, then broke off when he caught the eye of one of the young hoods.

"Forget it," he said.

"It's no bother."

"Look, mister, forget it, will you please?" he said, and wiped his face.

There were rows of tables, adding machines and typewriters. Paper shopping bags stuffed with policy slips were stacked in one corner. Piled high in cardboard boxes were hundreds of adding-machine tapes. Rubber stamps, boxes of paper clips, stapling guns, and extension telephones gave the large room the appearance of an industrious office. One of the men sitting meekly in a chair looked up at me.

I guess "nondescript" is the proper description for Gennaro. His blue suit, white shirt and blue tie, clean-shaven face almost without lines, and the ball-point pen precisely clipped on the edge of his jacket pocket gave Vito Gennaro the look of some impossibly grave bank clerk. It was only the eyes that gave the clue to the man; they were pale blue, distant and hard, and alert as a cat's.

"I think we got him this time," Murphy's voice said behind me. "We have the books, the slips, and the money. We were lucky they were just leaving with the ribbon when we hit. One of them gave us a little trouble trying to get out the fire escape, but on the whole they were quiet."

"Who's the woman?"

"Just a bookkeeper."

"It's—"

The bulb went off, and Bernie let out a wild cry. He grabbed a towel from the table and held it to his face.

"No pictures! Tell him he can't take my picture!"

"You silly bastard," I snarled at the photographer. "Couldn't you have waited a minute?"

The bulb clicked again. "Just take care of your job and I'll do mine."

By now someone had tipped the local precinct, and the room was filling up with uniformed men. They kept asking questions, but Murphy's men just shrugged. They grew silent and fell back as the inspector came out of the front room and motioned to me.

"It just came over the radio—there's trouble on the West Side. They asked for the Emergency Squad." He took a deep breath. "This is what I was afraid of."

"What happened?"

"One of the plainclothesmen knocking off that big drop on 138th Street got in a scuffle with a young runner. The radio says he shot him. . . ."

"Christ! Did he kill him?"

"DOA," Murphy said. "With cops crashing in doors all over Harlem, it's a miracle there weren't more casualties."

A plainclothesman came up to whisper in his ear. When he left, Murphy stared at me.

"Plan A," he said. "The whole west side of Harlem is going crazy." He said roughly, "Well, let's wind this up."

I suddenly recalled the savage, dark face of the Prophet, the shouting hate, the rearing horse, the slashing club, and the man clutching his battered head. And then Tilley's words that some night there would be blood running in Harlem and it won't be all black man's blood. . . .

The Prophet's Night of the Black Fire.

"I wonder if it's the Prophet?"

"I don't know," he said. "I hope not!"

"I heard that madman once. He was telling the people to carry pistols."

"He should have been grabbed a long time ago," Murphy said with unaccustomed vehemence.

"Well, why the hell wasn't he?"

Murphy gave me a bitter look. "And have every colored society and demagogue accusing us of brutality, discrimination, and everything else under the sun?"

"You going over, Inspector?"

"Just as soon as I wind this up."

"What about Gennaro?"

"I'll start him downtown after I book him at the East 145th Street house. You coming along?"

I hesitated only for a moment, and he reached out and caught my arm.

"Don't go over there, Duke."

"I just want to make sure my photographer knows where Gennaro will be booked."

He nodded and went back into the other room. I found my photographer in the hall.

"The cops say there's trouble over in West Harlem," he said.

"There may be a riot."

He was a middle-aged man with a thin, morose face. It became more doleful at the news.

"I don't want any part of that assignment. I covered the last one. All I got was a broken head and a busted camera. Where are they gonna book this bum?"

"East 145th Street. Get him in cuffs if you can."

"What do you know. Now we have reporters telling us how to take pictures."

He slipped the strap of his heavy bag over his shoulder, pushed his way through a wall of blue uniforms, and was gone.

I stood off to one side in the crowded hall for a moment, feeling more frustrated than at any time in my life.

The raid was a fantastic success—greater than I could have ever hoped for. Vito Gennaro, one of the most powerful gangsters in recent history, the target of numerous law enforcement agencies, state and Federal, congressional committees—had been at last snarled in his own policy bank—the favorite dream of any prosecutor. There was little doubt that Johnny would have a good case against Gennaro of contriving a lottery—a felony.

Action Jackson would get his wish. . . .

Yet, now it had all become secondary to something much more important. This is why newspapermen hate the joker who says, "Well, fellows, it looks like a dull day," and knocks on wood. There are no dull days in our world any more. A coup in Southeast Asia. A thousand prayerful Negroes march in some southern city and the sheriff's men grip their billies. A teletype suddenly clicks to life in the State Department. It's a world in which there is no control over events, happenings. Murphy said not to go over there. Strange, the thought never would have occurred to me—where there was news, that's where you went. I guess this is what I had tried to get across to Gwen, Johnny, Murphy: there's a little more to a newspaper than the eight-column headlines. . . .

"Mr. Malloy," a young plainclothesman was saying, "the inspector says he can give you a lift to the 145th Street house."

"Thank the inspector," I said. "Tell him I'll see him over in West Harlem."

Outside, I whistled down a cab and gave him the address of Jackson's drop on West 138th Street.

"Not me, mister," he said. "There's some kind of trouble over there."

I gave him a five-dollar bill. He looked at it, then shrugged.

"I'll take you part of the way, but first sign of trouble and that's it for me."

"Did you hear what happened over there?"

"A cabbie going downtown said a cop shot a jig during a policy raid." He shook his head. "I always said there would be trouble with those niggers. Ever since La Guardia took away the cops' clubs, they push you off the sidewalk. Black bastards!"

"One of them must have held you up."

He half turned in surprise. "Stuck me up! Hell, no, mister. I just don't like 'em."

We moved up Third Avenue, crossed the Harlem River on the 149th Street Birdge, passed Harlem Housing, and started down Lenox Avenue as the dusk slipped into darkness and the streetlights suddenly blinked on like the yellow eyes of a startled cat. We had gone a block when the night echoed the distant wail of sirens. The cabbie swung into the curb.

"This is it, brother," he said, turning around. "This is as far as I'm going. Something's goin' on over there. This is no company cab. I'm partners with the finance company. Sorry."

I took out another five. "Look, I have to get over there—"

"Not with this cab," he said stubbornly. "Not for a hundred. All I hear are sirens, and that means trouble."

In a way I couldn't blame him, so I threw him a bill and began a running walk west on 144th Street. Halfway down the street I was suddenly struck by the unnatural silence. The usual bumper-to-bumper parked cars, the blank windows, the pools of hard white light from the streetlights seemed lonely and severe. As I came up to a basement entrance, an old man popped up like a woodchuck from its hole.

"What's happening?" I started to say, but he dropped back among his ash cans.

I slowed to a walk, the monotony of my footsteps producing a quickening, hypnotic accompaniment to the fear growing in my mind. The eerie silence was suddenly broken by the screech of a car's brakes.

"Where in the hell are you going?" a harsh voice demanded as a flashlight pinpointed me.

It was a radio car, and an angry, heavy-jowled face was framed in the open window.

"I'm going over to—"

"You're not going anywhere! Get the hell back downtown! Fast!"

I started to walk toward the radio car, as I searched for my police card.

"Look, Officer, I'm a reporter for the *Blade-Leader*—"

"I don't care who you are!" the cop shouted. "Get downtown. There's a lot of trouble up here!"

I reached the car and held out my police card.

"I have to get over—"

The cop leaned out of the window.

"Get downtown! God dammit! Get downtown!"

There was a volley of shots down the street, followed by the sound of shattering glass and wild cries. The radio car leaped forward, and the red-faced cop shouted that I had better get downtown immediately or else he would run me in.

I started after the police car, which spun around the corner, sirens wailing. Seconds after it vanished, there were several sharp cracks followed by a crash. Instinctively I jumped into a doorway. Screams and wild howling rose from the far end of the dark street. I could feel the hair on the back of my neck begin to rise, and I cursed myself for a fool. After a few minutes the screams, the shouts, and the sound of breaking glass stopped. I looked out; there was nothing but the symmetrical row of brownstone stoops, the line of ugly ash cans like silent, stubby sentinels, the unwavering pools of light.

This was the jungle, without the banana cats. But it was a jungle in which black men were rising to kill.

I moved down the street, hugging the building line. I turned the corner and almost walked into the radio car. It was up on the curb and had smashed into a building front. The windshield was shattered, and I knew at a glance the driver was dead. The bullet had gone through one eye; the back of his head was a bloody hole. Shattering glass and high-pitched howls came from down the street.

Crouching behind the car, I could see the mob of about fifty, throwing ash cans through the windows of a men's furnishing store, while others were climbing out the shattered front windows of a liquor store, carrying armfuls of bottles and cases of beer. Only a few had clubs or bar irons; two or three had rifles. The men who were armed all wore red caps.

The Night of the Black Fire had begun.

There was no doubt about it, the Prophet ruled Harlem tonight.

Another big pane of glass collapsed with a shattering sound, and instinctively I ducked. It was then I heard the moan. Sticking out from under the car, almost at my feet, was a man's hand in a blue cuff. I knelt down and pulled him from under the car. It was the red-faced cop who had shouted at me. Only now his face was a pasty gray, and he had a horrible gash across his forehead where his head probably had gone through the windshield.

I had propped him up against the stoop, wondering what I could do, when I heard a cautious whistle above me. Inside the doorway was an old woman dressed in a man's sweater fastened at the neck with a safety pin.

"You better bring that man in here, mister," she was saying, "or those crazy people gonna kill you."

It was the only thing to do. I bent down, got the cop under the arms, and dragged him up the steps of the stoop. I thanked God for that liquor store down the street. From the looks of it, even the Prophet's men were having a hard time controlling the wild mob. One red skull-cap who was shouting and waving his rifle crumpled under an ash can that seemed to fly through the air. One man was screaming and methodically flinging cans of beer at a door of a tenement. Others were dragging mannikins from the men's furnishing store to a bonfire. A hydrant was opened, filling the gutters with garish-hued water.

"Those crazy fools," the old woman cried. "Come in, come in . . ."

I dragged the cop inside the black, foul-smelling hall. She slammed the front door and hurried down the hall to her apartment. I carried the cop inside, and she slid home a bolt lock, ran some chain through a hasp, clicked a big Yale lock, and slid home another bolt lock just above the floor.

"Women ain't safe in Harlem any more," she said.

The unshaded bulb showed me an old woman in her late sixties. She had gray hair combed back in a neat bun. Her skin was chocolate, her eyes an alert black, and she was wearing men's sneakers.

"I heard the crash," she said. "And when I looked out some men were running away. They took the cop's gun." She shook her head. "I don't know what Harlem's comin' to any more. All these junkies robbin' people."

"I'm afraid it's more than just junkies, ma'am," I told her. "It looks like a riot. Do you have a phone?"

She gave me a sad smile. "Widder ladies on welfare don't have phones, mister."

The cop moaned, and she hurried across the room to take several clean-looking rags from a sewing basket. "Wet these and put 'em on his head." She added proudly, "I worked practical at Harlem Hospital till my feet gave out."

I wet the rags and made compresses for the cop's head. But he seemed to be getting worse, and there was a slight bluish tinge to his skin.

"This man needs a hospital," I said.

"You better not go out there, mister. Those crazy people will kill you sure."

"Can you see out into the street?"

"From my parlor window."

I followed her through the darkened apartment, stumbling over cardboard boxes, chairs, and tables. Once a cat hissed in anger and clawed at my leg when I stepped on its paw. When I finally reached the window, the lady cautiously pried apart the slats of the old-fashioned wooden blind.

At the far end of the block the mob was still looting the stores; the bonfire was higher, outlining in its glare the dancing, whooping figures. But our end of the street was deserted.

"I'll try to find some radio cars and tell them," I told the old woman. "You keep those cloths on his head."

"You just tell 'em Mrs. Waters on the first floor," she said as she carefully unlocked the door and slid away the chains and bolts. As she closed the door, leaving me alone in the urine-strong darkness, she whispered, "Mrs. Waters, the widder woman in 1A. You tell 'em now."

I crouched on the stoop for a moment; the scene was the same. Sirens wailed blocks away but didn't come near. I slid past the smashed car with its dead driver and ran down the block. Midway in the next block a figure in the doorway of a store shouted at me, and a bottle whistled past my head to splinter on the street. It only gave wings to my feet. I was somewhere on Eighth Avenue when I saw a small crowd in front of what appeared to be a grocery store. Suddenly from the crowd a figure broke free and started to run.

He appeared to be wearing an apron and sweater. Something sailed out of the crowd and hit the man in the back. He stumbled, tried to catch his balance, but crumpled. Two men in the crowd ran over and systematically kicked the struggling man until he was quiet, then ran back to join the crowd pushing into the store.

I had sunk down among some ash cans and was about to dart forward again when several cars roared down the street, swinging into the curb with a screech of tires. The occupants of the cars began shouting and furiously blowing a horn. Men ran from the grocery store and flung themselves into the cars that roared away, while others who were left behind picked up an ash can, flung it through the big plate glass, and ran down the street. In the sudden, painful silence, a piece of glass that still clung to the shattered window fell with a brittle, tinkling sound. Several streets away there was a burst of shouting; then its echoes died out. I was wondering if I should try to help the man in the apron when a woman and another man crept out of the shattered store and helped the man in the street to get to his feet; then all three vanished in a nearby building.

People now seemed to be appearing in doorways and on stoops. One or two cursed me and one called to me to be careful. I ran until a pain like a knife made me bend to one side. I was afraid to stop. I had the eerie feeling I was fair game, and the hunters were somewhere behind me in the darkened streets.

Once I spotted a subway entrance but decided not to take a chance when I saw a crowd tearing a newsstand apart and hurling the boards at store windows. I felt the only thing I could do was continue moving. Near 125th Street and Eighth Avenue I saw the riot in full swing; a number of radio cars, red lights flashing, were parked up on the sidewalk, while farther down the block a fire truck poured several high pressure hoses into a howling, screeching mob that flowed and eddied up and down the street like a terrifying human sea.

Occasionally bricks smashed on the street. Once a piece of scrap iron ricocheted from a stoop to hit the side of one of the radio cars with a sickening sound of bending metal. The street was littered with broken glass, beer cans, bricks, clothing, and ash cans. The hiss of the high-powered hose, the incongruous, monotonous voices of the police radio dispatcher, the slam of bricks and crash of glass, the impatient cries of the police and the firemen, and the fierce, incoherent shouts of the mob filled the cold, clear night.

Hugging the buildings, I ran to the nearest radio car in a crouching run. A cop who was peering over the hood whirled around. There was a gun in his hand, and for a terrible minute I thought he was going to shoot me.

"I'm a reporter . . . there's a cop badly hurt. His partner's dead."

The cop, a young Negro, stared at me for a moment, then yelled at someone across the street: "Hey, Sarge! There's a reporter over here who says a cop's killed!" He turned to me. "Where about?"

I gave him the exact location. "The radio car's on the sidewalk."

"You say a cop's dead!"

"He was shot. His partner's badly hurt."

"Where's the other cop?"

"I got him into—"

A deep gruff voice called out, "Where's that reporter?"

"Over here, Sarge," the Negro patrolman cried. "Right here."

A powerfully built Irishman towered over me.

"How bad is he hurt?"

"He's unconscious and in bad shape. I think he has a fractured skull, among other things."

The sergeant said to the Negro patrolman, "You better pick him up, Davis, and get him to Harlem Hospital."

"You'll be all right, Sarge?"

"The 20th is sending up two more cars. Get going."

The cop holstered his gun, jumped into the car, made a wild U-turn, and disappeared down the street, his siren wailing.

"How the hell did you get here?" the sergeant asked. "I thought they weren't allowing anyone up here."

"I was across town when I heard about it. Those cops passed me just before they were hit."

A brick bounced along the street, and we both ducked.

"The bastards are up on the roofs," he said, "tearing the old chimneys apart. When the—"

He broke off as one of the emergency men ran up.

"We got to go down to 110th," he shouted. "They busted a gas main, and the whole damn' city might go up!" He started to run back but stopped and turned.

"Maybe you fellows better come along."

Suddenly, as if an answer to a prearranged signal, a hail of debris fell on the street. A brick whistled past my head and bounced off the car's hood. The rear window crashed, and an ash can bounced end over end. The fireman cried out and fell to his knees, blood running down one side of his face. The sergeant jumped up and pointed to the tenements across the street.

"Cappy! Get up there with some men and get those bastards!"

Four cops, guns drawn, rushed into the building. In a few minutes they came out, dragging two shouting, kicking men. One grabbed a cop's hand and bit hard. The officer cried out. A gun butt raised and fell sharply. The cop biter slumped down. The other man stopped struggling but continued to scream curses. Both were flung into the patrol wagon that seemed to be serving as a temporary jail.

The sergeant pointed to another tenement, and the four cops disappeared through its front door.

"What a night," the sergeant said. "Every nigger in Harlem's gone nuts."

"Do you know how it started, Sarge?"

"Downtown pulled off a numbers raid. One of the cops shot a prisoner, and all hell broke out."

More bricks fell, and the sergeant shouted his orders. When his men had disappeared into the tenement, he silently searched the empty roofs, like a foot soldier in a newly held enemy town.

"A sergeant from the 19th said it was started by that crazy bastard they call the Prophet. They said he was holding a meeting a few blocks away when the cops made their hit at one of the drops. Someone told him, and he came running down with those crazy black baboons he calls his Apostles. They came down the street like madmen. That started it." He turned to me and said bitterly: "There's been a couple of cops killed so far. Maybe more before this night is over. One guy's named Delaney from the West Forty-seventh Street house. He's got five kids." He slammed a fist big as a ham on the hood. "They threw him off a roof."

I had a terrible, sick feeling in the pit of my stomach as the thought kept running across my mind . . . Is all this because of me?

But the Irish sergeant was saying, "This has been a long time coming. If it wasn't that raid, it would have been something else. I was up here when the last one took place. Hell, that started because a kid stole a ten-cent knife."

Something made the crowd roar with rage. We both ran from around the radio car. Down the street several men had started to charge the firemen, using a shield made of old-fashioned French doors. A fire lieutenant and several firemen rolled out another hose. In minutes the powerful watery spear knocked the rioters off their feet and the French door flew up in the air.

"Where's the commissioner, Sarge?"

"He's over at the 123rd Street house. Half City Hall's there. Someone said the Mayor's going on TV." He gave a short, abrupt laugh. "That should be interesting. I wonder how those tinhorns are going to alibi this one!"

A cop came out of one of the tenements, half dragging another officer, who seemed to be unconscious. Two others ran to his assistance, and they carried the injured man to the radio car.

One cop said, "The bastards dropped a sink down a stairwell, Sarge, and it bounced off a banister and hit Denny. He fell a whole flight."

The sergeant stared down at the moaning man. "He needs a doctor bad. Get him over to Harlem Hospital right away." He turned to me. "Want a lift?"

"I'll be grateful, Sarge."

"On your way back, drop this reporter off at the 123rd Street house."

As we hurried to another radio car, a shotgun slammed. A roar rose from the mob as several figures moved out of the darkness into the searchlights' hard white pool. This time they were using a large kitchen table as a battering ram. The hoses rose from the street like live things to zero in on the bobbing white square of porcelain. It flew to one side and the figures bounced about the street like sodden bags of rags. An ash can hit the street, followed by several bricks. The sergeant bellowed through his cupped hands as he gestured upward.

"Dickens! Ross! They're crossing the roof at 320—the one with the chimney. Get 'em!

"What a night! What a lousy night!"

Harlem Hospital was in pandemonium. The intercom constantly pleaded for doctors and nurses to report. Men, women, and children packed the corridors, on benches, on chairs, some on the floor. They tenderly touched bruised faces, held bloody rags and handkerchiefs to gashed scalps, or just lay still, moaning. They were the victims who would be lost in the anonymity of the usual last paragraph that would report hundreds had suffered superficial injuries.

Stretchers with still forms in cocoons of sheets, with an impatient nurse pushing at one end and a doctor or another nurse holding high the plasma bottle alongside, rolled down the human aisle hacked out of the crowd by a harried orderly.

I helped the driver to get the wounded officer a bench. An intern hurried over, quickly examined him, and wrote out a tag.

"Concussion, maybe worse," he said.

"How many dead, Doctor?" I asked. "I'm a reporter for the *Blade-Leader*."

The intern looked up. "Where was your damn' newspaper when this thing was beginning, five, ten, fifteen years ago?"

"I guess he doesn't like your paper," the cop said. "Let's get over to the 123rd Street house."

The way to West 123rd Street was marked by the passage of the rioters; stores were sacked, streets littered with garbage, glass, bricks, and overturned cars. The night was filled with the constant wail of sirens. Patrol wagons and fire trucks screeched past. Now it seemed there were more people out in the street, arguing and gesticulating in knots at corners and on stoops. Once, when we slowed down to let an emergency truck pass, a group stared at us. I could almost taste the hostility.

The West 123rd Street precinct, Harlem's oldest and largest, was almost inaccessible. Radio cars, official limousines, and city vehicles clogged the street. Uniformed men and others hurried in and out of the dirty, ancient building. Two men came out, and photographers' light bulbs blinked their progress to a big black car. I pushed my way through the mob in front of the building and entered the precinct's main room just as an inspector in plainclothes began reading a statement for the assembled reporters who crowded about him.

There were now eighteen dead; several men and women were in critical condition in various hospitals; the injured ran into the hundreds; property damage was inestimable. The Mayor would be on television in fifteen minutes to address the city. The riot had been touched off by the Prophet and his followers, following the shooting of the policy runner. Police were looking for the Prophet, who had fled. Thirty of his followers were under arrest.

Someone tugged at my sleeve. It was the photographer who had accompanied me on the raid of Gennaro's bank.

"Where've you been?" he said peevishly. "I've been carrying these damn' plates of the raid all night. You're not going to get anything in tomorrow's paper with this thing—what do you want me to do with them?"

"Just give them to the city desk when you go down," I said. "What happened to you? I thought you were the guy who didn't want any part of this assignment?"

He raised his face, tired and empty in the harsh light, and ran his tongue over his lips.

"I guess we're just nuts in this business." Then dully, almost unbelievingly, he added, "It's been one hell of a night."

I didn't answer him. I couldn't answer him. I pushed my way through the crowd, knowing how the hangman felt.

[18]

I MANAGED TO get downtown by hitching a ride with a television news outfit. TV covered the events of that night in a superb, professional manner. Today those films are classics, and will be rerun in the years to come. The crews were battered; one man lost an eye, another was shot in the leg, but all of them stuck doggedly to their assigned posts, sending back film as soon as it was shot. It was one of those shuttle trucks that got me beyond the tight police lines set up at Seventy-second Street and stretching from river to river.

Like every other newspaper city room that night, the *Blade-Leader*'s was hectic, with the calm, sure hand of Turner Elliott funneling the high-pitched nervous energy into cold type. When I stepped off the elevator, I was greeted as if I had just returned to headquarters from the Lost Battalion. A photographer who was in the city room took my picture, and I have it before me now, a haggard, soot-smeared face, a slight gash on my cheek with dried blood running to my collar, a pocket torn away, sodden pants and shoes.

Julian Savage, Turner Elliott, and Bowers were in the publisher's office when I walked in. The room was sour with exhausted conversation. Bowers was standing off to one side somewhat uncertainly. Elliott was leaning forward in his chair, studying his folded hands, while Savage stared out the window into the darkness the way some men look into a fire. They looked tired and apprehensive. When they heard me they turned quickly, as if expecting vital news.

Savage moved forward quickly, a look of relief spreading over his face.

"Good God, Duke, we've been looking all over town for you! What happened?"

"I just had the hell scared out of me."

I walked inside and took the chair that Bowers pushed toward me.

"We've been calling Murphy every hour," he said. "He said he had alerted all radio cars."

"I just came from the West 123rd Street precinct," I said. "Somebody from headquarters was reading a statement. Eighteen dead."

"They just brought in two more to Bellevue," Bowers put in quickly.

"Twenty people killed!" Savage whispered, "God, what a terrible thing!"

We looked at one another. The unspoken words vibrated in the room—We did it; we were the cause.

"I told you before, Julian," Elliott said, "neither you nor the paper can be blamed."

"It just happened," Bowers murmured.

Elliott went on firmly, quietly, "Frankly, I'm shocked that neither the police nor Flaherty's office were aware of how explosive the situation really was." He turned to me. "Did they say anything at any time, Duke?"

"Yes. Inspector Murphy told De Lorenzo the commissioner had asked the Mayor to let him put in motion an emergency riot plan."

"What did the Mayor say?"

"He refused. He said it would give the city a bad name if the news leaked out."

"That idiotic bastard!" Elliott exploded with unaccustomed fury. "He should be booted out of City Hall!"

"We can't use that," I said hastily. "It was told to me in confidence by Murphy."

"What about this Prophet?" Savage said. "I've seen stories about him, but I never realized he was so dangerous."

"I guess we all took him for granted as a harmless fanatic," Elliott said.

"De Lorenzo asked me about him," I said. "It seems they had some complaints."

"But nothing was done about them?"

"Apparently not."

"In a way you can't blame them," Elliott said. "Their complaint bureau must be flooded with complaints about Harlem fanatics."

"But certainly the police should have had an inside picture of the situation," Savage said.

"I guess the bomb has been ticking so long we all have become accustomed to the sound," Elliott said.

"I don't know who is to blame," I said, "but I know this will haunt me for the rest of my life."

"Don't let it, Duke," Elliott said firmly. "We were just doing a job, and so was this paper."

"Don't forget, there have been other riots in Harlem," Bowers said.

Elliott said, "The last time there was a great deal of unrest because of civil rights."

Julian lifted his brows. "You think they feel differently now in Harlem? They're still using dogs, bullwhips, and cattle prods down South."

"That's true," Elliott said, "but I think we had better stop this breast-beating. None of us wanted this to happen, but it did. And, dammit, it could have been touched off by an ordinary street fight. Or some stupid fool looking for a woman. Look at some of the other Harlem riots. One was started by a rumor that a boy had been beaten for stealing a ten-cent knife!"

Julian walked back to his desk. He looked incredibly drawn and weary. His face was almost gray.

"I suppose so," he said. "Anyway, there's nothing we can say that will turn the clock back." He spread his hands palms down on his desk. "There's the immediate problem—tomorrow's newspaper." He sketched a tiny oval on a memo pad. "The only honest thing to do is tell the reader exactly what happened and why."

"There's no question of it, Julian," Elliott said.

Bowers said dubiously, "The other papers might cut our throats."

"I doubt it," Elliott said. "The newspapers in this town are a responsible lot. I doubt that with twenty dead they'll adopt a holier-than-thou attitude. However, if they do we will have to let the readers decide if we did the right thing."

"I'm only pointing out what might happen," Bowers said stubbornly.

"Well, you have," Elliott said shortly.

Savage slammed one hand down. "Will you people stop bickering! There are important decisions to be made! Now!"

"I guess we're all tired," Elliott said, "and worried. I'm sorry, Joe."

Savage went on, "As I said, we must state exactly what happened and how it happened and why it happened."

"The first two things we can do," Elliott put in, "but the last—the why of it—you must explain. I would suggest, Julian, that you do it in a page-one editorial, set in two-column measure in a Ben Day box."

"I agree with Elliott, Julian," I said. "We started this thing and we had better explain why, loud and clear, on page one."

Bowers added: "We should send copies to the AP and UPI and all the radio and TV stations. Let's get our licks in first."

Elliott said, "That's an excellent idea, Joe. Use one of the rewrite-men."

Savage, after a moment, nodded. "Very well. We'll do it on page one. Turner, I would like you to help me."

"By all means, Julian." He glanced at his watch. "Let's break down what we're going to do—Duke, you should do the main story. . . . Joe, you have all the outside people turn in their stuff to everyone on the rewrite battery. Let Duke talk only to the City Hall man, police head-quarters, and the men covering the West 123rd Street precinct." He turned to Savage. "I've ordered publication to go up two pages and to clear at least four pages of all ads, and to leave them clear."

Bowers said, "We should have three picture pages. The stuff com-ing up from the studio is sensational."

In those few seconds, while they were discussing the makeup of the paper, a strange light had come into the faces of Elliott and Bowers. Weariness and fatigue had vanished; they were animated, almost con-spiratorial. Their mutual dislike of each other had vanished; they were two veteran professionals at work.

"There's another thing to be decided," I said.

They turned to me, frowning and impatient.

"How will we treat the raids, the Gennaro arrest? Up until the first brick had been thrown, this was our big one."

Savage said, "We're certainly going to give it prominence—"

"We'll run it on page one with a picture of Gennaro," Elliott said briskly.

Bowers added, "We have a good shot of him in cuffs in the pre-cinct."

"Just a minute!" Julian said sharply. "I realize the gravity of the riots and the amount of coverage we have to give it on page one. But as far as I am concerned, our original intent of exposing a criminal con-spiracy in this town is still a very, very important story."

"It should be all one story," Bowers said.

Julian gave him a cold look. "Of course it shouldn't. This tragic riot should be treated exactly as what it is—a race riot that had its in-ception in poverty, a scourge of rats, rent strikes, official ignorance and apathy, and racial hatred."

"And the raids, Julian?" Elliott said softly.

"The raids and Gennaro's arrest should be a separate story and given equal prominence," he said. "As we agreed, we will withhold the police corruption angle, but I want it made clear that this newspaper's own investigation showed that the conspiracy has been operating untouched for the last few years. I don't want any punches pulled, and furthermore I want it on page one every day. If, for any reason, Duke's follow-up stories are to be removed from page one, I want to be consulted. Is that clear?"

There was iron in his voice, and everyone in that room recognized it.

"Yes, sir," said Elliott, and he meant it.

Julian walked me to the door. "Thank God you weren't hurt."

"I'm sorry it turned out this way . . . what a tough break. I know how much it meant to you."

"They say you test the strength of the metal with the way it resists acids. I guess this is my first big test." He added in a low voice, "I just hope the old man doesn't bend."

"Has he said anything?"

"He's been on the phone several times. I think the politicians are reaching him. Nothing serious, but he's worried." He paused at the door. "Well, I have to get to work."

When I passed the closed door sometime later, the typewriter was clicking industriously.

In a few hours the wire-service copy, the material funneled to me from our staffmen covering the riot and from the reporters stationed at City Hall, police headquarters, and the makeshift riot main base in the West 123rd Street precinct, gave me a crow's-nest view of what had happened.

A few minutes after the raiders had hit the West 138th Street policy drop, the Prophet had abandoned his favorite spot outside the supermarket parking lot to advance to where the unmarked cars of Murphy's men were parked. As the first prisoners were brought out, the Prophet began haranguing the growing crowd. There were jeers and curses and a few bricks were thrown, but it was the usual Harlem anticop demonstration. Murphy's man in charge of the raid ordered everyone to hurry up and clear out, and this was being done when one of the prisoners, a young Negro, broke free. Two detectives grabbed him after a short chase and began dragging him to a car. Then one of the Prophet's red-hatted followers struck one of the detectives with an iron pipe. His partner swung at the fanatic, knocking him back against the open door of the car, only to be grabbed from behind by another man. They wrestled, and the detective who had been struck over the head got to his feet, blood streaming from his smashed skull, and fired, killing the Negro, who had the other officer in a stranglehold.

For a moment the crowd watched the dying man; then, according to the witnesses, the Prophet screamed, "Get those white bastards!" Suddenly the whole street seemed filled with shouting, cursing red-hatted men who were armed with clubs, bricks, and some with rifles.

As I knew from personal experience, the inevitable Harlem shower of chimney bricks, lengths of old lumber, ash cans, old bedsprings, parts of ancient plumbing rained from the rooftops. Patrolmen went down, some seriously injured. The Prophet's men waded in, shouting commands for the crowds to join them. Some did and some didn't. The police fought back desperately, in many cases joined by colored residents of the block. Fortunately, the Prophet's men had more clubs than rifles, and the cops' aim was better. Two Apostles died on their feet when they fired almost point-blank at Murphy's men coming out of the drop. As one cop said, it happened so fast it was hard to believe. The rapid exchange of gunfire made the mob, including the Prophet's men, hesitate; and it was then that the cops wisely moved in with swinging clubs. It was this swift, offensive action that saved them; the crowd broke, and some of the red-hatted fanatics fled to other parts of Harlem to spread the news of the riot and incite other mobs to loot, burn, and attack innocent pedestrians, white or black.

Eyewitness reports showed how successful they were. The violence spread from street to street, avenue to avenue, leaping whole blocks across the rooftops, like exploding fires in a wind-fanned forest fire.

Mobs surged through the streets and into subways, clubbing and beating. Riot squads were powerless to stem the advance of the mobs that moved through the streets, laughing, singing, shouting, cursing the white man. Radio cars were particular targets. They were overturned and the patrolmen dragged out, clubbed with their own clubs or kicked unconscious. Liquor stores were quickly emptied, and big plate-glass store windows seemed to hold fascination; there was scarcely a block in all Harlem with an intact storefront. Fires were started in tenements, in the streets, and in overturned cars. One tenement was a roaring torch with men, women, and children trapped in the upper stories. When the mob refused to let firemen through, they attacked the mob with high-powered hoses, pikes, and even axes. But the delay was too costly. By the time they could raise their ladders the fire had burst through the roof and the building was totaled, with two families dead.

Employees of private protective agencies, which have a large business in Harlem guarding jewelry stores, supermarkets, business houses, and banks, were set upon and savagely beaten; two later died.

Every available policeman was recalled from vacation and other duty. Emergency trucks and fire equipment of every description virtually ringed Harlem before dawn, and fire trucks from as far as New Jersey came into the city to take over the posts of the absent fire fighters.

Ambulances from every hospital, private and city, raced through the streets, carrying the wounded. The dead were removed to Bellevue Morgue. Accident wards were so crowded that—as I had seen—beds were set up in corridors and halls. As the rioting increased, TV and radio stations began calling for private physicians.

Looting was widespread. Streets were littered with suits, luggage, smashed furniture, bathroom accessories.

"It reminded me of the Russians when they stripped Berlin," one reporter recalled. "The Russkies even ripped out bathtubs and carried them to the streets. No one knew then what they intended to do with them—they just dropped them in the street—that's what it looked like in Harlem."

At first the victims brought to the hospitals were those injured by clubs, rocks, and other debris; but as the night wore on and the violence and looting increased to a point never before reached in an American city, the police were forced to use their guns to protect their own lives or the lives of helpless whites or blacks.

Then the hospital reports bore the words "gunshot wound."

However, by dawn, with every patrolman available rushed from the other boroughs, the rioting began to fade. Policemen and plainclothesmen, along with firemen and Civil Defense workers, wielded nightsticks and fists without mercy on many of the mob who now were reeling drunk.

I have always written well under deadline pressure, and from experience I can intuitively separate the important from the trivial. I wrote steadily for hours, the longest news story I can recall. The Mayor made an unprecedented appearance on TV at 2:00 A.M. to report to the city. He appeared to be exactly what we had always known: a frightened, bumbling politician, an inept man at ease greeting visiting choral groups from overseas or opening the local boy-scout drive, but far beyond his depth when faced with anything significant.

The lights at City Hall burned until dawn, and the limousines of the party's leaders crowded City Hall Park. Among them was Big Jim McShane. Before he arrived, there had been rumors that Washington was pressing to send in Federal marshals, but after McShane appeared the Mayor held a brief press conference with his Police Commissioner in which he insisted that the police had the riot under control, and said a warrant for inciting a riot had been issued for the arrest of the Prophet.

After the riot story had been cleared, I turned to the story of the policy raids, how we had cooperated with the police and the District Attorney's office, and how this joint cooperation had broken one of the largest and most powerful organized syndicates in the city. The pictures of the raid were excellent, especially of Gennaro in the precinct with his hands held above his head as two officers frisked him. The mobster's face was tight with rage at undergoing such indignity.

As I studied the picture I thought of Jackson. This, he had said, would be his payoff. But God, what a price!

During the night I tried several times to get Johnny De Lorenzo, but the night lines to the D.A.'s office were either busy or else someone grumpily took a message and hung up. The hours passed, and that strange moment came when the high-pitched tension moved like a spirit from the city room to beyond the metal sheeted door into the composing room to translate words into type, forms, and lead pages. This is when men in the city room slowly inhale, gossip, impatiently eye the electric clock, contemplate breakfast, wife, the weary ride home, the unmowed lawn. It was during this lull that Hoff called, Gwen called, and I was passed a paragraph from the Associated Press.

I recognized Hoff's voice the moment I picked up the phone. He was trying hard not to sound triumphant.

"Tough night, Duke?"

"Not especially. What's on your mind?"

"You called De Lorenzo, remember?"

"But I didn't call you, remember?"

"Well, I do all the talking now. The boss called from Geneva. He wants to see you and your boy-scout publisher tomorrow at 2:00 P.M."

"There's one thing I didn't put in the story tonight. . . ."

"What's that—how your paper started this God-damned thing?"

"No. How we couldn't raise your tinhorn boss because he was shacking up with some floozie in Geneva."

One thing about Bob Hoff, I mused as he hung up; he's never at a loss for four-letter words.

Later, Gwen called, and for a long moment I just closed my eyes and enjoyed that rich, wonderful voice.

"Duke, are you all right? I've been looking at the riot on TV almost all night. It's terrible! One man said a reporter was shot."

"Don't believe all you see on TV. How are you?"

Her voice dropped. "I miss you terribly, Duke. . . . Come out here . . . just for a week, please—"

"Maybe—when it's all over."

"It's never over," she whispered.

"The publisher told me to take some time off in a few weeks."

"Who are you kidding, Duke?" she said. "This damn' thing will go on and on."

"When are you coming back?"

She hesitated. "I don't think I am coming back, Duke. Bunny's out here now, and he introduced me to another producer who's doing a movie in Greece in the spring."

"You going to get the part?"

"I have it if I want it." She hesitated. Then: "Please, Duke, come out; we can get married tomorrow."

I suddenly felt very old and very tired. "I don't know, Gwen; you hit me at a bad time—can I call you?"

"Darling, I'll be here nearly all day, and then I'm going to the studio for one quick scene. . . . Please, Duke, please call me. I love you, darling."

I held the phone tightly and told her that I loved her more than anything in the world. The click of the phone was devastating. Then I was staring down at the ink-smeared page one proof, and Gwen was lost as Bowers was telling me with his usual fierce urgency that the Mayor was having another press conference, another man had died, and I had better make three inserts for a replate that was going in within minutes.

Finally, at ten in the morning, it was over. I turned my late notes, wire copy, and dupes of my inserts over to a day-side rewriteman and hurriedly ran through the first edition with him. There was a fresh batch of local AP with a yellow piece of UPI on top. It read:

GENEVA (AP), Quinn Flaherty, District Attorney of New York County, left here today for New York where a race riot had reportedly resulted in the death of more than twenty men, women, and children, injuries to scores of others and caused damage estimated in the millions.

In a brief conference held at his hotel, Mr. Flaherty revealed he had instructed his office to issue a warrant for the arrest of Isaiah Redmond, a Negro racial leader known to police as the Prophet. Redmond's alleged attack on a policeman touched off the bloody riots. Mr. Flaherty predicted the Negro leader would be arrested within hours. A nationwide alarm, he said, would be sent out by New York City police.

Later, at the airport shortly before he took off, Mr. Flaherty told reporters he was "shocked" at the news of the riot:

"New York has been the world's melting pot for over a hundred years, and the people of all races live, work, and play side by side in our great metropolis," he said.

"For several months there has been a disturbing element in Harlem seeking to arouse race prejudice and hatred. We are not unaware of this faction, and in fact I have been conducting an active investigation into this matter for some time and was preparing to present it to the Grand Jury when I was summoned by our President to attend these very vital conferences in Geneva. Narcotics addiction has increased by leaps and bounds within the last three years, and the peoples of the world have at last joined hands to wipe out this menace which certain nations are using as a commercial enterprise."

Mr. Flaherty identified these nations as Castro's Cuba and Red China. He hinted that narcotics seized in big-city raids, including his own New York City, had been traced to these nations.

Mr. Flaherty said he has been in constant touch with his administrative assistant, Robert Hoff.

Mr. Flaherty, who appeared tired, said he had been up all night on the telephone, receiving reports and issuing orders to his office and concluding a final meeting with the delegates from France and Italy.

(TXH ADVISES NY, FLAHERTY ARRIVES 7:30 A.M. EST, TWA, FLIGHT 17, KENNEDY.)

I showed the dispatch to Julian and Turner Elliott in Savage's office just before I left. Julian's face was waxlike, and under his eyes there were deep smudges, as though someone had dubbed a thumb in soot and carefully made two half-moons.

I think it was at that moment I realized Julian Savage could be a sick man. It was also clear Elliott was aware of his exhaustion.

"There's no longer any reason for you to stay, Julian," he said. "In fact you should have gone hours ago."

Julian smiled. "I'll wait until the paper comes up. I want to look it over."

"I'll have a boy deliver it," Elliott said promptly. "I'll have a cab waiting outside the building for the first paper."

"Thank you, Turner." Then quietly, firmly: "I'll wait."

Who was it said give me a hundred butterflies with iron hearts and I'll conquer the forest?

"Any word from the D.A.'s office, Duke?" he asked.

"Hoff called a few hours ago," I said. "He would like you and me to meet him at 2:00 P.M. tomorrow—today."

I showed him the AP dispatch.

"I wonder why he didn't blame us," he said. "I thought that would be the first thing he would say. I wouldn't be surprised if this is a good indication of his strategy. What do you think, Duke?"

"I'm inclined to agree. Let's not forget that Flaherty is an excellent politician. He's a past master at taking adverse situations and turning them around to his advantage. I've seen him do it before."

"Let's analyze it," Julian said. "What in this adverse situation could be made to work for him?"

"The Prophet," I said.

Elliott broke in, "He can make the Prophet the scapegoat!"

"With all the trimmings of a Grand Jury investigation, a mayor's committee, a nationwide manhunt, raids on their headquarters," I pointed out, "this madman could be made into a perfect headline villain. And Flaherty could save a lot of political faces in this very sensitive year if his office did the probing." I counted off on my fingers, "First they could concentrate on the Prophet and ignore—"

Julian said quickly "—disgraceful housing, crooked real-estate operations, rats, police corruption, lack of jobs, schooling—"

Elliott smiled. "You're getting it, Julian. Cloud the main issues. Concentrate on the Prophet, his fanatical ideas, his crazy followers. Ignore the fact the city is really to blame for his being and the underlying cause of the riot."

"In other words the Prophet is a ready-made villain," Julian said.

"Exactly," Elliott said. "One you can make the people really hate."

I counted off again: "The second thing Flaherty could brush off is Gennaro's power in this town and, more importantly, cut short an investigation of McShane."

Julian closed his eyes and leaned back in his chair. "And hide McShane's connection with Gennaro. Is that it, Duke?"

"That's it. And if I know them they'll move heaven and earth to make sure the connections are never exposed. There's too much at stake. Who knows how far it might go beyond McShane?"

The room was quiet for a long moment.

"What about Johnny De Lorenzo?" Julian asked at last.

"Frankly, I don't know," I said. "He's the unknown quantity. He may stand up to them; then again he may be bought for a magistrate's job."

"Obviously, Flaherty won't let him continue. What do you think he'll do?"

"Play the politician. If he sees Johnny is getting stubborn, he may call him in for a cozy chat. He'll slap him on the back, praise him to the skies, and commiserate with him that the raids let to the riot. I wouldn't be surprised to see Flaherty announce that Johnny has been placed in charge of the Grand Jury investigating the riots. Of course, he'll recite Johnny's great family background."

"Suppose Johnny doesn't swallow that and insists on going ahead? Do you think Flaherty would sack him?"

"Flaherty is too much of an old hand to do that. If he fires Johnny he has a tough foe on the outside who could issue some devastating statements that the enemy would love to hear. Oh, no. Flaherty will never sack Johnny De Lorenzo—at least until November. If he can't buy Johnny, he'll sidetrack him in other ways."

"What about Tom Murphy?"

"Inspector Murphy is an honest cop. But the department is his whole life. If the commissioner orders him to keep his mouth shut, that's it."

"And the commissioner?"

"He's Tom's closest friend. They both came up the hard way. When the commissioner was a sergeant, he pounded a beat for a year in Staten Island because he raided a clubhouse. It happened to have been one of McShane's."

"Do you think he might order Murphy to continue?"

"He could, but there wouldn't be much point if Johnny was taken off the investigation or if he is stalled by Flaherty. The cops can dig up evidence, but they need a Grand Jury."

Julian gently rubbed his eyelids. He said nothing immediately; I knew once for all that he had to make his position clear, and I suppose important declarations create their own prologue of silence. Finally he spoke. "Well, I guess we know what to expect at our meeting. Speaking for myself and the paper, I will tell Mr. Flaherty we would be derelict in our duty in dropping the whole Gennaro investigation."

"We'll continue, then?" Elliott said.

"Not only continue," he said slowly. "I want to intensify our efforts. Duke, I want you to keep exclusively on Gennaro. I want a story every day—" He turned to Elliott, "Page one, and no excuses. I want editorials, hard-hitting—"

Elliott asked in his blunt way, "Why, Julian?"

"Because I honestly believe it is our duty," was the quiet answer.

Elliott pressed, "Is there anything that could force you to lay off, Julian?"

The answer was cold and harsh. "Nothing. And that includes my father-in-law, Flaherty, and the whole McShane machine."

We sat there, the weak sunlight pouring through the windows making us feel warm, tired and relaxed, and the sound of the impatient early-morning rush-hour traffic rising from the street below. When Julian did speak it was evident he had put his crossroads behind him.

"Just before you both came in, my father-in-law called and said he would have breakfast with me." He said wryly, "I can't remember when he missed reaching his office at nine."

"Do you think that City Hall has reached him?" Turner asked.

"Who knows? Somebody has. Well, we'll soon find out." He yawned. "I don't know about you fellows, but I've never been so tired. Why don't you all go home?"

"I'll stay until the Commuters' Special is away," Elliott said.

"Duke, there's no reason for you to stick around. Suppose you pick me up about one-thirty?"

"I'll be here. Good night."

"Good night—and thanks for a great job. Turner, will you tell Joe Bowers and the staff?"

"I'll post a note with what you said."

"That will be fine."

On the way out Elliott said, "An old friend called me a few hours ago. He's a retired Supreme Court judge, and close to City Hall. His son is also county leader in Brooklyn. . . . Beginning next Monday, all the Alcoholic Beverage Control liquor-license ads are being yanked from the *Blade-Leader.*"

"Do you think you should have told him?"

At the elevator Elliott pressed the Down button.

"After what he went through tonight? And now having to face that miserable old son of a bitch of a father-in-law?"

"I'm afraid he'll make Julian lay off—after all, he owns the paper."

"No, he won't do that right off. His way is to turn the screw slowly. He'll let Julian sweat and suffer; then he'll move in and take over."

"My God, the man's his son-in-law, his dead daughter's husband!"

"That's it exactly, Duke," he said. "The old man never got over his daughter's death. He has never said it in so many words but—" He shook himself and impatiently pressed the button again.

"I wish we could help him in some way."

"All we can do is to follow his orders completely."

"All the while suspecting that he will have his throat cut?"

"Would you rather not do what he wants, dog the whole thing, give him lip service?"

"It might stop him from being hurt."

He gave me a bitter look. "For God's sake, Duke, let him die on his feet and not on his knees. . . ."

The elevator door opened, and he turned back into the rising tempo of the city room where new minds and new events were beginning to reshape what we had created during the long hours of the night I will always remember as the longest and darkest of my whole life.

BOOK FOUR

THE PEOPLE'S CASE

[19]

THE *New York Times* editorial summed it up in a traditional low key; while the city had suffered a calamity so terrible its citizens, both white and black, would find hard to forget, this human eruption had been a long time in coming, so now the future must be faced by all, from the Mayor to the humblest taxpayer, or the second time might far overshadow the first in violence and in hatred. The rest of the city's newspapers commented in the same voice, all with overtones of sadness, horror, and indignation that it could have happened at all.

Obviously, the news accounts carried the fact that a raid made by police in conjunction with the *Blade-Leader*'s crime exposé touched off the initial violence. But as the *Trib* pointed out in fairness, there have been raids of all descriptions in Harlem down through the years without subsequent race riots. It simply had been the wind that fanned the sputtering fuse.

The news of Gennaro's arrest had been completely buried by the vast coverage of the riot. The tabloids used a picture of him leaving the precinct, and a brief story. The *Times* had four paragraphs and the *Trib* a half column with a one-column cut and caption, "Mob leader arrested in policy raid." Our story started on page one, above the fold under a three-column head, and jumped inside for a full column with three pictures of Gennaro and two of the actual raid. I even had the feeling we were forcing its importance in view of what had happened. It seemed lost on the page. Our front page was dominated by a photograph of Murphy's men and the Prophet's followers exchanging gunfire in the street, with one of the fanatics clutching his stomach and dying on his feet. It was one—and it won the Pulitzer—of several shots taken by the photographer assigned to the raid. Elliott had wisely used it eight smashing columns across page one, and my story, set in two-column measure, running down the page. It seemed a lost ironical touch—that I should help Gennaro escape the full impact of exposure.

Directly in the center of page one, also set in two-column Bodoni italics so that it jumped out at the reader, was Julian Savage's personal editorial.

Simple, forceful, it put forward the paper's statement that we had inaugurated the raids as a public service under strict police control and had done nothing of which we were ashamed.

I had the feeling that this editorial, along with the muted references to our part in the riot, could allow us to bow out gracefully—if that was what we wanted. As I reread the editorial, I wondered if the same thoughts were haunting Julian.

However, the news on the whole was terribly depressing: the death toll was now twenty-one; a second policeman had died; four were in critical condition; a whole family had been burned to death in that tenement fire, and hundreds of stores and business places had been destroyed and looted. The "Today Show" devoted all its time to a tour of the streets of Harlem; glass, debris, and burned cars were everywhere. The people stared out of my TV with bitter faces. One man spat at the camera.

I was carefully shelling a soft-boiled egg when the woman commentator was cut off by an urgent bulletin. Moscow was now in the act; *Pravda* was triumphantly giving Moscow a highly exaggerated account of the burning of New York City during a race riot; Tass was sending out reams of copy, and the Congo delegation had issued a denunciation of brutal police methods and was asking for a UN investigation. Of course, they made no mention that policemen had died. As I was finishing my second cup of coffee, another bulletin quoted a spokesman for the Attorney General who revealed that Department of Justice officials were in New York conferring with District Attorney Flaherty.

The events of last night had joined Birmingham and Mississippi in our history. . . .

I spoke to the office twice between catnaps. Elliott sounded worried. It appeared from the wire services that the Communist propaganda machine was churning at full speed, picturing New York City in ruins as white and black butchered each other, with the army called in to take control. Elliott also had more disturbing news. Shortly before he had left the office, Julian had been taken ill.

"Apparently it was his stomach," Elliott said. "He was nauseated and went down to the dispensary for a while. He insisted he was all right when he left, but he looked like hell.

"Apparently this wasn't the first time. On a hunch I asked his secretary, and she said she came in a few weeks ago and found him as white as a sheet. She wanted to call the nurse, but he wouldn't let her. I recall he left unusually early that day."

I suddenly remembered Julian mentioning his bleeding ulcers some time ago, and I told Elliott.

"Yes, I had heard something about it when he first came here." He added thoughtfully: "I'm going to make a point of insisting he slow down. No more nights like the last one. And look, Duke, try to make this an easy meeting for him."

I promised. Realizing sleep was impossible, I kept busy putting in order my transcripts and notes; the original tapes I placed in my private vault. The brisk walk to the bank several blocks away helped to clear the cobwebs, and by the time I returned to my apartment it was near noon and I was ready for Flaherty.

Before I left for downtown, I tried Jackson's rooming house, but Mrs. Zuccartelli was even more vague than usual until I told her who it was. Abruptly her immigrant English fell away and she was telling me in a heavy accent that Jackson hadn't been around for a few days but that his room was locked, which meant he still had the key. We ended by agreeing that Jackson should get married, preferably to a nice Italian girl.

Julian was dictating when I arrived, so I waited in his outer office. When I went in I found him looking tense, angry, and terribly tired.

"You look like you're ready to tee off on Mr. Flaherty," I said.

"I'm ready to tee off on somebody," he said shortly. "I've been on the phone twice with the old man this morning. They yanked the liquor ads out of the paper, and I'm having all kinds of trouble with my old classmate Jack Cummings."

"Cummings, I gather, is twisting your arm?"

"Not too much, just enough for me to get the message," he said. "I can handle Jack, but those politicians really disturb me." He fumbled with some papers, then threw them back on his desk with obvious exasperation. "The old man is suggesting I make peace with them! We have to be over there at two?"

"That's right. But maybe we can postpone it until tomorrow—"

"Why? Why not today?"

"Frankly, you don't look like you got a lot of sleep."

"I'm a bit off my feed, that's all," he said shortly. "It's probably the prospect of another session with the old man tonight." He said between his teeth, "Those damned politicians!"

"If I know them, this is mild compared to what will happen when they know we're going ahead."

"You can bet your life we're going ahead." He glanced at his watch. "We'd better be getting over there."

In the cab on the way over to Foley Square, he was silent and preoccupied. I didn't try to intrude on his thoughts. We went into the side entrance to Flaherty's private elevator and were whisked silently to the fifth floor. Walking down the corridor lined with portraits of the great D.A.'s New York has had from Whitman to Hogan, I wondered what had happened to all of us to allow Flaherty to walk in their company. Every political reporter in the city, veteran or tenderfoot, had been aware for years how the clubhouse lawyers and judges had been feeding here at the trough of justice. Why had it been allowed to continue? The voters? Perhaps, in the final analysis. The press? Of course. Why? Cowardice, economic pressure? Fear of the machine?

What would happen when that machine, in a frenzy of self-survival, began hurling its thunderbolts, making the whole structure of the *Blade-Leader* shiver and shake?

Flaherty's secretary, who knew me, instantly picked up the phone, whispered into it, and a moment later the door behind her swung open to frame Flaherty, smiling, exuberant, and seemingly brimming over with good fellowship.

"Julian, how good of you to come," he said, vigorously, painfully, pumping Savage's hand.

"Hiya, Duke . . ."

"Fine, Mr. District Attorney," I said with studied sarcasm.

We walked in, selected one of the comfortable chairs arranged in a semicircle, and murmured greetings to Johnny De Lorenzo, Tom Murphy, and Bob Hoff. Johnny looked tense and worn, Murphy impassive as always, and Hoff arrogant and tough. I introduced Murphy to Julian, and after the usual small talk Flaherty lighted a cigar, gave a gratified smile, and began talking.

"I don't think I have to mince any words," he said. "I think we are all aware the city's in one hell of a mess. Twenty-one dead, including policemen, inestimable damage, and God knows how many seriously injured." He tapped the ash into a large tray.

"The State Department had me on the phone three times this morning, and Justice wants to send down a flock of marshals. I told them we have the situation in hand and to keep their marshals down South where they really need them."

"From what I saw myself up in Harlem, we could have used them,"
I said.

He ignored me and went on. "It's unfortunate that God-damned
Prophet didn't wait. . . ." He cocked an eye at Savage. "You know we
were just about to move in on him?"

I broke in, "Oh, you were going to indict him?"

Flaherty stood up, leaned on the back of his chair, and stared down
at me.

"No, Duke, we weren't going to indict him." He tapped a yellow
folder on the desk. "Nobody is indicted by this office unless we have
evidence enough to support a prima facie case; *you* know that. What
we were going to do was begin issuing subpoenas for the books of his
organization and start questioning some of his people."

"I assumed your office only had some routine complaints."

The first trace of iron edged into his voice. "Well, let's say you
assumed wrong, Duke. And if anyone in my office led you to believe
that, I would like to know who he is. Now."

It was his first move. He was challenging me to publicly cut down
Johnny, expose him as the bumbling little boy.

Quite cheerfully I said, "Sure. In fact it was Bob here who said
you had some complaints."

Hoff almost leaped up in the chair. "Me! Where the hell do—"

I hated to do it, but I threw the ball to Tom Murphy, who I knew
wouldn't lie if every organ in his body was pulled out by red-hot pincers.

"I think Inspector Murphy heard Bob say that."

All eyes swung to Murphy.

"I believe Mr. Hoff did use that word."

Flaherty impatiently shut off Hoff's flow of words.

"Well, if Bob gave you that impression it was wrong. This office
was ready to go all out after the Prophet and his gang." He shrugged.
"But things got out of control when you people didn't play ball."

He softened it with a smile and looked directly at Savage to see
how he took the first blow.

"I'm sorry, Mr. Flaherty; I don't believe I understand you," Julian
said softly.

"Then let me spell it out. You let Malloy give my office information
about a criminal conspiracy operating in this city. I really believe you
should have waited until I came home, but that isn't the issue—"

"What is the issue, then?"

"You withheld pertinent information from this office until the last
minute. And this information changed the whole aspect of the investigation. If we had known about it, and if I had been aware of what you

had, I would never have authorized those raids!" He slapped the back of his thick leather chair. "Never! And this whole dreadful thing would not have happened."

His first offensive moves now were clear; we were the culprits who had dealt with a young, inexperienced member of his staff. Had the wise, older prosecutor been present, nothing would have happened. It was just too much to take, and I saw Johnny's hand clench until the knuckles were white as he stared straight ahead.

Flaherty was continuing: "I would like to know why—why did you keep back this information?"

"It wasn't ready, Mr. Flaherty," I said as bluntly as I could. "I was in charge of this investigation, and it was my responsibility to advise my office about what I thought. And I thought it wasn't ready. Is that satisfactory?"

He gave me a bleak look.

"No, it isn't, but if that is your explanation we will have to accept it."

"By the way," I said quickly, before Julian could speak, "I would like to know something about this Prophet investigation—"

"Off the record?"

It was my turn to elaborate.

"I don't like to talk off the record, but I guess this is an exception."

"What is it you want to know?"

"You say you were ready to present something to the Grand Jury. I assume it was evidence. Has your office an undercover man in the Prophet's organization?"

He hesitated, and Hoff gave me a cold smile.

"It just happens, Duke, we didn't. But we don't have to. This is a police investigation. We handle what they dig up."

"You would know, Inspector," I asked Murphy. "Did the department put a man in the Prophet's group?"

The stone face stared straight ahead. "That particular assignment was not given as far as I know. But we do have a file on Redmond, quite extensive I believe."

I said, "Would it consist mostly of Redmond's activities in Philly and complaints sent in and follow-up reports on these complaints? In other words, routine stuff?"

"I haven't seen the file in some time, Duke," Murphy said evenly. "It's in Criminal Identification, you know."

"We're going off the track, Boss," Hoff said roughly. "I don't know why we're discussing this at all."

"I agree," Flaherty said, "but Duke asked the questions, and I said I would answer them." He turned back to us. "But Bob's right: we were talking about your newspaper's part in this—not how this office is conducting itself!"

Julian's cold, even voice filled the room. "Let us get this straight here and now, Mr. Flaherty. I don't intend to be bulldozed by you or anyone else in your office. I consider what we did an excellent public service, which is one of the *Blade-Leader*'s principal functions. If you wish to start a Grand Jury investigation of our conduct, you are free to do so. In fact, I will accept a subpoena right now and so will Mr. Malloy."

For one brief second I thought I saw a flicker in Flaherty's cold blue eyes. It gave me heart. I could almost taste the electricity in the air. Flaherty appeared undisturbed; Hoff's eyes were narrow, but Johnny looked surprised.

"If we decide to start such an investigation," Flaherty said smoothly, "we will contact you immediately and invite you and Mr. Malloy to appear before the Grand Jury. Is that satisfactory?"

Julian gave him a nod. "It is, sir."

Flaherty came from around his chair and sat down. He flipped open the folder, studied it for a moment, then looked up.

"I think we should agree, Mr. Savage, that your newspaper and my office are partners in this mess. Your newspaper dug up evidence of a criminal conspiracy and gave it to this office. For the time we will put aside how it was given—and we acted. Unfortunately, a terrible race riot resulted. Not only is the public shocked; it is demanding action." He slammed his fist down. "And dammit, that's what we have to give them! Now!"

"I agree wholeheartedly," Julian said calmly.

Flaherty leaned forward, and that deep, rich orator's voice filled the room.

"There's one man responsible for this horrible human toll—that's Redmond. He's a vicious criminal, and his followers are a dangerous cancer in this city. He must be apprehended, indicted for murder, his whole rotten gang investigated by the Grand Jury, and every mother's son of them sent away. Or, gentlemen, the second time will be twice as horrible as the first!" He looked straight at Julian. "As I said a few moment's ago, we are partners in this mess. I hope we have the complete cooperation of your newspaper and your staff, sir."

"Absolutely. You are the District Attorney, Mr. Flaherty. Anything your office wants we will do."

Flaherty lifted a photograph of Redmond from the folder.

"I intend to ask the Board of Estimate this afternoon to vote a reward of $5,000 for the arrest and conviction of Redmond. Will your paper match it?"

"We will."

"Will you run this picture on page one tomorrow with a special phone number, no questions asked, for information as to where Redmond might be hiding?"

Julian turned to me, "Duke, will you handle that?"

"Of course." I took the photograph from Flaherty.

"That's an exclusive picture, Duke," Hoff said. "Nobody else has it."

Flaherty turned to Hoff. "Shall I mention the material, Bob?"

Hoff shrugged. "Why not? We have a confidential file on Redmond from Washington and from the Philadelphia and Detroit police department's CID. They have some sensational material. How he's been forming a small army of thugs to take over when he feels the time's right."

"How about that oath in the Philly report?" Flaherty asked.

"Three years ago the Philadelphia cops got someone in his organization," Hoff said. "He tells how they took some kind of a crazy blood oath in a kind of Black Mass ceremony. It sounds weird but it's all official. But get this—they had a list of city officials to be assassinated and a plan to use the race riots as a political movement. I told the boss you might consider doing a series on the Prophet and his gang. I know the *Journal-American* and the *Trib* have started looking into Redmond for a series, but they told us they're having a hard time. The facts are very meager about this guy. This could be a real plum—"

Flaherty carefully pulled out two thick stapled reports from the folder and handed them over to me.

I almost burst out laughing. It was a God-damned seduction scene with exclusive pictures and material as bait instead of wine, candlelight, and Brahms. When I sat back I stole a look at Johnny. There was a slight smile of cold contempt on his face. He really believes we've been had!

"You heard how Moscow's taking off on us?" Flaherty said. "Well, the police have tipped us off to expect mass picketing some time today. They're picketing police headquarters at this moment." He stood up again and dramatically looked out the window for a moment before he turned around.

"I'm not worried about those crackpots, do-gooders, and phony-assed liberals!" he thundered. "I'm thinking of the good, righteous people in this city—white and black—who have been shocked and stunned at what happened. They're the ones we're serving. They want

Redmond and his gang punished! And, by God, this office is going to do everything possible to bring that about!"

Flaherty seemed enchanted by his own performance, as if he dared us to challenge the premise that the Prophet was a major menace to the security and safety of the American way of life. Neither Julian nor I responded. As we both agreed later, we were almost hypnotized by his dramatics. Gradually the truth began to sink in: how frightened he must be that we might ignore the opportunity he offered us to save our country from a monster and continue with Gennaro.

At last he was finished. From his triumphant look I am sure he felt we were solidly behind him, that finding the Prophet and prosecuting him and his followers were the only things really important. There was silence for a moment as we waited for Julian, who was carefully studying his trimmed nails.

"I can't agree with you more, Mr. Flaherty," he said mildly. "The Prophet and his gang certainly must be brought to justice and, as I said, we will do everything in our power to help your office. My staff is at your call and so is my paper.." He seemed to straighten slightly in his chair. "However, there are two items which I consider very important, which have not been discussed here this afternoon."

"And they are—" Flaherty said in a voice stretched as tight as a rubber band.

"In addition to the activities of the Prophet, will your Grand Jury explore Harlem's miserable housing, who owns those rattraps, and how the landlords have been getting away with those violations?" He paused and stared hard at Flaherty. "There is also the rat problem, the school program, and the way police corruption has distorted the values of the young people of the Harlem community."

Flaherty's voice was cold and even.

"I am sure those problems will be ably taken care of by the city's departments."

Julian's reply was equally cold. "It would be interesting to study their past performances."

Hoff broke in, "You said there were two items—"

Julian nodded. "Vito Gennaro and the raids."

Flaherty leaned back in his chair. "The raids were made, the men arrested and charged. The matter will be placed before a Grand Jury. Undoubtedly they will be indicted and tried. If convicted . . ."

Julian looked up to protest such an inane explanation.

"Please, Mr. Flaherty—I know the fundamentals of the law."

"Sorry," Flaherty said. "I was only trying to sketch for you what my office had in mind for Gennaro."

"I'm not interested in that," Julian said doggedly. He gave Flaherty an odd, almost embarrassed smile. "Vito Gennaro. How certain officials in the Police Department protected his enterprise. Who is Mr. Big at police headquarters? And who is beyond Mr. Big? That's what we're interested in, Mr. Flaherty."

Flaherty shifted his bulk in the big leather chair. He closed the folder that held all his material on the Prophet and selected another folder, opened it, read some typewritten pages, then looked up.

"I just wanted to confirm my memory," he said carefully. "What we have here are a series of tapes alleging that certain members of the Police Department are accepting bribes. Correct me if I'm mistaken; the corroborative witness is anonymous. Mr. Malloy has refused to divulge his identity. Unfortunately, that was agreed upon in my absence."

A deep red flush slowly mounted Johnny's neck, and his fists were tight balls. He kept his dark, angry eyes glued on his boss.

"You forgot something," I broke in. "Hoff was present at the meeting, and he tried to get you all day in Geneva." Then I added, "The operator said you were out in the country with the Yugoslavian delegate."

It didn't get a rise out of him. He pursed his lips as though to inform everyone in the room he was dealing with an incorrigible.

"Johnny was acting District Attorney in my absence. Bob was only an adviser. Johnny gave the orders, and although I disagree with them I will not countermand them. He gave them, and that's good enough for me. As for not being able to reach me, it's a matter of record that I was at the home of the Yugoslavian delegate, with whom I prepared the conference's final report." He gave me a pleasant smile. "Any other question, Duke?"

"Did you question Peters?"

"That's a Police Department matter."

"Departmental matter! Peters is the bagman! Maybe the link to McShane!"

The name didn't ruffle Flaherty, although Hoff licked his lips.

"Jim McShane? If you really believe that, Duke, why don't you print it?"

"You know why."

"Of course I do. He would sue your paper for a million dollars, and collect. You would be libeling him. Is that correct?"

"At this point, yes."

He shrugged slightly. "You can't print it—just as I have no proof that Mr. McShane is anything but a fine politician and a well-thought-of member of this community."

"Have you asked Strasser how he can fix cops downtown?"

"Strasser has disappeared."

I almost shouted, "Strasser's gone!"

"Maybe I used the wrong word," Flaherty said hurriedly. "Officially he has told his office he's on vacation. Off the record, I have men looking for him."

"Looking for him! Why the hell don't you get a warrant and put him on teletype?"

"On what charge? Sleeping with a redheaded woman? Johnny talked to him before he left—"

"And—"

"Take it easy, Duke. Strasser admitted he was in the apartment the night you taped the call, but he said he was drunk and thought it was a joke. For your own information I have advised the Bar Association I will seek the appointment of a Referee to hear disbarment proceedings aginst Strasser. Personally I think he's just a shyster and nothing more."

"My God, man, he may be a shyster, but he's one of the keys to Gennaro's operations!"

Flaherty shrugged. "I told you I have investigators looking for him and the girl. What more can I do?"

"What about Peters and Inspector Barrist?"

Hoff broke in: "Barrist put in his papers today. By the way, they were both questioned and denied everything."

The way they so smugly accepted the denials infuriated me. "Why don't you ask Peters to waive before a Grand Jury?" I demanded. "He's the bagman for the Sergeants' Club and the precinct commanders."

"I've been hearing about this so-called Sergeants' Club for years," Flaherty said, "but no one ever proved it for me."

I was about to say I was present when Peters took the money from Jackson, but I caught myself. Peters would be questioned and would know immediately who the informer was.

"You know, Duke, it would help us all tremendously if you would turn over your informer to this office."

"It would be his death warrant!"

"We would give him police protection around the clock."

"That's what Abe Reles got, and he went out the window."

"You people are playing games," Flaherty snapped. His voice softened as he turned to Savage. "Believe me, Julian, what we have here is a simple misdemeanor and a whole basket of Police Department violations."

Julian said suddenly, "I wonder what Inspector Murphy thinks. Didn't he question the officer involved?"

"I went over the deposition of your men, Inspector," Flaherty said, "and frankly I disagree with you. Two of their stories, under questioning by this office, didn't jibe with their original reports. The discrepancies are few, but they mean the difference between a misdemeanor and a felony."

A slight, chilling smile stole over Murphy's blunt face. "So I understand. I talked to these two men, and their memories are refreshed. You'll find the items the same now as they were the night of the raids."

By God, this was a man, I told myself. This was a man! The fix was fixed before it could get rolling. Knowing Murphy, I would not want to be in the shoes of those two detectives who betrayed his trust, probably for the unspoken promise of a good transfer and perhaps a promotion.

Flaherty didn't appear upset. He only nodded and swung back to us.

"You know your own men, Inspector. Just make sure they repeat the same story on the witness stand that they'll tell the Grand Jury."

"Have no fear of that, sir."

"Well, let's say we do get a felony indictment. I'll do my best, but it will be one hell of a job getting a conviction. The last one was Jimmy Hines in Dewey's day. Let me say this, misdemeanor or felony, this office will do its best to put Gennaro away. And I promise you I will personally investigate every charge of police corruption. If I believe there's a case, I will order it presented to the Grand Jury. But if I honestly doubt we can get a conviction, I will refer the evidence this office collected to the Police Commissioner for department proceedings. Is that fair?"

For several seconds Julian didn't answer, but continued to study his clasped hands. Suddenly he spoke to the floor, to his hands, not to us, for his voice was very low; it sounded as if he were whispering, "No, it isn't," again and again.

Then he stopped, shook his head briskly, and then looked up.

"No, it isn't, Mr. Flaherty," he said. "It isn't by any means. Neither I nor my newspaper is interested in the conviction of Vito Gennaro, per se. What we are interested in is finding out what forces were behind this man which allowed him to operate freely and untouched one of the largest criminal conspiracies in the history of this city. That's what I want to find out, sir."

Flaherty's face slowly reddened. "There is no proof of such so-called forces—"

"The very existence of this syndicate is proof," Julian said. "Good God, are you blind, sir?"

Flaherty's voice rose. "No, I'm not blind, Mr. Savage, neither

am I damn' fool enough to put my hand in a fire to pull out your chest-
nuts. You blew this up out of all proportions to an inexperienced man
in my office—"

"He was your appointee, sir."

"And I plead guilty in overestimating Mr. De Lorenzo's experience," Flaherty shot back. "I accept that blame, but that's all water
under the bridge. I'll be damned if I'm going to put all the energies of
this office in trying to prove vicious gossip instead of going full force
after a monstrous black son of a bitch who has made a fool of this city
and country in the eyes of the world. Christ! Can't *you* understand
that? Are *you* blind, sir?"

There were two tiny bits of red on Julian's cheekbones. His face
was shallow and his forehead shiny with perspiration. For the first time
since I've known him, he looked angry and dangerous.

"If you're questioning my Americanism, Mr. District Attorney—
don't!"

It was Flaherty's turn to back a step. His voice dropped several
measures as he said: "No one is questioning your Americanism or your
integrity or the integrity of your paper or your staff. I'm simply telling
you as a District Attorney there is no evidence in this"—he slammed
his fist down on the yellow folder—"other than a misdemeanor or perhaps a felony charge against Gennaro and, at the best, departmental
charges against the cops involved!"

"Could I say I disagree with you, sir?"

If Johnny De Lorenzo had tossed a sputtering bomb into that
room it could not have created more of a sensation. Flaherty slowly
turned to him, a blank look on his face; Hoff jerked his neck forward;
Murphy's eyes widened; Julian carefully wiped his forehead with a
handkerchief, while all I could do was stare at Johnny and wonder at
the terrible conflict that must have been warring inside him all the time
he had been sitting there.

Then Flaherty said, almost disbelieving, "You can if you want
to, Johnny."

"I think we should tell Duke and Mr. Savage the result of a meeting
I had with Bernie Levin, Gennaro's business manager." Johnny turned
to me. "I brought Bernie to my office and read the transcript of your
tapes for him. He got very upset, and I sent him back to stew a while.
This morning he sent word he wanted to see me. Inspector Murphy was
in the office, and we both spoke to him. Bernie feels he's going to take
the whole rap and wants to blow the whistle. He admitted everything
and more. He gave names and dates and amounts paid to Peters and a
whole slew of cops." He bit his lower lip. "He also named McShane.
True, it's only hearsay, but he named him as Gennaro's partner."

"Good God," I could only say.

Julian said slowly, "Is this true?"

To give Flaherty credit, he had steel cables for nerves and ice water for blood. He simply nodded.

"What Johnny said is true. Every word of it." He paused. "But there's more, isn't there, Johnny?"

Johnny nodded miserably. "I'm sorry, but there is—"

Flaherty said to me, "Do you know Webster Pryce, in charge of frauds?"

"I do—for many years."

"And would you say he was an incorruptible man?"

"I would say he was one of the finest." To Julian I added, "He's the oldest man in the office."

"He's been in the D.A.'s office a thousand years," Flaherty added heartily. He picked up the phone. "Please ask Mr. Pryce to come in."

In a few moments Pryce came in. He was tall, thin, distinguished looking, with old-fashioned pince-nez glasses, a shock of white hair hanging down over one eye, and a very faint New England twang. He had always reminded me of a rail-thin Carl Sandburg.

Flaherty introduced us, then said: "We won't keep you but a moment, Webster. I should like to have you repeat for the record what Bernie Levin told you when you questioned him."

He peered over his glasses. "The one in for policy?"

"That's right."

"Well, I had Johnny's notes," he said, "and I started to go down the list, but the defendant just sat there, mute as a mule. Finally I asked him what was wrong, and he said he had changed his mind and I should pass along his regrets to Johnny and the inspector but he was sorry. . . ."

Flaherty said quickly, "In other words he didn't intend to be a cooperative witness?"

"He made that quite clear. Just for the record I went over each one of the points Johnny had sketched up."

Julian beat Flaherty this time. "I'd like to get two things clear, Mr. Pryce."

The shrewd gray eyes studied him. "I don't believe we've met, sir."

"I'm Julian Savage, publisher of the *Blade-Leader*."

Pryce frowned. "I take it this is an off-the-record conference?"

Flaherty looked a trifle uneasy. "Everything said here will be held in strict confidence, Webster. It's perfectly all right."

Pryce shrugged, but it was evident this unorthodox discussion of a case disturbed his orderly soul.

"What are your two points, young man?" he asked Julian.

"I'm afraid I'm not familiar with your procedure," Julian said apologetically, "but I am curious why *you* were interviewing this man?"

Pryce said sternly, "I was asked to by the District Attorney, because this defendant had informed Johnny he would turn state's evidence."

I interjected, "It's Mr. Pryce's job to interview all potential Grand Jury witnesses, Julian."

Julian nodded. "I see. Now I wonder, Mr. Pryce, if you could tell us what were some of what you have called points in Mr. De Lorenzo's notes?"

The old man looked at Flaherty, who nodded his consent.

"I haven't my notes—"

"Just from your memory—"

"Well, as I recall he had named about a dozen police officers who, he alleged, he had paid bribes. In some cases he had given their full names and home addresses where he said he had sent Christmas presents. When the full names weren't available, there were initials. As I recall, he had identified a sergeant named Peters who, he alleged, was Gennaro's principal contact at police headquarters. I believe he said Peters also paid off Insector Barrist of the Police Confidential Squad. This man, he said, accepted large amounts of monies on certain days each month—"

"How much?" I asked.

"I believe it was in the neighborhood of $2,000 a month."

Julian's voice was almost casual. "Was Mr. McShane named in Mr. De Lorenzo's notes?"

Pryce peered over his spectacles at Flaherty, who again nodded.

"Johnny's notes said the defendant stated Mr. McShane was Gennaro's"—he hesitated—"this is my memory now—Number One man in the city. And as long as McShane was around, Gennaro could operate as though he had a license—"

I asked, "Did he say how?"

Pryce carefully cleaned his glasses with a large linen handkerchief. It was obvious how much he disliked to answer.

"The notes quoted the defendant as stating McShane had the courts and cops in his vest pocket and the city in his hip pocket."

In the silence the old man's throat clearing sounded like a tearing rag.

Julian's soft voice went on: "Did you gather from the notes, Mr. Pryce, that this was just hearsay or did the notes specify that the defendant had personal knowledge of what he was charging?"

"The notes were specific that the defendant was present on several occasions when Gennaro spoke to McShane on the phone. I might add, a man he believed to be McShane."

"You didn't see any signed statement, Webster?" Flaherty asked.

The slender white, veined hand pushed back the shock of hair. "No, sir. There was a memorandum attached to the notes signed by Johnny that the defendant stated he refused to sign a statement, but would do so after he found out what kind of deal he was going to get."

Flaherty leaned forward. "Did you discuss any deal?"

"No, sir. As I said, the man remained silent all during my questioning, except to tell me to inform Johnny and the inspector he was sorry, but he had a wife and two children to think about."

Johnny's voice was harsh. "Did you get the impression, Webster, this man had been intimidated?"

"Yes, Johnny, I did."

Flaherty put in, "Did you see him again, Webster?"

"Three times. The last time he refused to see me."

Flaherty toyed with a pencil. "Did he deny he ever saw Johnny or the inspector?"

"He did. And when I pointed out he could be indicted for perjury, he just shrugged and said we had to prove it, and even if we did he could take a year on the island standing on his head."

Flaherty swung about to Julian.

"Well, there's your case, Julian. You don't have to be a lawyer to see there isn't one."

"What about Gennaro?" Julian asked.

"Johnny interviewed Gennaro—I don't think he changed expression or opened his mouth once."

"How about Ricky Strasser's girl?" I said. Flaherty reached inside his drawer and took out a stapled report. "I asked the inspector to check her out," he said. "His report shows she moved out and told the superintendent she was tired of New York and was going to Florida."

"When did she move out?"

He flipped through the report.

"The night of the raids. I know what you're going to say, Duke, that it's mighty funny—"

"The understatement of the year—"

"Perhaps. But it doesn't prove a case. And for your own information I have contacted the Miami police, the Florida State police, with a full description of this girl and asked she be held on an open charge if found."

Julian asked, "What about the FBI?"

"Fine," Hoff broke in, smiling. "If there was a Federal charge. But there isn't. In fact, there isn't any charge against the girl. If she was sleeping with Strasser, I would say the only thing she's guilty of was bad taste."

Out of the corner of my eye I was watching Johnny. He was hunched forward in his chair, almost impatiently waiting for Flaherty and Hoff to finish. Flaherty was putting the report back in his desk when Johnny spoke.

"Webster, I would just like to get one thing straight."

Pryce nodded in his dignified way.

"First of all, the notes you referred to are the dictated notes I made after a three-hour conference with Bernie. Inspector Murphy was present."

"That's correct. The notes were initialed by you and were transcribed by your secretary immediately after the interview."

"And you went over each one of my points with Bernie although he refused to talk?"

"That is correct. I went over page by page, point by point. There was a stenographer present."

Johnny inched forward in his chair, his elbows now resting on his thighs. Everyone in the room was looking at him curiously, while Flaherty was frowning as though annoyed.

"And he did say that he would deny that he ever spoke to me and Inspector Murphy?"

"That is correct."

"And he would also deny he answered freely the questions we asked."

"He said he would swear he never gave you the information you had in your notes."

Johnny leaned back. I had the feeling that something was about to break—and it did.

"Inspector, will you pick it up from here?"

Murphy carefully, almost meticulously, put on a pair of heavy framed glasses, took three small metal keys from a vest pocket, and slid one into the lock of the attaché case and snapped it open. I sat frozen as he opened the case. It was a tape recorder disguised as an attaché case. Flaherty flushed angrily, and Hoff looked startled.

"What have you got there, Inspector—a recorder?" Flaherty snapped.

Murphy looked up. "Yes, sir. I have always been instructed to try to make a tape recording of any conversation of a defendant arrested by the Police Department who wishes to turn state's evidence and become a people's witness."

"When the hell was that rule put into effect?" Hoff said loudly.

Murphy reached inside his jacket and took out a much folded letter, which he handed to Hoff.

Hoff read through it quickly and handed it to Flaherty.

"That God-damned thing's five years old," he said angrily.

The inspector said, "We operate under rules that are twenty-five years old or more." Flaherty silently returned the letter.

Johnny said, "The point is, we have a complete record of Bernie's conversation with me and with the inspector."

"Well, that's excellent," Webster said, looking bewildered. "His voice will indict him for perjury."

His voice trailed off under Flaherty's even stare. There was a deep silence; then Flaherty said quietly to Murphy, "Well, that's quite a stunt you pulled, Inspector. Was the Police Commissioner aware you were doing this without notifying this office?"

That iron face could not be stared down nor could the old cop be intimidated.

"I sent a communication to the commissioner through channels, pointing out I was following the rule of the department," Murphy said. "I brought this to Mr. De Lorenzo's attention as soon as I ascertained the tape was audible, and later Mr. De Lorenzo informed me you hung up on him."

There it was; Murphy was playing it by the book, by the cold, unshakable rules of his bureaucratic department. Nothing he had done was technically wrong, and Flaherty, who used the book when it suited his purpose, was forced to recognize a fellow conspirator and even had the grace to smile.

"If I ever thought I'd catch you napping, Inspector, I was badly mistaken," he said. Then, briskly, he added: "Very well, we now have a tape with the defendant's voice. Mr. De Lorenzo, you and Mr. Pryce are to play this tape in the presence of this man and a stenographer. If he insists he lied, or has the gall to state to you he never said these things, then you are to prepare a charge of perjury. Is that clear?"

Both Johnny and Pryce nodded.

To Julian he said: "I predict right now that this man will tell us he lied to save his own skin. And as far as I am concerned, all this smearing of our Police Department and a man who is a national figure is a shocking indictment of your newspaper! Frankly, I think you should start consulting your libel lawyers, because I am sure McShane will institute suit if he ever gets wind of what is going on." He turned to Hoff. "Do you agree, Bob?"

"Absolutely."

So there it was, all at once spelled out before us; the threat, now that the seduction had failed. I felt a quick dig of disappointment, which was rapidly replaced by a white-hot anger. I should have known what was coming; you just can't be a political writer and an investigative newspaperman in New York City for more than twenty years without developing a second sight about the way these people operate. The moment Murphy touched off the fuse with that attaché-case tape recorder, I should have heard the gears spinning in Flaherty's nimble brain, and guessed that he had us flanked before we even moved out to attack. Flaherty didn't come to this meeting without being sure that no matter what, perjury, contempt, or what have you, Bernie would never talk. Somebody got to him, as only the underworld can in jail, and the fear instilled in this already frightened man must be terrifying by now.

Julian was plainly outraged. Whether because of Flaherty's cheap seduction attempt or his blunt threats, it was impossible to say.

"What I have heard here, Mr. Flaherty, is an outrageous performance on your part," he said in a voice that trembled slightly but was still under control. "I spent most of last night and the night before going over the transcripts Mr. Malloy obtained and the reports he submitted with a classmate of mine who is one of the foremost criminal lawyers in the country." He held up a hand and said sharply, "Never mind his name—it's not important. His conclusions are that we have an unmistakable basis for an intensive investigation of the higher echelon of the Police Department, of Mr. Strasser's conduct, and certainly an opportunity to thoroughly investigate Mr. McShane, his bank accounts, his associates, his business dealings, and to place these findings before a Grand Jury and let the chips fall where they may! I might also add that this man who was formerly connected with the government as a special prosecutor feels that on the basis of the police work done in this case you have an excellent felony indictment, namely, contriving a lottery!"

Flaherty said with what seemed a genuine curiosity, "What made you go to this man?"

"I wanted assurance."

"In other words you didn't have faith in your own stand . . . you weren't even sure yourself you were right."

"You are correct in using the past tense," Julian said in a tight voice. "I might have needed bolstering up, but, by God, I don't need that now."

Flaherty smiled slightly. "I hope you will come around to our way of thinking."

"I don't think so, Mr. Flaherty, I don't think so."

He stood up and I joined him. "By the way," he said, "if the wire services announce tonight the sudden and unexpected resignation of Mr.

De Lorenzo, I will print a front-page editorial tomorrow denouncing you. Is that clear?"

For a long moment they eyed each other.

"I think we understand each other, Mr. Savage," Flaherty said in a curiously soft voice.

Before the door closed, Johnny and I looked at each other.

It seemed only a few short weeks ago that Johnny De Lorenzo had appeared to me to be a little boy. . . .

We received the call from Johnny later in the day. He sounded weary and puzzled.

"We played it for him, but Bernie just shook his head. All he said was, 'So indict me for perjury. I tell you right now I lied. I was hoping to make a deal.' "

"Is he frightened, Johnny?"

A groan came over the phone. "The poor guy kept asking Inspector Murphy to get him a glass of water. He was trembling so much it spilled every time he lifted the glass."

"Where do we go from here?"

"I'm going home tonight with these transcripts and make up a complete list of witnesses."

"Did Flaherty give you a hard time, Johnny?"

"Hoff started in on me, but Flaherty told him to shut up. He won't kick me out—yet. He'll wait until the dust settles." He paused. "Then he'll cut my throat as quietly as possible."

When I had repeated what Johnny had said, Julian nodded grimly. "Flaherty will do his best to get rid of Johnny. There's no doubt he will start the moment he sees we are losing interest. So that's one reason why I want us to keep hammering away."

Suddenly he got to his feet, but as I started to rise he motioned me back.

"No. Stay there. Please. I'll only be a minute. I'll be right back." He went swiftly into the small bathroom that adjoined his office, closing the door behind him, and I wondered if he was ill. Yet in a way, it was only what I had expected. I know that his illness must be only one of his troubles. Who knows what took place those late hours in that large and dreary Park Avenue apartment where he lived with old man Dolbar? And so I sat there and waited for him to come out. I tried to stifle the uneasy thoughts running through my mind, but all I could see was the image of Julian Savage, eager, confident, so full of hope and dreams, and now looking so—how I hated to even say the word—pathetic.

Finally he came out and walked quickly to the chair. I had the feel-

ing he reached for it, as though he couldn't wait to get to it. He sat down
with a sigh.

"Anything I can do?" I said anxiously.

"No. It's nothing. When I get tense my stomach acts up. . . ."

"You shouldn't let him upset you like that."

"Who? The old man? I can't help it. With him there's no fight. He
lets you get mad."

"Are the boys on his back?"

"He says they all are, from the Hall to Jack Cummings. It just so
happens that Cummings's father-in-law was slated for the Park Commission Board. Just a dollar-a-year, but the bluebloods love it. Well,
they're holding up the appointment—I imagine you know why."

"They put the pressure on Cummings, the big advertiser, and he in
turn puts it on you."

He said wearily: "It's so simple it's sickening. Well, I shouldn't
be crying on your shoulder. Let's forget it, Duke."

I listened in silence; there wasn't much to say. But for the first
time I had detected a quaver in his voice.

The Commuters' Edition had started, and the huge, ancient presses
were sending tremors through the building when I left for dinner. As
always, the street was blocked with our double-parked trucks standing
in line, waiting to be filled and to roar away with thousands of copies of
the paper for the ferry houses, the train terminals, the Port Authority
Bus Terminal, the stands in the financial district. Within the hour commuters would settle down in luxurious pullmans, club cars, crowded
buses, to open their paper and for the next hour grumble silently at
Washington's new tax setup, eagerly read the latest details of the Broadway star's spicy divorce suit—they'll later say that no newspaper should
print such filth—read the first two paragraphs of the President's speech
at the UN and skip the rest; race through the gossip columns, ignore the
book reviewer's selection of the big biography of an obscure Edwardian
poet, feel smug at the half page of pictures showing the city's traffic
jams, smile at a favorite comic strip, read the financial columns line by
line, and eagerly scan the closing prices on the New York big board. In
between all this they will have digested chunks of news from as far as
Hong Kong and as near as the next street. Some will remain with them;
a good part will have made no impression.

It was this man whose battle we were fighting; this was the man
Flaherty feared. . . .

As often as it occurs, this is a special moment for me, one that de-
fies routine; this moment when I walk through the grimy lobby of the

Blade-Leader and reach the open air with the sullen rumbling of the presses coming at me through the walls of the building. In daylight the building is dirty; the walls are cracked, the revolving doors sadly in need of paint. But at night it's quite different, and not merely in the sense that the darkness hides antiquity, dirt, physical neglect. Rather, the night brings a strange dignity to the place: the floors ablaze with lights, the hurried coming and going, the sense of urgency, the trucks, tailboard to tailboard, growling impatiently. Here the urgency of the night seems to have quite a different atmosphere from the shabby apathy of the day; now one feels it.

This night I was uneasy as I stepped out into the dark. I guess I had been avoiding the fact: Julian Savage was a sick man. I was in no mood to go home and face the loneliness of another night. I thought of calling Johnny but decided it would be unwise. For one swift moment Gwen's name hung in my mind, then passed. That issue couldn't be decided by an emotional phone call. I stopped for a few minutes on the corner of Broadway, watching the homegoing crowds and studying the darkened windows of what had once been the offices of the gallant New York *Sun*. Why had it died . . . more importantly, why had New York let it die?

Tonight I wanted to walk. At Centre Street I studied Foley Square where Justice was sleeping, then moved downtown. Tonight I walked more than usual, lower Broadway, Wall Street, the Battery, then back up Broadway. I couldn't lose the worn, tired face of Julian Savage or the scene in Flaherty's office. As I came abreast of Greeley's statue, I recalled the night Julian Savage and I had walked through the park after leaving Flaherty's Christmas party. How long ago that now seemed!

The press run was off when I returned to my desk. I was just staring at my typewriter, my mind a million miles away, when a copyboy tossed a letter on my desk.

"One of your fans called you, Duke. The city desk had a rewrite-man take the information."

"Did he leave any name?"

The boy grinned. "It wasn't a he—it was a she. She told the re-writeman she was just an Anonymous Friend. He also said to tell you she sounded like she had a lot of class and knew what she was talking about."

Anonymous friends calling me with tips and inside information was routine; disgruntled city workers, petty politicians envious of some-one else's success, angry girlfriends, even the honest municipal employee who will go so far but not far enough to divulge a name—all have either written or called in. When I'm out, the city desk usually has a rewrite-man take down the information and leave it for me.

The memo was on copy paper, and only a few paragraphs. It had to do with a housing project downtown, one of those enormous plans running into millions that will reshape the face of the city. I was so tired, so brain-weary, the words were almost a blur. I ran through it quickly, even impatiently. Something about a company called Three Harbors Dredging and an upstate senator who had accepted an enormous loan. A tiny bell rang in my memory; the senator was chairman of an important Congressional committee that might have some say in approving the Federal funds for the project. If true, this could cause a national scandal.

The last line of the memo read:

"Tell Mr. Malloy there is a tremendous payoff in this."

It looked very promising. I slid the memo in my desk. But it would have to wait until after McShane. . . .

I slipped on my coat and headed home at last, so exhausted I fell asleep in the cab.

BOOK FIVE

THE PIGEON WITH
THE BROKEN NECK

[20]

SOME DAYS REMAIN with a man. A taste, a wisp of perfume, a falling leaf, a scent of woodsmoke can suddenly re-create a day in such vivid detail it stands out like a pleading sapling against a winter sky.

This day will always be associated with the sweet smell of cinnamon.

It began with a screech of tires that jerked me out of a sound sleep. I stumbled out of bed and looked out the window to see a cabdriver and a motorist arguing loudly. I had just settled between the covers when the phone rang. All my adult life it seems that phones have been ringing for me in the dead of night; again and again I have said the hell with it, but I just can't let them ring—I know that will gnaw at me until daybreak.

And so I reached over.

"Is this the Malloy residence?"

The cautious, young official voice brought me up with a start. I swung out of bed.

"Yes it is. Who is this?"

"Patrolman Winters of Old Slip Precinct. Is this Mr. Malloy?"

"Yes it is. What's wrong?"

The voice moved closer to the receiver. "Do you know a Mr. Jackson, Mr. Malloy?"

"Yes, I do. What's wrong?"

The young voice hesitated.

"Well, Mr. Jackson had an accident, and I think you better get down here. He's—"

"Wait a minute!" I shouted. "This is Duke Malloy, a reporter on the *Blade-Leader!* Is that man badly hurt!"

It must have shook him up. This wasn't the usual anxious father or the stunned relative.

"Well, yes, Mr. Malloy. I would say he's hurt pretty badly."

"Look, Winters," I said slowly, "is he dead?"

"Well, no, but very near—"

"I haven't time to talk. This man is a Grand Jury witness. Is there an ambulance there?"

"Beekman Street, just came up."

"Where are you?"

"Fulton and Stone Slip—right outside the Clifford Meat Company—"

"Please tell that doctor to do everything he can, will you, Winters?"

Things were now falling into the traditional routine. "Sure, we'll do everything that can be done."

I hung up on the solicitous voice, fumbled for Johnny's phone number, and dialed. It rang a few times, then a low, sleepy voice asked who was calling.

"Johnny, this is Duke. I just received a phone call from a patrolman at Fulton and Stone Slip. They got our informant!"

Johnny's voice was suddenly brisk and clear. "You're talking about the man on the tapes?"

"Right. His name is Jackson. He's a gambler and has been in the Gennaro setup for years."

"Give me the rest later. Where's your car?"

"In a garage on East—"

"Forget it. You may have trouble getting a cab. What's your address?"

I gave it, and he told me to wait on the corner of Lexington and Thirty-eighth Street.

I was slipping into my overcoat when, almost as a reflex action, I dialed the office and ordered the city desk to assign a photographer. I hung up and paused in the darkness for a moment, recalling the old chestnut of the two Hollywood producers who were in the thick of an argument when one suddenly rolled over with an apparent heart attack. The other was dialing the doctor when the news came on, announcing the nominees for the Academy Awards. The producer put down the phone, and, ignoring the stricken man, turned up the volume. It was a grim joke of what comes first in Hollywood. . . . But what comes first with me. Good God, would I have been measuring the groans at the Crucifixion?

Outside it was snowing, a wet, silent snow of wafer-big flakes that vanished as soon as they touched the street. Under the lights, asphalt gleamed like a dark, glistening river. A sleek Cadillac passed with an arrogant hiss of snow tires. I huddled in a doorway, watching the big flakes fall and feeling dull and empty inside.

An unmarked car from Homicide East on night standby for the D.A.'s office swung into the curb. The driver had a small plum of a nose, and in silent rage cut off a bakery truck. He was a skillful driver, who apparently had made a life study of how to beat lights, of sliding malevolently up to the red, then gleefully taking off at the green without touching his brakes.

We picked up Johnny, who was stamping impatiently in the doorway of old Jefferson Market Court. He slumped back into the seat, both hands still in his pockets.

"Keep it low," he said softly. "Who is he?"

"Action Jackson. He's been a gambler for years. After the war he organized the West Side for Gennaro."

"Why did he blow the whistle?"

"Gennaro's ribbon-car driver—a pimp named Frank the Sheik—tried to force Jackson's niece into prostitution. When she refused, he beat her. She died in Harlem Hospital."

"Did you check that?"

"I have the Medical Examiner's report. It was a ruptured spleen."

"Who called you, Duke?"

"A cop named Winters."

"Is Jackson still alive?"

"The cop said he didn't think he would last long."

"Who besides you knew you were working with Jackson?"

"The publisher and two other executives."

"No cops. Inspector Murphy?"

"No one else."

"Were you up in Harlem with Jackson?"

"He showed me everything."

"Are you sure no one made you up there?"

"I'm positive."

He said slowly, "You realize now, Duke, the wraps are off."

"I don't think it matters any more, Johnny."

He sighed deeply. "I wish I had been able to talk to him. I don't have to tell you what it would have meant to you—and to me."

"I asked him, Johnny. He said no—" The car spun on two wheels into East River Drive from Houston Street, and I almost slid onto the floor.

"Hey, Louie, let's get there in one piece," Johnny cried.

Plum Nose looked up into the overhead mirror and gave us a triumphant grin. He had frightened us; his day was full.

We raced down the Drive. The only sound was the measured creaking of the wipers. On our left a tug hugged the shore as she laboriously beat her way downstream.

We smelled Fulton Fish Market before we saw it; then suddenly we were in a bedlam of shouting, cursing, laughing men, of barrels rim-ful of cracked ice and fish, entrails and prowling cats, bonfires in ash cans, men in hip boots who bent over tubs and emerged with arm-fuls of pinkish, rubbery octopi. Then it was behind us and we were moving through a black tunnel under the elevated highway. Near the Battery we swung right into a wide street or slip.

"Christ, looka those lights," the driver cried.

Two spotlights from emergency trucks were focused on a building. For a moment a wild thought ran through my head that there had been a chase through a dark building and a gun battle. As we drew nearer the scene became clearer. Radio cars with red lights flashing were parked haphazardly about a stone building with iron shutters staring into the hard white lights like ancient, hooded eyes. On the Fulton Street side of the building was a long shed. Several figures in raincoats were gathered in a knot at one end. A man in white pants under a raincoat ran in and out of an ambulance.

Several ladders leaned against the shed. Firemen ran along the roof, leaned over its edge, then raced back to the street. As we approached, a cop in a glistening raincoat stopped us.

"D.A.'s office," Louie snarled.

When Johnny rolled down the window, a weather-beaten face peered in.

"Do you have Mr. Malloy?"

"I'm Malloy," I said. "What—"

"You a relative, Mr. Malloy?"

"No. Just a friend."

The cop looked uneasy. "It's pretty awful . . ."

"Did you talk to him, Officer?" Johnny said.

"No, sir. He was too far gone when I got here. A watchman found him. He climbed up on a box and tried to help him. The man just kept whispering 'Malloy—Malloy.' The sergeant said to call all the Malloys in the book. I tried five before I got this gentleman."

"How did you know the other man's name is Jackson?"

"The sergeant found a plane ticket with that name."

"Okay, Winters." Johnny swung open the door. "Let's go, Duke."

The damp air was heavy with the smell of herbs and spices brought here by clippers when bowsprits towered over the East River docks. I took a deep breath and tasted the cinnamon. Wooden crates and broken barrels were stacked on the sidewalks, along with small iron-rimmed

wagons chained together by their distrusting owners. About a foot below the roof was a long line of ugly meat hooks. Faded yellow lettering
on one side of the building said CLIFFORD WHOLESALE MEAT COM-
PANY. A monotonous, incongruous noise pierced the heavy wet stillness.
Johnny said it sounded as if someone was filing through a safe. As we
approached, the circle of glistening raincoats slowly parted, and I
looked up at a scene I shall never forget.

They say Jackson was still alive. I don't see how. He had been
beaten until he was unrecognizable. One eye had been torn out; his
mouth was a bloody gash, his face a swollen, purplish mask. Both arms
and a hip had been broken from being run over with a car. He was
dressed in a pair of pants and a torn shirt. He had been shot three times,
but it was the beating that had done the real damage. He had been
clubbed almost methodically, police later said, probably with a baseball
bat. Hanging from around his neck was something that looked like a
dark rag. Directly below his body a broken box was stained red by the
dripping blood.

Most horrible of all, he had been impaled on one of the hooks like
a slab of beef.

Two firemen on the roof of the shed had a hawser taut under his
buttocks, pulling the body upward, while on a pyramid of boxes another fireman frantically sawed at the heavy hook.

An intern perched on a ladder pressed a hypodermic into Jackson's arm.

"My God," Johnny whispered in a voice filled with horror. "My
dear God!"

Then he hurried forward and ran up the ladder. He said something
to the intern, who moved to one side, and Johnny bent toward the battered, bloody face. It looked as if he was whispering in Jackson's ear.
The intern reached over him and carefully explored Jackson's chest
with a stethoscope. Then he took it away, shoved it into his jacket
pocket, and looked down into the wet, staring faces. He shrugged
slightly and slowly descended. I saw Johnny remove the thing I thought
was a rag from around Jackson's neck. Then he too came down.

"What do you say, Doc?" one of the cops said.

"He's dead," the intern said. "I don't know how he lasted this
long."

Then Johnny came up. "He's dead, Duke."

"I know. Did he say anything?"

"I tried to get a dying declaration," he said. "But I was too late."

He held out what I had thought was a piece of rag.

It was a dead pigeon with a broken neck.

Johnny talked to me; we both talked to the young cop, Winters, and the sergeant in charge of the Emergency Squad. We stood there a long time; I can dimly recall the flashing bulbs of the photographers and talking to my city desk. I don't remember feeling pain, shock, or anything at all. And to this day I don't recall watching them break off that ugly, ghastly hook, lowering the body to the stretcher and the trip with Johnny to Beekman-Downtown where someone gave me a phone and I was talking to Julian Savage. Then I went home. What happened afterward I remember perfectly. But there is a gap in my life—a gap of perhaps an hour, a gap in which my mind and memory came to a halt and my instinct took over, a gap that actually began when Johnny whispered that awful, chilling prayer: My God, My dear God . . .

Later, Inspector Murphy told me what had happened.

"The old Italian lady who runs the place where he boarded said Jackson had informed her he was leaving in a few days. He paid his rent and gave her a set of copper pots as a good-bye present. Apparently the old lady really liked him."

"He was a likable guy, Inspector. . . ."

He looked at me curiously, then went on. "The old lady said she was waiting for him to come in and say good-bye, but he never showed. She said she even had a bottle of wine for a toast. After a while she said she opened his door with her key and saw his bags in the corner. This didn't bother her; she was used to Jackson coming and going. She said she never left the house. After I called her she looked again in the room just to make sure; the bags were still there."

"We checked the neighborhood, and got the usual; nobody saw a thing. I had a couple of stoolies working on it, but they got nothing. One called me back after a few hours and said he wouldn't touch it with a ten-foot pole. I think the word is out. . . ."

"That it was ordered?"

"No doubt. Gennaro. Somehow he got wind of what Jackson was doing." He gave me an intent look. "Are you sure you weren't made up there?"

"Positive. Jackson would have been the first to sense it. If he missed, Tilley would have asked questions."

"Tilley, a Negro about five foot six, weighing about one eighty? Sort of assistant to Jackson at his drop?"

"Jackson trusted him—and he didn't trust many people. How do you know about Tilley?"

"We grabbed everyone in that drop."

"Tilley?"

"We found him at his apartment. He told us nothing."

"What about Johnny?"

"I hear he's having a hard time." He cleared his throat. "The commissioner called me in this morning. It seems the District Attorney complained about my recorder. I pointed out to the commissioner the section of the Department Rules that covers such a situation. I assured him the department was correct."

"I'm sure you did," I said dryly. "How about the department—will it stand behind you?"

"City Hall was on the phone this morning. The commissioner told him I was under his orders to continue my investigation. He also offered to send over his resignation." He added musingly, "I guess when you reach our age the job isn't that important. Well, I'm going to the funeral parlor. Want a lift?"

And so Tom Murphy and I went to the bleak, dingy parlor near Bellevue where they had Action Jackson. The coffin was closed, an American flag draped across it. I had made sure of that with a call to the Veterans Administration. Jackson would be buried in the National Military Cemetery on Long Island where they didn't care about police records.

I was surprised at the bank of flowers. They gave dignity to the barren room.

Johnny and a plain-looking woman in her forties who spoke with a Midwestern accent were sitting on the folding chairs when we arrived. She looked toil-worn and bewildered. Before Johnny introduced me, I knew who she was, Jo, Jackson's sister. We sat in silence until the minister and the honor guard supplied by the Veterans arrived. After a brief service we drove out to the cemetery. The grave was on a slight rise; the frozen ground, hard as iron, was piled in chunks. Two elderly gravediggers stood off to one side muttering to themselves. The coffin was lowered, the minister said a few words, and the rifles cracked.

And so I said good-bye to Action Jackson.

Inspector Murphy offered to take Jackson's sister to the airport— she was leaving on the afternoon plane—and Johnny offered to drive me back.

"She's a nice woman," he said. "While we were waiting she told me about Jackson. She called him a wild young scamp. I haven't heard that expression in years. Jackson a wild young scamp." He stared out the window. "She said he was planning to go back."

"So he told me."

"He would never have made it," Johnny said. "They would have found him. They always do."

"He said he was willing to take a chance."

"He had moxie, lots of it."

"What are the chances of breaking it, Johnny?"

"We'll never know unless we get a squeal."

"Murphy said he had a couple of stoolies on it but they wanted out. Too risky."

He started up the car. "There's no doubt Gennaro ordered it. Maybe McShane, for all we know. By the way, I told Flaherty I was continuing my investigation."

"Oh? What did he say?"

"He just wished me luck. Then he thanked me for sending him an invitation to my engagement party—"

"He is coming?"

"Oh, sure. There's no open warfare in the office. He's gone out of his way to keep things on an even keel. I even think he's told Bob Hoff to lay off."

"There's only one thing that keeps me awake these nights, Johnny."

"What's that, Duke?"

"That Gennaro might beat it and we'll never get McShane."

He stared out at the passing landscape, the winter-ravaged grass, the endless rows of crosses and marble slabs.

"All I can promise, Duke, is to do everything short of perjury to get that bastard and his partner McShane." He gave a short, harsh laugh. "Frankly, I don't know how the hell we can do it with my office. So start praying for a miracle."

We stopped at the cemetery gates to let a funeral pass. Looking back to the rise, I could see the two gravediggers shoveling the dirt back into the grave. They seemed to be in a hurry. I guess they were cold.

The day hadn't ended yet; there was more. About nine that night the downstairs bell sounded, so loud, so unexpectedly I jumped. I touched the button, and waited. I heard the cautious steps, then the buzzer. I opened the door. It was Tilley. He was wearing a battered old fedora and looked twice his size in an old Air Force jacket. He was carrying a small package in brown wrapping paper. For a moment we just stared at each other; then he smiled.

"Hiya, Duke." He walked in, took off his hat, and looked about in open admiration.

"Man, quite a pad."

"Take off your jacket. Want a drink?"

I went to the refrigerator and came back with a quart of milk and put it next to the Scotch decanter.

"You a numbers man?" Tilley said chuckling.

"Just as good as Tarcey's," I said, mixing the drinks.

We silently touched glasses. "I didn't see you at the funeral parlor."

"I went down before it was open," he said. "The only one who had balls enough to go with me was the guy from 145th Street. Remember him?"

"The one who makes love to Jack Daniels?"

"The same. We gave the undertaker a pound and he let us in."

"I saw the flowers."

"We hit everyone on the Avenue. I only used a few bucks for the flowers. The rest was dropped off at his sister's hotel. About five hundred. We left word it was insurance." He tested the whiskey, rolled it around in his mouth, and swallowed.

"Jackson told me he was going to tell you everything before the raids," I said.

"He did. I cursed him out for a stoolie, but then I saw it his way. I knew he had to burn Frank the Sheik and the Wop some way. He just had to."

Curious, I asked why. "The girl wasn't much. Even Action said that."

He gave me a startled look. "Man, you don't kill a jerky kid because she ain't gonna hustle for you! She's got a right—even a jerky kid up in Harlem." He added in a bitter voice, "And no curly-haired pimp or wop numbers boss is gonna take that right away."

I quickly changed the subject. "I guess you wondered what I was doing up in Harlem, Tilley."

The hat stopped moving between the big black hands. "Yeah. Why you come to Harlem? Why you mess with numbers?"

"It's my job."

"What's a newspaper care about numbers?"

"Not numbers. But the people who are protecting it, making money out of it."

"Yeah. Yeah. But you put some guys out of work." He shook his head. "Whitey's newspapers get nosy, and a lot of guys are sittin' on stoops, just lookin'."

"Jackson said you would take over."

"Won't be me, will be somebody else." He juggled the worn hat. "Look, man. You don't have me on those tapes you write about in the newspaper?"

"We were not interested in the guys in the drop, Tilley. Just the crooked cops and politicians."

"Can't move on the Avenue these days," Tilley said bitterly. "You give the cops a look, and they'll go up beside your head before you can say anything."

"Just for nothing!"

He gave me a faint smile. "Man, that ain't unusual. But now it's worse. They're scared. Even the member cops. They go up beside your head in a minute. 'Take this nigger,' they say. Then goes the billy. Bang. Bang. Then you find yourself in Harlem Hospital with the nurse wrappin' up your head."

I poured him another drink, and waited.

"Who did it, Tilley?"

He stared down at the glass for a moment, then looked up.

"The Wop. He got a couple of guys from the East Side. They made the hit."

"Who tipped him? It's personally important to me."

He shook his head. "Man, nobody made you. We really thought you was from Jersey goin' over there with Jackson's backin'. It looked right to me. He was always talkin' about how easy it was to move over there if you had connections."

"Well, then, who tipped Gennaro?"

The stained brown hat slowly revolved between the big dark hands.

"Remember the Dummy?"

"The humpback in the bar?"

"He tipped off Frank the Shiek."

"But what—how could the Dummy possibly know about Jackson?"

"The little son of a bitch told the Sheik he saw Jackson with a little iron box in a phone booth," Tilley said roughly. "He said he was emptyin' garbage when he saw him takin' a wire from the receiver that was attached to the box."

And I remembered Jackson telling me in this very room how he had caught a flash of the Dummy's plaid shirt just as the back door to the alley closed.

"After the raids the East Side went crazy," Tilley went on. "Guys were worked over but nobody knew anything, so they couldn't say anything. The Wop was offering all kinds of dough for someone to name the fingerman. Jackson even told the East Side he was pulling all kinds of wires downtown to find out what they had, but the Wop told him to forget it, he was doing his own wire pulling with Peters." The big hand crumpled the hat. "That phony bum!

"The way I figger it, the Dummy tipped the ribbon car and the Sheik told the Wop. At first it didn't mean anything. Then the Wop found out, from Peters or someone, that the D.A. had wire recordings of his telephone calls. Then they remembered what the Dummy said. As I heard it, the East Side put a tail on Jackson. They followed him

to the East Side Terminal and found out he bought a ticket to Missouri."
He looked up. "One way. That was bad. Then they got into his room."

"The old landlady said she never left the house."

"That's true—except for an hour every afternoon when she goes
down the block to the Italian grocery store and drinks coffee with the
old woman who makes the ravioli. You can set your watch by her trip.
A couple of guys got in and found Jackson's bags packed. That did it.
The word on the Avenue is, they grabbed him the night he was supposed to leave. . . ."

We both sat there, the tick of the clock loud in the silence. I think
Tilley was not only shattered but also embarrassed and not a little
curious: Who was I? Why had I been there to snoop in his world? And
I for my part knew I could never offer a satisfactory explanation.

He was slightly hunched over in his chair, looking down intently
at his worn hat. Then the question came, hard and blunt.

"You see it?"

"Yes. It was awful."

"The guys on the Avenue said they worked him over with a couple of baseball bats."

I told him about the butcher's hook. The felt crumpled inside his
big fists.

"The bastards. The no-good lousy bastards!"

"I've been sitting here thinking maybe it's my fault."

"Why you? Jackson was around a long time. He knew better'n
you what happens when you buck the East Side. You hurt their dough,
they kill you."

"You know why he came to me?"

"Sure. The Wop. You did just what he wanted. Bust the Wop and
put him in stir."

"But we didn't count on the Prophet."

He shrugged. "If it wasn't the Prophet it would have been something else. Like I told you, Harlem's ready to blow—Prophet or no
Prophet." The black hands smashed together. "Bang. Like that."

I changed the subject.

"How's your wife?"

"Fine. Oh, fine. You single-O?"

"So far. How are the kids?"

"Ain't easy to bring up kids in Harlem. Man, you know how many
pushers there are on my block? I hate those cats. Man, how I hate 'em!
I see a lot of kids up there hooked. If it's not horse, it's wine. The kid
downstairs, he was on tea and wine. Last week he thought he was a bird.
Only, he ain't got wings. Man, he hit that sidewalk!"

"You going to stay in numbers, Tilley?"

He gave me a sincerely startled look. "Remember when I told you Whitey has us in a big black cage? Well, in that cage, man, there just ain't no jobs. You come downtown and Whitey gives you a dishrag or a mop. Maybe a pick. Maybe a monkey suit. But no money. So when you live up in that cage for a while, you get to know the only money you can make is in numbers or pushing junk. Or makin' a heist. Or runnin' an after-hours place. Man, I hate junk and pushers. I'm scared of guns. And maybe I would drink up the profits in an after-hours joint. So it's numbers for me. Whitey ain't gonna give me a break, so I stay in numbers. I get two C's a week. I give the wife a little each week. Maybe we can send our kids to a good school. I know a guy who's a lawyer. His old man runs a numbers joint. How the hell do you think his kid stayed in college?" He shook his head. "Yessir. When you live in that cage you only got numbers, junk, and after-hours joints. Or else you take Whitey's shovel, dishrag, and monkey suit. Me, I like numbers. It's been good to me and a lot of other guys on the Avenue."

"Jackson said he thought you were going to take over."

"What take over? It never stopped. Nobody can keep policy out of Harlem. We were back pickin' up the day after the hits. Not as big, but it was goin'. . ." He tossed off what remained in the glass, and stood up. "Jackson made me promise I'd get his stuff to you. As I see it, I kept my promise."

He paused at the door, gave the room a last admiring look, then with a curt nod went out. From the window I watched him cross the street, a powerfully built black man in a faded bomber jacket who kept his head down to buck the wind. He turned the corner, and disappeared.

The package came next. For a moment I weighed it in my hand wonderingly, then opened the heavy brown paper. There was a thick white envelope with my name. Inside was a sheaf of ordinary looseleaf paper held together by three paper clips. Attached to it was a brief note written in ink. It read:

DUKE:

I got to thinking about what you said on the phone about evidence to clinch Gennaro. Maybe you're right, about having some insurance on the bum. I wrote out everything I know about him and the cops and the payoffs. Including the ones I made for him. To be on the safe side, I took a bus across the bridge to Jersey and had it notarized. Tell De Lorenzo he can grab Ricky Strasser by the stuff he has in a vault at the Gramercy Chartered Bank, Uptown Branch, 78th Street and Broadway, under the name of Richard Dove. I give you this but I know you will never call on me unless it's only me that can turn the key on the Wop. Otherwise, forget it.

I'll be shoving off in a few days. I will call you when I get to the land of cotton.

Good Luck,

J.

I recall how surprised I was at the handwriting. It was neat and clear, like a product of the old-fashioned Palmer method. I forced myself to go from word to word and not race along the pages to keep up with my growing excitement. There were more than fifty, with a neat blue notary's stamp on the last page.

There were names, dates, payoffs, orders from Gennaro, Strasser, and Bernie; Bernie's bank where he and his girl friend had a safety deposit box, his unlisted home phone number, the East Side restaurant where they met every night, the nickname and description of Bernie's favorite cabdriver who drove him to the Westchester and Jersey policy banks to check their books; the Eighth Avenue pawnshop where Strasser's girl usually pawned her mink when she went to Miami; pages of payoffs to Peters and others, including a financial rundown on how the syndicate bought protection. There was an account of how Jackson, on Gennaro's orders, had visited Magistrate Lou Janus with an envelope containing five thousand dollars one Christmas Eve. Jackson shrewdly and vividly gave an intimate description of the Janus living room and study, including a small, expensive table lighter which Janus boasted was a Tiffany Christmas present from McShane, as was the five thousand.

It was a shocking eyewitness document of official corruption.

But that wasn't all.

There was a second package, roughly five by seven and tied with heavy cord. Before I had ripped the paper away, I knew what it was.

Jackson had not forgotten. The photograph was clear and distinct; it showed Big Jim McShane, Vito Gennaro, Magistrate Lou Janus, and several other city politicians seated at a small table. The photographer had wanted to please Gennaro: he had snapped the picture just as McShane placed his arm around Gennaro's shoulder and was whispering in his ear.

The kingmaker of New York's politics. The man who would do most to elect the next President of the United States. The vigilant protector of our morals.

And the gangster.

I dialed twice before I got the right number, and when I finally heard Johnny's voice I had to force myself not to shout. I will never know how I said very calmly his miracle had just arrived—neatly wrapped in brown wrapping paper.

[21]

BERNIE TALKED. At first it was only a few grudging admissions, and reluctant confirmations of last names and policemen; then with a gush came the whole story. Once he started he never faltered. As Johnny said later, Bernie talked through breakfast, lunch, dinner, and past supper. It took three stenographers, including Tom Murphy's confidential secretary, to record it all.

Ironically, it was not Jackson's statement that forced Bernie to talk. Johnny had read it to him, and he just shrugged. But what Johnny had not told him was that his girl friend, Stella Schwartz, the bail-bond woman, had been quietly taken into custody on evidence Tom Murphy and his men had uncovered after researching through hundreds of bail bonds Stella had written for members of Gennaro's policy syndicate. Miss Schwartz, as Tom Murphy said, had been just too greedy; she had forged the names of defendants, some fictitious, some so ignorant they couldn't sign their names, and had violated almost every statute of the state banking law in her issuance of bail bonds. In addition, Murphy had followed Jackson's tip and found Bernie's and Stella's safety deposit vault. There was more than one hundred thousand dollars in cash, stocks, and bonds.

Stella, a middle-aged, brassy blonde, automatically denied everything until they produced the evidence: Jackson's recorded conversation with Bernie; a breakdown of the forged bonds and a listing of both state and county bail-bond violations. Stella listened to it all, then asked for her lawyer. At 2:00 A.M. she signed a full confession and agreed to become a state's witness.

Bernie was brought out of the Tombs to the D.A.'s office where he met Johnny. As Tom Murphy said, Johnny De Lorenzo by now had the bit in his teeth. He no longer pleaded, cajoled, promised—he shouted, snarled, demanded, threatened. At one point he had Bernie in tears when he picked up a phone—it was dead—and told a detective to stand by and be ready to bring in Bernie's wife. He was a confused, frightened man when they finally brought in Stella.

As Tom said, "She didn't waste any time. She told him not to be a schlemiel and take the rap. The D.A. had found out everything, and if he thought she was going to spend five years in the pen he was crazy."

That did it. Bernie started to talk.

When I saw Johnny the next day at his house, he seemed older, grim.

"Did Tom give you a rundown on Bernie?"

"He gave me the highlights. From what he said we're on our way."

He shook his head. "There's no doubt we have a big police scandal. But believe it or not, I have to agree with Flaherty—"

I was stunned. "You mean—turn it all over to the department for action?"

"I spent most of the night going over reports on police corruption in the 1938 Amen investigation."

"I recall the *Times* had a magazine piece on it, but it was before my time."

"Frankly, mine too. The gist of it is, Amen, who was a terrific prosecutor—he was Jackson's assistant at Nuremberg—turned up one of the biggest police scandals in New York's history. He even made movies of cops on the take. But after doing an analysis of the results of official bribery trials he turned over everything to the department. They had an honest commissioner who threw the books at the cops. Most of them got kicked out."

"But, Johnny—what about Jackson's statement?"

"It's a good statement, Duke," he said, "but not good enough."

"Why?" I demanded. "He names names. It's notarized—even out of the state. It's in his own handwriting. His landlady has the rent book. She saw him sign it. Any handwriting expert can compare—"

"I know, Duke," he said wearily. "I know. It's not that. Do you remember when you drove up and I was on the ladder—"

"You mean down at the slip? When Jackson . . ."

"That's right. That's right. I told you I was trying for a dying declaration. I knew I had to get it. It was the only thing."

"But this statement is in his own words, Johnny! Christ, the guy wrote it knowing that they might knock him off!"

"I realize all that, Duke. But in the eyes of the law it's all one-sided. This statement can't be cross-examined. The law says you must cross-examine all sides—not only one. The people must show motivation for their witnesses, why they testify. Jackson had an ax to grind. His motive was clearly revenge. Therefore everything he wrote is questionable. Look, Duke, I didn't write the law. But there it is."

I felt something draining out of me, leaving everything inside cold and empty.

"And the tapes?"

"I went over and over and over them, Duke. Frankly, I'm afraid of them."

"Why? I can testify I was present when some of them were taken."

"That's not the problem—"

"For Christ's sake, what is the problem?"

He gave me a long, calm look. "Look, Duke, I'm on your side. Take it easy. I know how you feel, but I have to go into a courtroom with this stuff. I want to go in loaded for bear, not rabbit."

"I'm sorry, Johnny. It's just tough to hear this from you—"

He said harshly, "Why don't you lay the facts before some big-time criminal lawyer and get his opinion?"

The look on his face and his tone of voice jarred me back to reality. "I'm sorry, Johnny. I really am sorry. Go ahead."

"Forget it. As I said, the tapes would have been wonderful a few years ago. But not with the high courts changing the law every month or so. I don't think any defense counsel would have much trouble getting a judge to throw the tape out as evidence. In fact," he said, "I think we would have a time getting them introduced as evidence."

"But on what grounds?"

"Invasion of civil rights," he said promptly. "Just bring in any kind of a tape recorder, and up pops the defense, citing all kinds of decisions. There have been so many even the lawyers are confused."

"Can't they be used at all?"

He grinned. "Play the tapes and get an admission."

I gave him a look of disgust. "All we have to do is play the recordings for Peters or Barrist at headquarters and they'll break down and tell us, yes, they fixed the cops. Is that it?"

"Kid all you like, but those are the facts of life. Since the Mapes decision no judge wants to take a chance on any type of recording."

"Before I first used a recorder I looked up the law," I said. "What about the Lopez decision in that Treasury agent's case. The court said if a tape recorder is used and one of those using it gives his permission, the tapes are within the law and can be introduced as evidence. Right?

"Right. Still no judge wants to take a chance. As evidence the tapes are too risky. Judges today are looking at their batting average. They hate to be reversed. They only want to win."

"So you think the best we can get are departmental trials?"

"Frankly and honestly I do. Let's say we indict them. We have a dead man's statement, a convicted thief as the people's witness, and the tapes—which may not get in. Bribery is damn' hard to prove. Bernie gives names, dates, and places, but he'll make a poor witness. He's frightened to death, for one thing."

"What about his girl?"

"Stella knows only what Bernie told her."

"What about Peters and Barrist?"

"I think I have a good conspiracy case against both of them. I'm sure I can send them away."

"Seriously, is there any chance of them talking?"

"Not a chance. It's ironical—crooked cops and mobsters don't talk."

"And McShane?"

"Duke, I haven't a thing I can present as evidence linking him to Gennaro."

"How about that picture?"

"It's quite a picture for a newspaper. But it's not evidence, Duke."

"One of the biggest political figures in the nation with his arms around a mobster!"

Johnny rubbed his closed eyes. "The picture was taken secretly, at a fund-raising dinner for a church. We checked everyone out who is in that picture. There's a monsignor, a legislator with an unblemished record, and a Papal Knight who spends all his waking hours raising money for churches and orphanages. They're in addition to Janus, McShane, and Gennaro and the other politicians. Sure it's shocking, but these are the facts."

"Didn't Bernie say he overheard Gennaro telling McShane he wanted some policy cases fixed?"

"When I pinned Bernie down, he admitted he couldn't hear the telephone conversation. Gennaro made that crack after he hung up."

"Isn't that something?"

He shook his head. "Bernie would have to pick up the phone and recognize McShane's voice. McShane would then have to ask for Gennaro, and Bernie would have to turn the phone over to Gennaro. Then, under the law, a connection has been made."

"It's incredible that with all the breaks we've gotten there's nothing to link McShane—"

He had walked to the window and was looking out.

"I told you I believe McShane is behind Gennaro. So does Tom Murphy. So does your publisher. So do you. But believing is not evidence. We must present to the Grand Jury cold, unalterable facts that show beyond a reasonable doubt that Jim McShane is receiving financial profit from protecting Gennaro's policy syndicate. And that we don't have."

"What about that thief Janus?"

"I think I can make out a case against him with Jackson's statement and something I dug out of Bernie. He had to deliver some money once in a hurry to Janus's home. He used a ribbon car to get there. Now, in this case we have one of the hoods who drove the car and Jackson's statement."

"Will Janus talk?"

"He might, but it will take a long time. If he's convicted he'll appeal the verdict up to the Supreme Court. If he is sure he's going to jail, he might talk. But I wouldn't build any hopes on that. Janus is an old clubhouse lawyer. He knows the score. And besides, he's almost seventy."

"Certainly the charts I made of that bastard's court performances in policy cases can be used for something."

"It sure can," Johnny agreed. "For the Bar Association's Grievance Committee for one thing. There's no doubt I will get him disbarred, but again the guy's seventy. What does he care?"

"I'm beginning to wonder just whose side the law is on?"

He said soberly, "Our side, Duke, believe me."

"Have you spoken to Flaherty?"

"I went in to see him this morning. Bob Hoff and Webster Pryce were with him. I went over the entire investigation. When I finished he just said, 'What do you want to do, Johnny?' When I said I really hadn't decided but I thought I would turn over the evidence to the department for trial, he just nodded. Hoff started to laugh, but Flaherty shut him up with a look. Then he asked Pryce for his opinion, and Pryce said he agreed with me that if we wanted these men punished we could get much more through department trials than risk jury trials. I flatly told him I was continuing on the McShane angle, and he didn't blink an eye. He told me to keep on it and to let him know if I needed any help. He also reminded me of the agreement I had made with you people to give the *Blade-Leader* the exclusive on any part of the story. He even told me to prepare a summary for Bob Hoff. Then he turned to Hoff and said, 'When the first edition of the *Blade-Leader* comes out, you can release it to all the papers.' "

"He's as smart as a fox. He's going to let you run the course by yourself. He figures you'll come up with nothing."

The phone rang, and he picked up an extension, listened for a moment, then said softly, "I'll take it upstairs, Mom. . . . Yes, please hold for a minute. I'll get you on another phone."

He turned at the door.

"Wait here. . . . I'll be right back."

The big house was strangely silent when he left. I studied the fierce old Italian faces in the ancient gold frames, particularly the one dressed in judge's robes and seated at a desk. There was something familiar about the picture; then I realized what it was; the desk I was sitting at looked like the one in the picture. This, then, was Johnny's famous grandfather who had paid with his life for defying the Mafia before the turn of the century. I was still studying the curiously gentle face when Johnny returned.

"Looking at the judge, Duke?"

"Isn't he the one the Mafia shot in New Orleans?"

"The same. He sent fifteen of them to the pen for murder and forced a Grand Jury investigation. He was a tough old guy. My mother tells a story how he threw one Mafia mobster through a store window. You know the story? They shot him as he was going to church."

"Didn't that stir things up?"

"That's an understatement. A mob lynched the prisoners in jail; the governor sent in troops; and the Grand Jury really cracked down."

"Isn't this the same desk that's in the picture?"

"Yes. When the family moved the produce business to New York, this desk came along. They gave it to me when I graduated from law school."

I suddenly had the feeling that Johnny was suppressing something. He seemed tense and less reflective than before.

"What's up, Johnny?"

He grinned. "Does it show?"

"Well, let's say you wouldn't make a very good gambler. Was it the call?"

"Maybe I'm getting soft in my old age. . . ."

"Something on the case?"

"This morning, just before I got into the office, my secretary received a call from a lawyer named Biglatti. The name won't mean anything to you and for a while it didn't to me. I was walking down the hall when it hit me. Biglatti was the attorney who handled Gennaro's deportation appeal in Washington. He's one of the most respected lawyers in Washington."

"So what? Gennaro probably retained him."

"There's more to it. Biglatti told my secretary he would call me at home this afternoon and I should wait for the call, it was very important."

"And was it important?"

Johnny swung around in the chair and gave me a long, tantalizing smile.

"Biglatti said he wanted to come down and see me—here, not at the office. He said he wanted to discuss what considerations his client could expect if he cooperated—"

"Good God! Gennaro—"

"Hold on. I didn't say that."

"No. But we both know what you mean—"

"Hope is a better word."

"If Gennaro makes a deal—"

Johnny said flatly, "There's no telling where we'll go. The governor would have to act."

"It's hard to believe that an old Don would play informer."

"Not too hard," Johnny said, "if you never forget those grandchildren of his. Vito's crazy about them. We've found out he's established three trust funds for them in an out-of-town bank. Here's a true story that might interest you. It was told to Murphy by one old Don. When Vito's son was seventeen, the kid began cutting military school. The headmaster sent a note to Vito, who made inquiries. He found the kid playing cards in the rear of a candy store where some pushers hung out. Vito caught the kid there and belted him from one end of the store to the other. Then he drove him back to school. The next day the store was closed. The guy who owned it was given the message. The kid stayed in line and graduated with honors. When he was married, Vito sent him and his bride on a honeymoon trip to Europe. When they came home he had a house already built for them in Westchester. He set the kid up in business and gave them everything they needed. When his first grandson was born, Vito acted like it was his own child. The christening was like a summit meeting of the Mafia; every hood in the country sent a gift. The second and the third were just the same. Tom has a file on Vito and so do the Feds. Most of their tails say that's all Vito does on Sunday—take the kids out."

"I guess Jackson had it pegged right; he said Gennaro would die if he knew he couldn't fix the case."

Johnny smiled. "It's not that he didn't try. You would be surprised at the reputable attorneys who approached me. It was suggested that I might be interested in running for District Attorney."

"Are you, Johnny?"

"No. And I'm not interested in the judgeship I was offered two weeks ago."

"You didn't tell me about that one."

He said bluntly, "It wasn't any of your business."

"You might be interested in knowing I once told Savage you possibly could be bought for a magistrate's job."

"Well," he said matter of factly, "I once told you I didn't know how honest I was. I had never been tested."

"I'm curious as to why you are going on, Johnny."

"Nobody has ever forced me to do anything wrong," he said simply. "I'm not going to start now."

"You know if you get Gennaro to talk and continue, you will be bucking the biggest and the toughest people in the country."

He slapped me on the shoulder. "As of now, there are only two things on my mind—the meeting with Biglatti and my engagement party Saturday night at the Stuyvesant. You and Julian are coming."

"We wouldn't miss it for the world. It must have taken a lot of coin to build that hotel. From what I heard it's the biggest in the city."

"Connie's father is president of the syndicate that built it, you know. Our party will be the first affair to be held there after the opening on Friday." He glanced at his watch and leaned over the desk. "Now let's get things straight, Duke. I'm going to see Biglatti, and anything he offers I'm going to tell Flaherty. He's still my boss, and no matter what I think of him I don't intend to knife him in the back. Okay?"

"Of course. Let him knife you first. Will you call me and let me know how you made out?"

"I don't think so, Duke. Biglatti is one of the finest lawyers in the country. If he thought for a moment that after he left me I would be talking to a newspaperman he'd go into shock. Wait until everything is set. Now, are you going to tell your publisher?"

"Of course."

"Please don't give him any false hopes. Biglatti's call may mean nothing."

"Look, Johnny, please do me one favor," I said. "Saturday night at the party, if the news about Biglatti is good, say something like—'Be sure and look over the hotel, it's beautiful,' or some other nonsense. I'll get it."

Johnny walked me out into the quiet hall, now filled with the aroma of cooking.

"Mom must be worried about me," he said. "It's veal parmesan . . . my favorite."

BOOK SIX

THE DON

[22]

THE ENGAGEMENT PARTY of Constance Ryder and John Anthony De Lorenzo was not the casual affair that Johnny would have led you to believe. It had been mentioned many times in the Broadway and society columns. Actually, Colton Ryder, as well as his beautiful daughter, was hard news, as any city desk would tell you. I dislike the word "fabulous," but I guess it really fits Ryder. It always seemed to me he was building the largest of something, either hotels, motels, or just plain skyscrapers. Next year the Ryder Building on Third Avenue will make the Pan Am look positively squat. When I had the time I examined the reference-room file on Ryder; the *Fortune* piece told it best.

Ryder had apparently been born into construction. His grandfather had helped to build the old Astor House and was in charge of the advance party that laid track west of Omaha. His father had built the One-Nine Building on lower Broadway and most of the big hotels in the twenties. In the early thirties, after his father died, Ryder finished building Puerto Rico's first luxurious hotel. He almost lost everything but held on until he recouped. After the war his company expanded until he was building from Tokyo to New York. Connie's mother died when she was a child; she was his only child.

Anyone who builds big buildings in New York knows politicians and city officials. Colton Ryder knew them all—not only in New York but in Washington. He had been on more than one White House Committee and twice had appeared before a congressional committee to give his recommendations about urban renewal.

Julian filled me in on Colton's political connections when I picked him up. It was a black-tie affair, and he poured drinks for us.

"I had a call from Ryder this afternoon," he said.

"Oh? Did he want to make sure we were covering?"

"Ostensibly that was it. But he finally got around to the real reason he called. He said he was having a private cocktail party for a few of his friends and he wanted to make sure we would be there early enough to make it."

"We?"

"He made a point of asking you. Here's another tidbit for you. He and my father-in-law had lunch.

He neatly tied the black tie. "They had an interesting lunch."

"Does Ryder know your father-in-law, Julian?"

"I regret to say—yes. Several years ago they had some sort of deal in Chicago. Ryder was head of a big syndicate, and Pop was trying to get his hands on some of the *Chronicle*'s stock. I delivered some sort of message to Ryder at lunch. I gathered later he helped the old man buy in. Ryder was very powerful out there at the time."

"Well, then they're far from total strangers."

"They're probably partners in crime—"

"Since Ryder did your father-in-law a favor, obviously he's now asking one in return. Do you have any idea—"

"Yes, I know what it is," he said roughly. "Next month Ryder and Associates will present a plan to the city to construct a Metropolitan Business and Housing Center on the lower West Side. It is one of the biggest projects he ever tackled. It will mean the razing of blocks of warehouses, piers, business houses, and so on. The final cost will be in the hundreds of millions." He lifted his glass and peered at me over the rim. "Do I have to spell it out?"

Of course he didn't. In a city where a single variance in the standard building code, such as a cut in the sidewalk for a parking lot, could be a major task for even a lawyer with connections, Ryder had to swing enormous power to get this staggering project off the ground. In touching all bases, from the formal lunch at Twenty-one to the carefully guarded meeting in the out-of-town hotel room, someone had whispered in Ryder's ear that the way could be made easier if he could— "persuade" is the proper word in political circles—the publisher of the *Blade-Leader* that there were more important things for a metropolitan newspaper to do than investigate the character and activities of one of its outstanding leaders, Big Jim McShane.

The title, Metropolitan Business and Housing Center on the lower West Side, echoed in my mind.

"That project somehow rings a bell. I must have been reading something about it."

"Oh, it's not exactly a secret," he said. "There have been hints in the real-estate columns."

But I wasn't interested in Ryder's building plans. What I wanted to know was how far Ryder got with Sam Dolbar. . . .

"I would say he had his foot in the door, at least," Julian said. Then he saw the dismay on my face. "Oh, don't for a minute think that he made any threats or promises—nothing of that sort. This is high-echelon pressure. It's not what's said, but what's not said that counts."

An ice-cold kernel began to form in the pit of my stomach.

"How far do you think that foot is in the door?"

He slowly put on his overcoat. "You're the last one I want to double-talk, Duke. No matter how many are in it, you and I started it. There's no doubt Ryder made an impression on the old man. He seemed upset when he came home. Among other things, Ryder told him how they felt in Washington about what we were doing."

"And how do they feel?"

"Ryder said the people in Washington feel we put them in a terrible spot before the world. He had photostats of some European newspapers he said a friend in State gave him. The old man told him to show them to us tonight." He went on more bitterly, "If it was only the international reaction, I think the old man might have simply shrugged it off." He added with a tight smile, "No matter what you say about him, he's not a superpatriot. What did disturb him was what Ryder hinted at—"

"McShane, of course."

"Of course. Ryder left it until the last. As I said, there were no outright threats. But the old man's been around as long as Ryder. He got the message. In a nutshell the feeling in Washington is that a lot depends on McShane this year, and if anything happens to him the people down there will have a long memory."

We paused at the old-fashioned clock in the hall and waited for the elevator.

"In other words they'll put the screws on him."

"I'm going to tell you something that only four men in the country know," he said at last. "We have made a deal with the opposition in Ohio to combine the morning and the evening. It's been a carefully guarded secret; even I don't know all the details. Well, just before he said good-bye to the old man, Ryder congratulated him on taking over the whole field in Ohio. I don't have to tell you how that shook him up."

Outside, the doorman saluted smartly, then ran out into the street, whistling for a cab.

"Perhaps this time I have to spell it out?"

"No," I said. "Not this time either. The merger in Ohio will mean the Dolbar Enterprises can dominate the Midwest. But a government antitrust suit would certainly muddy the water."

"There are times you are given to understatement, Duke. You might be interested in another item, purely local. Last night I received a call from our prize new account, Jack Cummings. He went into great detail how Jim McShane was such a great asset to the community. I hung up on him."

"Well, there goes that account."

"I don't think so," he said briskly.

"You mean because of auld lang syne?"

"Don't let anyone kid you, Duke. In business the old school tie doesn't carry much weight." He said with a slight, distant look on his face, "What does sometimes are a few dirty aces up the sleeve."

I took a deep breath. "Look, Julian, you're the publisher—if you want to call it off . . ."

"Don't be ridiculous," he said. "Are you ready for item Number Two?"

"No. But go ahead."

"The building superintendent paid me a visit this afternoon. With him were two city inspectors. They had just spent a few hours going over the plant, particularly the press room. I don't think it's any secret we have one of the oldest buildings in the city, but the way they shook their heads I thought the roof was about to cave in."

"Did they give you a summons?"

"Nothing as crude as that. They indicated it was far more serious. One of them was an engineer; he really put on a show. He had notes and figures and the damnedest doleful voice I've ever heard." He said with irony, "They said they had to go back and consult with their boss." He looked at me. "Commissioner Aymes. Wasn't he our drunken friend in the elevator who had the charming wife?"

"The same boor. I told you then he was City Hall's hatchet man."

"Well, I called Aymes. He was friendly enough. He suggested you might want to run over and see him next week. . . ."

"The squeeze is on, Julian," I said.

"Do you think they will try to shut down the plant?"

"Why not? Technically they could. Any old building in the city has fire and building violations."

"That worries me."

"You had better face it, Julian," I said. "The day may come when the walls will fall in."

"When it does," he said quietly, "they'll have to bury me. Well, let's go and take on Ryder and get Johnny engaged."

What had that statesman said about our wonderful privilege of daily reading about life, the world, to witness in our newspapers great events, see strange and beautiful things—machines, armies, moonshots, shadows in the jungle; the delightful laugh of a child, the sob of a woman, the numbing impact of a catastrophe, the hopes and dreams of mankind . . . ?

This privilege sometimes comes high.

[23]

THE STUYVESANT WAS New York's largest and newest hotel. It had everything from a bridal suite with gold-plated faucets to a doggie salon where a manicurist painted your hound's nails. Nothing was too luxurious, too costly, or too frivolous. There were seventy-six stories, thousands of rooms, ballrooms just under the size of Madison Square Garden, and three nightclubs.

Perched on top the hotel, like a glowing queen's tiara, was the Grand Vista, exclusive, expensive, ridiculous. The smallest dish was ten dollars, a thimble of liquor, five or more. Here you paid for prestige and the large-sized match cover with your initials. (No matter what your name might be, the management had initials ready.)

However, the view was stunning. Here you could watch the Dipper march across the sky, the matchpoint lights of the laboring tugs hauling reluctant barges to the Bay, and Masefield's coasters with salt-caked smokestacks beating through the channel.

This was where Johnny and Connie's party was being held.

I knew this was going to be a big one when we stepped off the elevator; waiting to check their coats were the state legislative whip; the chairman of the state finance committee; a former chairman of the Stock Exchange; a cool beauty who only this morning had lifted her skirts for the photographers in the press room of New York's Supreme Court; and a swarthy-faced man in an expensive dinner jacket who dictated what records were to be played on the city's jukeboxes—not through any superior appreciation of music but simply because he had more hired guns than anyone else in the racket.

Well, I thought, you certainly can't say Ryder isn't democratic.

Connie, standing just inside the door, was a vision in pink. Johnny, looking slightly flushed, towered over her.

His beaming mother and sister stood next to him. On Connie's right was her father.

When we reached her, Connie held out both hands.

"Duke!" She turned to her father. "Daddy, you remember Duke Malloy?"

Ryder's grip was firm, his smile easy, his eyes searching.

"Of course. Flaherty's Christmas party." He turned to Savage. "How are you, Julian?"

"I was telling Duke we first met in Chicago," Julian said. "It was at Walsh's, wasn't it?"

"Good memory. That was the afternoon you gave me the message from your father-in-law." He added almost casually, "By the way, he looks wonderful."

Ryder had stated it very diplomatically: Julian had once been his messenger. He had seen his father-in-law.

"Yes, he does," was Julian's unruffled answer. "But he can't take those heavy lunches any more."

Ryder raised his brows. "Oh. Too rich?"

"The dessert usually upsets him."

Ryder smiled. "Perhaps he should refuse the dessert."

"We discussed it," Julian said.

"I hope you had an interesting discussion, Julian," Ryder said softly.

"I assure you we did," was Julian's firm reply. Then he said, "You have a beautiful daughter, Mr. Ryder."

"Obviously she got her looks from her dear mother. Do you know Mr. De Lorenzo, Mrs. De Lorenzo . . ."

The introductions were made, and we moved down the line. When we reached Johnny, he gripped my arm and said jovially, "Duke, be sure they give you a tour of this place! The view is fantastic."

"I bet on a night like this you can see all the way to the bridge," I said quickly.

"Bridge, hell," he said softly, and the grip on my arm was like a vise. "I bet you can see all the way up to Albany!"

"Albany?" Julian murmured, as we walked away.

I steered him to a corner and gave him a brief summary of what Johnny meant. He listened intently, and I had just finished when we were greeted by an effusive Flaherty.

"Did Johnny tell you what he had decided about the cops?" He stabbed me with his finger. "It's his decision, you know. We had nothing to do with it. I want *you* to know that."

"Johnny told me."

"And you agree?"

"If Johnny says so."

"And you, Julian?"

"I'll accept any recommendation Duke makes."

"If you fellows were lawyers, I could talk to you much better," he said seriously. There are so many damn' legal precedents when it comes to bribery."

There was a pause. Was Flaherty still uneasy? Apparently, for he said again, "Well, it's the law. That's the way it goes."

"We all sympathize with you, Quinn," Julian said gravely.

Flaherty gave him a cold smile.

I said, "I wonder what would happen if a certain gentleman might wish to make a deal?"

"Scotch and water, please," Flaherty said to a passing waiter. He accepted a glass and gave me a dazzling smile.

"I'm surprised you haven't heard, Duke. My office doesn't make any deals."

Julian looked startled.

"You wouldn't consider a proposition from a man who is in a position to expose—"

Flaherty said briskly, "By the time we check out his lies, it would be next summer. But if he wants to plead guilty and save the state a hell of an expensive trial . . ."

So this was the latest word: Gennaro could cop a plea and probably get an SS.

"He's a three-time loser," I said.

"The courts are always prepared to listen to the District Attorney's recommendations." He added magnanimously, "It's what you people wanted in the first place. If he did take a plea, I would certainly point out to the court it was the *Blade-Leader* whose public service . . ."

Julian looked at him with disgust.

Flaherty had the grace to flush. Then, with a show of anger, "I told you before, Gennaro is not going to occupy my office twenty-four hours a day. You know what I consider important. Every news broadcast tonight mentioned that African minister's speech at the UN," he said hoarsely. "They're making me look like a damn' fool. Washington's been on the phone five times. They'd like to see the FBI take over."

"Frankly I think it's a Federal case anyway," Julian said.

"My office will find the Prophet," Flaherty said. "And we don't need any God-damned FBI accountants to help us."

"As always," Julian said, "we get off the track. We want to put McShane in jail, and you want to find the Prophet."

"I don't know what ax you have to grind with McShane," Flaherty said bluntly, "but you're going to do it all by yourself."

"And if Gennaro is willing to talk—"

"Every defendant is willing to talk to avoid going to jail."

"But this is not an ordinary defendant," I broke in. "This is Vito Gennaro, the same man you called King of the Rackets five years ago!"

"We have a good case against him and we'll put the king in jail. Isn't that what you want?"

Without another word Flaherty turned and pushed his way through the crowds.

"I just can't get it through my head, is he crooked or just plain stupid?" Julian asked as we moved to one of the huge windows overlooking the city. I noticed he was drinking only ginger ale. I guess he was taking care of that stomach.

"Let me explain something," I said. "Politicians are mostly lawyers who have one objective in mind: the bench. Everything they do is geared for that wonderful moment when they can put on a robe and hear the attendant cry, 'All rise for his Honor.' Flaherty is just another lawyer yearning for that robe."

"But does he want it that badly?"

"He doesn't think he's doing anything wrong," I said. "He'll put Gennaro in jail. He'll find the Prophet and send him to jail. Then he'll retire to his judgeship, hand down important decisions, mingle with the judiciary, be on the Bar Association committees, issue momentous statements to the press—and still slap Jim McShane on the back when he meets him."

The party was beginning to grow, and the large room was filled with the babble of voices. Above us in the Grand Vista ballroom, the orchestra had begun to play. Guests were beginning to move up the short wide staircase to the ballroom, while still more continued to emerge from the elevators. The worlds of society, sports, politics, theatre, and law were fully represented. There was a relaxed air, with a great deal of laughter, the tinkling of ice in glasses, the catchy beat of a Latin rhythm, and the sound of dancing feet. This is one that will last until dawn, I told myself. I wondered how Johnny and Connie were standing up on that reception line.

"When do we start that private party?" I asked Savage.

Julian said, "I've had my eye on Ryder, and here he comes now."

Still smiling faintly, Ryder pushed his way slowly toward us, stopping every foot to shake a hand, bend slightly and listen, nod and pat a shoulder, then move on. You could almost judge how much

power he had in city politics by his progress; at least three commissioners and the Mayor's private secretary hastened forward to shake his
hand as he inched past them. And the leader from lower Bronx, the
man Washington had designated as the dispenser of Federal patronage,
put his arm around Ryder and whispered in his ear. For those in city
government Ryder, at that moment, had been officially dubbed the
king's own.

"I just left the kids. They're bubbling over," he said as he finally
reached us. "Look, can we have a drink in private?"

"Of course," Julian said.

He linked his arms with ours and started to lead us through the
crowd. I saw the Bronx leader, who was intently watching, lean over
and say something to the Mayor's secretary, who in turn said something
to the leader from lower Manhattan, who also happened to be the secretary to a Supreme Court justice who was standing at his side. The
justice, nudged, also turned to stare.

"Half the city government is wondering what's up," I said.

"Typical newspaperman's exaggeration," Ryder said. "According
to my secretary's guest list, only a quarter of the city is here." He nodded
to the stairway. "My private office is just off the ballroom."

As we moved upward, single file through the jammed stairway,
I looked down. The Mayor's secretary had joined the two city council-
men and a powerful Brooklyn leader. Then from the bar, I saw Hoff
making his way toward the stairway. It was going to be quite an affair.

We skirted the fringe of the ballroom, with Ryder never losing
that faint, almost arrogant smile as he waved off repeated invitations
and questions, then moved into a small elevator that took us to a penthouse.

"How high do you go?" Julian asked.

"I love height," Ryder said quietly.

Julian said, "I imagine it can give you a sense of power."

Ryder said, "I'm never content to build the second-largest
building."

We stepped out of the elevator into a large room, which actually
seemed to be a huge slab of deep red carpet floating on the heavens.
There were no walls, only glass. The lights were subdued, and all about
us were stars and the faint moaning night wind. In one corner was a
large desk with an onyx top like a reservoir of black ice, a bar, several
deep lounge chairs, and a sofa that circled half the room. Almost
automatically Julian and I walked to the windows. Below us, Manhattan was a vast sea of twinkling lights, the George Washington Bridge a
delicate tracery against the night.

"Do you spend much time up here, Mr. Ryder?" I asked.

He came from the bar with a tray of glasses. "I transact most of my business up here when I'm in town," he said. "I guess a few billion dollars in construction has gone out of here. I would think—"

"Mr. Ryder, what can we do for you?" Julian asked candidly.

The faint smile returned, and I thought he shrugged slightly.

"I thought we could wait a few minutes for Mr. Hoff."

"What does the Director of Community Relations for the D.A.'s office have to do with this meeting?" Julian asked. "You told my father-in-law you wanted to talk to me and Mr. Malloy."

"Your father-in-law is a wonderful old gentleman," Ryder said casually. "He has a marvelous grasp of current affairs, particularly politics."

There was a knock at the door. Ryder leaned over to the desk, pressed something, and the door opened and Hoff entered. He looked sober and tense.

"Have a drink, Bob?" Ryder asked.

"A light one, please. Just a little Scotch and water and lots of ice."

Ryder gave him his drink and then waved us to the chairs and sofa.

"I, too, have always believed it's best to get right to the heart of the matter," Ryder said.

"In other words you want to talk about our investigation of Jim McShane?" Julian asked.

The reply was just as blunt. "Exactly."

"What is it you want to know?"

"What have you people got against McShane?"

"He's a thief; worse than that, he has politically protected a gangster. Does that answer your question, Mr. Ryder?"

"Can you prove he's a thief and a protector of gangsters, Mr. Savage?"

"We will."

"But as of this moment you have no proof," Ryder said. "In other words you're really slandering the man?"

"Technically I guess I am," Julian said. "And if Mr. McShane wishes me to repeat it in public so he can sue me, I will gladly do it."

"Don't be ridiculous, Mr. Savage. McShane doesn't want to get on a witness stand any more than I do. Does that shock you?"

"Lately I'm finding few things shock me," Julian said. "Now let me ask you a question."

"By all means."

"What business is it of yours?"

"In a few weeks I'm proposing to the city one of the largest building programs in its history. The cost will run into the millions. For five years I've gathered this capital together from Hawaii to Canada. Obviously, to get this project off the ground I've had to have Washington's blessings and that of the local leadership. That happens to be Jim McShane."

"In other words, Mr. Ryder," Julian said, "if you can persuade me to get off McShane's back, it will make things easier for you both here and in Washington."

"I would say that about sums it up."

Julian said quietly: "The thieves could rob the city blind. Minorities could be squeezed in a wringer. The whole damn' inside of the city could be decaying, and it would be all right with you as long as we had the beautiful billion-dollar projects, these God-damned obscene big buildings . . ."

Ryder stared at him. "You're making it so simple it is ludicrous, Julian, but in a nutshell what you are saying is true. I'm not interested in some local politician acting like a dictator or some niggers sleeping ten to a room. Hell, no. I'm interested in getting a billion-dollar project started that will change the shape and destiny of the biggest city in the world! Jesus Christ, man! Where the hell would this country be if the industrialists, the robber barons, the railroad builders worried how their porters lived and whether some local politico was lining his pockets with the taxpayers' money." He leaned across his big desk. "We haven't got time. The world is moving too quickly. Everything is changing. Towns. Villages. Cities. Today it's not the individual who counts, Julian. It's the project! And the bigger, the better!"

Julian turned to Hoff, who was sitting uncomfortably on the edge of the sofa.

"Well, Mr. Director of Community Relations for the District Attorney's office of New York County, just what do you think of Mr. Ryder's philosophy? It concerns your office as well as my newspaper."

Hoff cleared his throat. "I'm only here as an observer. Mr. Flaherty didn't think—"

Julian's voice was so low and savage it startled me. "For Christ's sake, Hoff, why don't you get your boss up here? Hasn't he got the guts to talk for himself?"

I sensed, rather than saw, Ryder slightly stiffen. When Hoff looked over at him, he nodded.

"I was only trying to avoid embarrassment," Ryder said. "I don't think it will accomplish anything, but if you want him up here, we'll have him." He lifted a phone from beneath the desk and spoke into it.

Ryder ignored the awkward silence that followed and turned to

Julian. "Your paper is looking very bright these days, Julian. Have you changed some of the type faces?"

"We had an expert typographer in for a few weeks. He gave us some excellent suggestions."

"I see you now have the Cummings store."

"Yes. We're very proud to have them aboard."

"I know Jack Cummings very well. He's in our syndicate, you know."

Bob Hoff looked over at me with a slight, knowing grin.

"Really?" said Julian. "Jack and I roomed together at Yale."

"I didn't know that."

"Jack's a wonderful fellow." He stared at Ryder. "But slightly peculiar when it comes to women, don't you think?"

"I wouldn't know."

"The family's paid a lot to hush some things up. Last month it was something with a young girl. We wouldn't print it, of course."

Ryder studied Julian with that faint, cool smile. "You wouldn't be pulling my leg now, Julian?"

"Why don't you ask Jack about a certain blonde teen-ager from Queens?"

I looked at Julian as I would a stranger. So this is what he meant about having a few dirty aces up his sleeve!

There was a faint knock. Ryder pressed the buzzer, and the door opened to admit Quinn Flaherty, who, in trying to look jovial, succeeded only in appearing tense and worried.

"Gentlemen, how about one more fast one?" Ryder said, moving to behind the bar. He ignored any refusals and quickly filled the glasses and passed them around.

Julian moved in for the attack.

"I asked that you come up here, Quinn, because this conference is touching your office."

"If it has anything to do with Grand Jury testimony," Flaherty said firmly, "count me out!"

Ryder said, "Of course not." For the first time an edge of irritation entered his voice. "Just for the record, I'm not here to fix any case. I'm simply a businessman trying to get a point across."

"The point in question, Mr. District Attorney"—Julian deliberately underscored the title—"is my newspaper's investigation of Mr. McShane. When Mr. Ryder asked if we could prove that McShane was a thief, I thought that you should sit in."

"And we told you—" Hoff started to say, but Julian pointed at Flaherty.

"Are you going to do the talking or is he?"

"No one has to talk for me," Flaherty snapped.

"Well, suppose you begin by answering my question," Julian said.

Ryder held up both hands. "Please, gentlemen. Let's not get hot under the collar." He glanced over at Flaherty. "Suppose you let me begin, Quinn. . . ."

"I said no one has to talk for me," Flaherty growled, "and I mean it."

Ryder said soothingly, "We know that, Quinn. No one is trying to talk for you. But I'd like to put things in their proper perspective." When Flaherty shrugged, he went on:

"As I said, I have a syndicate that has put almost a hundred million dollars into this West Side project. A big chunk of this will be in Federal funds. We're all over three times seven and we know Washington can give me a hard time before they approve my project. We also know that this is going to be a tough election year." The voice hardened a bit as it became brisk, businesslike. "The people who count told me right from the shoulder they need McShane to deliver New York and they need him badly."

"Do the people who count know that McShane is tied in with a gangster whom Mr. Flaherty once called King of the Rackets?" Julian asked.

Ryder said, "Do you think you're going to prove that, Julian?"

"I'm going to do my damnedest."

"And you know what may happen while you're doing your damnedest?" Ryder carefully took a sip of his drink. "You may disturb a very delicate and vital election. You may also delay one of the biggest projects for this city ever to come down the pike." He turned on that faint, cool smile. "But more important, you may prevent me from making a few million dollars."

Julian said, "And that you will never let me do?"

Ryder's tone was almost impersonal, like a compensation nurse making a routine inquiry of a bruised foot. "I'm afraid not. I think I might almost cut your throat if I seriously thought you would."

"Would you do it here or in Ohio, Mr. Ryder?" Julian said quietly.

Ryder shrugged. "Wherever it would be most convenient." Suddenly he turned to me. "You're an old pro at politics, Malloy, what do you think?"

"Frankly," I said, "at this point I think your syndicate would be an excellent subject for investigation."

Ryder shook his head. "You wear that God-damned crusader's outfit like a belief."

Flaherty's harsh voice rose a pitch. "You mean like a disease."

"Gentlemen, we're not getting anywhere," Ryder said. "I want to know about McShane. Let me ask you, Quinn, are you going to indict McShane?"

Flaherty slowly lowered his glass to stare at Ryder.

"Are you serious, Colton?"

Ryder snapped, "I was never more serious in my life."

"Does Washington think I'm going to indict him?"

"The last time they called, you laughed it off. But there have been a lot of rumors. We want to know just what you intend to do."

"My office never indicted anyone on hearsay or malicious gossip," Flaherty protested. "And that's all we have on McShane."

Hoff added quickly, "And that's all there will be."

"There's a little development that might change all that, Flaherty," I said.

"As far as I am officially concerned, there is no change," he said flatly. "I told you that downstairs and I'm telling you again. I want the Prophet and his gang—not go on a fishing expedition after a man who's been a leader in the city for a quarter of a century!"

"Just for the record again," Julian said shortly, "we think this man is a madman and should be put away at once with his whole gang. However, at the same time we believe that conditions in the area which allowed the Prophet to exist should also be looked into by a Grand Jury."

Ryder asked quickly, "And those conditions are?"

"Bad housing, corrupt police, rats." Julian smiled faintly. "Also the corrupt influence of certain real-estate syndicates."

Ryder said impassively, "Yes, I have heard of some."

Julian said innocently, "Yes, I imagine you would have."

"Suppose a Grand Jury investigated those conditions," Ryder said intently. "Would that be enough—"

"—to get me to lay off McShane?" Julian asked.

"That's right. To get you to lay off McShane."

"No," Julian said. "I want all those conditions looked into. But I also want McShane the subject of a Grand Jury investigation."

Ryder swung about in his chair and gave Flaherty a look of disgust.

"Just what the hell do you want me to do?" Flaherty cried in frustration. "Ignore the law? Indict a man without evidence? Do a hatchet job on my own party?"

Julian leaned forward and pointed a finger that trembled slightly.

"I want you to continue to let Johnny De Lorenzo do his job. That's one thing we want."

In a low and bitter voice Flaherty said, "I don't think De Lorenzo is going to be on this case much longer. I think he needs a change of pace."

Incredulously, I said, "You mean you're taking him off the investigation?"

"Why not? Come to think of it, it's the only answer."

Hoff said, "It makes sense. Don't you see it?"

"Not even remotely."

"That's because you're handicapped," Flaherty said. "You're a newspaperman; you see the D.A.'s office as a news source. Well, he's not a news source; he's a prosecutor responsible to the people. And the trouble is, he's lost that viewpoint. He sees this whole thing purely as a big exciting news story and he's in the middle. You people have mesmerized him. I wouldn't have said that about Johnny a few months ago, but I do now." He spoke forcefully, and mostly to Ryder, who sat back and listened to him impassively. "You know something, Colton? These people have seduced this kid into thinking he's a shining knight and I'm a God-damned villain!"

Julian gave him a look of pity. "My God, man!"

"Let's get back to the main subject," I said.

"God damn it!" he said angrily. "You're one of the main subjects."

Ryder interrupted, "I'm inclined to agree with Duke, Quinn. What about my future son-in-law?"

It was evident, not only to us but to Flaherty, that Ryder wanted a showdown; he had flung the challenge.

"Just what I said; I think I'd better give Johnny something else to do. I have a competent staff of assistants; anyone could handle this matter."

Julian's voice was almost casual. "I don't think so, Flaherty."

Flaherty turned to him and almost snarled, "You're not trying to tell me how to run my office now—are you?"

"I'm just telling you, you're not going to take De Lorenzo off this case."

Flaherty's voice rose. "If you—"

Ryder was plainly curious. "Why won't he take De Lorenzo off this case, Julian?"

"Because if he does I will have an editorial, six and a half inches deep, in two-column measure, set in a Ben Day box so that it jumps out at you, placed on page one, denouncing Mr. Flaherty. I will also devote the entire upper half of my editorial page to this case, enclosing two coupons, one to the Governor, the other to the majority leader in Albany, demanding that Flaherty be superseded and an Extraordinary

Grand Jury investigation of official corruption in New York County be appointed at once. I am sure the Governor—"

Ryder, smiling, held up his hand. "I know. I know. This is an election year and he's the opposition."

Flaherty blustered, "You can't—"

Ryder ignored him. Still directing his attention to Julian, he said, "Would you really do that?"

"Absolutely."

"Even though you admit you have no proof—no real proof?"

Julian smiled. "Let's say there are new and potentially explosive developments—"

The slight burr under Ryder's desk was almost too faint to hear. Ryder spoke into the phone, lifted his brows a trifle, then handed the phone to me.

"For you, Mr. Malloy."

Over the phone there was a faint roar of sound: clicking typewriters, shouts, feet, paper rustling. Then a voice:

"Duke? Is that you, Duke?"

Turner Elliott's voice was unusually shrill. Although the room was still, I pressed the phone closer to my ear.

"This is Duke, Mr. Elliott. What's up?"

"Vito Gennaro's just been knocked off in an espresso shop off Delancey Street."

I said foolishly, "Is he dead?"

Elliott's voice dropped a pitch. "They used a sawed-off shotgun, Duke. Is Julian with you?"

"He's right here."

"Well, look. I'm sort of tied in a knot without you people. You know the whole story, and Julian had better—"

"Wait a minute." I looked at Julian. "Gennaro's been murdered."

Out of the corner of my eye I saw Flaherty start. I wasn't sure, but I thought he and Ryder exchanged swift glances. Julian came toward me and took the phone. He listened, broke in to say he would be down shortly, and hung up.

"Two men came into an espresso place and killed him." Then to Flaherty, "Where does that leave us?"

"There was no deal made with my office."

Julian's voice trembled slightly.

"You know damn' well De Lorenzo was talking to his attorneys." He turned halfway to Ryder. "It's not finished, Ryder."

"Perhaps," Ryder said calmly. "But isn't it all academic now?"

"In other words, you knew Gennaro was ready to talk," I said.

"I never said that."

"But you implied that." I said to Flaherty, "Why don't you get him before the Grand Jury and ask him under oath?"

Flaherty stared at me as if I had gone mad.

"You're hot under the collar, Duke," Ryder said, smiling. "I didn't need any inside information. Julian said there were some big developments. The call comes in that they killed Gennaro. You and Flaherty talk about deals. What kind of deal could it be? Come on, fellows, give me some credit for brains."

Julian ignored him and said to Flaherty, "I want to know where does this leave us now?"

"The investigation will continue."

"With De Lorenzo?"

"I don't know. Maybe."

"We don't want any maybes. We—"

There was a soft but insistent knocking. Ryder leaned over and pressed the buzzer. The door was flung open, and Johnny entered with Connie.

"Boss!" he cried. "Gennaro's been murdered downtown. I called Trench. He's on night Homicide. They're sending a car for me."

"Now I know what the wife of a D.A. goes through," Connie said, looking beautiful and just a trifle petulant. "And I'm only engaged to one!"

But we were all waiting for Flaherty. Johnny looked puzzled and questioningly at the lack of our response to the news.

"My office just called me, Johnny," I said.

"I'd better get down there," he said. "The cops said they had a witness—"

Julian said evenly, "Well, Quinn?"

"Okay, Johnny," said Flaherty abruptly. "You tell Trench to take over Homicide and you sit in on the questioning of any witnesses."

"There must have a leak," Johnny said bitterly. "They knew he was going to talk. I'll hop right down there." He turned to me. "Duke, I'll call you."

"I'm sorry, Johnny," Ryder said. "Connie, you better see to your guests."

Connie clung to Johnny as they hurried out.

"Come on, Duke," Julian said. "We'd better get downtown. Good night, gentlemen."

Ryder rose, but remained behind the desk. "It's elementary that a good businessman has to protect his interests and those of his investors," he said. "You can't blame me for that, can you?"

Julian said, "It depends on what methods you use."

"Any method that produces the results I want is the one I will use," was the cold answer.

"There's just one thing I can't understand."

"If I can be of any help . . ."

"Johnny's going to be your son-in-law, yet he may be the man who will dig deep enough to bury your Mr. McShane."

"And you want to know if this bothers me?" Ryder asked. "Frankly, no. Johnny's as honest as the day is long. That's the kind of man I want for my daughter. It means they have a better chance for happiness. But you and I know that Johnny's only a hired hand. I don't bother with hired hands; I never did and I never will. I find it's more profitable to deal with the top. . . . Next week why don't you give me a call and we'll have lunch up here. On a clear day—"

Then suddenly it came to me: the rewriteman's memo, the information phoned in by my anonymous female informer. The Three Harbors Dredging Company soon to begin work on the Metropolitan Downtown Business and Housing Center, and the upstate senator, chairman of that committee, who had been granted a million-dollar loan from Three Harbors . . . What was the last line of that memo? "Tell Mr. Malloy I believe there is a tremendous payoff somewhere . . ."

I could almost hear the pieces click as they fell into place. Thank God for Anonymous Friend, whoever she was. I hesitated for a moment. Should I use this as our final ace? It was only a tip; I had not confirmed the facts. If they were wrong or exaggerated . . . But something told me our tipster was authentic. I took a deep breath.

"I have one thing I'd like to ask you, Mr. Ryder," I said.

It took them all by surprise, even myself at the way it came out. It sounded harsh, arrogant, even threatening.

"Yes, Mr. Malloy?"

"You said that you would use any method that produces the results you want."

His eyes narrowed slightly. "That's my philosophy. Why?"

"I have a similar one."

Flaherty, Hoff, and Julian were staring at me. Ryder was too much of a veteran at infighting to change the life mask that had slipped down over his face.

"Threats, Mr. Malloy?" he said softly.

"No threats. I just remembered something. It's a piece of information which I thought may be valuable to this discussion."

"What's that, Duke?" Julian said wonderingly.

"There's an outfit called the Three Harbors Dredging and Surfacing Company," I said. "I think it's a company that belongs to Ryder Associates."

"That's right," Ryder said, "it does. It's a twenty-five-million-dollar business, if you're interested."

"I am. In fact, that's why I'm puzzled why your company made that million-dollar loan to that upstate senator. Isn't that senator chairman of some important committee in Washington? A committee that might have something to do with the Federal financing of your project?"

A melting piece of ice fell into a glass, and in the sudden quiet it sounded like a crashing girder. Ryder stared at me impassively. I was wondering how long I could match that steady gaze when he said to Julian, "Good night, and thanks for coming."

We walked out, and the door clicked softly behind us.

"He's as fine a man as ever robbed a city," Julian said, as we edged our way past the dancers and down the stairway, which seemed as crowded as before. "Now what's all that about the senator and the loan?"

I told him the story.

"How does so much corruption and violence come out of one decent impulse?" In the beginning of the evening he had looked refreshed; now there was a grayish tinge to his skin.

"We should play this story big," he said. "We'll have the main news story, then twined along with it the whole inside story of our investigation of Gennaro. I want a team of reporters to start interviewing the important leaders in the community, civic, religious, merchants, and so on. Beginning tomorrow we're going to make this city mad—"

He broke off abruptly to stare at someone over my shoulder. Before I turned I knew, from the faint, delicate perfume, who it was.

She was more beautiful than I had ever seen her. She was dressed in a green velvet sheath that set off her deep, even tan. Her hair was long and sun-bleached and held in place with a wide green ribbon. Gwen never went in for jewelry; she was wearing only a single strand of pearls I had given her a few years ago. And that damn' full-length mink made her look as if she had just stepped out of *Vogue*. She was so beautiful I couldn't say anything for a moment, but let her bask in the attention she was attracting—from the Commissioner of Highways to the Governor's newest political adviser who turned away from the National Chairman to stare.

Julian broke the silence. "Well, Duke, aren't you going to introduce me?"

But I was just looking at Gwen. "I guess I forgot how beautiful you are," I said, and it took an effort to get the words out.

"I tried to reach you at your office," she said softly. "They said you were here."

Julian cleared his throat, and I apologized and introduced them. They shook hands and smiled at each other, almost conspiringly, I thought.

"Can I get you a drink, Gwen?" he asked.

"Rye, just a little water."

"She drinks like a longshoreman," I said.

"My father insisted good liquor should never be mixed—not even with water," she replied.

"Your father sounds like a wise man," Julian said. "I'll be back in a moment."

I knew from the look Gwen had given him he would take as long as possible.

"No call. No telegram," I said. "Just dropped in. I could have met the plane."

"I wrote three letters, and tore them all up."

I felt my stomach begin to turn.

"You met someone? You're going to get married?"

She gave me a startled look, then smiled, her eyes glistening.

"I came back because of you—you big clown. Yesterday on the set I blew every line. When Bunny came into my dressing room I just cried. I couldn't stop. He threw up his hands and told me to take off until Monday. He said the best thing I could do was come back and see you. He called you an idiot."

"Tell Bunny he's the nicest fag I know."

Two tears rolled down her cheeks. "So I swallowed my pride and I came back to see you."

"All I can tell you, Gwen, is that I love you very much."

"You never even called . . ."

I took her hand. "Gwen, what can I say? I'm in one of these damn' situations. It's one thing after the other. The office just called—"

"I heard it on the radio," she said. "And the cabdriver told me."

Julian came back with three drinks. He was trying to look cheerful, but he looked ghastly.

"Now I know how old Charlie Connery felt many a Sunday afternoon," he said. "Half the city must be at the bar."

"Look, Julian," I said, "I want to bring Gwen down to the office. I can finish my piece in a few hours and give Turner Elliott all he needs." I slipped my arm around her. "She's just not safe in this dress."

"By all means, Duke," Julian said quickly. "I'll be in the city room most of the time, and you and Gwen can have the office to yourselves.

Suppose I ask Connie to come down and keep Gwen company? Johnny will be calling you anyway, and she can talk to him." Before we could say anything, he turned away and was lost in the crowd.

"Duke, this is crazy," Gwen said. "I can't come down to your office like this!"

"Why not? It's one way to awaken the night side. Those ancients will never be the same."

I pulled her closer and kissed her lightly. The perfume and the fact she wasn't wearing a hell of a lot under that dress made me tremble. "I was a fool to let you go," I whispered.

"I couldn't stay away," she said. "The people out there were wonderful, but I missed you, Duke. I had to come back even for a few days." She kissed me. "Here they come," she said. "Who's Connie?"

"Connie Ryder. This is her engagement party."

She gave me a surprised look. "But Duke, what about her fiancé?"

"This will sound stupid, but he's viewing a corpse. Look, dear, it's a long story and a little complicated. We'll fill you in on the way down."

We managed to make our way through the crowd, which by now was at its peak. Ironically, none of the guests seemed to be aware—or care—that their hostess was leaving; in brief it was a typical New York party: the guests greeted the host and hostess on arrival, then left to join their own worlds—the politicians to talk politics, the theatre people to slander the newest stars, the society types to seek out the columnists, the press agents to maneuver their clients into the lenses of the bored photographers.

"I understand this is your engagement party," Gwen said to Connie as we went down in the elevator.

"It is, but I'm glad to be leaving. The party is getting just too big," she said. "And besides, Johnny was called away. When he calls you, Duke, will you let me talk to him?"

"That's a promise."

We used Ryder's chauffeured limousine, a long sleek car, almost obscene in its luxuries. It was the first time I had a drink at a bar in the rear of a car taking me to work. The uniqueness of the situation and the alcohol relaxed Gwen, and before we reached the office she and Connie were chatting away like old friends.

When I said to Gwen that her appearance in the city room would undoubtedly wake up the night side, it was the understatement of the year. We stepped off the elevator to hear the high-pitched tempo of Editorial, turning out a fast-breaking big-city story. But the moment Julian stood at the threshold with Gwen and Connie beside him, it slowly subsided, ground to a halt.

Even old Pop Elders, an ancient copyreader who had boomed his way back to New York from the Laramie *Cowboy* when most of us were learning to talk, turned in disbelief.

Turner Elliott, a sheaf of dupes in his hand, hurried across the room.

"I'm terribly sorry I had to break in on the party," he said, "but you certainly had to be told. We'll need a few minutes of your time to go over everything."

"Give me a moment to show the ladies to my office," Julian said.

I winked at Gwen, who had been studying the city room with a bewildered look, and hung up my coat and dinner jacket. When Julian returned, Elliott and Bowers joined us in the deserted Society Department off to one side of the city room.

"Joe, give us a rundown on how the story shapes up now," Turner said.

"I have two men at the scene and one at the precinct," Bowers said. "The shooting took place at Julio's, a small espresso place less than a block from police headquarters. For the last thirty years the old Dons have been coming down here to this place to talk things over. The cops say there's been more knockoffs planned there than any other place in the country." He glanced at a sheaf of notes, and I thought Joe Bowers could have been an excellent cop. "At about eight o'clock Gennaro came in with two Dons. One guy runs a bank on the coast, and the other a number of nonunion dress shops in Easton, Pennsylvania. They sat down and began talking. About ten minutes after they were served, two young torpedoes walked in."

"How do the cops know they were young?" I asked. "These Dons never talk."

"A witness saw the whole thing."

Elliott said impatiently, "Go ahead, Joe."

Bowers grunted. "They walked in, and one let go with a sawed-off shotgun. I guess the Wop saw them, and ducked, because the first blast only caught him sideways. It almost tore off his shoulder, but he was still alive. . . ."

Turner said, "This is the cold-blooded part, Duke."

"That's right," Bowers said hastily. "Listen to this. He hit the floor and then staggered up. The two button men seemed to wait; then one shot him—.38 special—in the hip. The Wop again hit the floor, and started to crawl. Then these two guys walked up to the table, and one guy leaned over and shot him again. The Wop grabbed the table and started to pull himself up. Even the cops say he must have been a tough old bastard. When he got halfway up, the other guy pumped in another slug. This time when he hit the floor one leg was up on a chair. He held up his hands said something in Italian. One of the triggermen just took aim and emptied his gun into Gennaro's groin. The other guy blasted his head off. Then he took Gennaro's hat and tossed it on his foot. It caught like a ring on a peg, a cop said. The one who seemed to be the spokesman said in Italian that this was what informers against the family could expect. They turned and walked out. The cabdriver, who was hiding behind his cab, said they didn't seem to be in a hurry." He shrugged. "Typical mob knockoff. No fingerprints, no nothing. Every old guy in the place talked to the cops in immigrant English. They didn't see anything; it seems the whole place was in the men's room when it happened."

"Hold onto your hats," I said. "Gennaro was ready to make a deal with Flaherty's office."

Elliott gasped. "Duke, are you sure?"

"Johnny De Lorenzo had talked to his attorney, Biglatti, from Washington."

"Francisco Biglatti!" Bowers cried. "The big Washington lawyer! He handled Gennaro's immigration case five years ago."

"The same one," I said. "I'll put in a call to him right away."

I could see the clouds forming on Bowers' face, so I explained: "The only reason you didn't know about this was I scarcely knew about it myself. I happened to be with Johnny at his home when the call came in. He just gave me a brief summary and said nothing was definite. It was all in the talking stages. Tonight at the party Johnny hinted it might be big."

"I only knew about it myself when we walked into the Grand Vista," Julian said.

"That's incidental," Turner said. "What we have now is a story that should rock this town and put Flaherty's office in one hell of a bind." He turned to me. "Flaherty, of course, knew about this deal, Duke?"

"Johnny filled him in the moment he got the call. He can't cry innocence."

Elliott had a makeup pad, and began sketching the *Blade-Leader*'s front page for the next day.

"This is the way I see it. We'll take two lines of 120-point railroad, start Duke's story down columns one and two, in two-column measure, use one of the pictures in the coffee shop, four columns, and another story—probably Gennaro's importance in American crime, reading right out from under the cut."

Julian studied the sketch. Taking a pencil, he drew a rough box across the top of the dummy.

"How about this? We take the best picture and spread it eight columns across the top of page one, then superimpose the vignette. Keep Duke's story in two-column measure, but instead of another picture below the fold, what do you people think of an editorial, calling on Flaherty and the Mayor for action?" He turned to me. "I have a few things I'd like to tell Mr. Flaherty in print."

Turner said, "But even a shallow cut might push the two lines below the fold."

"Then go with one line of 120 point," Julian said. "Incidentally, I want us to start immediately on a series on Gennaro, no cops-and-robbers thing, but one backed by solid research, putting him in the proper social perspective; his growth in the postwar era, the easy money, the affluence in the city, his nonunion trucking racket, how he took over the city's gambling rackets, the public apathy, and his close political ties . . ."

Julian stood up. His face matched the starched whiteness of his evening shirt. I had a sudden desire to reach out and steady him.

"I think we had better get to work," he said. "Turner, I'd like to see the dummy of pages one and three when they're ready. Duke, ask a boy to shoot me your dupes. I'll give all of you dupes of my editorial. There's no pride of authorship tonight. Let's change it until it's exactly what we want—a demand by this newspaper to the leaders of the community once for all to smash this gangster-politico alliance, to stop this wholesale murder, and also to the citizens themselves to wake up and do something about it."

"You might call it a war of extermination," Bowers said hesitantly. "That's what it is . . . first Jackson, then Gennaro."

Julian said, "Excellent, I'll use that, Joe."

Julian now had welded us into a team; each had his assignment. When I sat down at the rewrite battery, I could sense the high-voltage excitement fairly crackling. Even the ambassadors from the composing room came out to spread the news through the mechanical departments that the *Blade-Leader* was going with a big one in the first edition.

I had sent over the fifth take of my story when Johnny phoned. The city desk switched him to Connie, then back to me. He filled me in with some details I didn't have, and cautioned me not to identify the witness as a cabdriver.

"He's so damned scared he's changed his story three times," Johnny said.

"None of the old gents talked, of course?"

"I talked to them in Italian. One old guy said he was so tired he slept all through the shooting."

"From what the cops gave us, they certainly made sure."

"They stalked him from table to table," Johnny said. "It was like going after a wounded rabbit. They just did an autopsy. The M.E. found eight bullets, all dum-dum. There wasn't anything left between his legs. In the old days they would have used a knife. There's no doubt Gennaro's murder is a warning."

"But, Johnny, who knew he was ready to talk?"

His voice sounded dull and weary. "I called Biglatti. He was shocked. He's coming in on the first plane. He swears he didn't say a word to anyone, but he does point out that Gennaro must have hinted his decision to someone. Someone he trusted. Maybe in his own family. Who knows?"

"What a horrible thing to believe."

"My grandfather used to say that Italians in crime are not like any other race. With them it's a brotherhood, almost a religion. The oaths, the promises. Well, you know the whole bit. What can I say?"

"Johnny," I asked, dreading to hear the answer, "does this wind us up? Isn't Gennaro the end of the road?"

"For God's sake," he cried, "don't you realize what they must be hiding to kill a big Don like Gennaro? He was killed because we were getting near a raw nerve. Maybe we even touched that nerve. Duke, they're geting frantic! We can't quit now. We must go on. Dig deeper."

"I'll never quit, Johnny. I swear on it."

I can't remember when I wrote so well at such a steady pace and with such intensity: five columns of type, fifteen full pages of copy. In addition, a two-column box with the highlights of Gennaro's criminal career and a five-column box inside on the jump page from testimony pointing up Gennaro's influence, given by law-enforcement officials, Federal and state, at one of the congressional hearings.

There was one story that was a labor of love; I made sure Elliott gave it a good start on page one: the part Action Jackson played in the entire investigation. Later we chewed over Julian's editorial for almost two hours until we had what we thought was needed.

Finally, as always, the news editor indignantly cried that he wouldn't take another line, it was all past the deadline anyway, and how in the hell was he ever going to make press time? Under his wrath even editors quail, so the last take was rammed through to the copydesk, slipped into the pneumatic tube, and we were finished. The rim of the copydesk emptied; the picture editor and his assistants left to join the bustle and tension outside in the composing room; while in the city room there was a sudden quiet. Shapeless old women in faded house-dresses mysteriously appeared with their ragged feather dusters and tin bins and began making their aching way from desk to desk. Torn papers vanished into their baskets, spikes were cleaned, ashtrays emptied. Weary veterans closed their eyes, while young reporters tried to sneak a look at the proofs of their stories to see how the insensitive copyreaders had trimmed their polished gems.

Before joining Gwen in Julian's office, I walked through the composing room to the small ad alley in the rear. I was looking for Gus the jeweler. His type is traditional in every composing room, a virtual Yankee peddler who can produce from his locker anything from contraceptives to jewelry. Gus was the *Blade-Leader*'s all-around merchant. He was a short, stocky man in any inky apron. I am sure he will be buried with the cigar stub stuck in one corner of his mouth.

"Hiya, Duke. How's the boy?" he asked from behind his stove. The stub never moved.

"Gus, do you have any rings?"

He cocked an eye. "You mean like poil rings?"

"Like poil rings."

He slid a galley of type contemptuously to one side, reflectively chewed on the stub, then brushed past me. I followed him into the deserted locker room and watched him laboriously try several keys on a huge Yale lock. It finally opened, and reaching down he came up with a handful of small velvet boxes. He snapped one open, studied my face, then snapped open another, then another. The third held a really exquisite tiny pearl ring.

"I'll take this one."

"Twelve bucks too much?" He said tentatively.

I started to say something. "Okay, okay. Make it ten."

When I gave him the money, he asked, "Going to see a broad, kid?"

I winked and he chuckled.

Well, I thought, as I walked back to the city room, I can always tell Gwen, as Charlie MacArthur told Helen Hayes, that the next time it will be diamonds. . . .

Julian, Gwenn, and Connie were sipping coffee when I walked into his office. Gwen just shook her head.

"Darling, I'm afraid you no longer look as though you just fell off a wedding cake," she said. "Your arms are all black."

"That's from the proofs I had to correct," I said. "Do you mind waiting another half hour? I want to check a page-one proof."

"I waited all night, Duke," was her soft answer.

I didn't care who was there. I just had to lean down and kiss her.

"You lovebirds make me jealous," Connie said. "You know, I was just thinking—here I am in a newspaper office two miles west of the Great Wall of China instead of being in the arms of my betrothed while the orchestra plays 'Stardust,' and here's Gwen, the bright new

Broadway star, drinking coffee out of a cardboard container with a guy who didn't even fall off a wedding cake!"

It broke us all up.

"I was telling Gwen how much I enjoyed her show," Connie said. "When she sang 'I'm Waiting, Always Waiting,' I almost cried."

"Now you know I wasn't kidding when I sang that one," Gwen said dryly.

"Do you really have to go back to the coast tomorrow night, Gwen?" Connie asked. "You could stay with me for a few days."

"I'd love to, Connie, but I made a solemn vow to be on the set by Monday at ten. I missed one day, and I was shocked to discover it cost the company thirty thousands dollars."

"A Swedish Scotchman," I said.

"Darling, I've eaten too many times in Nedick's not to appreciate money. I love hot dogs, but three times a day . . ."

Abruptly Julian said, "Duke, would you like to go back with Gwen for a few days? I'm sure we could handle it for that time."

Gwen's hand found mine and she squeezed hard. "Duke, please say yes." .

I hesitated, but I knew what I had to say. None of them—not even Julian—knew what this night had meant to Johnny. He just couldn't be left alone, especially now.

"I'd love to, Julian, but I promised Johnny I would stay by a phone. You know, he'll have a problem."

"A bad one?" Connie asked anxiously.

"Nothing he can't handle, Connie."

Julian slowly rubbed his eyes. "For all your trouble I wonder if you people really realize how lucky you are. . . ."

There was a knock, and the boy entered, gingerly holding a page of proof sleek with ink. He let it ripple to rest on Julian's desk. Here at last was our creation; this was what 827,000 New Yorkers would read sometime today.

Connie gave a shudder as she looked at the picture spread across the top of the page.

"Is that where Johnny is?"

"It's his job to be there, Connie."

It was indeed a grim picture; Gennaro was lying half under a table. One leg was resting on a chair. On the foot was his broad-brimmed hat where his killer has tossed it, like a ring on a peg, as the cop has described it. The one line of 120-point type rammed home the story. My story ran down the page in two-column measure. Julian's editorial, entitled by Turner "WE DEMAND," was set in century-bold italics, 24 point, and clanged like a bell. The story of Action Jackson's role began under my main story and jumped inside.

"Can we go now, Duke?" Gwen whispered. "I'm terribly tired."

"My car's downstairs," Julian said quickly. "I can have someone drive you home." Then he came from around the desk and took Gwen's hand in both of his. "Gwen," he said softly, "marry him."

"Maybe," she said.

He reached out and took Connie's hand. "Remember to save me a dance at your wedding, Connie."

Connie reached over and impulsively kissed him. "It's a date."

"Aren't you coming, Julian?" I asked.

He shook his head. "I'll wait until about eight and call the old man. I also want to make sure the city desk starts a canvass of our leading citizens. Duke, they must be made to respond!" Then to Connie and Gwen, "Cheers now, both of you. Gwen, good trip."

In the lobby, waiting for the car, Gwen said fiercely, "What is in this crazy business that makes a man kill himself like that? That man's sick, Duke.

"What do you mean?"

"He's very sick," she repeated. "Once he excused himself and went down the hall. I knew he was in the Ladies' Room, because when I went in there later I saw a paper towel with blood on it. When he came back he looked white, didn't he, Connie?"

"He said coffee didn't agree with him, but it wasn't coffee."

Gwen said in a resigned voice, "That poor man will work all night until morning. Oh, Duke, why?"

"I guess you could say it's a matter of conscience."

We sped up the West Side Highway and cut across Seventy-second to the East Side in excellent time. The city was sleeping, the streets dark and deserted. We dropped Connie off at her place. As she got out she held my hand.

"Duke, remember when I asked you a long time ago not to let Johnny get hurt?"

"I remember, Connie."

"Please, please don't forget."

"I won't."

Gwen leaned over and touched Connie's cheek. "I'll never let him forget for a moment. And we'll be at your wedding even if he's covering the Second Coming."

When she was gone, Gwen leaned her head back on the seat.

"I'm at the Carlyle, Duke."

I ignored her and gave the boy my address.

[24]

THE WEATHER FITTED in with my mood when I took Gwen to the airport that night in a thin, melancholy rain. We had had a leisurely supper complete to champagne.

I was pouring when suddenly I remembered the ring. I jerked the bottle away and jumped up.

Gwen looked startled.

"Duke, what's wrong?"

"I have something for you and I forgot all about it." I found it in my jacket and snapped open the small velvet box. The tiny, spurious pearl shimmered and glowed in the gold light of the fire.

"I stole this from the royal barge as it floated down the Nile. It cost two Nubians their lives for trying to protect the treasure box, but I was like a cat on their backs."

"Duke, you're crazy. It's beautiful, darling. Really beautiful," she cried.

I slipped it on.

"It's the only engagement ring I could find in a composing room at three o'clock in the morning. Monday I'll drop in Tiffany's."

"Never, never, never," she cried. "I'll never take it off. It's beautiful."

In the cab when Gwen slipped her gloved hand in mine, I could feel the ring; now that the time to say good-bye was fast approaching, I felt a hollowness forming in my stomach. Out of the corner of my eye I could see Gwen doing her lips. I leaned over and kissed her; two fat tears rolled down her cheeks.

"It will be only a short time, Gwen."

"You make the time, Duke." She fumbled in her bag and handed me a torn newspaper clipping. It was an airlines ad for California flights.

"Be sure to take this one," she said with a forced smile. "The kids on the coast call it the Martini Special. It's a real swinging trip."

Then that phony, cheerful voice told everyone Flight 100 for Los Angeles was ready and would passengers please start moving aboard.

"Good-bye, darling, I love you . . ."

Her lips met mine, and then she was hurrying through the misty rain toward the plane. Behind me someone whistled softly. It was a short, stocky, white-haired priest. He winked, and I grinned back at him. Gwen would have good company.

When I returned to the apartment, the faint scent of her perfume depressed me still more. Almost in desperation I plunged into the first Monday editions I had picked up at the airport.

The one-star *News*—their first edition—had gone big on Gennaro, picking up most of my Sunday story on how Gennaro had started to make a deal with the D.A. The early *Trib* and *Times* also had it on page one, the *Trib* giving it a big play. They all pointed out the significance of Gennaro's move; it was one of the few times a power in the syndicate had offered to make a deal with the law. The *Times*' lead editorial was on this subject:

WHAT DID VITO GENNARO WANT TO TALK ABOUT?

It was a vigorous one, calling on Flaherty to follow through on what Gennaro was ready to talk about, particularly on any links between politicians and organized crime.

I made a call to the D.A.'s office, the precinct where they had set up headquarters for the Gennaro investigation, and to Johnny's home. A gruff desk sergeant said he had not seen Johnny for hours; his office reported the same thing; and his mother could only tell me Johnny had called her some time ago and said not to wait for him, he wouldn't be home for some time. A terse old man's voice at Julian's apartment said he was asleep, and hung up. I assumed that was Sam Dolbar. The city desk did say they had been trying to get me; they had a message from a man named Johnny. He had said simply I was to wait for a call.

On this note I gave up. Although I desperately wanted Johnny to know every detail of what had taken place in Ryder's office, the lack of sleep was making me stagger.

I fell into bed and slipped into a deep, bottomless pit of black velvet.

It seemed I had been asleep only a few hours when the phone rang. Almost automatically I picked it up.

"Duke? I'm terribly sorry to disturb you," Turner Elliott was saying. I glanced at the clock; it was a few minutes after 7:00 A.M. I shook the fog from my brain and swung over the side of the bed.

"That's quite all right, Mr. Elliott. What's up?"

"The city desk was notified during the night. Flaherty is calling a press conference."

"Flaherty!"

"That was my reaction when they told me. Hoff himself called about 4:00 A.M. He said it concerned a vital matter."

"He doesn't say what the matter is?"

"No," Elliott said wryly, "but we can guess."

"Where will it be held, sir?"

"At Criminal Courts."

"I'll be there," I said.

"I'm sending a photographer."

"Did Hoff ask for a photographer?"

"He hinted there would be a page-one pictures," Elliott said grimly.

"Then it's big."

[25]

IN THE LAST few years the official and political press conference has become part bedlam, part circus, part moose-call contest, and part Actors' Equity fallout. Without question the growth of television in covering public affairs is responsible. In the old days a press conference with an important official issuing an explosive statement was always a wild affair, especially during the daytime hours when the reporters for the afternoons had to meet their last-minute deadlines. But when the electronic press made its appearance, things just fell apart. Now crews snake cables across press rooms and up and down halls and corridors like nonchalant ranch hands cutting out steers for branding, so their man with the mike can thrust it into the face of a newsworthy citizen and snap out the damnedest questions. To the murderer being arraigned: "What did you have for breakfast?" To the shattered, onetime financial genius accused of robbing his partners: "What's your wife's first name?" I will never forget the shocked expression of a young TV reporter when a hardened jewel thief replied to one of his questions so that thirty million people could hear, "——— you, sir. And that's upper case."

I checked my city desk and learned that Flaherty's press conference would be held in a General Sessions courtroom on the third floor. This confirmed the hunch that it would be very important; in all his years in office Flaherty had never held a press conference outside his spacious office.

I entered Criminal Courts and passed the press room. Every large public building has one, usually dominated by a dean (a reporter who has covered the same building for more than a century), and here the local and alien newspapermen gather when something unusual is about to happen "in the building," as they like to say.

Frankly, I have never cared much for press rooms or local beat reporters. I have always felt they should be changed every six months on the simple theory that familiarity breeds contempt. So I found a seat in the General Sessions courtroom and read the *Times* review of a new Broadway musical.

The room filled up rapidly, and I was soon trading insults with old friends.

"Hiya, Duke," said the *Times* man, with whom I once chased fires. "What does it look like?"

"I'm hoping it might be on Gennaro."

"That was quite a piece you had."

"Maybe Flaherty will announce he's running for President."

"God!"

The television crews were setting up their lights and hauling their cables across the benches and rails, right up to the judge's bench, where it appeared Flaherty would sit. The TV reporters huddled with their sound men, and the room soon echoed with sound-level testing.

Promptly at three a court attendant locked the door, and a hush fell over the packed room. A door opened, and Flaherty and Hoff walked out of the judge's chambers onto the judge's bench. Flaherty looked eager and triumphant, Hoff just arrogant.

"You television men will have to wait until the D.A. reads the first announcement for the PM's," Hoff said. "After he reads it, all afternoon men can leave; the doors will then be locked."

"Will he repeat it?" one TV reporter called.

"Definitely—as many times as you want," Hoff said. He nodded to Flaherty, who rose with a paper in his hand. He seemed in a jovial mood.

"I had a meeting with the men who regularly cover this building," he said. "The attendant will open the doors for those reporters for the evening papers who wish to call their offices. The doors will then be locked, and the press conference will continue."

"What about the evening-paper reporters who want to get back in?" someone asked.

"You will be admitted through the clerk's office," he said, "but no one else will be allowed to leave." He added with a grin, "It's always easier to get in than out." He glanced down at the paper. "Now, gentlemen, the announcement."

I had a few sheafs of copy paper, and despite myself I could feel a tension, a quickening inside, as I poised my pencil.

Flaherty's strong voice rolled across the room:

"At 10:15 A.M. yesterday, Isaiah Redmond, alias Isaiah, the Magnificent, alias the Prophet, was arrested by investigators attached to the

New York County District Attorney's office, at 413 Commerce Street, in Baltimore, with the assistance of the local police. The Prophet was immediately taken into custody on a warrant issued by General Sessions Judge Franklin LaCourt and booked at the local precinct in Baltimore, on charges of being a fugitive from justice.

"The defendant has signed a statement to the effect that he knowingly started the riot of the 29th with the purpose in mind of focusing national attention on the plight of the Negro in Harlem. He has admitted that he held meetings in various sections in the city in which he discussed with his followers details of how a race riot could be touched off to create the greatest amount of citywide confusion."

Several reporters already had bolted out of their chairs and were angrily tugging at the door, ignoring the attendants, who tried to order them back to their seats.

"My investigators also found in the defendant's possession a list of fifteen congressmen and senators, along with their home and office addresses."

Flaherty paused theatrically and stared hard at the upturned faces of the press.

"The defendant has told us," he said slowly, emphatically, "that these American statesmen were marked for assassination. Other details obtained by this office cannot be divulged but have been turned over this morning to the Washington office of the Federal Bureau of Investigation."

Reporters at the door were shouting their demands at the attendants to open up; others joined them. Some stood on their seats, screaming questions at Flaherty, while television reporters leaped over benches, holding high their mikes like so many wild-eyed hurdlers reaching forward with their relay sticks. The besieged court attendants at the door yelled something to Flaherty, who waved his consent. The door swung open and they poured out, racing to reach the bank of phones at the end of the corridor. The doors were then closed.

I almost felt physically ill. This was the answer to everything, to why Flaherty looked far from the man who had been in Ryder's penthouse, why he couldn't care less now about removing Johnny. With the Prophet's arrest—and within the hour there would be new, blaring headlines—he knew that Gennaro would soon be just another underworld murder soon to be forgotten.

The Prophet, the dark man of evil, the menace to our democracy, would be the new darling of the headlines.

Flaherty dramatically held up his hands.

"Gentlemen! Gentlemen! Please! There is another part to this press conference. Please return to your seats!"

The court attendants, conscious of their new responsibility—and conscious that the TV cameras were sweeping the room—began shepherding the gesturing and angry reporters back to their seats.

Flaherty continued.

"Since he has been returned to New York in our custody, the defendant has insisted almost hourly that he be permitted to speak to the New York press. I have informed him that it would not be ethical for me to allow a defendant under such grave charges to talk to you men.

"However, this morning he engaged counsel, who, after conferring with his client, asked that he be allowed to make a public statement.

"I again refused. But a few hours ago confidential information obtained by my office indicated that charges of massive police brutality on the defendant, accompanied by demonstrations which could result in violence, were being prepared by irresponsible sources.

"I immediately conferred with his Honor the Mayor, some of my distinguished colleagues in the District Attorney's offices of other boroughs, wise and learned heads of our Bar Association, and finally with the State Department. They have all agreed that it would be wise to show you, the spokesmen for our community both in public print and on our television screens, that this defendant has not been harmed or coerced by any member of the New York City Police Department or this office."

Flaherty paused and slowly accepted a glass of water from Hoff. He took a sip, delicately touched his lips with a handkerchief, then went on:

"I have been advised that if the defendant is accompanied by his attorney, his constitutional rights will not be violated. So, gentlemen, you will now meet Isaiah Redmond, alias the Prophet, indicted by the New York County Grand Jury on charges of first-degree murder, twenty-one counts, and seventy-six counts of conspiring to start a public riot."

He turned to Hoff and whispered something. Hoff hurried to open the door of the judge's chambers.

Then in walked the Prophet.

Curiously, there wasn't a whisper. The cameras swung to him, and he turned to stare at TV's red eye, arrogantly, unblinkingly. With open contempt he accepted the chair Hoff offered. Behind him trotted a small white-haired Negro in a shiny blue suit.

Flaherty turned to the white-haired man.

"Mr. Robinson, isn't it?"

The Negro nodded.

"I have informed Mr. Robinson, gentlemen," Flaherty told us, "that it is his responsibility to guide his client at all times while he is present. I have informed him that he need not answer any questions after he reads his prepared statement. Is that agreed, Mr. Robinson?"

The white head nodded.

"Your client may have the floor, sir."

The attorney bent over to whisper to the Prophet, who only impatiently pushed him aside. He walked to the edge of the bench and studied the room with hard, glittering eyes. There was a strange, theatrical majesty about him that could not be denied. He looked the same as he had those nights outside the Harlem supermarket when the mounted cops were so uneasy and the footmen gripped their clubs just a bit tighter.

Then suddenly he began speaking. The powerful, incongruous voice roared out of that thin, black pipestem neck to lash us with the sting of a whip; white fiends, bloodsuckers, killers of the black race. Twice his attorney tugged desperately at his sleeve, but the Prophet snatched his arm away.

His statement was long, rambling, and full of invective.

The question-and-answer period was the wildest I have ever witnessed. The Prophet never answered one reporter; there were usually three on their feet. And almost every question produced a headline. He admitted his organization was terroristic and dedicated to the elimination of the white race. There was a revolting blood oath, classes in mayhem and arms, a no-alcohol, no-meat program that was supposed to be in obedience to the law of some god named Dri-Kov, and numerous other wild statements. As it went on, reporters kept running in and out of the room while the TV reporters frantically tried to get the Prophet to repeat some deadly statement he had just made. There was only one trouble—the Prophet changed his statements every time he was asked to repeat them.

Within an hour he was shouting, almost incoherent. It must have been evident, even to Flaherty, that he was completely mad.

What made it doubly tragic was that everyone at the press conference, including myself, thought only of the Prophet and the violence he had brought to our city. No one raised their voice to question the forces that had brought him to prominence, that forced ordinary men and women to listen to him and, in desperation, believe.

And neither did Flaherty, our representative of justice.

I had enough, and pushed my way through the mob of newsmen in the aisles. Just before I reached the door, I looked back. Flaherty had been watching me. He gave me a meek salute. . . .

On the phone Turner Elliott told me what was happening.

"The services have been coming in with bulletins every few minutes," he said. "What is going on over there?"

When I told him he whistled softly.

"There's nothing we can do, Duke, but play it like the rest. I had to take the main lines off Gennaro and put them on the Prophet. You can't deny it; that's a shocking story about the list of congressmen he wanted to kill off."

"You don't have to explain, Mr. Elliott," I said. "It's a big story even though he's nutty as a fruitcake. Does the publisher know?"

"I called him the moment we got the first AP bulletin," he said. "And I've been reading every bulletin and piece of copy that has come in. He hasn't said much, just told me to play the hard news but keep the Gennaro story prominent on page one."

"Flaherty will stretch this out as long as he can."

"Of course. The arraignment will be tomorrow. Flaherty will save something for that."

"Wait a minute, Duke, here comes something." There was a pause, then, "He's just admitted he had a meeting with one of the attachés of that new African minister."

"Flaherty must be crazy to let him go on."

"He's not so dumb. Juries come from newspaper readers." He sighed. "Despite this, you'll have a story on Gennaro for tomorrow, won't you?"

"I'll write one, but if I don't get De Lorenzo on the phone it will be mostly a rehash."

"Well, I'll leave a note over for the night side to give whatever you turn in a good play on page one. If anything else big comes out, I'll have the city desk call you."

I tried Johnny again, both at his office and at his home, but there were no messages. On an impulse I called Inspector Murphy's office and found that he too hadn't been in since the murder. Idly I wondered if they were together.

Then I called Gwen to tell her how much I loved her and missed her. Like the minx she was, she reminded me that the low fares were still available along with the martinis. My heart ached when I hung up, but just hearing her voice made me feel better.

I guess Gwen's voice and knowing subconsciously what she expected led me to the bookcase to pull out the old copy of the Foley Collection and open to "Capt'n Sam." Lying inside the page like a bloated bookmark were the notes and rough outline of a three-act play. I settled back, ready to greet old familiar faces, but they were gone. Instead, all I could see, sharp and clear, was a mad, black face and the hard, open mouth. What does Whitey care? Whitey burns black men with gasoline, Right? Right.

BOOK SEVEN

BATTLE OF TORYTOWN

[26]

IT SEEMED AS though I had only closed my eyes when the phone rang. I awakened, listened for a moment to the dogged, dull ring, then rolled over. If it was the office, the hell with them. Gennaro could be resurrected for all I cared. But my caller was insistent; he refused to give up. I cursed him to his cradle, and reached out.

"Duke. Hello, Duke?"

It was Johnny's fierce, intense voice.

"This is Duke, Johnny. What's up?"

"Get a pencil. Quick."

"I have one."

"Go downstairs to a street phone booth and call Morgan 3-3463. Ring two. Got it?"

"Sure. But where—"

"Call me at once. I'll fill you in."

There was a sharp click.

I dressed in a matter of minutes, my mind whirling with a shower of thoughts and conjectures, none of which made any sense. In the phone booth on Lexington Avenue I poured out my change and dialed the operator and repeated the number. There was a pause, then:

"That will be thirty-five cents, please."

The solemn clang of the quarters filled the booth.

"Where is that, Operator?"

"That is northern New Jersey, sir. Shall I ring the number?"

"Please."

The faint buzzing and mysterious rattling and far-off voices of operators dragged on, then the faint one-two, one-two . . .

The receiver was lifted, and Johnny's voice poured through the phone.

"Duke!"

"Where have you been, Johnny? I thought you were—"

"Look, I have a million things to tell you," he said. "But some of them must hold until I see you. First, hold your hat—"

"Go ahead."

"Ricky Strasser has surrendered to me. He came in with his girl."

"Vickie Simms?"

"Right. The one he was with the night you taped his call."

"Tell me the rest, quick."

Excitement pitched Johnny's voice a note higher.

"He's going to blow the whistle on McShane, Duke! This is our miracle, boy!"

I could only stare at the ugly black mouthpiece.

"Duke, you there? Hello . . ."

"I'm here, Johnny. I just don't know what to say. How did it happen? When?"

"I won't go into details. I just can't. But, very briefly, Vickie called me. Rickey knew he was slated next to go after Gennaro. In fact, I'm sure we were followed when we left their fleabag in Trenton."

"Trenton?"

"That's where I picked them up. We went down to the station, and just before the train started moving I pushed them aboard. Two young punks came running up the steps. Maybe it's my imagination, but Tom raised hell—"

"Tom! Is Murphy with you?"

"He picked me up in Hoboken and then we came up here."

"Here? Where's 'here'?"

"Torytown. It's a grocery store and a couple of cabins up in the Jersey mountains. The place was started by the Hessians and the Indians in the Revolution. The old man showed me a story *Life* did on the place in 1942. It's like living with Li'l Abner."

"You're going too fast for me Johnny. Who is the old man and what—"

"Cut it off, Duke; there's too much. Look, I want you up here as soon as possible."

"Fine. Fine," I almost shouted. "But where in the hell is Torytown and how do I get there?"

"Take it easy and I'll tell you. You go through the Lincoln Tunnel, up Route S3, then 46, and follow it right through to 23, at the Mountain View Circle. Know where that is?"

"I covered a small-town triangle murder up near Newfoundland when I first came on the paper. Is it near there?"

"It's three miles past Newfoundland. Go through the town and watch for a large inn on the right called The Hunter's Inn. A half mile beyond that is a small gas station. The sign says Adam's Service. Got that?" He continued, "Drive in there, and a young fellow named Adam will guide you up here. He's Vickie's brother."

"God, you sound like you're in the woods!"

"An hour and a half from Times Square and it's like the Ozarks! No kidding!" He became brisk. "Look, Duke, I'm down at the station now. I have to get back. Start out right away, will you?"

"As soon as I hang up."

"One other thing. Don't tell anyone where you're going."

"I have to give some excuse to the office."

His answer was blunt. "Tell them anything, but not the truth. And there's one more thing."

"What's that?"

"Bring your tape recorder. Do you have extra tapes?"

"I have about five."

"Bring all of them. Do you have a portable?"

"Sure."

"Bring that too."

"Johnny, is he talking?"

"I have learned so much about McShane, Duke, I'm afraid. Does that answer your question?"

"I'll be leaving in ten minutes, Johnny."

Back in my apartment I packed my tape recorder, portable typewriter, paper and carbons. I changed to corduroys, boondockers, a heavy sweater, and lumber jacket. A sullen attendant pulled out my car. I gassed up on Eleventh Avenue near the tunnel, then started out.

I wasn't unfamiliar with northern New Jersey, especially the small towns along the scenic Route 23, a part of the East that always reminded me of Devon's rich dairy country. The triangle murder I had covered in this section had been a routine, week-long sensation. It was right after the war. The outraged husband who killed his wife and her lover had been attached to the Manhattan Project, a disclosure that sent the FBI combing the hills and the scientist's background. Ripples of excitement went through every newspaper office in the East until a berry picker found the husband's body and rambling, incoherent suicide note.

It had been spring, and after filing my overnight story for the next day I acompanied a vigorous old girl from the *News* who was also an antique collector. She explained she loved out-of-town assignments because it gave her a chance to shop for antiques. For a week we visited every small village and farmhouse in a radius of fifty miles. By the time I returned to the city, I had a fair idea of Sussex County's backwoods.

As I drove along the dark and empty highway, I fumbled about in my memory for a clue to where I had heard of Torytown. Suddenly it came back to me. Several months before, while idly watching TV one Sunday, some fine camera work in a small village had stopped me. The camera was focused on a proud and ancient weather-beaten face. From the narrator I gathered it was a documentary on a little-known northern New Jersey hill-and-mountain village called Torytown. I was particularly struck by dark eyes, the high cheekbones, and the arrow-shaft posture of the old man. Then the cameras took in the man's sons; they were light, almost blond. The narrators explained that the inhabitants of Torytown were descendants of Leni Lape and Delaware Indians and Hessians who had deserted the British when Burgoyne's army was making its pitiful march from Saratoga to Boston. Before World War I, a famous anthropologist from Harvard had published a story of the Torytowners, as they were called, and it had created a mild sensation. I also recalled with some slight uneasiness the narrator stressing that visitors were not welcome in Torytown; the mountain people were suspicious of the world outside their Bearfort Mountain home. Their hostility was underscored when a phalanx of state police had to usher in the draft board to register the males in World War II. The Torytowners lived mostly by poaching, fishing in the state reservoirs, dairy farming, and breeding a small tough pony called the Callender Buckskin, which, ironically, they shipped west.

I kept going over the program in my mind as I moved along the highway. It was a lonely, monotonous drive after I swung into Route 23 from 46, with only a few milk trucks rumbling on to New York. It was so tiresome I stopped at an all-night diner to get coffee and cigarettes and confirm Johnny's directions.

I finally passed through Newfoundland and the darkened Hunter's Inn. It wasn't long before I spotted the small service station with the battered tin sign, Adam's Service. It was little more than a cinder-block shack, a tin roof, an outhouse with "Gentlemen" and "Ladies" stenciled on the wooden doors, a grease pit, and three gas pumps. A single naked bulb hung over the head of a young man with his feet on a greasy table. A checkered hunting hat was pulled down over his eyes. A lean, wolfish-looking dog was asleep. When I knocked on the door the checkered hat jerked upward and the dog raised his head to bare his teeth. The boots came down with a clump. A big hand pushed back the hat, and I was studied by a pair of lazy black eyes set in a dark face.

"You want gas?" he called out.

One eye on the dog, I shook my head and answered through the door, "I'm looking for Adam."

"Who wants him?"

Irritated, I snarled, "If you open this damn' door maybe I'll tell you."

The dark face split in a grin. "I guess you're the guy I'm waiting for," he said as he rose and unlocked the door. The deadly-looking animal started to rise.

"Down, Bravo," the young man ordered. The dog reluctantly lowered itself to the floor.

"Don't worry about him," he said cheerfully. "He'll only tear you apart when I tell him to."

"I hope that won't be necessary. Are you Adam?"

The smile faded. "I'm still waiting to hear who wants him."

"My name's Malloy."

"You got something to prove it, mister?"

It was a reasonable request but it irked me. For a moment I was tempted to tell him to stop playing cops and robbers and get Johnny on the phone, but the swarthy-skinned young man was deadly serious. I fumbled in my wallet and gave him my police card. He read it carefully, turned it over, then handed it back.

"It ain't signed where it says to sign your name," he observed. "But I guess you're the guy I'm waiting for. You ready?"

"As I'll ever be."

He flipped off the ceiling light and snapped on a small light over the desk. Then from a tin clothes closet he took a rifle.

"You watch the till, you hear, Bravo," he said, gently nudging the dog with his toe.

Bravo languidly moved his tail and kept his eyes on me.

"Do much hunting?" I asked as we walked across the station's yard.

"Yeah—for skunks," was the terse reply.

He threw the rifle into the cab of a small panel truck.

"You better lock up your car and leave it here," he said. "I'll pick it up in the morning and bring it back to the house."

"Why? Any reason?"

He jerked open the door of the cab. "You want to get a broken spring, mister, it's okay with me."

I knew I was beaten. "Okay. I'll be with you in a minute."

We rode down 23 for about two miles, then swung left onto a narrow blacktop road. There were a few darkened farmhouses, and long stretches of trees broken by an occasional deep meadow. I learned that my driver owned the gas station. Everything else was a grunt or a perfunctory answer. Finally I settled back into a deep silence. The only time Adam showed any emotion was when he suddenly swung his wheel to one side. I caught a brief glimpse of a big bushy black-and-white tail in the headlights.

"Polecat. Hit one of those and you'll stink for a week."

I had noticed when we were on 23 that Adam once or twice studied the highway in his overhead mirror. We had traveled about three miles on the side road when suddenly he jammed to a stop.

"Did you see if you were followed?" he snapped.

"I checked but I don't think I was."

"Mister, I hope you're right," he said, half to himself as he gunned the motor. The light truck took off like a startled animal. We rattled over a small bridge and swung onto a dirt road, where he shut off the lights.

"I'm just going to see who the hell this is."

We stared out the rear window. The cab now seemed to be filled with the smell of oil, grease, and stale cigarette smoke. Outside, there were only blackness and the cold chips of stars glinting through the leafless branches.

"Hear 'em?" Adam asked softly, and when I didn't answer he impatiently rolled down the window. When I strained my ears I could hear the distant sound of an approaching car. It was moving slowly, cautiously, down the winding road. After a few minutes I could see the glow of the headlights against the treetops as the car climbed a rise in the road.

"Watch it," Adam whispered, and we drew back from the window.

The car passed. It appeared to be a heavy sedan traveling at about twenty miles an hour. When it was out of sight, Adam backed out of the road and turned back in the direction of the highway we had left.

"Nobody I know," Adam said.

"How could you tell?"

"Everybody around here's been moving up and down this road so long they do it dead drunk," he said. "They don't move no ten miles an hour, mister. Those people were looking for somebody."

"Maybe me?" I asked.

The silent shrug answered me.

We took the first crossroad, which Adam said wound over the mountain. It would take longer but would get us to Torytown. The road was rutted from the winter, and we bounced inside the cab like two old sailors in a bucking longboat.

I estimated we had traveled about ten miles when suddenly we entered a larger road, now blacktop, which circled a lake that lay like a sparkling pan of silver in the moonlight.

From the blacktop we entered a dirt road again, passed a few farmhouses, made an abrupt U-turn, and backed into a driveway. Behind us, silhouetted by the moonlight, was a squat house with a slanted roof and a chimney pointing a stubby stone finger at the night sky. A chorus of hounds greeted Adam when he opened the truck door, but the baying broke off with a yip and a shouted curse.

"Wait here," Adam said as he jumped out of the cab.

Alone in the darkness I wondered whether I had really left Times Square less than two hours ago. This is just too damn' melodramatic, I thought, and got out of the cab. I had closed the door and was about to walk across a wide lawn to the house when a soft voice called out, "I'd stay put if I were you, mister."

I froze. What I had thought was a tree trunk was a man. When he moved, moonlight glinted on a rifle barrel.

"I was just going in," I said.

The soft voice said, "They want you, I guess they'll call you."

I was debating what to do when suddenly the door of the house opened and a man's figure filled the doorway.

"Duke? Is that you?"

It was Johnny, and I hurried toward the house, still conscious of that rifle barrel behind me.

I stepped inside, and he slapped me on the back.

"God, it's good to see you, Duke. Here he is, Inspector."

Johnny looked as if he hadn't slept for a week. A dark stubble covered his chin, and his eyes were smudged with fatigue.

Inspector Tom Murphy, weary looking but still impassive, smiled at me from behind a table. Beside him was a small, sullen, rather good-looking dark-haired man in his early thirties. I didn't need any introduction; I had seen Ricky Strasser many times in the city's courtrooms.

Sitting alongside Strasser was a striking young woman. She was taller than Strasser, slender, and with a breathtaking figure. Her skin was swarthy, her shoulder-length sable hair glossy and curly, her eyes polished onyx. She gave me an open, minx-like grin. I had the immediate feeling that as a child she could dive deeper and run faster than any boy she had ever played with. I liked Vickie Simms from the moment I met her. Behind her, leaning on a windowsill, were a lean, dangerous-looking pair of twins. Their blondness was startling. They were dressed in worn overalls and woolen plaid shirts. Adam had joined them. Seated in a worn easy chair was an older man who looked like a weather-beaten Lincoln in dungarees. He gave me a grave nod of welcome.

I was in an enormous log cabin. In one corner was an old-fashioned floor heater. A fire crackled in a fireplace that appeared large enough to burn Adam's panel truck. Throw rugs covered the wide planked floors. The imprisoned ruby light from the fire glowed in the polished log walls. Beyond the circle of light was a small kitchen. A split-log stairway led to a sleeping balcony, with a bearskin hung over the balcony rail. Above the fireplace were crossed snowshoes and a brace of oiled rifles and shotguns. The only other decoration was a framed picture of a jaunty FDR, head tilted back and cigarette holder pointed upward. Above the picture was the faded legend "Our Friend."

"Duke, I'd like you to meet the Simms family," Johnny said. He gestured to the weather-beaten Lincoln. "This is Mr. Simms," and to the blond twins, "Asa and Ben. You know Adam. And this is Vickie." He put his hand on Strasser's shoulder. "I imagine you know Ricky."

The old gentleman stood up. He was over six foot, lean and hard. His hand completely enveloped mine.

"We're happy to have you here, Mr. Malloy." He turned to Johnny. "We'll just go over to the old house, Johnny. You have a lot of talkin' to do." The blond twins and Adam followed him out without a word.

When they had left I looked at Johnny.

"Is that the tape recorder, Duke?"

"It is. But look, somebody has got to fill me in. What's going on?"

Strasser leaned forward and glared up at me.

"Look Johnny, I told you I don't feel right about having this guy here."

"I explained everything, Ricky," Johnny said soothingly. "Duke has been on this thing since the beginning—in fact, he started it."

"Then he should have his—" Strasser started to say, but Vickie gave him a sharp dig in the ribs.

"I told you I didn't want any of that talk when you're in this house," she said in a husky, attractive voice. "Pop don't like it."

"Okay, kid. Okay," Strasser said. "But I still don't like a newspaper guy around. That's all. Can't I even say what's on my mind any more?"

She leaned over and hugged him gently. "Sure, honey, but say it in a nice way."

"He's really a nice guy, Ricky," Johnny said.

"Okay," Ricky said, exasperated. "He's a nice guy. But if anything gets out where I am—I'm dead. You know what they'll do to me, Malloy?"

"What do you think I'm going to do, Ricky"—I gestured at the phone in the corner—"call West Fifty-fourth Street and tell them you're here?"

"Come on, Vickie, let's have some coffee," Johnny said, giving me a warning look. "Vickie makes the best damn' coffee in the mountains, doesn't she, Inspector?"

Murphy rose and stretched. "She certainly does. No sugar for me, Vickie."

While Vickie went back to the kitchen, Johnny waved me to a chair.

"Wait until you see this place in the daylight," Johnny said. "It's beautiful. They have a trout stream halfway up the road. You know this cabin was built just after the Civil War?"

Ricky said with a note of pride, "In the winter of 1867, to be exact. That fireplace is the original one."

I said I remembered seeing something on TV about Torytown.

"Don't say anything about TV to the old man," Johnny said. "He never got over that show. Tourists began coming up here. And some guy with a tape recorder kept bugging him to sing some folklore songs." He called out, "Wasn't that it, Vickie?"

"What's that?" she called back.

"The fellow that came up here with the tape recorder and wanted to tape your father's singing?"

She came to the door of the kitchen. "Don't talk to Pop about that guy! The boys got real mad and wanted to kick him down the mountain."

"I saw Flaherty's press conference on TV," Johnny said. "What do you think?"

I gave him my version of the Prophet's press conference and told him how it had completely obliterated the Gennaro story.

"I had a feeling something was up, when I went back to the office after working at the precinct," Johnny said. "Flaherty called me into his office. Hoff was there, and they both looked like the tiger who had just eaten the keeper. It took only a few minutes. Flaherty said he just wanted me to know I was to conduct the Gennaro investigation as I saw fit, and if I needed any assistance I was simply to ask him for it. He asked Hoff if he understood, and Hoff said he did."

"Then Vickie called," Strasser said nervously.

Johnny repeated, "Then Vickie called. Murphy and I were going over that eyewitness's statement when the call came in. The operator said someone from Baltimore had been trying my house all morning. It was Vickie. She only told us where she was, and hung up. The inspector and I were on our way in five minutes. I just left a note for Flaherty that we were going out of town to check a tip.

Ricky said savagely, "It was that Giovanni bastard! He turned me in!"

Johnny said patiently: "After your story of the raid, Gennaro told Ricky to hide himself in Baltimore for a while. They all thought it was going to blow over. One of his friends, a mobster named Giovanni, who owns a nightclub down there, put Ricky and Vickie up in a small motel outside the city. To Vickie, Giovanni didn't seem kosher. One day she was going down a hall and heard Giovanni talking to somebody. She couldn't get the whole thing, but she heard him say something like 'our boy and his dame.' It didn't really mean much, but Vickie insisted they blow."

Strasser took out a handkerchief and wiped his forehead. "Christ, am I glad she heard the bum!"

"They pulled out that night. They were just leaving the motel when a car with New York plates passed them."

"There were two gorillas in the car," Ricky said nervously. "One guy looked familiar. I think Gennaro used him for muscle."

"It looks like they were on their way down to take care of Ricky."

"Looks like!" Ricky exploded. "There's no doubt about it. For Christ's sake, man, do you know what they would pay to find me?"

Johnny said soothingly, "No one is going to find you, Ricky. No one."

"You'll have complete protection at all times, Ricky," Inspector Murphy said.

Ricky gave him a scornful look. "What—for the rest of my life?" He stared broodingly into the fire. Johnny looked at me and shook his head. He seemed relieved when Vickie came in with a tray of cups and some cookies.

"Honey, you're not worrying again?"

"I can't help it," Strasser said. "Every time we talk about it I see that guy in the front seat of the car. He's a crazy guy—the mob calls him 'The Bug.'"

"No Bug will get in here," she said cheerfully. "You saw how Adam and the twins can shoot?"

"They have a little shooting range back in the woods, Duke," Johnny said with awe. "You ought to see those guys!"

Ricky said proudly, "They don't use beer cans or anything like that—just a piece of wood stuck in a post. And this dame can shoot just as good as any of them!"

"Every kid in the mountains shoots rabbits and chucks by the time they're eight," Vickie said as she poured the coffee. "Milk, Inspector?"

For the next half hour we sat around the fire, sipping coffee and discussing hunting, fishing, the mountains, a variety of subjects. I could see what Johnny was doing—getting Strasser to relax before he began any tape recording.

Finally coffee was finished and Johnny gave me the eye.

"It's very simple to record," I said casually. I plugged in the speaker. "Here, let me show you." I put it on record and spoke briefly into the mike, then switched it on. My voice came through loud and clear.

"That's marvelous," Vickie exclaimed. "I should get one for rehearsing."

Ricky eyed the machine and wet his lips. "Yeah. Yeah."

"You have the typewriter, Duke?" Johnny said.

"Right here."

"Good. What I would like to do is have Inspector Murphy take shorthand notes as Ricky is talking. Later he'll type them up. That way we get it down twice." He went on. "I think, Ricky, we should start at the very beginning, just as you told us."

"You mean about meeting the Wop in West Side Court the day they pulled him on that vagrancy rap?"

"That's it. And then how he called up and you went over to that restaurant—"

"Frank's, down on Baxter Street," he said. "That was my first real contact with him."

"That's it," Johnny said. He was trying to be nonchalant, but I could see that underneath he was tense. Even Murphy looked on edge.

"Pull your chair up closer, Ricky," Johnny said. "Duke, how long is the tape?"

"Two hours," I said. "I have plenty more."

"Christ, to tell the whole story you need ten," Strasser said. "That right, honey?"

Vickie nodded. "We said we were going to tell everything, honey, so you go ahead."

"Okay. Okay. Turn it on Malloy."

[27]

RICKY TALKED FOR hours, he was still talking when the sun was up. I will never know how Tom Murphy kept taking shorthand, but he did. I took notes, a million notes, more notes than I will ever use. But I couldn't help myself; I was listening to one of the most incredible stories of American crime I had ever heard. I have heard veteran reporters reminisce about the famous Kefauver hearing and the Valachi testimony, but they paled next to what Ricky Strasser told us in that log cabin in the heart of Torytown.

Ricky traced his life with Gennaro from the morning of his first meeting in New York's West Side Court. He described the syndicate's meetings in New York State, New York City, Ohio, Florida, California, and even Seattle and Toronto, in which the top mobsters of the country reported on their profits and their losses in every imaginable racket. Reports on corruption of judges, whole police departments, prosecutors, even the military, were given; the syndicate was deeply involved not only in the illegitimate but also in the legitimate, such as government contracts. Names, dates, places, bribes, private telephone numbers, phony holding corporations, the legitimate companies and how the syndicate operated them. Ricky told everything.

Vickie stayed awake as long as she could, and finally fell asleep, her head on Strasser's knee. At his urging she gave us a bleary good night and went upstairs to bed, promising to get up and cook us breakfast.

As the darkness paled to gray, then to creeping light, Johnny began slowly, tenaciously, bringing Ricky around to New York City and McShane. There was no doubt that Strasser feared McShane even more than the mob's killers.

"That son of a bitch never gives up," he said over and over. "Gennaro always said he's worse than two Sicilians, and what the hell is worse than that?"

But Johnny was relentless. He kept probing, digging in deeper. Ricky flared up at him several times, but Johnny patiently continued. In the end even I knew that while Gennaro had told Ricky everything there was to know about McShane, there was only one tangible link that legally chained McShane to Gennaro and the policy racket.

It had happened one day in the policy bank; Ricky had come over at Gennaro's request and was waiting when the phone rang.

"The guy at the other end of the phone just said, 'Let me talk to the boss.' I recognized McShane's voice. He has a rasping voice like a longshoreman. I said, almost without thinking, 'Hiya, Jim. This is Ricky Strasser.' He just grunted something, and I said to myself if he doesn't want to talk to me, the hell with him. So I called the Wop, and he talked to him. I asked Gennaro if it was McShane, and he said it was; in fact, he had to get up five G's right away for him. I was standing there when he counted out the dough and put it into a plain envelope and sent one of his flunkeys out to get Frank the Sheik—that's the pimp who drives the ribbon car."

"In other words you could identify McShane's voice as the man who asked for the boss?" Johnny asked.

Strasser gave him a weary smile. "Come on, Counselor, I'm still a pretty good lawyer. I'm giving you your conspiracy count."

"That's the only time you ever spoke to McShane, Ricky?"

"If I had any personal meetings, don't you think I would have told you about them long before this? McShane's the smartest crook in the country. Nobody is going to get him hooked. I spoke to him only a few times, and those were at social events. He told Gennaro he didn't want any part of me. In fact, I think I'm the only one in the setup besides Gennaro who ever spoke to McShane outside of saying hello at a fight or a political rally."

"Did Vickie ever talk to him?" Johnny asked.

Strasser gave Johnny a long cold look.

"No. And if she did I wouldn't let her talk to you. We made a deal, remember?"

Johnny nodded. "I promised you I would never call Vickie as a witness. I'm just looking for leads, Ricky."

"Well, look for them somewhere else," the lawyer said roughly.

Abruptly he stood up. "I don't know about you guys but I'm bushed. I'm going to hit the sack. I'll see you later." He added to Murphy in a low voice, "Just make sure those hillbillies are on the lookout."

The inspector said evenly, "Don't worry, Ricky—nobody's going to get you."

"You just better make sure of that, Murphy."

When the bedroom door closed, we looked at one another. My eyes felt gummy, my mouth stale from too much coffee and cigarettes. In the daylight both Johnny and Murphy appeared incredibly haggard.

"I don't know about you guys," Johnny said, imitating Strasser, "but I'm going to have a snort."

He came out of the kitchen with a bottle and three glasses. It was some local product and burned all the way down, but it made my blood run again.

"Isn't this the damnedest setup you've ever seen, Duke?"

"I still don't know the whole story. How did—"

He held up his hand and made a gesture to the balcony.

"Let's get some air. You going to call in, Inspector?"

"I'll take a run down to Irontown and call from there," Murphy said. "I'll bring back some groceries."

"Murph, will you call my office?" I asked. "Just tell Turner Elliott I'm out of town with you and Johnny on a Gennaro tip and I'll call just as soon as I can."

"Okay. Anything you fellows want from the village?"

"Get some beer and cigarettes, Murph," Johnny said. "That local booze would melt iron."

"There's one more thing," I said. "See if you can buy me a small camera and some film."

"Duke, you take any pictures of Vickie or Strasser, and I'll throw you and that camera in the lake." Johnny looked at me. "Is that understood?"

Murphy said, "And I'll hold his head under."

"I simply want to take some pictures of the countryside, that's all," I insisted. "Come on, let's take that walk."

In the early-morning light the log cabin was enormous. There was a wide open porch with a set of worn summer chairs and a tired-looking glider. The cabin was on a grassy plot easily a half acre, screened from the road by trees and brush. Through the branches I could see sunlight sparkling on water. In the rear of the house were a smaller cabin, a big old barn, now a garage; what appeared to be a small racetrack, and then the forest, which rose to a sharp ridge. One of the twins was walking a small buckskin-colored pony in the corral, while the other twin sat on the rail.

"That's one of the famous Callender ponies," Johnny said. "They're small and tough, marvelous with kids. Vickie's family has been breeding them for over a hundred years. Here's the old man now."

Mr. Simms was dressed in a heavy plaid shirt and pressed chino working pants. When he came near, I could see his weather-beaten skin had a bronze tinge, while his eyes were startling gray.

"Good mornin'," he said. "The boys said you fellows were up most of the night. Did Vickie fix breakfast?"

"We sent Vickie up to bed, Mr. Simms," Johnny said. "She was exhausted. I don't think she's had four hours' sleep in the last three days."

"Well, me and the boys will fix something. It looks like a nice mornin'. The ponies smell the spring. They're frisky as puppies."

"We're going to take a little walk down to the lake," Johnny said.

"Sure. There's a little path across the road," Simms said. "There's one thing I'd like to get straight."

"By all means," Johnny said.

"When Vickie called and said she needed our help, I told her to come right away. I didn't know what trouble she was in until she told me. But that doesn't matter. We'll do everything we can to help her and that fellow she's got. But I want you to remember the promise you gave me—"

"I promised you, Mr. Simms, as I promised Mr. Strasser—Vickie won't be called as a witness. And just to get the record straight: she didn't commit any crime. I guess the only thing she did wrong was fall in love with Strasser."

The old man shook his head. "Nobody could ever tell Vickie what to do. I remember when she was just a kid, I told her a hundred times not to dive in the lake from that tree over there. Well, she did. The doctors say they never knew how they put her head back together."

"How did Vickie ever come to New York?" Johnny asked.

"That damn' newspaper over in Paterson had a beauty contest. Even the boys didn't know she entered. She won, and then there was no holdin' her. After she went to New York, we heard from her every few months. Sometimes in the summer she would come up here for a time, but then she got in a show and all we saw of her was her pictures in the papers. . . . What do you think will happen to that fellow?"

Johnny shrugged.

"We're just people who live in the mountains and make our own way. Some of the things you told me . . ." The old man shook his head. "Well, I'll go in and get the coffee on."

"They're wonderful people," Johnny said as we walked across the road and down the narrow path to the shimmering lake. "I tried to explain to the old man why Strasser is so important, but I don't think I got through to him. But that kid, Adam, knows what it's all about. He only got out of the army a few years ago, and he's been around."

"Did Adam tell you he thought we were followed?"

He stopped short, and I told him about the sedan on the road.

"That's what the inspector was afraid of," he said as we continued walking. "He twisted and turned for an hour before we drove out of Baltimore."

"But why would anyone follow me?"

"Why not? They know you're working with me. If they missed me they might tail you to get to me. By now they must know that Strasser has flown the coop." We paused at the edge of the lake. The sun had cleared the rim of the surrounding hills, and the water shimmered with golden light. A school of sunfish was feeding at the end of a small dock, the tiny splashes the only sounds in the morning quiet.

"McShane was important last week, Duke," Johnny said suddenly, "but he's twice as important now."

"How come?"

"Just before you arrived last night, we watched the news. The White House announced he will be the new National Chairman. Huntley and Brinkley gave him most of their half-hour show. There is no doubt he'll be the key figure in getting out the New York City vote."

"Flaherty doesn't have an idea of Strasser?"

"You're the only one outside of Murphy and myself who knows."

"God, I wish I could let my publisher know."

Johnny tossed a pebble into the water. "We can't take a chance, Duke. Even Murphy isn't telling the commissioner."

"What about you? I remember you telling me Flaherty had to know everything."

"I thought about it, God knows I did, Duke, but I can't tell him now. Before I tell him I want this one wrapped up and tied with a ribbon."

"What you are saying, in effect, is you don't trust him."

"Maybe I don't want to tempt him." He tossed in another pebble, and we watched the ripples widen out beyond the dock. "A phone call to the right person with what you and I and Murphy know . . . Christ!"

"That phone call could get him a lot of goodies."

"Like a judgeship," he said shortly.

"Fill me in on what happened to Vickie and Strasser after they left the motel," I said to change the subject. "Where did they go?"

"They had got to a rooming house in Baltimore when Vickie called me. I don't have to tell you Strasser's no hero. When we arrived he was shaking so he couldn't lift a cup. Vickie is the one with the guts. She met us on the highway and drove us over to the rooming house. I thought we would have to break down the door before the bastard would open up."

"I'm surprised he talked."

"Vickie laid it on the line for him—either cooperate with us or she would ditch him. By the time we got to him, he would have made a deal with the devil to turn in his own mother if it meant saving his own skin."

"He's certainly a creep."

"When we got out of Baltimore and things looked better, he started yelling about a deal," Johnny said. "I told him I would put my fist down his throat if he started anything. But I didn't have to. Vickie just talked to him for a few minutes, and he was straightened out."

"She's really a dish, Johnny. What does she see in Strasser?"

He shrugged. "I tried to find out, but all she said was that Strasser treated her like a lady when she was in the Starlight Club line. Maybe he appeals to her motherly instincts."

"There are a few things I had better fill you in on."

He gave me a grim look. "You mean what you and your boss and my boss were doing in the office of my future father-in-law?"

"Exactly."

"Be my guest."

We sat on the dock, and I told him in detail what had happened in Ryder's office. He listened intently, without interrupting. When I finished, he stared out across the lake.

"I've been hearing rumors about Ryder for a long time, but they were only rumors, and nothing more. Connie has mentioned that downtown project. In fact, I always felt she was worried about it. Once I thought she was about to tell me something but didn't."

"As I pointed out, Johnny, he really wasn't trying to fix anything."

"Come on, Duke, you're a big boy. You don't think he was going to come up with a bundle of money in a white envelope, did you? He's the Washington type. They're shocked at the word 'bribe.' They either do it by making sure you get a bank loan without collateral or by swinging some Engineer Corps project over to you, or making sure that if there is a project, the trucking, the insurance, the construction go to the right people."

"Clean graft," I said.

"Of course. In this instance he couldn't throw anything your way, so he dropped a few flares to your publisher; the Cummings store was one, the Ohio newspaper merger the other."

"I wonder if that dredging-company and bank-loan crack I made pulled him up short."

"Are you kidding?" Johnny said. "That is going to be one hell of a thing to fix." He squinted out across the lake. "Whoever gave you that tip must certainly be on the inside. Ryder would never get into a deal like that unless it was with people he trusted."

"Apparently the loan had been arranged."

"What's the difference?" Johnny said. "His problem right now is to make it appear it was a purely business arrangement. Everything aboveboard. Everything a matter of record." He shook his head. "This is going to be a tough one for Ryder to square both here and in Washington. There wasn't any hint as to who your tipster might be?"

"Not a hint."

Johnny gave me a tired smile. "Knowing Ryder, I'll give you ten to one he was on the phone with his flunkey, trying to figure how they could get the senator off the hook, the minute you left the penthouse."

"Sometimes I think McShane is a choirboy compared to your future father-in-law," I said.

"You know something, Duke," Johnny said softly, "that's exactly what I have been thinking."

"You certainly don't think we'll hook Ryder to McShane!"

"At this time, legally, no. Morally, yes. Remember the German munitions makers? Anything to keep the boat from rocking. And that anything turned out to be—"

"Hitler," I said.

"They were his godfathers," he said. "When he failed, they dropped him like a hot stove and joined the Allies in denouncing him. After a respectable period they went back into business. Isn't that like Ryder? Don't rock the boat because it might disturb the profits, and to make sure, protect the local dictator so he will keep the boys in line. If he flops, drop him. What have you lost?"

"What do you intend to do about it, Johnny?"

"Let's say that Mr. Ryder and a certain senator are high on my list," was the quiet answer. He added: "But for the moment McShane is our prize target, and I'm going to indict the son of a bitch if it's the last thing I do. With that phone-call conversation I have one good solid conspiracy count. I'm going to throw in bribery, extortion, and everything but the kitchen sink after that."

"I want to make one thing clear, Johnny. I have a job the same as you and Inspector Murphy. My job is to get this into the paper. Exclusive. Not when forty-eight thousand reporters and photographers pour into this Irontown place."

"Can't we wait until we get back? Who's going to know it up here. There's no newspaper—"

"There's a justice of the peace who might be a stringer for AP or the nearest weekly, or he may even know a friend on the state police who will tip off the local guy who gets his wife's picture in the society page. I'll phone in when you're arraigning Strasser."

He bit his lower lip, then threw the remainder of the pebbles out into the water. The splashes scattered the school of sunfish, and their tiny, brilliant bodies exploded in all directions, like fragments of colored light in the mountain-clear water.

"Okay," he said at last. "You call your paper just before we arraign this joker. Then we move out fast. I don't want any trouble with the state cops over here."

"That reminds me, Johnny. I'm scared."

He smiled grimly. "That makes three of us. So is Murphy. But I can't call in the cops. Strasser will clam up, and if we don't get the statement we might as well all resign."

"How much longer do you intend to stay here?"

"Today and tomorrow. I want the inspector to type up that statement and I want it signed and I want you to witness it. Then we'll go down to Irontown and arraign Strasser on a fugitive charge. The justice of the peace is Simms's cousin, so we can do it one, two, three and be on our way back to the city."

Behind us a bell clanged.

"I think that's breakfast," Johnny said. "Let's go."

[28]

INSPECTOR MURPHY RETURNED loaded down with bundles. He had beer, cigarettes, and a small camera and two rolls of film for me. Mr. Simms protested that it was unthinkable for guests to buy their own food, but Murphy glibly informed him he had an ulcer and needed a special diet. We all laughed when the old man wryly held up a can of corned-beef hash. Strasser and Vickie slept through breakfast; when we finally got started again it was late. We worked through the afternoon and again far into the night until Strasser shouted that he'd be damned if he was going to say another word. Frankly, I had to agree with him. Strasser's voice was hoarse, but we had more than eight hours on tape. Johnny had been relentless in his questioning. He had brought out things even Strasser had forgotten.

He refused to accept such statements as: "Then we met and agreed that the cops would get a thousand a month." Johnny would go back and insist, "Now what did Gennaro say and what did you say to Gennaro?" Or, "When you talked to downtown on the phone, what did you say to the operator at headquarters?" "What time of the day did you always call?" "What did Gennaro say when he counted out the money?"

When finally he had finished we knew everything there was to know about crime and crooked politics not only in New York but in several other large cities. Strasser was a shrewd lawyer, and always prefaced his remarks with "Now this is only hearsay evidence, Johnny," or, "You can corroborate this if you bring in that collector from 123rd Street. I think his name is Johnny D . . ." Unfortunately, while we knew everything, we also realized some of it would never stand up in court.

What it did produce, however, was a shocking indictment of McShane's machine, which obviously had grown fat and powerful by its alliances with the underworld.

As Strasser continued, Murphy's face grew grimmer by the hour. He was hearing men whom he had trusted branded as corrupt. Sergeant Britt Peters and the shadowy "downtown" clique were not all; at least ten high-ranking police officials would be indicted on the basis of Strasser's testimony, most of which could be corroborated.

But there was one mystery that even Ricky Strasser couldn't solve: Where were Gennaro's books?

"I know he kept a personal book," Strasser said, "because I saw it. One day he was drinking wine. I think it was the day his son had another kid, he brought it out. He was drunk or he would never have done that. He threw the book down on the table and said this was his insurance policy. I flipped through it, but it was written in Italian. There's no doubt he wrote it."

"How do you know it was in Gennaro's handwriting?" Johnny asked.

"He wrote like a kid in the fourth grade. He gripped the pen like he was milking it." Strasser held up his pen to demonstrate. "He didn't like to be kidded about it."

"What kind of book was it?"

"A regular kid's homework book. It had a black-and-white marbleized cover. I remember thinking that this was like the books I used to buy when I was in grammar school."

"Anything written on the front?"

"Nothing. The first few pages are written in Italian. I think he did this to throw off anyone who might open it accidentally."

"What did he do with the book after he showed it to you?" Murphy asked.

"When I started to go through it, he snatched it away. I think he was sorry he showed it to me. I asked him what was in it, but he just waved his hand and went into another room. When he came out he didn't have the book."

"What room was that?"

"It was a bedroom. Some of the collectors used to knock off a piece there when Gennaro was out of town."

"A few weeks before the raids Gennaro went out of town, apparently in a hurry," I said. "We understand he did this a few times a year. Do you know where he went?"

Strasser shook his head. "Nobody knows. He just took off and returned in about a week." He hesitated and looked at us. "Did you know the guy loved to fish?"

"How do you know that?" Johnny asked.

"For Christ's sake, stop trying to pin me down, Counselor," Strasser snapped. "I'm not on your God-damned witness stand yet!"

Johnny's lips thinned. By this time we had all had Strasser up to our ears.

"I only asked you, Ricky," Johnny said. "You know better than all of us how important any bit of information is at this time."

Ricky slid down in his chair. "Yeah, I know, but don't pin me down for every little thing." He stared at the floor for a moment. "Like I said, I know the guy liked to fish only from what he said one night. Once or twice we went out for dinner. I was always surprised because he never wanted to go to an Italian restaurant; it had to be fish. I hate fish, but to humor him I went along to one of those big fish places on Third Avenue. He ate fish like it was going out of style. Every time he said the same thing, that there was nothing like fresh-caught fish. The last time I asked him how he knew, and he said he liked to fish because that was the only thing that took his mind off bums and crooked cops."

"Did he ever say where he went fishing?" Johnny gently pressed.

"Believe me, if I knew I would have told you long ago."

The thought suddenly came to me, and I asked, "Ricky, did Gennaro ever mention he had real-estate holdings in Harlem?"

Strasser slowly shook his head. "No . . ." Then his face brightened. "Wait a minute. I remember—this is hearsay—but one of the collectors once asked me what the old man was doing buying some tenements on Lenox Avenue. But that's all I know."

"Didn't you ask him about it?" Johnny asked. "After all, you were his attorney."

Strasser gave him a patronizing look. "It wasn't the usual client-attorney relationship. Gennaro and I had what I guess you would call a unique working arrangement; I did what he wanted, and got paid for it. I never asked any questions about anything else. That's what the Wop liked." He added in an elaborate Italian accent, "Ask-a no questions."

"Why did you stay with him for so long?" I asked.

"I was a punk kid when he gave me my first break. After that, the money rolled in. For a kid that worked in a tailoring store and went to law school at the same time, this was living for the first time."

"Did you ever think of leaving the syndicate?" I asked.

He stared into the fire for a long time. Vickie, who was sitting on the floor, reached up and took his hand.

"Sure I did," he said slowly. "After I met Vickie we talked it over and I decided to cut out. I had more than enough cash stashed away so we could go to California or somewhere. I called up Gennaro and told him I wanted to see him. He said okay, and I went over to the bank. I walked in just as he was talking to some guy on the phone. Then he went into the john. The other guy in the room was a comptroller waiting for the night numbers to come in. He leaned over and whispered that it was all up with the collector on 108th. I asked him what he meant, and he said Gennaro had just ordered somebody to burn him. When the Wop came out, I made up some story about having to see him. The next day I read where they found this guy from 108th Street looking like a sieve in a hallway. . . . From then on, I forgot about leaving the setup."

"What about District Attorney Flaherty, is he on the take?" I asked.

"I'd like to tell you he is—but he isn't. Not for cold cash, anyway. But in a way I think he's a bigger thief than I am."

"How can you say that if he never took a bribe?"

Ricky said scornfully: "Because he never kicked over the rocks to see what was underneath, that's why. Sure his office was busy: homicides, 1897's, a few grafters. . . . All you have to do is look at his office record. It's terrific! But did he ever overturn the apple cart? Did he ever invite Big Jim McShane in for a little Grand Jury session? You know better than I do, De Lorenzo. Did he ever tell his staff to snoop into McShane's affairs or even Gennaro's? Of course not! These boys were big!" He leaned forward. "Look, Johnny, I've been as crooked as a pretzel, and the kind of a lawyer no one should ever be. But at least I admit it. Your boss wants that judgeship so bad he can taste it. And he wants to make sure you or anyone else don't kick over any rocks this year, not even a little pebble."

He stared into the fire for a moment, then turned to Johnny.

"There's only one more thing I know; I'm going to tell it to you and that has to be the end." Strasser took a deep breath. "McShane has a dame. Who she is, I don't know."

Johnny spoke softly. "Can you give us a little hint why you think so, Ricky?"

"All I know is, one night Gennaro was talking about the big shots. He called them 'the big-a shots downtown,' and he somehow brought up McShane's name." He held up his hand in a warning fashion. "Don't ask me if I questioned the guy—I didn't. I told you before, I never asked questions. . . ."

"Okay, Ricky, go ahead."

"Well, Gennaro said that when he first met him, McShane's wife had died. He was 'a-sick in the heart,' as he put it. Then he met some woman, and now 'she's-a his girl for a long-a time.' That's the way the

Wop put it. So help me, Johnny, don't ask me any more because I don't know anything else. At the time I couldn't care less who McShane was shacking up with. I got the impression—no facts, Counselor—that she was probably a middle-aged woman. After all, McShane is in his sixties."

He stood up and said abruptly, "I'm going to bed." This time he didn't even look at Vickie, but she hurried after him and tugged him down to kiss her. They whispered something; then he went upstairs.

"He's starting to brood about it," she said when she rejoined us. "I got up in the middle of the night and found him sitting on the edge of the bed, just staring out the window."

"I want to be very honest, Vickie," Johnny said carefully. "If he jumps now, he'll go to jail when we catch him."

She ran a hand through her thick hair. "You don't have to worry about him running away; he's too afraid of them out there. He's like a little kid when it comes to pain. Last year it took me all week to drag him to a dentist. Even then it took the dentist all week to fill a little cavity. He would only let him drill a little bit each night."

"What's worrying him?"

"It's not the future, but the past he's thinking about. Ricky could have been a great lawyer if he never met Gennaro." She looked up at Johnny. "Level with me, Johnny, what will they give him?"

"He's a people's witness, Vickie. If he goes the limit with me, I'll practically get on my knees to the judge."

"I always can write a sympathetic story about him," I put in.

"Thanks, but don't," she said. "No matter what you write about him, it comes out bad."

"Let's say he gets an SS," Johnny said. When Vickie gave him a startled look, he added quickly, "I'm just supposing. But *if* he did, what would you two do?"

"Get married," she said promptly, "after he gets a divorce."

Johnny was surprised. "I never knew he was married."

"He has a son," she said. "They were married when he was going to night school. I think she's a schoolteacher."

"Will you live here?"

She gave him a sardonic look. "Ricky and Vickie's horse farm?"

"It doesn't look like a bad life to me, Vickie."

Impulsively she leaned over and put her hand on his shoulder.

"I'm not laughing at it, Johnny. In a way I'm sorry I ever left it. But I've been around New York too long. Three weeks with nothing to go to but the bar in Irontown would make me a candidate for Bellevue psycho. During the summer I always manage a week out here to keep Dad happy, but I need the big city. Well, good night, all."

Vickie went upstairs. I didn't have to look up to see which door she would open.

Ricky slept through breakfast and lunch. When he finally got up, he was in a foul humor. Obviously it was no time for Johnny to tackle our last chore, getting Ricky to read, approve, and sign the statement Murphy had typed.

While Johnny stole a nap, Murphy and I walked down to the lake. The warm sun was penetrating and the quiet was almost hypnotic. We sat on the small dock watching the widening ripples when I tossed in a tiny pebble.

"That's the way it will be when this thing breaks," Murphy said unexpectedly.

"How do you mean?"

"The repercussions will ripple out from New York right up to the White House. McShane's a power in this city. If we hurt him, they'll never let up on us."

"What will they do to you, Inspector?"

"I'm putting in my papers," he said with a slow smile.

I was surprised. "Because of this case?"

"Not necessarily. I'm a little too old for getting pushed around. When I was younger I pounded a beat in the woods out on Staten Island after I knocked off one of their clubhouses. It was bitter winter, and they sent a mickey mouse to check on me every hour. I battled them toe to toe. But I was young then. Today I don't think I could take it. I know what this man McShane can hand out." He shook his head. "That's why I'm worried."

"About the setup here?"

"I can see Johnny's point. If we had the state police or local cops running about the place, Strasser might get hysterics. I know Johnny wants to keep things nice and easy until he milks him dry. That's fine with me, but every minute, every hour, I'm getting more uneasy."

"You didn't see anything when you went to the village?"

"Not a thing. But after forty years in this job you can smell trouble." He gripped the edge of the dock. "We have the biggest pigeon of them all, Duke, right here in this coop. A hundred men, less important than McShane, would gladly take the chance to send a couple of torpedoes or junkies over here to burn him. God, man, do you know that this man can disturb the next presidential election! He's giving us enough to indict the National Chairman! And in the toughest election year in more than two decades!"

Murphy suddenly hit the edge of the dock with his fist. "I told Johnny last night we just have to wrap this thing up fast! I wish you would talk to him, Duke. Seriously. I'm not being melodramatic. We know they were looking for him in Baltimore."

"I told you about that car—"

"Adam and I and the old man hit every back road the night you came in. He also passed the word to some of his relatives to watch out for strangers. God, they have more relatives than gypsies!"

"Did you find anything?"

He wet the tip of his finger in the lake and drew a few lines on the planks.

"Here's Route 23. This is Beaverdam Road where you were and where it eventually connects with the George Washington Bridge. You were about halfway up this road when you saw the car." His finger made a half circle. "Then you circled back and came in by a side road. The sedan following you went straight down the road to the other highway."

"How did you know?"

"We hit the gas station nearest to the other exit of Beaverdam Road. The owner knew Adam. He described the car, and said two fellows asked him if he had seen a panel truck pass." He gave me a cold smile. "He described them as 'city fellows.' One an 'Eyetalian,' as he put it. That's why I want to get Strasser out of here."

"The old man seems to have the place well watched. . . ."

Murphy gave a snort of disgust. "These people are country people, Duke. They think everything is still cowboys and Indians. They wouldn't know what you meant if you said a junkie might come in for a fast knockoff. Hell, there are three old roads you can use to get on this property. One is an abandoned charcoal road, and then there are two footpaths back in the woods just over the ridge."

"How do you know all this, Inspector?"

"That Adam's a real hunter. Yesterday, just before it got light, he and I did a little exploring. The kid's been in the army; he understands more than the others do."

"And so, security wise?"

"It's a sieve." He stood up. "Maybe nothing will happen, Duke, but we have to wrap it up tonight."

I followed him up the narrow path, trying to argue with myself that cops naturally always look to the darker side of any situation. But my common sense didn't buy it. Ricky Strasser could tell too many secrets to hurt too many men.

[29]

THE TAPING WAS finished, but we worked all afternoon and into the evening on the statement. Strasser was now the attorney, not the witness. He changed words, phrases, argued with Johnny until we all groaned aloud our protests. They fought over what I considered trivia, but which Johnny said he considered important. The original copy was marked and changed until it was barely discernible. Then at last they were satisfied, and Murphy began retyping the forty-page statement for Ricky's signature.

"I want his statement to be ironclad," Johnny explained. "It's good enough to indict Peters, Barrist, and the others, but I want it spelled out when he talks about the phone calls from McShane."

"When you come right down to it," I said, "if we hadn't gotten Strasser to talk there would have been absolutely no link between McShane and Gennaro. Apparently Barrist and Peters never talked with McShane."

"Of course not," Johnny said. "McShane is too smart for that. He spoke to only one man—Gennaro. Luckily, Strasser happened to be in the bank that day or there would not be one damn' thing I could indict him for in the eyes of the law."

"Are you going to indict Peters and the others?"

"Peters, Barrist, the whole syndicate," he said. "I want to show exactly what has been going on for so many years." He looked at me. "I don't have to tell you, Duke, what will happen when this thing blows."

"Murph and I were talking about that."

"You and I, Savage, Murphy will be well beyond the point of no return."

"What about Flaherty?"

"Let's face it: to the leaders, he's failed. They said no scandal this year and they meant it."

"That means no judgeship?"

"He may still be able to pull it off," Johnny said. "But he'll have to pull every wire he has. They will scream plenty when McShane is indicted." A shadow passed over his face. "Don't think I feel good about this, Duke. After all, Flaherty opened a lot of doors for me. I just can't help but feel I sold him out."

"Would you want it any other way?"

"No, I guess not." He added bitterly, "But from now on I might as well have a leper's bell and keep yelling, 'Look out, here comes an honest man.' "

I wondered about Ryder, and after a moment's hesitation, asked Johnny how he thought his future father-in-law would react.

"He'll jump with the winners, of course. That's been a way of life with him ever since he made his first dollar."

"Will Washington let him?"

"Politicians are a realistic breed, Duke. Ryder did his best. The way they see it, he went out on a limb for them, so they probably will give him what he wants and turn their attention on the jury, and principally the judge."

"You've lost a lot of baby fat in the last few months, Johnny," I said.

"And gained a few gray hairs," he said wryly. "One good thing: I'll never have to worry about Connie."

"I was going to ask you about that—"

"She's been on her own since she was thirteen when her mother died. She was brought up in boarding schools here and in Europe. Ryder's only been a visitor, seldom a father."

"There's little doubt he'd do anything for her, Johnny."

"Of course," he said. "Don't they always? Forget about the kids while you're making the millions; then come back and give them charge accounts at Saks, Corvette convertibles, and coming-out parties at the Plaza. The wonderful thing is, Connie couldn't care less for that stuff but still loves her old man. Look at that moon!"

It perched on the treetops, flooding the forest with bright yellow light.

"Murphy is nervous as a cat, Johnny," I said softly.

"He's nervous!" he said fiercely. "What do you think I am?

Dammit! I wish I could call in the state police or the local cops, but that's all Strasser needs. And then again, whom can we trust?"

Murphy's tired voice rose behind us, "Johnny, there are honest cops."

"Maybe," Johnny grunted. "But I figure I got them right here in this cabin."

It was after midnight when the statement was finally finished. There was another hour of lawyer-wrangling between Ricky and Johnny. The old man came in with Adam; behind them trotted the lean, wolfish dog I had seen in Adam's service station. He eyed the room, then sank down with a sigh near me.

"Full moon tonight, Mr. Simms," I said, for the sake of conversation.

"It's bright on the road."

"Everything all right, Pop?" Ricky called out.

"Yes," he said sharply, "I guess everything's all right."

This seemed to satisfy Strasser, and he returned to his discussion with Johnny. The old man lowered himself into a chair, while Adam sat on the floor and stretched his feet out. I noticed his soles were caked with mud.

Finally Strasser and Johnny agreed on the wording of the statement, and Ricky signed with me and Murphy as witnesses. I could sense the sigh of relief when Johnny held up the last page, studied the drying ink, and nodded approval.

"How about some coffee?" Vickie said cheerfully, and went into the kitchen.

I was sitting on the floor opposite Adam, and suddenly the room seemed restful. Tonight I would sleep like an innocent. . . .

I must have dozed for a few minutes. At first I thought someone had touched off a firecracker that had shattered some glass. I sat up with a start. Ricky Strasser apparently had just come out of the kitchen, where the light was strongest, when they got off the first shot. It smashed the coffee cup in his hand, cutting his fingers but not injuring him seriously. He was a picture of a man frozen in his tracks by terror. He stared down dumbly at his right hand, where the blood was beginning to well.

I saw all this in a flash. Murphy leaped through the air, slammed Strasser against the wall, and covered him with his body. I heard his muffled shout: "Down! Down!" when the second glass shattered. The bullet made a dull thud into the thick log over my head, just where Strasser had been standing. Out of the corner of my eye I saw Johnny's hand in a wide arc tear at the long chain of the kitchen light; socket and light bulb shattered to the floor. Adam was in a half crouch, two rifles in his hand. I wondered why I hadn't noticed they were out of the rack and stacked in a corner.

"Everyone all right?" Murphy called.

"My hand's cut," Strasser's muffled voice quivered. "I'm bleeding. . . ."

Vickie said quickly, "Are you hit, honey . . . are you hit?"

"It's only a scratch," Murphy said calmly.

"I'm trying to see out there," Johnny said from a back room. "The moonlight is strong. I thought I saw someone running."

"Get away from that window," Murphy snapped. "Johnny, Adams, Mr. Simms, Duke, crawl into the kitchen."

The cop had taken over; he had this plan all worked out in his mind . . .

In the kitchen we crouched in a football huddle. Johnny was explaining that he had seen shadows moving past the house in the woods when we heard two sharp cracks, followed by a third.

"What's that?" he said.

"That's the twins," Simms said. "I had them posted up on the rim near the old charcoal road." There was another crack. "I guess they're driving them back off the road into the woods."

"Any chance of them flanking the boys and getting to one of the deer trails?" Murphy asked.

"I've got Henry up by the trails with his oldest. They both can pick a hair off a woodchuck's chin, if need be."

"Who's Henry?" I asked.

"That's Uncle Henry," Adam said. "He runs a 'dozer for the county."

"So we can assume they can be kept in this patch of woods behind the corral, is that right, Mr. Simms?" Murphy said.

"That's right, Inspector."

"Let's move out," Murphy said. I could hear him click off the safety on his .38. A rifle was thrust into my hands, and Adam quietly said it was loaded. There was no question that I could handle the rifle; in their world everyone could shoot.

"The moon's on the other side of the house," Murphy said. "Hug the garage and go along the fence where the rosebushes are and wait for me in the woods." He raised his voice slightly, "Ricky . . ."

"I'm with him," Vickie said in a composed voice. "His hand is cut but it's not bad."

"Ricky, if you go outside they'll kill you," Murphy said harshly. "If you stay here you'll be safe. Understand?"

"Get those guys, will you?" Ricky's voice was husky with fear. "They want to kill me."

"Vick."

"Yes, Adam."

"The rifle in the rack is loaded."

"Don't worry about me."

We slipped out one by one, hugging the dark side of the house and the garage and the thick rosebushes that wound in and out a split-rail fence, then along the small corral. Two shots sang overhead, but the firing broke off when the twins answered their muzzle blasts. By the time we gathered at the edge of the woods, there was a heavy sound of firing to our right. Uncle Henry's heavy .44 made the woods echo.

"Is that dog any good?" Murphy whispered to Adam.

For the first time I noticed that Adam was holding the dog by its collar.

"He's the best hunter we ever had."

"Shall we move out, Inspector?" Johnny asked.

"Spread out in a wide semicircle; use the trees. Adam, Mr. Simms and I and the dog will go ahead—"

There were several sharp cracks.

"They have a rifle and a handgun, Pop," Adam said.

"Duke, you and Johnny spread out and take cover. If they get past us—"

The heavy rifle slightly above us slammed; two more cracks answered.

Murphy and the old man moved forward in a deep crouch. Adam slipped the collar off the dog's neck, slapped it on the rump, then followed like a moving shadow. The woods were suddenly silent. In my mind's eye I could see them ahead of us, carefully picking their way through the heavy carpet of dead leaves and brush. Johnny whispered he would move off to one side; then I was alone.

Even the moon seemed changed now. Hard and yellow raw gold, it bathed the cabin in an eerie glow.

Then, what the Sunday supplements called "The Battle of Torytown" began.

There was a crash of glass from behind us in the house, followed by a scream, then two shots so close they could have been one. Simultaneously, rifle fire opened in the woods. For a moment I was stunned; then it came to me:

"Johnny," I shouted, "It's a diversion. Somebody is back there in the house!"

Johnny was already hurdling the fence. I followed, and almost screamed as my hand slammed down on the heavy thornbush. But I hit the ground near the garage and began running. Behind us the woods echoed with gunfire. As we reached the side of the house, a light went on. I was only a few feet behind Johnny when he yanked open the kitchen door and leaped into the house.

The lights were on in the living room. An empty garbage can was in the middle of the floor. Over it stood Vickie, a dazed look on her face, a rifle in one hand. Ricky sat in a chair beside her, his bulging eyes fixed ahead of him, one bandaged hand clasped in the other. Hanging half through the smashed window was a man in a gray lumber-jacket. A fedora and a gun lay on the floor in front of his dangling hand.

"I was bandaging Ricky's hand when there was a big crash and the garbage can came through the window," Vickie said breathlessly. "Then he started to climb in. When I screamed he fired at us. . . . I shot him."

Ricky said, "It went just over my head . . . just over my head . . ."

She leaned the rifle against the fireplace and reached over and held him.

"I could hear it, honey," Ricky kept saying, his voice muffled by her arms. "I could hear it. . . . It went just over my head."

Johnny and I ran into the room and pulled the man through the smashed window. I had seen and handled enough dead men to know he was ready for the coroner's slab. Vickie's bullet had torn through one eye.

Vickie cradled Strasser, rocking him gently back and forth like a frightened child. "We would have been better running away," she said bitterly. "I was a fool to think you could help him."

"It's my fault, Vickie," Johnny said as he stood up. "I should have called in the state police. I'm going to call them now."

"Cops," she said wearily, "what will cops do? Push him out a window?"

There was a scurry of footsteps outside and the door was yanked open. A slender, dark teen-ager looked in.

"We got 'em both!" he shouted. "One bastard shot Bravo. Adam got—"

He stopped to stare at the dead man and the widening pool of blood.

"Christ! Did you get him, Vickie?"

"Duke, will you get Mr. Simms and Murphy right away?" Johnny said. Then to the boy, "Who are you?"

"I'm Claude. Pop and I were up on the ridge—"

"Get me a blanket, Claude, and fast," Johnny snapped. "Better get them down here, Duke. God, what a mess!"

I took the boy's flashlight and in a few minutes found the men in the woods. They were two hired killers. Apparently when they had heard the shots in the house they made desperate attempts to break out of the woods by rushing forward, shooting as they came. Simms and Murphy killed the first one; the second almost reached the edge of the clearing in the confusion and darkness, but the dog discovered him. He tried to club the dog, and finally shot the fiercely attacking animal. Adam's shot smashed his shoulder as he was climbing the fence. When I came up he was sitting in the dry leaves, a snarling, tough young hood dressed in dark-blue pants and what appeared to be a new suede jacket. He was holding his shoulder and cursing Murphy and his partners.

Adam was kneeling over his dog. It was still alive, breathing in short rapid bursts.

"If it wasn't for that mutt," the hood snarled, "I could have cut—"

Adam rose silently. His heavy shoe was only a blur in the dim light. Bone snapped, and the hood fell back on the leaves. Murphy lunged for the boy, but he brushed aside the hand, then pressed the rifle muzzle to the dog's shaggy gray head and pulled the trigger. Without a word he walked off into the darkness.

"What happened inside?" Murphy asked.

"One almost got into the house."

"Wounded?"

"Dead. Vickie got him."

"The girl's a good shot," the old man said. "Could shoot better'n her brothers when they were little."

"We'd better get this one inside," Murphy said.

The three of us lifted the now unconscious thug. It was obvious he would need a new set of teeth for his trial, and it would be very difficult for him to testify through the wiring needed to put together the shattered jaw.

"Adam liked that dog," Simms said, as we followed the bouncing beam of the flashlight across the lawn. "He's been with the boy since he got that gas station. They've done a lot of walking together. . . ."

From off to one side a voice said, "My beagle's havin' a litter, Asa. He can have the pick."

A tall, elderly man with a rifle cradled in his arm had come out of the woods. Uncle Henry. Behind him were the silent, blond twins.

"Thanks, Henry. I'll tell Adam," the old man said.

"There's nothing more we can do, Johnny," Murphy said. "We must notify the state police and the commissioner. I advise you to call Flaherty immediately."

Johnny nodded. "Go ahead and call New York."

Murphy shook his head. "It's your case—you're in charge. You should make the calls."

Johnny made his first call to Flaherty's office. The D.A. wasn't in but Hoff was; I could visualize his shocked, disbelieving face. Johnny just gave him a brief rundown, informed him he would arraign Strasser on the fugitive charge, and bring him to New York City at once. The second call was to the colonel in charge of the New Jersey State Police in West Trenton. He was brief and to the point; the colonel said he would notify all barracks in the vicinity and order troopers to the scene. Calls to the nearest doctor and the coroner were next, the last to the justice of the peace at Irontown. He wasn't very helpful until Mr. Simms got on; then he promised to hold court as soon as Johnny and his prisoner arrived.

Murphy found the Police Commissioner at a social affair, and made his brief report. Now it was being told in terse police language; it no longer belonged to us. I don't think I will ever forget that room: Johnny, bone-weary and staring into space; Murphy making innumerable notes in a small black notebook; the impassive twins leaning against the wall; Henry and his son, both still cradling their rifles, awkward and ill at ease; Adam tight-faced, slumped on the floor, his back to the wall; Ricky Strasser, his head buried in his hands; and Vickie sitting on the arm of his chair, whispering to him in a soft voice and slowly, methodically, running her hand over his hair. The dead thugs were covered with a blanket, but blood was edging from under it. Someone had put the garbage pail to one side.

I had no time to brood. I had to get to work. I first used the two rolls of film. With Henry and his boy as my assistants, I shot the dead thug, then went out to the woods and got the bullet-scarred trees, Henry and his son, and so on. I was tempted, but I never brought the camera back inside the house. After I had finished, I started to write the story in the garage, writing as I have never done before under deadline pressure. With two pages finished, I persuaded Adam to drive me to the nearest telephone—I didn't want to call in with Strasser listening—which was in the home of a farmer named Mercer.

Thank God, Turner Elliott didn't ask questions. I gave him a brief preface; then he switched me to the fastest rewriteman we had, who took the pages I had typed. I dictated the rest. It wasn't the greatest, but it would beat the town.*

Adam had waited outside in the truck. When I climbed back in

---

* Mr. Malloy is too modest. His story won the Pulitzer Prize for writing the best news story of the year under deadline pressure; the Headliners Award, the New York City Reporters Association Gold Typewriter Award, etc.—ED.

and asked if he knew anyone who would want to make a trip into New York for a hundred dollars, he stared at me as if I were crazy.

"What does he have to do?"

"Just deliver this camera and film to my office. They'll hand over a hundred-dollar bill."

"What's the matter with me?"

"Your father needs you; besides, the state police might want to talk to you."

"Mister, the state police can talk to me any time."

"Let's do it this way," I said. "You get the man to run this into New York and we'll pay him a hundred and you fifty."

"You have yourself a deal," he said, and leaped out of the truck. He returned with a tall, rawboned young man who was wearing motorcycle boots. He had the longest sideburns since Valentino.

"This is Tom Mercer," Adam said. "He's your man."

"You're not kidding, a hundred bucks just to drive to the city?" Mercer asked.

"You will get a hundred dollars the moment you give this camera to this man." I scrawled Turner Elliott's name and the *Blade-Leader*'s address. "And they will give you fifty dollars more for Adam."

"I wish you city people would come up here more often," Mercer said.

From down the road came the first faint wail of a siren.

"Must be an accident," Mercer said.

"Yeah, probably a crack-up," Adam drawled. "Tom, you get going, hear?"

I gave him the camera and a brief note to Elliott, advising him I might not be near a phone for hours but I would call him at the first opportunity, and the details of my deal with Mercer and Adam. When we turned down the road, Mercer was backing out of his driveway in a small ancient black sedan with a faded white number on one door.

"Tom drives stock over in East Paterson," Adam said. "He'll burn up the road for you."

When we arrived, the state police had the entire Simms place so tightly cordoned off it took a message from Murphy to get us through. We could see the headlights of more cars coming up the road. I entered the house as Captain Dan Marquette, who was in charge of the local barracks, was dressing down Murphy and Johnny like a top sergeant chewing out his rawest recruits. He looked like an angry Fiorello La Guardia in robin's-egg blue.

"I can only be kind and call you men thoughtless idiots or fools!" he shouted. "You had this man in this place without police protection!

You never gave us the courtesy of notifying us you were interrogating this important witness in our state!"

"We intended to call your office in the morning, Captain," Johnny said. "But things—"

"Things! Things!" the little captain roared. "You had a God-damn shootout here and two men were killed and another wounded. Things! Damn you people from New York! I'm going to make a formal protest to our Governor and to our colonel and demand that some action be taken by your superiors."

Murphy started, "Now, Captain . . ."

The little man whirled on him. "And you, Murphy! You certainly should know better!" Just then the captain discovered me. He pointed. "Who is this?"

"He's a newspaperman who has been working—"

That was all Johnny was able to get out before the captain exploded.

"A newspaperman! Out! Out! Sergeant! Throw this guy out of here!"

A husky sergeant took me by the arm and half lifted me outside, while behind me the roaring voice continued to denounce Murphy and De Lorenzo. That's how I spent the second phase of the Battle of Torytown.

[30]

RICKY STRASSER WAS arraigned at 5:00 A.M. in the living room of Iron-town's justice of the peace, Gottfried Von Hagger, in a virtual sea of TV cameras, shouting reporters, cursing photographers, and furious state policemen. Ricky received the same judicial format accorded the drunken farmer who beat up his wife or the speeder from the city. Judge Von Hagger proved to be a slow, methodical man who refused to be rushed. He posed a thousand times, holding up his gavel which the first Von Hagger had used in the first court of Irontown; it was said to have been carved from a Hessian blunderbuss and was a prize of the local historical society. In his billowing black robe, Von Hagger, a big man, almost three hundred pounds, looked like a figure out of Daumier.

He nodded to all Johnny's intense requests but quietly told the court clerk, who was a Simms—fourth cousin—to read the short affi-davit, which stated simply that Richard Lewis Strasser was charged as a fugitive from New York justice and, under the reciprocal agreement of 1867, had to be returned to said New York authorities and face that state's charges.

No one could hear the clerk—this was the fifteenth time he had read the short white paper—over the uproar in the small room. At one point Judge Von Hagger questioned Murphy, who had co-signed the affidavit, as to what he did in New York police headquarters. While Johnny fumed, Murphy explained.

Von Hagger shook his head. "Inspector," he said solemnly. "I think the whole problem of New York's traffic is to give those truck drivers tickets!" He leaned forward. "And then fines!"

"Judge, I couldn't agree with you more," Murphy said with a stone face.

Von Hagger gave us a triumphant smile; here was a colleague in law enforcement who really knew what was going on. . . .

During the arraignment Ricky was virtually supported by Johnny and Murphy. It was obvious he was on the verge of collapse. The gunfight, then the fierce interrogation of the state police captain—who denounced us all to the New Jersey newspapermen—had shaken him to the roots. Vickie was the iron one; she calmly answered a million questions, posed for pictures, parried the digs, joked with the photographers, and within a half hour won herself an admiring audience in that boisterous and slightly ridiculous gang. I hung in the background, but the UPI man found me.

"The *Blade-Leader*'s all over town with your story," he said. "My desk said it's real top stuff. How the hell did you get out here so fast?"

"I just happened to be passing."

He grunted an obscenity and walked away. I don't think he believed me.

It wasn't until after 7:00 A.M. that we finally got Ricky and Vickie into a car and headed back to New York with a state police escort.

We didn't do much talking during the trip. At the Lincoln Tunnel entrance we were met by the New York cops and a delegation of reporters and photographers. We went through the tunnel at top speed, down the West Side Highway, around the Battery, up the East River Drive, and then over to Foley Square. Ricky was quickly arraigned before an incurious General Sessions judge, then whisked away by Murphy to a small hotel in Westchester. We were all wobbly with fatigue when we finished. On the way out we met Hoff.

"The boss wants to see you in the morning."

"I'll come along," I said.

He slowly turned to me. "I wouldn't let you in our men's room."

I guess this was the place for a smart remark, but frankly I didn't have a smart remark in me. I was ground to a fine edge and would have probably cut his throat if he had climbed on my back. But he didn't; he just stalked off down the long, deserted corridor.

"I'll see you tomorrow, Duke," Johnny said. "I'll call you after I see him." He gave me a weary smile. "If you're worried, don't be."

"I'm not worried," I said.

When I passed the Centre Street entrance, TV cameramen were rolling out their equipment. There was a small crowd near the curb. I walked across Foley Square, and in a few minutes arrived at the *Blade-Leader*. I knew I had scored big when the elevator man silently held up the front page. The headlines were big and exciting; the dead thug was spread across the top of the page. Tom Mercer's stock-car racer really had made it in record time; I certainly hope they paid him.

Then I entered the rising tempo of the city room, and Julian Savage was silently walking toward me, his hand outstretched and a big smile on his wan face. . . .

BOOK EIGHT

THE TRUE BILL

[31]

ON THE FOLLOWING day Flaherty held his press conference. He was solemn, righteous, high in his praise of Johnny. He read a copy of an elaborate apology to the Governor of New Jersey and the colonel of the state police for the failure of his office to notify the proper authorities, pledging continued friendship and cooperation. What it said between the lines was to place blame on the assistant in charge of the investigation. When he was asked about my story that Strasser had given a complete and shocking statement revealing the extent of crime and corruption in New York City, Flaherty, according to *The New York Times* account, pointed out that there is an enormous difference between a statement and a conviction in the democratic process.

He didn't denounce the *Blade-Leader*. On the contrary, he was high in his praise of my work and my newspaper's "never-ending fight" against the forces of the underworld. He called me a valiant newspaperman, and added some other nonsense so bad the reporters didn't even take notes.

"After he finished I thought you two guys were queer," our Criminal Courts man told me.

Flaherty gave out rogues'-gallery pictures of the dead thugs and the wounded man along with their police records, and then added a vigorous account of his office's investigation. The essence was that Strasser had become the target of the underworld—not because of the official secrets he held but simply because the underworld bosses knew he was ready to turn them in. A power struggle in the underworld. The usual war of extermination. The traditional policy of seeking out and destroying the informer.

It was a good conference; it produced new headlines. The regulars swallowed it in one gulp, but the *Trib* and the *News* kept up a barrage of questions about the officials Strasser named. Who were they? What did he accuse them of? What did he have to say? When was he going to present the case to the Grand Jury?

At the last, Flaherty leaned back and smiled that charming smile; did the press expect him to smear men who might be innocent by accepting the uncorroborated word of a crooked attorney who admitted to breaking every law in the city, except possibly murder?

It was a superb performance. Flaherty could not be pinned down; you could sense the frustration of the more sophisticated reporters in their stories. It's the old dodge; the newspaper must quote the official source.

"He said all the right things. Nothing you could argue with," Johnny said bitterly. "It's a stall."

"My God, how can he stall on this one?" I asked. "The story is in every metropolitan paper in the country. He must act."

"There are three reasons," Johnny said heavily. "First, he just refuses to believe it all. He told me Strasser is nothing but a little Jew bastard who took everything while the getting was good, and now he's trying to use McShane to get a break."

"You're kidding!"

"No, I'm not. Then there's that God-damned nut, the Prophet. Flaherty has everyone in the office working on the case. Washington is throwing him all kinds of bouquets, and they have him convinced he is the savior of the country. One of the fellows on it told me he's going to hit the Prophet with every crime in the statute book."

"You said there were three reasons, Johnny."

"Flaherty wants out. He wants the judgeship. He is determined not to lose it. They told me that he was like a crazy man when he heard about what happened in Jersey."

"But, Johnny, he can't ignore the statement, the recordings! Christ, the second man in the New York Police Department was there as a witness!"

"He went over that damned statement with a fine-tooth comb," Johnny said. "He put Murphy on the griddle until I thought Murphy was the defendant." He gave me a tight smile. "He tried like hell to knock down that conspiracy count—"

"The point where Ricky said he recognized McShane's voice?"

"Right. He got our trial assistant in and made him agree it would be a risky case." He slammed his fist into the palm of his hand. "The man just stared at me, and shrugged!"

"What about Ricky?"

"We have him up in Dewey's old singing school in the Bronx, but it's impossible to have a maximum-security jail in this city. We have him isolated with twenty-four-hour-a-day guards that Murphy himself picked." He shook his head. "But someone got to him. It was a warning on the inside of a match cover."

"He can't back off on that statement, Johnny. He just can't!"

"A man can renege on anything, and usually does if he's pushed far enough," Johnny said roughly. "And Strasser's no hero. The only thing that's holding him together is Vickie. He's as much afraid of losing her as he is of the mob."

"What's the next move?"

"Murphy has every reliable stool pigeon he can lay his hands on to get a lead on Gennaro's books."

"What about Ricky? Does he—"

"I went over and over that with him all last night. What he told us in Jersey is all he knows. He was on the verge of tears when I left him. The guy just doesn't know any more, that's all."

When I got back to the office, Elliott silently held up the late editions; the afternoon papers were all carrying Flaherty's announcement: The Prophet had been indicted on 218 counts of inciting a riot, murder, arson, felonious assault, conspiracy, and just about every felonious crime in the New York State Penal Code. It was one of the biggest indictments in the history of the city. Five of his lieutenants were also indicted with him, separately and as co-defendants.

Of course, Hoff had prepared a terrific eight-page statement for the press to go with the handout of the indictment, in which the District Attorney's office revealed that two of the Prophet's lieutenants would plead guilty on the following day and serve as the people's witnesses. But that was only part of it; they had turned over documentary evidence proving that some of the Apostles had been trained in Cuba as guerrillas. The Prophet's organization, they said in statements, had been selected as a spearhead for the systematic campaign of terrorist activities in American cities along the East and West coasts. Cities and the targets were named along with the officials who were to be killed and the civic buildings to be destroyed.

It sounded like a nightmare, but I knew Hoff; he would never put this out unless they had it all wrapped up.

The story was sensational; there were official comments by the Secretary of State, the President discussed it at his press conference, and *Pravda* shrilled that it was all an imperialist fantasy. Castro himself spent five hours denouncing the investigation, then, as usual, blundered badly by confirming the plot when he demanded that the United States return his Cuban Nationals.

It was a wild few days. Flaherty was interviewed on television and radio, and his popularity was never greater. Hoff was sober and shrewd; he spread out the punches, dropping one after the other until there was only one name in town—Flaherty.

The white-haired, smiling Lochinvar, America's bulwark against the black Communists.

It was slightly blown up and exaggerated, as the much later reports of the FBI proved. But it was the old, old case of the official version. When the editorial dust settled, there were some analytical stories and columns questioning the more nightmarish angles of the plot, but they were largely ignored.

Forgotten, of course, was the bullet-splattered night in the woods of Torytown, the bewildered and almost hysterical Ricky Strasser; Gennaro was already a memory of garish headlines; and now, when Johnny sought to get an audience with Flaherty, Hoff's excuse was that the boss was too busy preparing for the Prophet's trial.

"He just sat there and told me the boss wanted me to continue the investigation," Johnny said angrily after one session.

"What about the Grand Jury?"

"I'm to wait until I get more evidence."

"You can't force it yourself before the Grand Jury?"

"He would love to see me try just that. Then he would have ample reason to sack me with the approval of every D.A. in town. I have never heard of an assistant going over the D.A.'s head to the Grand Jury. There has to be an office vote."

"Who votes?"

"Flaherty, his trial assistant, the appeal man, the Grand Jury assistant—"

"You don't think they would vote Yes with what we have now?"

"The timing is bad," he explained. "It would be bad psychology with all this Prophet stuff going on. It's not that Flaherty would try to coerce them; all he would have to do is make a spiel about the weak link, the stature of McShane as against Strasser. Assistant District Attorneys may be honest but they are also human; they want to win. So it's a good chance they would vote with Flaherty to wait. And for any case, that is deadly. The edge is taken off, enthusiasm dies, witnesses begin to have doubts. . . ."

"It just doesn't seem possible."

"But it's all nice and legal, and probably in Flaherty's estimation he's following the letter of the law."

"Well, as your faithful press agent, Johnny, I can advise you to do only one thing."

"What's that?"

"Wait him out. The greatest story in the world one day slips off page one."

He gave me a gloomy look. "Maybe you're right, but in the meantime let's hope Vickie Simms has enough guts for both of them."

Ten days passed, and as usual the big story was taken over by a bigger story. One day Flaherty's statements were not page one of the *Times* or the afternoons. Hoff, as an old pro, retreated with a final statement that the District Attorney was now ready for trial.

"Now we have to begin," Julian told us. He ordered a relentless daily campaign of news stories, editorials, a series on crime and corruption in the city, and even editorial-page cartoons.

"If we don't get some action soon, the case will die," he told us at an editorial conference. "We must force Flaherty to allow Johnny to present the case to the Grand Jury."

"He's stubborn, Julian," Turner said.

"Come to think of it, so am I."

"Have you had any pressure yet?" Turner asked.

"Some—"

"You'll get more before this week is out."

He smiled. "If I don't, I'll be surprised."

The others left, but he waved me back to my chair. "Stay a bit, Duke. I really haven't spoken to you since the night you came back from Jersey. How is Johnny?"

"He's worried. I told him we had to wait until Flaherty ran out of ammunition."

"Even if Johnny gets an indictment, Duke, it's a long way from a conviction," he said. "From what you told me, he really has only one good legal connection between McShane and Gennaro."

"It's a prima facie case; but, as Flaherty points out, in the courtroom it will be a leader of the community against a cheap little man who has made a lot of money out of crime."

"No sign of Gennaro's books?"

"Not a trace. Inspector Murphy has been working around the clock with Internal Revenue. They've been looking for Gennaro's safe-deposit boxes since he was killed."

Then he said almost casually, "I'd like to see Johnny get the case before the Grand Jury before I go into the hospital."

I was stunned. I could only repeat stupidly, "Into the hospital?"

"Just for tests. My stomach has been bothering me lately." Abruptly he changed the subject. "From now on until I give the word, this is our big story. We'll play the breaking news, but I want this on page one every day. A continuous barrage of page-one stories never fails to get under the skin of most politicians."

Later, in the city room, I asked Turner Elliott if he had heard that Julian was entering a hospital.

"He told me yesterday that his doctor has been after him to take some tests," he said. "But he seemed indefinite."

"Has he been ill?"

"He hasn't said anything to me, but his secretary told me last week he was sick in his office." He leaned forward and said softly: "He's under tremendous pressure from City Hall. There was a delegation of two in yesterday."

"Did they get anywhere?"

"I asked him what happened. He said they told him the last thing they wanted to do was tell him how to run his newspaper, but did the *Blade-Leader* have to continue playing up corruption? Julian advised them to get rid of the corruption and then there wouldn't be anything to write about. They left, but I understand the old man paid him a visit in the afternoon."

"Down here? He hasn't been here since he bought the paper."

"He wasn't here long. They left together. Betty said that when Julian came back he looked ill. When she went in to see him, he was lying on the couch."

"I just hope nothing—"

He said quickly, "Don't say what I've been thinking."

I didn't. I couldn't.

For the next week we pounded Flaherty with everything we had. There were copyrighted stories dealing with the details of the syndicate's power in New York City politics and how it had corrupted the Police Department. Julian had three page-one editorials demanding that Flaherty do something. Then suddenly the Police Commissioner announced one of the most sweeping shake-ups in the entire Police Department, with Murphy placed in charge of a new squad, assigned to ferret out crooked cops. In two days Murphy lodged charges against twenty-five lieutenants, captains, and inspectors.

The relentless campaign began to bring results; even the Mayor announced the appointment of a new commissioner and the formation of a new city department to be called the Bureau of Official Investigations. It was to sift all charges of official corruption. It was greeted with a yawn in Room 9 at the Hall, the City Hall press room.

Then on Thursday afternoon the urgent bells on the UPI and AP machines rang frantically; a bulletin was coming over. In Albany the powerful majority whip had taken the floor to publicly denounce Julian, the Dolbar Newspaper Enterprises, and the *Blade-Leader* as cesspools of sensationalism, mediocrity, and devotees of the Big Smear. He charged Julian and his editors with slanting headlines, leads, and phony juxtaposition of facts.

The majority whip had a thunderous voice, and he used it to the best of his ability. Our campaign, he said, was an attempt to inflame the public and increase circulation so that Julian would not have to appeal to his father-in-law for financial support. He was careful to point out that the Dolbar interests were founded on the heartaches and tears of small businessmen and widows who had lost their savings in Dolbar mortgages many years ago.

The majority whip, an old-time politician, obviously was doing a major chore for the party, but like many a veteran Albany hack he was seduced by his own golden voice. He concluded his long, vicious attack by pointing out that everyone knew the target of the *Blade-Leader*'s campaign was one of the most respected figures in American politics. There was stunned silence. He tried to correct the last sentence but the word was out; the reporters in the press gallery who had been mechanically taking notes straightened in their chairs. They pounced on that one pungent paragraph. Bulletins clattered in every wireroom of every major newspaper. When the speech was ended the whip tried to sneak out, but he was cornered. The more he tried to explain, the more he blundered.

The moment the bulletin hit the city desks, phones began ringing in the Criminal Courts press room. Within minutes Hoff was besieged. He advised Flaherty not to hold a press conference, and instead issued a terse statement denying that the New York County District Attorney's office was investigating any major national politician.

But no sooner had Hoff issued his statement than the usual "spokesman" at police headquarters told reporters covering that building that Strasser had named a powerful political figure in the United States as the political protector for the Gennaro syndicate.

That evening headlines from New York to the West Coast asked who was the powerful political figure who had been named in Flaherty's investigation?

"The reins have snapped and the horses are running wild," Julian said. "I wonder who will make the next move?"

It came—not in New York, but in Moscow. *Pravda*'s front-page editorial, later to become the celebrated "America's Other Side of the Coin" editorial, began:

Why does America boast of its Justice when it refuses to let its citizens look on the other side of the coin? Are the American leaders afraid of the putrid cemetery smell which emanates from the Office of the New York Prosecutor who has nothing but bourgeois morality, the iron law of which says the Negro, the workingman, the poor and the helpless, the plain people of America, will be tried by our laws, but the rich Imperialist, the powerful politician, must never be disturbed?

It would not be an exaggeration to say that the American people, in the vast majority, are shocked by the refusal of the New York officials to expose the political criminals who have been involved with gangsters. The Soviet Union has fought hard against the maklak* and the bribe taker. Unlike the American public, Soviet citizens have always condemned bribery or contribution to bribery.

The closer the peoples of the Soviet Union approach Communism, the higher will be the wave of resentment against predatory people of any kind. The citizens of New York must end their self-complacency, or such criminals and public officials will continue to commit their misdeeds for a long time.

Accompanying the editorial was an article from New York detailing the entire Gennaro investigation and written, significantly, by one of the Soviet editors who had recently arrived in the United States to write a series on America facing the crucial November presidential election.

Then the London newspapers picked up the story. As one London bureau chief told me, "It's the Christine Keeler case all over again, only with gangsters and big-time politicians; American politics instead of sex. And this time you chaps are on the receiving end."

This was too much for the party to bear in an election year. From somewhere on high came the order to Flaherty: Let De Lorenzo put the case before the Grand Jury. It's not the most airtight, and maybe he'll fall on his face, but it's the lesser of two evils.

This time there was no elaborate press conference. Hoff simply phoned down to the press room in Criminal Courts Building and dictated the brief paragraph. Additionally, he issued the statements late in the afternoon, which meant he missed the big editions of the afternoon papers and caught only the shank of the AM's. But even then he failed to catch all the city desks napping. In their last editions the *Times* had a superb story that included some analytic comments on the far-reaching

* The middleman, or fixer.

effects such a Grand Jury investigation could have not only on New York politics but on the national election.

Flaherty remained aloof, but Hoff kept trying to stir interest in the Prophet's coming trial. Even the regularly assigned reporters accepted his calls with a yawn.

After the crisis, the headlines, the excitement, and the initial taste of victory, like tart, bubbly champagne, had worn off, we settled back, looked at each other, and wondered aloud just where did we go from here.

"We'll have the Blue Ribbon jury next week," Johnny said. "I'm going to throw in the extortion cases first."

"Peters, Barrist, and the others?" I asked.

"Exactly. I want a whole string of them. It has to be impressive. I'm hoping that maybe Barrist will take a plea and come over to our side."

"Any hint that he might?"

"Murphy said he had a feeling Barrist might jump. But here's the surprise. He thinks Peters might beat him."

"Peters!"

"From what I gather, Peters is a very realistic guy. If he thinks he's in the bag, he'll make a deal."

"But what can he make a deal on, Johnny? He has nothing on McShane."

"Maybe more cops, more higher-ups. Who knows? It won't be McShane but it will be part of the overall picture."

"No word on those books? Or McShane's girl friend?"

"Not a line. I dragged in everyone. Bernie, his girl friend, all of them. The only books that Bernie knows about are the payoff books for the cops. He hasn't got a thing on McShane—only hearsay. And he never heard of McShane going for a woman. Murphy and I went over this angle with Strasser until we are both blue in the face. He just doesn't know any more."

"Did you ever get a line on Frank the Sheik—the ribbon-car driver? Jackson once said he was Gennaro's stooge."

"Murphy sent out a quiet pickup on him but they never caught up with him. Murphy said he just dropped out of sight. One of his stoolies claimed the Sheik was knocked off for fingering Jackson, but who knows? There's more gossip in the underworld than in a ladies' room."

"Did BCI come up with anything on the hoods who tried to knock off Strasser?"

"It was an out-of-town assignment. The yellow sheet of the one Adam kicked in the jaw shows he worked for a slot-machine mob in Detroit."

"I suppose he gave you a long and satisfying interview."

"Yes. He told me his name after we showed him his print sheet. Can't say I blame him for not talking. His jaw is wired like a TV set. Vickie's my only hope with that bum lover of hers. I got to let him out a couple of hours a day so they can get together. Murphy's with them all the time, but I sweat it out."

"Isn't that dangerous—"

"For God's sake, Duke!" he exploded. "Of course it's dangerous! But he says if he can't see Vickie he'll go out of his head." He underscored each word with a brief jerk of his fist. "This guy is our whole case against McShane!"

"All right, Johnny. Okay. I'm with you, man, remember me?"

He grinned sheepishly. "I guess I'm getting jumpy."

"What you need is to see more of Connie."

"I had dinner with her last night. She said she's seriously thinking of marrying an Arctic explorer. At least she'd see more of him than she sees of me."

"She's a great girl, Johnny."

"Well, she's smart enough to think you're crazy for not marrying Gwen."

"Gwen's fine," I lied. "I spoke to her last night."

Later, on the way home, I wondered why I lied to Johnny, of all people. It made me feel so ashamed I changed a five-dollar bill and found a phone booth. But with the clang of the first quarter I knew I couldn't talk to Gwen—not yet. She had said all there was to say. The next move was up to me, but it had to be a decisive one. I could stay in this damned business, or I could make a break and she'd be there to hold my hand if I fell on my face. She wanted a forever decision. But I wasn't ready. Not yet. If she could hang on a little while longer. Just a little while longer.

[32]

THEY SIT IN A small amphitheatre, like solemn, middle-aged interns listening to a mildly interesting lecture. A few ask questions, but the majority are silent. The Assistant District Attorney briefs them before the witness enters. He asks the questions and his witnesses answer. The fingers of the stenotypists move swiftly, expertly over the keys. In the Grand Jury there is only one accusing voice. The People.

The New York County Grand Jury considering the prima facie evidence was an afternoon jury, which meant it gathered at 2:00 P.M.

Johnny went in a few minutes before two, like a master of ceremonies; then the guards brought Ricky from the Tombs to the small witness room. With its rows of hard benches it always reminded me of an army chapel. Bernie, his fat girl friend, and several policy collectors were called first. Then came Strasser. In the beginning he was tense and nervous, but as the days passed he grew arrogant, even proud of the role he was playing. After a few weeks he told Johnny he would pose in the corridor for the photographers and TV.

"What the hell, they have to make a living," he said magnanimously.

Johnny looked at him with disgust.

There is nothing dramatic about a Grand Jury handing up a true bill. The foreman notifies the Assistant District Attorney, and the true bill is handed up to the judge in General Sessions. Warrants are issued for the defendants, and they surrender for booking or they are brought in by the District Attorney's investigators or the detectives attached to the bureau.

Peters and Barrist were the first indicted. Johnny wisely charged them with extortion in addition to bribery; the former charge, he thought, would be easier to prove. Peters' indictment had twenty-two counts, Barrist's, fifteen. There were several other indictments, mostly of policy figures, which were purely routine. They already had agreed to act as state's witnesses, but Johnny wasn't taking any chances.

Magistrate Lou Janus was next. Johnny hit him with eight counts of bribery; to me the case looked excellent. Bernie could not only testify about the time he paid Janus but could also describe the judge's room in minute detail. Berta was an excellent corroborative witness; she had driven to the judge's home with Bernie and had looked into the envelope that contained the bribe money. Strasser again was the star witness; he really pinned the fat little judge to the cross. He named times, places, amounts.

I have always considered New Yorkers shockproof, and I wasn't surprised when the first stories created scarcely a ripple. Crooked cops? No news to the storekeeper who pays the cop on the beat to open a few hours before legal time on Sunday morning to sell beer. Nor to the cabdriver who slips the cop a few dollars to escape the wrath of the Hack Bureau. But as the weeks went on and the stories continued, the indictments mounted, there was a whisper, then a grunt of surprise. I could feel it in readers flipping open to page three in the *News* without moving from the stand; the absorbed faces in the subways as they automatically swayed with the curves; the voluble cabdrivers—"Looka that guy they indicted yesterday—a cop working with the gangsters! And that phony judge! I bet that creep musta fined a million hackies."

I was working around the clock, squeezing every ounce from our agreement with the D.A.'s office that the *Blade-Leader* was to get first news of any indictment. Johnny played it square; he told me only enough to catch a one-edition beat before Hoff released the indictment. There were arraignments to cover, bail-reduction hearings in Supreme Court, press conferences with the Police Commissioner, with the defendants, even with Flaherty.

Scandal continued to flicker along the edges of the city like a tiny flame nibbling the edges of a dry leaf pile, but Flaherty publicly never lost his smile, his poise, his air of self-assurance. In his press conferences he denounced the thieves, the betrayers of public oaths. He never failed to praise his valiant young assistant profusely. Privately he was a lion with a thorn in his paw. Johnny said their meetings were cold and formal.

"He refuses to talk to me alone," Johnny said. "When I do get in, he makes an elaborate display of gathering the other assistants, Grand Jury, appeal, trial, and so on. Then he tells me to begin. The others hate it, but he drags it out as long as possible. He makes no bones about how he hates my guts. Sometimes I think, Duke, that if I could have known what was going to happen I would have thrown you out the window the first day you walked in here."

One good indication of how Flaherty felt could be detected in the way Bob Hoff had changed since the gun battle in Jersey. He had cut down his drinking and sent the redhead back to the Tax Department in Albany. Not a line went out of the D.A.'s office without his okay. Every report Johnny made he examined, every edition of the *Blade-Leader* was on his desk within minutes after it left our building. Cold sober he was a dangerous professional who was fighting for survival. He never hid his hate for me.

Rumors were spreading across the city, and some of them were getting close to McShane. One day Room 9 at City Hall buzzed like a hive with reporters trying to check a story that the administration's two top men were in town to see Flaherty. You could never pin this one down with a telephone; legwork was the only way to get the real story.

It was:

Washington was uneasy; the professionals whose job it was to make sure the present occupant of the White House was not dispossessed conferred with Flaherty on the strength of the case against Mc-Shane. They were told it was a lousy little Jew racket lawyer against a kingmaker, a tower of strength in the community. A man Catholics, Jews, Protestants called on for help. He made Presidents and they were his friends. Not even a rumor had ever besmirched his reputation.

The professionals then went to McShane and gave him the word; make them fish or cut bait. Too much is known; if it comes out in the campaign it could murder Washington. But even the top guns from Washington could only suggest to McShane, never order. McShane told them in Ninth Avenue prose what they could do with their suggestions.

That is, until:

The fight at the Hottentot Club was brief. The husky, handsome young man in the dinner jacket escorting the striking young deb to the swank supper club threw just one short punch which caught the playboy on the point of his chin. He was out before he hit the floor.

A woman at a nearby table gave a brief yelp, but outside of that and a few broken glasses the efficient waiters hid the scene from the other guests before they were aware of what had happened. Unfortunately for young Tony McShane, a Broadway columnist was at an adjacent table. He later wrote how he had heard the drunken playboy ask Tony how many tin boxes his father had hidden in the cellar and was he going to take them to jail.

That is, until:

Fran McShane resigned by request from the Tower Club, one of the oldest blueblood clubs in the city. There was no reason. A society columnist who broke the story gave one; the McShane name just wouldn't do.

"I think we're going to hear from him," Johnny said. We did.

Turner Elliott was the first to tell me. It was seven-thirty when my phone rang. Turner was the only managing editor I ever knew who not only came in at 6:00 A.M. but was civilized at that hour.

His soft voice was apologetic. "Duke? I'm terribly sorry to call you at this early hour but I have something important."

I was awake immediately. "That's quite all right, sir. What's up?"

"A telegram was sent to the city desk late last night. It's from McShane. He's having a press conference this morning."

For a moment I was stunned. I just didn't know what to say.

"Did you hear what I said, Duke?"

"Yes, I did, but frankly I'm amazed."

"I think you had better be there. I've called Julian, and he agrees. He asks that you call him as soon as you find out what he has to say."

"Of course. Where is it going to be?"

"Rose Room of the Peter Stuyvesant."

"That's Colton Ryder's hotel."

"Is that significant—or am I missing something?"

"It's only a hunch. There may be something between them."

"You have had some good hunches down through the years, Duke. Anyway, it's nine-thirty at the Rose Room. The city desk is handling it with a reporter and a photographer."

"Fine. I'll call both you and Julian."

All through a shower and breakfast I tried to guess what McShane wanted to tell the press, but nothing sounded logical. When I called Johnny he was as mystified as I was. All we could do was wait.

I reached the Rose Room at nine. There is nothing more barren or melancholy than an empty ballroom in the morning; the stacks of music stands, the piles of chairs, the few colored streamers in the cor-ner—all yesterday.

I took a seat in the front behind a *News* man who didn't have a hint of what the conference was about. Neither did the *Trib* or AP's City Hall men. Then the TV crews came in and took over with cables, cameras, mikes, and one of their celebrated reporting teams. They have always reminded me of actors and like actors they looked grumpy and angry at the early hour. The room was soon crowded, and someone made the observation that this was the place where McShane held his private celebrations for the party wheels after the city elections. The

Post man was reminiscing about the year he had almost crashed the party when McShane walked in, flanked by two aides, who looked as if they had stepped out of the pages of *The Last Hurrah.*

This morning McShane was dressed in a custom-made blue suit; the button-down blue shirt was Brooks Brothers and so was the tie. There was authority in the way he waved his flunkeys aside and walked up to the microphone. For a long moment he studied us, then slowly, dramatically, put on horn-rimmed glasses and took a single sheet of paper from inside his jacket.

"I am going to read a statement for you gentlemen and then I'll answer your questions. My associates will have copies . . ."

His associates zipped open folders and took out a sheaf of mimeographed statements. There was a slight impatient stir, and a few throats were cleared.

McShane said abruptly, "Is there a representative from the *Blade-Leader* here?"

"There is," I said loudly.

The blue eyes swung to me, and he nodded.

"I don't want to embarrass the representative of the District Attorney's office by asking if he is here," he said. "I know he is."

There was much creaking and turning of heads. I wasn't paying any attention, I was thinking of this deep, gruff voice with the unmistakable rasp—as Ricky Strasser had described it. . . .

He went on to say:

"This is my statement, gentlemen. A few months ago the *Blade-Leader,* an afternoon newspaper in this city, owned by the Samuel Dolbar Newspaper Enterprises, Inc., published a series of articles on the activities of an alleged gambling syndicate.

"I don't have to dwell on the sorry repercussions of the irresponsible actions of that newspaper and its reporters. As a direct result of their intrusion in an enormously delicate section of the city, a bloody race riot took place which shook to its very roots a far-reaching civil rights program which has been praised by every race, creed, and color as the most progressive in the land. As I said, I don't intend to dwell on that; Moscow radio has done a good-enough job.

"A few weeks ago this same newspaper, acting in concert with an irresponsible member of the New York County District Attorney's office, embarrassed both officials of this state and her neighboring state, New Jersey, when they failed to request proper protection for a man hiding in that state who claimed to have important information for the District Attorney's office. This man, incidentally, is a disbarred New York attorney, the subject of a twelve-state alarm, and a man who has associated with the most notorious members of the underworld. With him was a woman. I will be kind and say simply, a woman well known to Broadway.

"I have read of these sensational stories with a great deal of distaste. I felt that this newspaper was deliberately smearing our city and its Police Department purely for the purpose of gaining an increase in their fading circulation.

"As a citizen, I disliked what I read, but lacking public office I could do nothing but maintain my silence. However, the events of the past week have changed this." He raised his head and his tight face looked out over us. "It has changed this very much.

"The *Blade-Leader,* during the past several days, has hinted that a political figure is the protector of organized gambling in this city, that this figure collects large bribes, that this figure has corrupted sections of the New York Police Department, that this figure has judges in his vest pocket.

"The political figure, of course, was not named. The *Blade-Leader* chose to hide behind the cloak of anonymity. In other words its owners and editors chose the cowardly, traditional journalistic dodge to avoid a suit for libel, both criminal and civil.

"When these articles first appeared, I was warned by close friends that the *Blade-Leader* was implying that I, James X. McShane, was the political protector of the rackets—"

There was a stir, and several reporters darted from the room. I kept writing in a heart-pounding daze.

"—that I corrupted the Police Department and our judges. I laughed at my friends; I thought them preposterous. But then items began appearing in gossip columns, particularly in columns written by political writers.

"The items were getting warmer, if you can call it that, and more brazen. At one point I consulted my attorneys, who pointed out that the articles and items were still too vague to bring action.

"However, gentlemen, the scandalmongers at the *Blade-Leader* finally hit home. They have attacked my family. My son, now an honor student at law school, was forced to resign from his senior class because of an incident in a respectable supper club in which he provoked by an intoxicated person who repeated the scandal about his father which had appeared in this newspaper. My daughter also has been injured by this filth so that she has been placed under the care of a physician.

"As a result of these outrages I now challenge the editors, the publishers, the owners of the *Blade-Leader* to publicly apologize both to me and to the citizens of this city for their scandalous behavior with a promise to dispense in the future with printing such trash or to publish my name and identify me as the political protector of the gambling syndicate in this city.

"However, I must warn them that if they take the latter course I have instructed my attorneys to file a ten-million-dollar libel action against them with a demand to the court for a detainer and accounting of all profits, and furthermore I have also advised my attorneys to communicate with the District Attorney of New York County with a demand that he seek an indictment from the Grand Jury for criminal libel against this newspaper.

"I shall expect an answer on their front pages within twenty-four hours."

He carefully folded the paper and slowly took off his glasses.

"Now, gentlemen, if you wish to ask me any questions."

The ballroom broke into a chorus of questions and demands from the TV crews. Finally McShane held up both hands. There was a grim, no-nonsense air of authority about him that gradually quieted the room.

"If you wish to ask a question, raise your hand," he said.

Okay, teacher, let's get this one on the record, I told myself, and stood up. I think McShane was waiting for me, because he ignored the frantically waving hands to stab the air in my direction.

"I represent the *Blade-Leader* and I would like to ask you the following questions," I said. "One. Did you accept a weekly payoff from Vito Gennaro for protecting his numbers racket?"

The answer was a deep growl, "I did not."

"Two. Did you order Magistrate Lou Janus to give suspended sentences to important members of Gennaro's syndicate who appeared before him?"

"I did not."

"Three. Did you send word to a city department to tell its inspectors to ignore violations in Harlem buildings owned by a certain real-estate syndicate?"

The answer was just as emphatic. "I did not."

I took a deep breath. This was now all-out war, so I might as well fire the last round.

"Mr. McShane, did you order the murder of a gambler known to police as Action Jackson—"

I never finished the sentence. McShane, for one brief second, lost his composure. He was shouting to his stooges above the uproar.

"Get him out of here! Get him out of here!"

His two aides, like angry old bulldogs, started down the platform steps, but I had squeezed out between the benches to face the platform. One started to grab my arm, but I brushed him aside. If I couldn't take

care of him I had better turn in my track shoes. For a moment the uproar died down. I guess they all thought we were going to square off.

"McShane," I said, "you're a God-damned liar and a thief. You
want to sue me, go ahead."

And with that I walked out, the two bulldogs trotting at my side and
McShane's last words in my ears that he would see me in court.

Within the hour after the explosive press conference with Mc-
Shane, we had gathered in Julian's office; Sam Parsons, the paper's libel
lawyer, who had brought a new face from his firm; Joe Bowers, Turner
Elliott, Julian, and I. There was no doubt we all had been caught flat-
footed by McShane's challenge. The AP and UPI machines were clicking out bulletins and new leads to their running story every few minutes,
while out in the reception room a small army of reporters awaited our
decision. I knew now what it was like to be on the other side of the
fence; I felt like an idiot saying "no comment" to reporters I had worked
with for more than a decade.

Every piece of wire copy on the running account of the press conference which had gone on after I had left was sent in; it was silently
passed around, then returned to the small mound on Julian's desk.

He looked more tired than worried, but he had managed a smile
when I entered.

"It appears he gave you a rough time, Duke," he said, and held out
his hand. I knew it was more than a handshake. It was a declaration to
all that nothing had changed as far as he was concerned.

"How are we playing it, Mr. Elliott?" I asked.

"We're playing it hard in two-column measure with two lines. Just
reporting what he said. The *Telly* and the *Journal* replated. It's all over
the city by now."

Parsons cleared his throat, and the young assistant gave me a cool,
appraising look.

"What we have to decide, Julian, is what we're going to do. I just
spoke to Sam—"

Julian snapped: "I have informed my father-in-law that I will make
the decisions, Mr. Parsons. No one else. Is that clear?"

The shaggy old head nodded. "It is, but I do think you should consider his views. After all, he is still president of the Dolbar Newspaper
Enterprises—"

"And I am publisher of the *Blade-Leader,*" Julian said evenly.

Parsons went on doggedly, "We have to consider the parent corporation, Julian, and when you—"

Julian waved his hand impatiently, "Let's forget about the parent
corporation, Sam, and come back to our problem."

"I advised Mr. Parsons the first thing to do is to seek out a meeting with McShane," the cool young man interjected.

"Seek out a meeting for what?" I said.

Sam said, "Duke, I don't think you have met Cyril Townsend, our new junior partner."

I didn't like his first name or his face, and it was just as evident he liked nothing about me.

"As I was saying," Townsend went on, "we could seek out a meeting with McShane and talk it out."

Julian said, "But what would be the purpose, Mr. Townsend?"

"Mr. McShane is far from being a saint, and I think with the material we have on hand we might be able to effect a compromise."

"Compromise with a scoundrel, Mr. Townsend?" Turner said softly.

The neat shoulders shrugged. "As I understand it, the District Attorney's case will depend completely on Strasser." He looked over at me. "Is that correct, Mr. Malloy?"

"Strasser and some others."

A cool smile. "Come on. It's Strasser, isn't it?"

"Strasser will be the People's principal witness."

"Strasser has been disbarred. In the eyes of the law he is a polluted source of testimony. McShane ostensibly is a pillar of the community, a powerful political figure. When it comes down the last stretch, it will be Strasser's word against McShane's."

"That's true, Julian," Sam rumbled.

"If the District Attorney is foolish enough to proceed on this course and McShane is acquitted—"

"Julian, he'll take out the presses," Sam said roughly. "So help me. The paper will be ruined. He'll even attach our corporate assets. And with the plans we have—"

"On the other hand, if McShane is found guilty," Julian said quietly, "the *Blade-Leader* will be the most important newspaper in the city, if not the country. Is that right, Mr. Townsend?"

"That is correct. But you're rolling against tremendous odds, sir."

Sam exploded. "Good God, Julian! This is a business! We can't afford to play against such odds. This man can ruin us!"

"For Christ's sake, Sam," I said, "you talk about McShane as though he was invulnerable. I guarantee if you stick him with a pin, he'll jump."

Townsend said coldly, "Any man is vulnerable, especially if he is in politics. That's my point."

"In other words you want to make a deal," I said.

"I think with this press conference you have him on the defensive," Townsend said. "I understand Washington is jittery and wants him to make a stand. Fine. Editorially, I believe we have made our point, and at a meeting with McShane I am sure we can come to some understanding."

"We'll have to eat crow."

"Perhaps—a bit. But look what you have done to him, Mr. Malloy. He has a good argument with his son. That must have hurt, don't you agree?"

"Not as much as the man who was murdered in the investigation."

"Mr. Parsons has brought me up to date on the whole case."

"Doesn't that mean anything?"

"Jackson? He was an underworld figure. He knew what he was getting into. He came to us; we did not seek him out."

I said, "You don't think we have any moral responsibility to uphold what he did?"

"No," Townsend said stubbornly. "Perhaps I'm prejudiced. I dislike informers. But I think we are getting away from the main subject. What do we do about McShane's threat? I say we meet him and make a deal so we both save face."

Sam said vigorously, "I can't agree more, Julian."

Julian was leaning back in his chair, his eyes half closed. "What do you think, Mr. Elliott?"

"I think we should pick up McShane's challenge and print everything we know. I say run what we have today on the press conference, then advertise on every radio and TV station in the city that beginning tomorrow we will print the true, inside story of McShane and his underworld connections. I would also advertise in every paper in the metropolitan area."

Townsend's voice dripped with contempt. "In other words, the whole treatment?"

"It's routine in the Editorial Department, Mr. Townsend," Elliott said dryly. "Let's say routine when there's a thief involved."

Julian swung to me. "Duke?"

"I would turn over the whole paper to this story. I would disregard everything but the most vital international news."

"Mr. Bowers?"

Joe ran his hand through his bristly crew cut and kept shaking his head.

"I like Mr. Townsend's idea of a meet. I think we can wheel and deal this guy . . ."

Joe's voice trailed off. There was a hush. We all stared at Julian in his chair, his eyes still closed.

"Gentlemen, give me ten minutes," he said.

Betty's voice broke in on the intercom to tell him our advertising manager was on the phone. Julian picked it up, listened, then hung up.

"The *Blade-Leader* no longer has the Cummings store," he said. "They just pulled out. Please come back in ten minutes, gentlemen. . . ."

We filed out and followed Turner Elliott into Julian's outside office. Cigarettes were passed around, but it was a long ten minutes. We all jumped when the buzzer sounded.

Julian was sitting in the same chair. His face was pale, and there was a sheen of perspiration on his forehead.

"My decision is that we are to go ahead and print every line we have on McShane," he said in a low voice. "I do this with the full knowledge of the consequences. . . ."

"May we have a letter to that effect, sir?" Townsend said quickly.

"I will dictate one immediately and send it by messenger to your office, Mr. Townsend. Is that satisfactory?"

"It is, sir. I would like to add—"

Julian held up his hand in protest. "Please, Mr. Townsend. Please. I have made my decision. Right or wrong, it is mine. Mr. Elliott, I want you to instruct the Promotion Department to launch one of its most vigorous campaigns on all radio and TV stations along the eastern seaboard. I want half-page ads in the *News, Times,* and *Tribune.* Also in the important suburban papers."

"I'll do it at once, Julian."

"Duke will write the stories," he contined. "I want one every day, beginning with our investigation in Harlem and including all the tapes and conversations, and so on. I want McShane's name in the lines. Is that clear?"

"It is."

"Very well. I guess that's it. Sam, I'm sorry—"

Sam shook his head as he snapped shut his battered old attaché case. "I hope you know what you're doing, Julian."

"So do I. I guess we won't know until it's all over. Mr. Townsend, I'm sorry I have to disagree with you."

"I rather think, sir, we'll be back down here after McShane's lawyers get busy."

I couldn't help blurting, "McShane's lawyers may be too busy keeping him out of jail."

"Perhaps, Mr. Malloy. But I don't think so. Good day, gentlemen."

They walked out, but Julian asked me to stay a bit.

"Just some tea with a bit of cream, Betty," he said to Betty, who had come in.

"I could get you some boiled eggs, Mr. Savage." Betty looked worried. "Poached, on a piece of toast, the crust trimmed."

Julian smiled. "Just tea, Betty—and thanks."

"She doesn't think I eat enough," he said when Betty left.

"Frankly, I don't think so either."

"Perhaps after I get those tests," he said vaguely.

"When are you going in?"

"I have to see this through, Duke. The tests can wait."

Betty came in with the tea, poured it, and left.

"Jack Cummings threatened to take some others with him," he said, testing the tea.

"You had a trump card," I reminded him.

"Jack Cummings knew I would never use that. I told myself I would be tough and hard, but even in Ryder's office I knew down deep I would never use that story."

"I have no doubt he or the others would."

"I guess that's the difference between our side and theirs, Duke." He finished the tea and placed the cup aside. "I want to get this story in the paper as soon as possible."

"Mr. Dolbar?"

"Exactly. In the last few weeks we haven't been exactly bosom pals. In fact last night he gave me an ultimatum. Lay off McShane—"

"Or?"

"Or he would fire me."

"I'm surprised he hasn't done so already. When he sees the late-afternoon editions—"

Julian smiled. "He'll have to catch up with me first. Betty has orders to put through no calls to me except from you people upstairs. Tonight I'm staying at a hotel. Betty will have the number. I'll see him in the morning. By that time we'll be committed."

He walked to the window, and we looked out on the busy street choked with the *Blade-Leader*'s trucks inching up to the delivery platforms.

"What was the motto of the Nisei regiment in Italy?"

"Go for Broke?"

"That's it. That's what I'm going to tell the old man tomorrow morning. The *Blade-Leader* is going for broke."

We went for broke the next day, and McShane's attorney immediately filed a ten-million-dollar libel suit against the *Blade-Leader*. They also visited Flaherty, who announced that he was examining grounds for a criminal libel action against us. That was the least of our worries; any lawyer knows it's one hell of a job to get a conviction for criminal libel. It was more bluster than reality.

The meeting between Julian and his father-in-law was almost violent. Julian said little, but Sam Parsons, who was called to the apartment with Townsend, filled in Turner Elliott.

"Sam said the old man was almost beside himself," Elliott told me. "He called Julian all kinds of fools and idiots and finally almost pulled Julian into another room where he slammed the door. Sam said all he could hear was the old man shouting and pounding a desk. When Julian walked out he looked like he had been put through a wringer. He told Parsons and Townsend that if Dolbar tried to remove him he would file court action. Apparently his wife left him a good chunk of the family's stock. That brought the old man up short. I guess he knew Julian meant it."

I didn't see Julian for the next few days, but Betty kept me informed; he had broken two appointments to enter the hospital, and the last time she broke his date his doctor slammed down the phone.

"He's a sick man, Mr. Malloy," she said. "He's been living on tea and toast."

I could almost hear a puzzled and indignant Gwen asking: Why on earth is he going through all this? Why is he risking so much? What possible end can these stories serve?

Alone in my apartment I watched Turner Elliott on TV read to the other reporters the brief page-one editorial Julian had signed. His answer to Gwen lay in the final lines:

"In the last few years the bright, gleaming sword of the press, as Lippmann called us, has been dulled by politicians who would manage the news, by censors who would tell us what we can see or read, by pressure groups, both white and black. I am determined that my newspaper shall stand free of these influences and truthfully present the news, objectively and without bias."

We hammered at McShane, day after day. Every line of my copy was read by Julian—and I might say edited. Not a line, not a word of what might be considered editorial intrusion was allowed in the stories; they were coldly factual and objective. Every paper in town and all the TV news broadcasts quoted us—and McShane's lawyers.

Then the politicians bent to the task. Three of the paper's biggest advertisers pulled out; but, surprisingly, three refused to be intimidated. One even increased his yearly budget; unfortunately, he was the smallest.

Next came the petty, almost laughable political pressure; the fire inspectors appeared; Buildings came over and decided our pressroom was dangerous. As our luck would have it, just then one of the annual cracks in the building's base appeared, and this was pounced on by

Buildings, who virtually predicted the entire structure would soon tumble down about our heads. A private engineering firm surveyed the building and announced that, while it was old, the usual repairs would make it safe for many years.

The inspections were more annoying than anything, but they irritated Julian, and at this point I wanted to shield him from any further harassment. I decided to pay a call on our drunken friend in the elevator, Commissioner Aymes.

I found him in his office in the Municipal Building, looking smug and confident.

"Well, what can I do for you, Malloy?" he asked with an air of the bishop welcoming the little curate from the tumble-down church in poverty's east end.

This was the worst attitude he could have adopted; I sat down in the chair he offered and stared hard at the bloated jowls, the watery eyes, and the loose lips. I should have been ashamed; it was no contest.

"I understand you're on a campaign against the *Blade-Leader*," I said.

He tried to look surprised. "I have nothing against the *Blade-Leader*, Malloy."

"Then why annoy us with those inspectors?"

He selected a cigarette, found a light after several strokes, inhaled, and tried to look official.

No, this was no contest. "The Departments have had complaints," he said at last. He squinted at me through the smoke. "You understand, don't you?"

"I thought I would take a run over to the Hall," I said, humble as the little curate.

"Why don't you?" he said. Then, eagerly reaching for the phone, "Do you want me to call the Hall? I'm sure he'd be glad——"

I wondered how that patrician woman we had met in the elevator suffered him.

"You just reminded me of something," I said.

"Yes," he said. "What's that?"

"The day I dropped over to the basement in Surrogate's Court, it was the day the Mayor went into the phony annual budget retreat. You know something? That basement is quite a place. Every bill from every city department is filed there."

"So what?" he said. "We know that."

"I just happened to check some automotive bills," I said. "By a strange coincidence some were from your department."

He looked startled and ground out his cigarette.

"We use city cars," he said. "Every city department does."

"That's true. But just for the hell of it I compared your department with a comparable group for expenditures in the army and navy car pools." I stood up and gave him a cheery smile. "One of these days I'm going to check back with the Comptroller's Office. I've always wondered how you account for those long and intensive hatchet jobs your office does. . . ."

With Aymes it was only a guilty conscience. He blustered and bellowed, and I left when I couldn't stand it any longer. Poor Aymes. I hadn't been to Surrogate's Court in years.

But even though we stopped those idiotic visits from the city's inspectors, we were still harassed. McShane's constituents started a mail and phone campaign, and for a few weeks we were inundated with letters and calls accusing us of being Communists, Socialists, anti-Negro, and anti-white. But the real crusher came from Washington; the Department of Justice, in a brief, formal announcement, revealed it was conducting an investigation of the Dolbar Newspaper Enterprises, Inc., for possible violation of the Antitrust Act.

"They underscored the word 'possible,' " Julian said. "That's our fire escape."

"Are you going to use it?" I asked.

"Remember what Cortés did?"

"Burned his boats?"

"That's what I did that day in my office. From now on, we have to swim home."

Although I talked to Johnny every day, I didn't get to see him until a week or more had passed. I had a hint of what he was going through when I ran into an assistant from the D.A.'s office I had known for years; in fact, I had persuaded the Women's Editor to include his bride's picture among the bluebloods, even though she had only graduated from Bushwick High School and lived near Atlantic Avenue. I started to greet him, but he froze me fast.

"That's nothing," Johnny said when I told him. "They won't even stand next to me in the men's room."

"When do we go to town, Johnny?" I said. "I'm beginning to relish writing that James Xavier McShane has been indicted."

"Monday, 10:00 A.M., Ricky goes before the Grand Jury again."

"How is he? Standing up?"

"I had to take him out of the Singing School."

"What happened?"

"He got another threat. This time it was on a slip of paper between two pieces of toast. It just said, 'Enjoy your meal, stoolie,' but it was enough to throw that guy into a tailspin for two days."

"How did they get in?"

"Who knows? Murphy had three of his best men sitting outside the cell. They examined every piece of food. The jail's too damn' big. We need an army."

I asked where he had him now.

Johnny leaned back and clasped his hands behind his head.

"Believe it or not—Ellis Island."

"Ellis Island! That's been abandoned for years!"

"Since 1960, to be exact. There's been only a caretaker, and five of the most vicious dogs in the world. A classmate of mine in General Services in Washington arranged it. Murphy himself is over there with five men he would trust his own life with. One was a cook in the army. He's the chef. It's not Twenty-one, but they have everything this bum wants."

"Vickie?"

"I explained that for a while she's *verboten*. All we have to do is let them spring a story I'm feeding a piece of tail to Strasser. Wouldn't Flaherty like that?"

"What did he say about moving Strasser?"

"He turned it down until I put on some heat. I told him I was going to release a statement to you that Strasser's life was threatened and he wouldn't do anything about it. He okayed the transfer but only after I submitted a signed statement, giving my reasons and accepting the full responsibility for the security arrangements. He also put the Police Commissioner in a bind, but the commissioner backed Murphy." He looked at his watch. "Do you want to take a run over there?"

"I wouldn't miss it for anything."

"I don't have to tell you it's all under wraps, Duke."

"Absolutely. How do we get out there?"

"The Coast Guard down at Pier A takes us out. Let's go."

I had been out to Ellis Island only once to cover a story; I have even forgotten what the story was about, but what always remained with me was the striking sight of downtown Manhattan's towers from the ferry, the jumble of ugly buildings on Ellis Island, and the busy throngs who hurried in and out of them.

The spires of downtown were just as unforgettable, and the ugly, squat buildings were still there, but the throngs were gone. There was nothing but a vast, eerie silence broken only by the mewing cries of the gulls and the impatient snort of a freighter beating its way to the sea past an indifferent little tug. The whole island looked like a vast stone ghost town.

We clambered aboard the dock and walked less than a hundred feet when Johnny waved; a detective with a rifle waved back and vanished in the doorway of a building.

"Murphy has it so that even the sea gulls have to get permission to come ashore."

Walking up a long driveway that was overgrown with weeds and tufts of grass, we entered the Administration Building. Another detective waved us on, and we started down a winding corridor. Strips of paper hung from walls; plates were set at a table as though waiting for guests to arrive; a book lay open on a desk; a man's hat was on a chair.

"It's like coming back after the first blast," Johnny said.

It was so true my skin crawled.

We turned a corner, and seventy snarling pounds slammed against a barred door. I automatically leaped to one side. Beyond the door a detective snapped a leash on the huge German shepherd that was fighting to get at us. Behind him was a grinning Inspector Murphy.

"I thought I would just let you see how prepared we are," he said as he unlocked the door. "How are you, Duke?"

"Outside of a heart that almost just stopped, fine."

In a low voice Johnny asked about Strasser.

"He's bitching about everything. Now it's rats. He claims one ran across the room last night. It was a mouse, but he carried on like a woman."

We followed him into a room. It was large, with windows facing the bay. It contained a TV set, a stack of paperbacks, newspapers, a bed, easy chair, and a table. It wasn't the Waldorf, but it certainly wasn't spartan.

Strasser appeared thinner and more haggard since I had last seen him. His eyes were puffy and his hair shaggy. He had lost that sleek, arrogant veneer. Now he was more like Delancey Street. He was playing cards with a detective when we came in. Murphy nodded, and the detective left.

"It's about time you came over," Ricky said to Johnny. "I called three times yesterday."

"I told you I would make it today. I brought an old friend—Duke Malloy."

For the first time he seemed to recognize me. His face twisted, and he slammed his fist down on the table.

"You brought this God-damned newspaper creep! What the hell did you do that for? He'll blab this all over the front page, and I'm dead! They'll come out and . . ."

"No one is coming out here, Ricky," Johnny said wearily. "And Duke won't tell a soul where you are."

"You jerk! Of course he will! He's the cause of this whole damned—"

"Shut up!" Johnny shouted. "Do you hear me? Shut up!"

The pin had pricked the balloon, and the air slowly oozed out. Ricky slumped back in the chair on the verge of tears.

"You think I like to stay out here?" He sobbed. "You think I like to stay in this creepy hole? There's rats around here as big as cats! They're running all over the place."

"It will only be a few more days," Johnny said calmly. "And then we'll get some place in the city."

"Those God-damned dogs," Ricky said. "I'm afraid of them. I was always afraid of dogs; now you got the biggest damn' mutts in the world. Every time I go by I think one is going to take off my leg."

"They're as good as five cops," Murphy said. "They wouldn't let a tank get past us."

You poor, miserable bastard, I thought. Mouthpiece for the mob. Pal of the tough guys . . .

"When am I going to see Vickie?" he demanded.

"She's staying with a friend of mine in Westchester," Johnny said. He took something from his pocket. "Here's a letter. She's going to call you tonight."

"Why can't I see her here?" Ricky whined. "Why?" She's not a witness." He said quickly, "You're not going to put her on the stand?"

"I promised you and her father I wouldn't. Ricky, you were going to make some notes on Gennaro's book."

"I was too tired," Ricky said belligerently.

"Look, will you do it tonight? I'm just trying to get some leads."

"We went over it a thousand times, Counselor," Strasser said sarcastically. "Remember?"

"We'll go over it a thousand times more if I think you can come up with anything," Johnny said coldly. "Understand?"

Ricky dropped his eyes, and nodded.

"I'm telling you I don't like this creepy place," he said. "I should have gone to McShane, put my cards on the table, and joined him."

"And he would have killed you," Johnny said evenly. "The dirt would have been on top of you by now."

Ricky licked his lips. His face was as white as his shirt. "Don't talk like that," he whispered. "Please."

"We're doing the best we can to make sure they don't kill you," Johnny said. "You fell apart up in the jail when you got that last note.

I don't blame you. You're under a terrible strain, Ricky. But I want to get one thing straight: when you take that stand you are going to repeat exactly what you told Murphy and me. Is that correct?"

"I'm not recanting, Johnny. I never said that."

"I know you didn't, Ricky. I just want to make sure. Now we have to get back. Is there anything you want?"

He looked so pathetic I felt sorry for him.

"Just Vickie, Johnny, only her."

Johnny put his hand on Strasser's shoulder.

"It won't be long, Ricky. I promise."

"I'll see you out," Murphy said.

Outside, on the steps of the Administration Building, Johnny pointed to the other buildings.

"Are they all empty, Inspector?"

"Every one. The government man is on the other side of the island. We see him only when he makes his daily tour."

"Ricky sounds pretty ragged, Inspector," I said.

"I can't say I blame him. It's God-awful lonesome here at night. And those army dogs are vicious. One gave one of my detectives a nasty nip the other night."

"Well, where else can we put him?" Johnny asked impatiently. "You have any ideas?"

"How about the Federal pen on West Street?"

"The Feds gave me a long excuse why they couldn't help us. I was thinking of the Danbury pen up in Connecticut."

"I guess it's either here or one of the city jails," Murphy said.

"Another week in a city jail and he'll clam up," Johnny said roughly. "He stays here."

"Well, it's a seashore vacation," the inspector said. "I'll try to keep him happy."

On the way back we stood in the bow of the cutter and studied the cluttered tip of Manhattan.

"I wanted you to get an idea of what we are up against," Johnny said.

"He'll whine but he'll never renege."

"Even if he doesn't he will be in terrible shape to take the stand," Johnny said thoughtfully. "He'll fall apart under cross. The word I get is, McShane is prepared to hire that guy down in Washington. He's deadly at cross. Poor Ricky will collapse unless we get some iron in him. Damn! If we could only find that book! It could bolster his testimony."

"No luck yet?"

"Just between us, I told Inspector Murphy to offer anything to his stoolies for a lead on that book," he said. "But nobody came up with a thing. I told Bernie I would give him a medal on City Hall steps, but he swears he never heard of the book. I believe him." He shook his head. "It was just one drunken moment that Gennaro let his hair down. Apparently he never did it again."

"There's another thing," I said. "McShane's girl friend."

"We sniffed around that one too. Nothing. The guy's a widower; he has those two kids he idolizes; and he lives quietly. For your own information, he doesn't drink. He doesn't gamble. Politics is his life."

"And power."

"I guess that goes with it, Duke."

"When do we go to bat?"

"Monday morning," he said grimly. "McShane will be indicted on Wednesday."

James X. McShane was indicted on Wednesday afternoon. He was charged in the True Bill with four counts of violating Section 974 of the Penal Law, conspiring to form a lottery. He was also charged with two counts of violating Section 378 of the New York Penal Law, bribing a public official. He could receive a total of twenty years in prison and fines up to $75,000.

The indictment itself was almost anticlimactic. From the morning Strasser appeared before the Grand Jury, the papers were openly mentioning the possibility of McShane's indictment. When it came, Johnny called McShane's attorney to appear at the District Attorney's office with McShane. After the indictment was opened in court, McShane insisted that he and his attorney walk to Oak Street precinct, where the formal booking took place. It was a brilliant piece of public relations. The walk downtown was almost a triumphant procession. City workers poured out of the Municipal Building to shake his hand, and he soon had a small crowd following him.

"It was just as though he had returned from a space flight," Johnny said bitterly.

That evening the news broadcasts had the brief statement from Washington. It was cautious and was a far cry from any all-out endorsement of McShane. I would have been worried if I had been McShane; as any old pro, he knew the most ruthless men in the world are Washington politicians. They never go with a loser and they want no business with anyone in trouble.

Certainly not in an election year.

[33]

FATE IS A terrible temptress; she will lie in wait for a man, slip behind him when he is least prepared, and ask him to make an agonizing choice. . . .

A few weeks after the McShane indictment, a copyboy casually told me there had been a call earlier from a man who said he had been trying to get in touch with me. The boy said the caller had left no name but would get in touch with me that evening at home.

But that evening Johnny was going up to Westchester to see Vickie, and I was to go along. I hadn't seen Vickie in weeks, and this could be important. Johnny's pipeline told us McShane's Washington attorney was going to subpoena everyone he could contact, and this could include Vickie. Our plan was to publish Vickie's story, in which she would tell everything, in her own words, under her own by-line, with nothing held back. Vickie was willing, but it had taken a lot of persuasion by Johnny to convince Strasser. He finally agreed if he could first read the story. Her family and Torytown would not be mentioned.

The endless meetings with Johnny and Murphy, the consultations with Parsons and Townsend, who were getting more gloomy as the days went on; the bickering with Strasser and the frantic search for some of our policy witnesses who kept disappearing—all were now part of our hour-to-hour existence. Johnny said Connie was complaining she was a widow before she was married. I tried to write Gwen a few times, but gave up when I found my mind wandering.

This was the situation when Fate came up with her sly offer: go home and wait for the call from a vague stranger or go along with Johnnie and see Vickie. I brushed off the call, told Johnny I would join him for an early steak at the Pen and Pencil before driving to Westchester, and sat down to write my story for the next day.

Nothing went right. The lead wouldn't come; I had mislaid my file of clips from previous stories; the copyboy brought me coffee intsead of milk. The garage called to say I needed a new water pump. Yet despite all this the thought of that strange caller plagued me until finally I brusquely called Johnny and told him I would make the visit to Vickie later in the week. Then I rattled off the overnight story, flung it on the city desk, and went home.

About nine I was ready to give up and call myself a fool when the phone rang.

"Is this you, Duke?" a deep voice asked. Then a chuckle, "The guy from Jersey?"

It was Tilley.

"Tilley? How are you?"

"Fine, man. I think I better see you."

"When?"

"Want me to cut out now?"

"I'll be here all night."

He hung up. I got out the Chivas Regal and a pitcher of milk. Something was up, and nothing was too good for Tilley this night. Shortly before ten the doorbell rang, and there was Tilley, round and black and still wearing that stained brown fedora.

He grinned when he saw the Scotch and the milk.

"I call it Tilley's Special. The whole office is drinking the stuff."

I poured him a double and he added the milk. He took a deep swallow and smacked his lips.

"How've you been, Tilley?"

"I got a good chunk of the Avenue: 111th to 115th."

"Cops still taking?"

"They're careful but they're takin'. You ain't gonna put that in the paper?"

"We're not after the little fish any more, Tilley. Only the big ones."

"Yeah. I've been readin' about that guy McShane." He gave me a hard look. "You think he had the East Side knock off Jackson?"

"Who knows?"

"I think he did," he said harshly. "The bastard."

I wasn't going to hurry anything. I knew Tilley would never come down to see me on anything trivial. I had to wait until he was ready to talk.

He studied the glass between his big black hands.

"Remember you askin' me if I ever heard the Wop or Jackson talk about Sugar Daddy?"

"Sure I do."

"I told you I didn't, and that's the truth. But somebody else did—"

My mouth went dry.

"Oh? Who was that, Tilley?"

" 'Member Frank the Sheik?"

"The ribbon-car driver?"

"Yeah. Well, one day I was walkin' down the Avenue and he comes along in the Wop's Caddy. He used to put on the dog with that car. He stops and says, 'Hey, Tilley, where you goin'?' I says I was goin' downtown, and he says, 'Hop in and we'll ride Pullman.' But first he says he got to go to the post office on 125th Street. I said okay, and we drove there. On the seat was a big fat white envelope. 'What's that?' I said. 'The Wop's,' he said. Then he says the Wop wants to send it air-mail special delivery, and starts to tell me about a colored girl he was boffin'. I kept sayin' yeah . . . yeah, but I don't like to hear about any whitey boffin' a colored dame, so I didn't pay any mind to what he was sayin'. When he reached the post office, there's no place to park. 'Hey, Tilley,' he says, 'you go in and mail the Wop's letter. Okay?' Okay, I says, and he gives me a dollar. So I go in and mail it."

He finished the glass and I poured him another double. I had to bite my tongue from shouting the question as he deliberately poured in the milk.

"It's a long line, see, and I waited. While I wait, I wonder who the Wop knows out of Harlem, so I look at the letter. Man, I'm surprised. On the back it says Sugar Hill Financing Company, and it's addressed to a box number in Laurel, North Carolina. I'm wonderin' what business Sugar Daddy's doin' down in Laurel, but then my turn comes and I mail the Wop's letter."

"Did the Sheik say anything about the letter?"

"I asked how come, but he just kept talkin' 'bout that colored gal he was boffin', so I forgot it."

"You never heard anything before about Sugar Hill being down south?"

He shook his head. "I told you, man, I tried to dig out that landlord to fix that bathroom, but all I found on Twenty-third Street was a little girl who knew from nothin'. Nobody in Harlem ever found Sugar Daddy."

"What ever happened to the Sheik?"

He gave me a blank look. "Frank the Sheik?"

"Yes, Frank the Sheik," I said impatiently. "The ribbon-car driver. The pimp. Where's he hanging out now?"

"He's in the river," Tilley replied matter of factly. "Somebody found out he fingered Jackson. When he got out on bail they dumped him."

"Who dumped him, Tilley?"

He gave me a vague look. "Some of the guys on the Avenue."

"Where did they dump him?"

He finished his milk and Scotch and smacked his lips. "You know guys with ulcers drink this?"

"Tilley, where did they dump him?"

He looked down at his old hat. "Man, you want me to point it out on a map?"

"You have your ears to the ground, Tilley. You must have heard something."

"Watch the papers," he said. "One of these days they'll pick up a floater." He stood up and put on his hat. "That will be Frank the Sheik." He looked around the room with open admiration.

"Man, I bet this place ain't never seen a rat!"

It was a Harlem accolade.

As I walked him to the door, I had a final question.

"One thing, Tilley—when did this business about Gennaro's letter happen?"

"Maybe last summer. I know it was hot. Me and the wife took the kids for a ride." He scowled. "You think this is bullshit?"

"No. I was just wondering how you remembered the name of the town."

"Laurel?" He stared over my head. "I lived with my folks in Vance. That's just three miles away. One night when I was a little boy they lynched three niggers in Laurel." He searched my face for a moment. "One was my old man."

BOOK NINE

THE LADY IN THE DIARY

[34]

Over the phone I suggested to Johnny that while he threw some things in a bag I would find just where Laurel was located and the fastest way to get there. After a series of calls the city desk reported that Laurel was in Yancey County near the Tennessee border. It was a small town in the foothills of the Black Mountains, a short cross range of the Blue Ridge that split the county. Total population 3,300, a library, two churches, two schools, a courthouse, and a main street. There wasn't anything listed about the three Negroes lynched more than forty years ago; I guess Laurel's Chamber of Commerce didn't go in for that type of tourist promotion.

The nearest airport was Asheville, Tom Wolfe's town. From there we could hire a car. Laurel was about fifty miles away. There was a plane at 7:00 A.M. leaving from Washington. I called Julian, who wasn't home, and Turner Elliott, who wished me luck. I had the night city desk call Washington for reservations, and I was in Johnny's house within the hour. We debated about taking Murphy but finally agreed it might throw Strasser into a frenzy.

"What do you think Sugar Hill is doing in Laurel, North Carolina?" I asked him.

"Gennaro either has an accountant or a front man," Johnny said, "or"—he zipped closed the small overnight bag—"a safe-deposit box."

"You mean the book?"

"I'm afraid even to say it."

The phone rang, and Johnny grabbed it.

393

"Hello, Inspector? Yeah, I see. No luck. Okay. If we get anything we'll let you know as soon as possible. Right. Good night." He said to me, "I asked Murphy to feel out Ricky on Laurel. Not that I think he is holding anything back, but I thought the name might jog his memory."

"And it didn't?"

"He never heard of it. Neither did Vickie. The same goes for Bernie."

"You've been working—"

"The minute you called I was on the phone," he said. "Duke, now tell me again about Tilley. Take it nice and slow and tell me everything."

I went over the scene in my apartment, quoting Tilley and even describing his battered hat.

"That explains why you haven't been able to pick up Frank the Sheik."

"It confirms what Inspector Murphy's stoolies reported. They have insisted all along that a colored mob got Frank the Sheik after the East Side put up his bail. The story is that they got a beautiful colored dame to act as a lure. She got the Sheik up to her apartment and used knock-out drops. Murphy said he was strangled and dumped in the Harlem River. Before they tossed him in, they cut off what was always most important to Frank the Sheik."

We caught the 7:00 A.M. out of Washington and arrived in Asheville shortly after nine. In the airport we shaved, freshened up, and had some breakfast. There wasn't much business in the dining room, so we had the waitress all to ourselves. I told her we were in furniture. She was talkative, and we managed to get an idea of Yancey County and how to get there. Then we hired a car and were off.

After the tour around northern New Jersey years ago with that *Daily News* antique buff, I always maintained that Sussex County in that part of the state was one of the most spectacular scenic spots I had ever seen. But from now on it will have to place second to Yancey County, North Carolina, a breathtaking world of rolling timberland, deep narrow gorges, and mountain waterfalls. In the early afternoon we rode through Vance, and for a wild moment I could picture Tilley as one of the ragged black urchins who stared at us from the doorways of the pitiful shacks just off the highway. It was hard to decide which was better for Tilley's kids, the black streets of Harlem with its pushers and junkies and switchblades and zips and rumbles with antennas that cut to the bone like Frenchmen's foils, or the potbellied, rickety youngsters with glaucoma, in the piny backwoods of North Carolina. Johnny didn't know either; maybe, he said, it was Harlem—at least there they let him vote and go to school. But I once had written a series on New York schools, and remembered the kids who told me how they smoked pot and drank Three-fingered Brown, as they called the cheap wine, under the stairs and under the eyes of the teachers who hated to rock their principal's boat. . . .

We found Laurel to be a beautiful little southern town, about a mile off the main highway. There were the inevitable grassy square with the stalwart Confederate soldier, a tree-shaded Main Street, the small modern bank, the supermarket, and the furniture factory on which the town depended. A pleasant cop directing school traffic suggested we stay at the Laurel Motel near the highway or the big Victorian-style house that advertised tourist accommodations. We decided on the motel.

The motel owner was a friendly enough fellow who fortunately seemed to be too busy painting and caulking a swimming pool to be curious about us. We did ask him if he had ever heard of the Sugar Hill Financing Company, but he only scratched his head and said that was a new one on him. The county telephone book, a yellow book, and a county business directory didn't offer anything.

"I don't think Gennaro would have been idiot enough to list a racket outfit, but you can never tell," Johnny said as he tossed the phone book aside. "Personally I think we'll just have to ring doorbells."

"Are you going to contact the sheriff?"

"I don't see how we can avoid it," Johnny said. "Sooner or later someone will tip him off there's two strangers asking questions."

"What story will you tell him?"

"Simply that we are looking for this company that has been violating New York City building and tax laws. And we suspect that Vito Gennaro, a New York racketeer, is connected with it."

The sheriff turned out to be a fat six-footer who reminisced about the '64 election. He was surprisingly apathetic about Johnny's query and the fact that Vito Gennaro might be connected with a racketeering outfit in his county. He spent more than an hour on the phone, asking builders, bankers, fellow sheriffs, and businessmen in the county if they had ever heard of Sugar Hill. They hadn't. But he said he had to go over to the state police headquarters the following day and would ask their CID if they had any information.

After dinner we explored the town; it took less than a half hour. Lights went out after nine o'clock, and in the bar even the motel owner, who doubled as bartender, was half asleep. Laurel definitely wasn't a place for dissipation.

The furniture factory's seven o'clock whistle got us up, and most of our morning was spent waiting for the sheriff to return from the state police headquarters. He did, but with no news. We also checked the Secretary of State's office for possible papers of incorporation, the state tax bureau, and the Better Business Bureau. Again blanks. Then Johnny and I got on the phone and systematically called every businessman and company in the county. Nothing.

"Let's take a ride out in the country," Johnny said after lunch. "This place is giving me the creeps."

We rode aimlessly for a while, over back roads and secondary highways and parts of the breathtaking Blue Ridge Parkway. Spring was in the air, and you could almost feel the land ready to burst into bloom. We crossed a small river and had taken a road along its banks when I spotted the boy fishing. Suddenly it hit me.

"Johnny! I got it!"

Johnny spun the wheel to one side and the car skidded to a stop. "What's the matter with you!"

"Johnny, look," I said, and pointed to the boy.

"So what?" he said, puzzled. "It's only a kid—" He stopped. "Fishing!" he whispered. "That's what Strasser said Gennaro liked to do, fish!" He added excitedly, "He might have come down to fish." He swung the car about. "Let's get back to that hick sheriff and find out where you fish around here."

When we told him, the sheriff lumbered to his feet and pulled down a county map; he ticked off one by one the best fishing spots in the area. There were twenty-two, and they stretched from the northern end of the county near the Tennessee border to the southern tip near the Catawba River.

"You boys have a lot of traveling to do," he said. "Better start down at the Catawba country and move up to us." He marked off the routes on the highway map and gave it to us. "If you have any trouble you give me a call, you hear?"

We heard.

"We'll hit these places one by one," Johnny said back at the motel, "and just give it to them cold." He took out Gennaro's picture. "This ought to help."

It took us three days to check off seventeen fishing places. Owners, guides, baitmen just looked at Gennaro's picture and shook their heads. We went on from early morning until dark. Some of the places were in remote back country near Mount Mitchell State Park, and difficult to find. More than once we were blinded by a powerful flashlight with a soft drawling voice against a chorus of baying hounds asking just what the hell did we want. On the afternoon of the fourth day we found ourselves on a highway with signs directing us to Pisgah National Park. We were both exhausted and depressed; even the spectacular scenery had become commonplace. The place we were looking for, according to the sheriff's map, was on War Bonnet Lake, near a village called Crossfire. A highway gas station not only filled our tank but gave us a history lesson on the origin of the lake and the village. War Bonnet was the name of some Indian chief, and Crossfire a spot where a Confederate guerrilla outfit had wiped out a Yankee patrol. The owner of the gas station said he knew the fishing camp because the owner was one of his customers. Then he added, he was an "Ah-tal-yan."

"An Italian?" Johnny repeated.

The muffled voice from under the hood said, "Yeah. An Ah-tal-yan from New Yawk. Nice fellow. Name's Minnotti. You could do with a quart..."

Back on the highway Johnny said, "Minnotti. I know that name. Although it's a common Italian name, like Smith or Jones. We'll see."

We reached Crossfire, a sleepy little village, and got additional directions from a passing farmer. The road was blacktop for a short distance, then dirt. It climbed considerably for several miles, then wound around a stunning lake that the sinking sun was turning into a bowl of burnished copper. A sign, "Minnotti's Lodge, Prop. A. Minnotti," directed us up a narrow road lined with pine trees. The air was fragrant with pine and just edged with a chill.

The Minnotti lodge was reminiscent of the Simms cabin in New Jersey, except that it was larger, newer, and surrounded by several small clapboard houses, all newly painted; a table of planks stretched over horses held splattered cans of paint. The inevitable hound chorus rose as we parked, and a man came out of the main house. He was wearing paint-splattered dungarees and a blue shirt and was holding a big German shepherd on a short chain.

"Mr. Minnotti?" Johnny called out.

"That's me," was the answer. I was immediately struck by the lack of the soft North Carolina drawl we had become accustomed to.

"This guy sounds like New York," Johnny whispered as he came closer.

Minnotti was in his early twenties, dark skinned, with a new painter's cap, like the kind paint stores give you with a purchase, stuck on a tangle of black curls. He was a good-looking boy, but he seemed uneasy and unsure of himself. He kept tugging at the dog and muttering commands.

Johnny must have sensed the uneasiness because he dropped the casual, friendly manner he had been using with the natives.

"Your name Minnotti?"

"That's right," the boy said. "Who are you?"

Johnny walked nearer and flipped out the black wallet with his D.A.'s badge.

"I'm from the New York County District Attorney's office," he said. "My name is De Lorenzo. This is Mr. Malloy."

The boy did his best to appear nonchalant.

"So? What do you want with me?"

"Can we step in for a moment?"

He hesitated, then said, "Why not?"

We followed him into the lodge. The knotty-pine walls glowed with new varnish. A cheerful fire crackled in the enormous fireplace, and there was a superb bar to one side of the room with framed pictures of fishermen in the usual poses holding up their catch in a boat or in groups. On the floor were other paint pots, sanders, and brushes in glass jars. The air was heavy with the smell of alcohol, turpentine, and paint.

"I just finished shellacking the walls," the boy said. "We'll be opening for trout next month. Let me get you a drink. . . . What's this all about?" he asked as he went behind the bar to fill our orders.

"Are you Anthony Minnotti?" Johnny asked. I looked at him in surprise; there had been just "A. Minnotti" on the sign.

"That's right," the boy said. "Anthony Minnotti, owner of the Minnotti Fishing Lodge, one of the oldest and best in the State of North Carolina." He came from around the bar with the drinks. "I guess you're not here to ask how the trout will be next month."

Johnny took out the picture of Gennaro. "Did you ever see this man before?"

Minnotti studied the picture and slowly shook his head. He looked tense as he gave it back to Johnny.

"Never saw the guy in my life. Who is he?"

"Did you ever hear of Vito Gennaro?"

A faint shrug. "Who hasn't? He was bigger on television than Wyatt Earp. Last month the local station had a show on gangsters, and he was all over the screen. Right?"

"But you never saw him in person?"

The boy tried to laugh. "How would I know him, De Lorenzo?"

"Maybe he came down here to fish."

"A gangster like that? What are you guys—nuts?"

"You talk like a New Yorker," I said.

"West Third Street in the Village," he said, "until a few months ago when my father died."

"Were you working in New York?"

"I was in my last year at Columbia Law. After the season I'm going back and finish out."

"Oh, then you're Anthony Minnotti, Jr.," Johnny said.

"That's right. But where did you get the idea Gennaro came here?"

"Information which came to the attention of our office," Johnny said formally. "Did you ever hear of the Sugar Hill Financing Company?"

Minnotti shook his head, a bit too vigorously, I thought.

"Your father wasn't in any company setup with Gennaro?"

For the first time the boy looked angry. "What the hell are you talking about?"

"I'm asking you questions, Minnotti. If the answer is No, just say so."

For the next half hour Johnny shot questions at Minnotti, simple routine questions, but the boy either laughed them off or denied them. Johnny appeared to be making elaborate notes, and finally, when he had finished, he told Minnotti he would have a statement prepared the next day for his signature.

"Sign a statement? What for?"

"It's only routine," Johnny said casually. "We'll get a notary and it won't take but a minute. The sheriff will witness it."

"The sheriff?"

"He's an officer of the court. He makes it legal. Then we give your statement to the Grand Jury—"

"The Grand Jury! What the hell for?"

Johnny smiled. "As I said, Tony, it's only routine—if you didn't lie. If you did I'll indict you for perjury, and the next time you come to New York I'll grab you. As a law student you certainly know what perjury is." He stood up. "Come on, Duke; it's going to take all night to find our way out of here." He looked at Minnotti. "Unless you can put us up for the night."

Young Minnotti was now obviously ill at ease. He kept licking his lips as though they were unusually dry, and looking from Johnny to me.

"Well, maybe I can. There are some sheets and some blankets in the cabins—"

"Fine," Johnny said. "What's for dinner?"

"I've got some lasagna I was going to heat up."

"Lasagna! Wonderful! We'll be your first guests this season," Johnny said. "Where's the cabin?"

Minnotti showed us the way. The cabin was chilly, and smelled of paint and varnish. The mattresses were cold, and the piled-up sheets, blankets, and pillowcases looked anything but comfortable.

"What's going on?" I asked Johnny when Minnotti left.

"Doesn't the name Minnotti mean anything to you?"

I shook my head.

"If you were Italian it would. Tony Rabbits Minnotti. Back in the twenties and early thirties he was a big man in the Brooklyn rackets. Remember Frankie Yale?"

"God, you're going back to prehistoric times!"

"Tony Rabbits and Frankie Yale were fighting for control of all the whiskey that came into New York from Canada. Yale was killed, and Tony took over. From whiskey he went into produce. Every Italian family in the city that had anything to do with trucks or produce paid him tribute. I can remember my mother cursing Tony Rabbits when I was a kid. He was deported before World War II. I guess he slipped back in and came here."

"Why did they call him Tony Rabbits?"

"When he first came to New York he got a job in a produce store in Brooklyn where they sold rabbits."

"But is it the same Minnotti? You said the name is common."

"The kid's from New York. The first name—too many things click."

"You think his father knew Gennaro?"

"Give me two Italian mobsters in New York who don't know each other and I'll eat them." He waved me away as I started to spread out a sheet. "Don't bother, Duke."

"I'm not going to sleep on a cold mattress, not even for the New York District Attorney's office."

"You won't have to. I have a hunch he'll be back soon."

"What for?"

"To talk. He knows something. And he's studying to be a lawyer. Doesn't that mean anything to you, Duke?"

"Only that he'll be twice as smart and won't talk."

"If we strike out here," Johnny said, "that's the ball game. I probably can get two more adjournments, but McShane's lawyers have already told me they want an immediate trial. After a month on that damned deserted island with only Murphy to talk to, Strasser will probably be ready for the gas pipe—"

We both spun around as the door opened. For a wild moment I thought I would see old man Minnotti standing in the doorway with a gun, but it was his son and he looked worried.

Johnny said rapidly in Italian, "Potete avere fiducia in me. Ditemi la vert verità. Sonotuo amico." Which Johnny told me later was: "You can trust in me. Tell me the truth. I am your friend."

The boy nodded. "Dice verità . . . I will speak the truth."

"Let's go back to the main house," Johnny said.

The story was simple; the older Minnotti had died of a heart attack at the lodge and had been found by the mailman. Young Tony, who was living with an aunt in New York while he went to school, came to North Carolina and buried his father. He dropped out of school but notified the authorities he would return the next year to graduate; in the meantime he had taken over the lodge, which had an excellent clientele, and made preparations to hire a manager for the next season.

The week after he had buried his father, there had been a long-distance phone call. The voice, speaking Italian, asked for Tony. The boy answered, and the man from New York identified himself as Don Vitone and said the letter was on its way down and to take care of it.

Johnny asked, "Did he think he was talking to your father?"

"I guess so. When I answered in Italian he just rattled this off in Italian and hung up. He never gave me a chance to say anything."

"But you knew Vito?"

"Every year he would come down for a few days, and fish. I really never knew who he was. I thought he was just a friend of my father's from the Old Country. In fact, I used to be glad to see him because he and my father would really enjoy themselves. They would drink wine and play bacci and talk of the old days. When he came down I took over the place. I guess that was another reason I liked to see him. It gave me a chance to play the boss."

"When did you know he was Gennaro?"

"When he appeared on television. I was sitting right here, and I almost fell over. My father didn't say anything for a while, but when I began pressing he said Vito was an old friend."

"Did you know that your father and Gennaro—"

Minnotti said bitterly, "When I opened the safe-deposit vault in the Crossfire bank, I found out a lot of things."

"What did you find, Tony?"

"Gennaro kept a book in which my father's name is mentioned."

"Is it a notebook with a black-and-white cover?" I said quickly.

Tony looked suprised. "I think so. How did you know?"

"We just happened to know, Tony," Johnny said. "Why did you go to the bank and how did you know your father had a vault?"

Tony went behind the bar and brought back a torn envelope.

My heart jumped when I read the address written in a laborious, crabbed hand: "Anthony Minnotti, General Delivery, Laurel, North Carolina." And printed on the back flap was, "Sugar Hill Financing Company, Box 74A, General Post Office, New York City."

"Where did you get this?" Johnny asked.

"A few weeks after my father died, the mailman called me and said there was a letter in the Laurel post office. That puzzled me, because we always got our mail delivered from Crossfire. I picked up the letter, and they told me my father used to get one or two letters like this a year. Later our lawyer called me about the estate and I went down to the bank to sign some papers. That's when I found out about the deposit box. I found the keys and opened it."

I found myself on the edge of the chair.

"What was in the box, Tony?" Johnny asked.

"More money than I have ever seen in my life," the boy said. "A lot of letters from a bank in Switzerland, that book I told you about, some letters from Gennaro to my father, and a roll of movie film."

"Movie film?" I said.

He handed me a small yellow box, the kind in which home movies are returned after being developed. I held the strip to the light, but the frames showed only what seemed to be a man and woman standing outside a motel, then going aboard a small yacht. I handed the film to Johnny, who gave it a quick look.

"All these family films, Tony?"

"No. The only pictures we ever take are of the clients and their catches. And those are usually color slides unless they ask us to take movies. Then we send the film on to the factory, and they are delivered to the customer." He turned the box over. "This film was developed in Rochester, New York. We send our stuff to Winston-Salem."

Johnny put the box in his pocket. "Did you take anything else out of the box?"

"Only the film and this old envelope. I knew something was wrong when I saw all that money. I tried to count it, but I stopped after fifty thousand. There must be at least a hundred thousand. I know the Internal Revenue should be notified. . . ." He threw up his hands. "I didn't know what to do! He was my father! Everyone around here knew and liked him. He was a director of the Crossfire First National Bank. He was head of the County Fish and Game Association. Once one of our big clients wanted to bring down a photographer from a big magazine to do a picture layout of our place, but my father refused. He didn't give any reason; he just said No. I was mad as hell. I couldn't understand." He added bitterly, "Now I do. He didn't want any pictures in a national magazine. Someone might remember Tony Rabbits."

"Why did you finally decide to tell us?" I asked.

"I guess I'm going to be a lawyer with a conscience," Tony said.

We reached the sheriff as he was having breakfast, and he in turn called the Supreme Court judge in Laurel, who gave Johnny a court order to open the vault on the grounds that the book was a tool of trade and held facts of crime in New York City. The order allowed us to have the book, letters, and all documents photostated on the proviso that Internal Revenue be notified. This Tony did himself.

The box was then opened in the presence of the bank officials, an IR man from Asheville, Tony, the sheriff, Johnny, and me. I had thought it would be a supreme moment, but I guess that belongs to Hollywood; in fact, there was only bickering between the Internal Revenue agent, the bank, and the sheriff. Uncle Sam's representative wanted to take everything away on the grounds that the Organized Crime and Racketeering Section of the Department of Justice would want to study the documents, but Johnny and the sheriff told him bluntly the cold cash and nothing else was his responsibility.

The photostating was another problem, but the sheriff told the local photographer that if he wanted to photograph any more highway wrecks for the county he had better put everything aside until he had copied the book and the various documents and letters that were in the vault.

Gennaro's diary or account book for some reason reminded me of something from the twenties. The pages were unlined, and smelled musty. Some pages were blank; others had a few lines; many were filled with Gennaro's small, crabbed writing, like that of a grade-school child gripping his pen, as Strasser had described. Everything was in Italian. As I flipped through the pages, I could visualize Gennaro, alone in a room, bent over the book, carefully writing down his secrets for God knows what purpose. . . .

"It's going to take a day to translate this stuff," Johnny said. "Another headache."

By nightfall we were hungry, harassed, and irritable. The Internal Revenue agent had called Washington, and as a result we were dogged by an officious little man at IR headquarters in Washington who kept leaving messages all over the county for us to call him.

We stayed in the studio, virtually breathing down the photographer's neck as he dried each stat. Finally, by early evening, the job had been finished.

"The fellow in Washington has been calling every hour," the sheriff said over the phone. "I think you boys better scoot right back to New York. If these Federal people come down here . . ."

We didn't need any urging. We said good-bye to Tony, turned to our car to the rental agency in Asheville, and picked up the last night plane to Washington.

During these long hours I was haunted by the thought that some local reporter would turn up the story and it would get on the wires to New York. Johnny was for not using anything on the diary until Monday when he appeared in court, but I had to point out that I was still working for the *Blade-Leader* and not the D.A.'s office and that, additionally, my story would give young Tony the better of it. We compromised on Sunday. Earlier I had the local photographer take some shots of Johnny holding the diary, and these I gave to the photographer's assistant, who handed them over to a hostess on a plane bound for New York. I wired Turner Elliott I had a big one coming up for Sunday and gave him the name of the hostess and the plane's arrival time. A copyboy would pick up the pictures and make the hostess happy with twenty-five dollars.

The sheriff and the judge had agreed not to talk until Sunday, and all I could do was hope the Crossfire bankers, the Internal Revenue man in Asheville, and the local photographer didn't have any friends in the press room of the Laurel courthouse.

News is perishable, and I had two days—forty-eight hours—to hover over, protect, and keep cool a secret that was now known from Washington to Asheville.

We arrived in Washington late and decided to stay at the Congressional. We had just checked in and were walking to the elevators when we passed the newsstand. Automatically I started to read the headlines. I stopped and grabbed Johnny's arm. He stared down for a moment, then whistled. I bought the *Washington Post* and all the New York papers and we sat down in the lobby.

The stark headlines told us the story: the Prophet had gone berserk in his cell. When they finally got him into a straitjacket he was a raving maniac. There was the report of the court-appointed team of psychiatrists, which said very simply, in between the medical and legal language, that this skinny little Negro, with the golden voice and the tormented mind that told him he was a Pierre Toussaint and Harlem his golden Citadel, was hopelessly mad and should be committed for the rest of his days in Dannemora's Hospital for the Criminally Insane.

There were pictures of Flaherty at a press conference and of the Prophet, trussed like a fowl, being carried into Criminal Courts Building, and of the team of psychiatrists and the judge who had sentenced him. There were also stories of reported demonstrations scheduled to be held outside the courthouse, but apparently the news that the Prophet was only a madman and not a messiah had punctured the plans, and less than twenty-five pickets showed up.

Flaherty had a great deal to say in court; the AP dispatch said he spoke for more than an hour, crying out his defiance at those who would use racial unrest to promote violence and hatred among the people of the greatest city in the world. He praised the police, the White House, Congress, the courts, City Hall, and just about everyone else he could think of. As the AP man wrote, the applause was spontaneous.

We sat in silence, reading every line. Finally we rolled up the papers and deposited them in a wastepaper basket.

"Well, that's the end of that," Johnny said. "The great big black problem has been conquered."

"You mean that's the end of it?" I said. "The end of the race riot, those people in Harlem who were killed, the cops who had their skulls cracked by ash cans flung off a roof? You're kidding!"

"You're supposed to be the cynic," he said, "not me."

"Cynicism or idealism has nothing to do with it," I said. "A number of people were killed in the largest city in the world. A madman goes stir crazy. That can't be the end of it! Just can't be!"

"No, it's not," he said. "There'll be great plans made so that it doesn't happen again. The cops'll say they need more money, more facilities, more policemen. And everyone will deplore the situation and make great promises. Then the civil-rights groups will hand out their usual about how this would never happen if people had gotten their rights. The city will hold a meeting with them—preferably at City Hall—so that the statements will be read to the press and be seen on the late news. It will all blow over. We'll forget about it, and then it will happen again someplace else."

He shook his head.

"We can't forget about it, Duke. The Prophet is now where he should have been in the first place. But the conditions that allowed him to exist are still there—ready to spawn another Prophet. And the only way we are going to stop more Prophets is to do what Julian suggested: force the city to act. Cut out the cancer. Now. Or the second riot will be far worse than the first."

"And who will make the city act?"

"The law," he said. "It's all there in the books. Once you asked me whose side the law was on, Duke. Well, it's on our side, and that includes Tilley and a lot of other people like him. But, damn it, someone has to invoke that law!"

"Okay, I'll bite. Who? Flaherty?"

He groaned. "It will take a special prosecutor. An Extraordinary Grand Jury. Perhaps a Moreland Commission."

I picked up the paper. "The *World-Telegram* says Flaherty will arraign the Prophet's lieutenants within a few days and will also ask the

Governor to reconvene the legislature. Something about a new law he wants against terror groups."

"That's good politicking," Johnny said. "This will put the Governor on the spot. Well, let them play politics. We have our work cut out for us."

How true that was! I had to write the story for Sunday, and Johnny had to translate the diary. We had two single rooms with a connecting door; Johnny sprawled on his bed with the bundle of photostats, and I sat down with a rented typewriter. I don't think we exchanged two words all night. I wrote a detailed story of the search for Gennaro's diary from New York to the small North Carolina town, and then stopped; the rest of it had to come from Johnny and what he found in the diary. I looked in on him a few times, but he only grunted in answer to my questions. Some time about two in the morning we had a pot of coffee and a sandwich; then he returned to the photostats and his notes. I fell asleep, and woke at dawn to find Johnny had stopped writing.

"You finished?"

"Yeah," he said wearily. He slapped the photostats. "It's good and it's bad."

"What's good and what's bad?"

"Well, he doesn't mention McShane by name."

"He doesn't mention McShane!"

"He talks about the Patrone—that's Italian for Boss, the Big Guy —and how together they control the whole city. But he doesn't mention McShane by name!"

"What does he say? My God, the damn' thing is over two hundred pages!"

"Racket stuff," Johnny said. "The most exhaustive inside picture of what's been going on in the city—even the country; what Don is in junk, numbers, gambling. What companies they have taken over. The dress houses. The unions. The pension funds. The cops. Even his political contributions—"

"But, my God, Johnny," I cried, "you have the basis for one of the biggest scandals in the history of New York City."

"Sure I have," he shouted back at me. "Sure it's there! But what am I going to do with it? Give it to Flaherty? Say 'Here it is, Boss, the whole stinking mess, all tied up for you with red ribbons!' What do you think he'll do, Duke? Run out and convene a brand-new jury? Is that what you think?"

He turned to the window, and we both watched the sullen sky slowly dissolve into little-girl pink and gold ribbons.

He said in a quiet voice, "When Gennaro says Patrone he means

McShane, but McShane's lawyer would never let me try to prove it in court."

"You said there was a good side."

He turned around. "Two good sides, in fact. One, Gennaro owned Sugar Hill. Some years ago, at one of the mob conventions, he persuaded the syndicates to invest money in old Harlem real estate. He had met McShane, who agreed for a price to keep the city departments off his back. Apparently this was after the mob had lost a fortune in Vegas and the boys were not too keen on any more investments. But I guess Gennaro's success in numbers, plus the fact he had McShane as a silent partner, persuaded the mob. They bought big chunks of Harlem. From the papers they have dozens of holding companies. No wonder Tilley could never find his landlord to fix that pipe . . ."

"How much did Gennaro and McShane split?"

"It must have been hundreds of thousands a year."

"Does he mention McShane by name in this angle?"

"No. Again just Patrone. If we had the time and the facilities, we could grab McShane. It would have to be done by the old Dewey method: convict an underling and throw the book at him; when he talks, convict the next higher-up. Eventually you'll get McShane. Not only McShane but a whole ring of crooked city employees, probably commissioners. Another Tweed ring, perhaps."

"But we haven't got the time, Johnny. You said so yourself."

"I know," he said wearily. "I know. But there's one more bright side that may tie everything together."

"And that is—"

"A name," he said slowly. "A name."

"Whose name?"

"McShane's girl friend."

"And she is—"

He took a deep breath. "Lydia Aymes."

Suddenly, in my mind, I was back in that small elevator, smelling the heavy, sweetish smell of whiskey, seeing Aymes's red, puffy face with the rolls of fat hanging over his collar, and the mixed look of disgust and apprehension spreading over his wife's face.

"Lydia Aymes. The wife of the commissioner," I said. "The lush behind the desk who wanted to fix everything with the Hall?"

Johnny looked puzzled, and I told the story of my visit to Aymes's office.

"I guess now we know how he's been holding on to his job," Johnny said. "The Hall's hatchet man, and his wife the sweetie of the local kingmaker. Quite a package."

"But how did Gennaro ever find out?"

"Apparently by accident," he said, and glanced at his notes. "He said the Patrone's girl friend is Lydia Aymes, who lived on Central Park West and Seventy-fourth Street. A few years ago he had them tailed by a private detective who took a roll of 16-mm. film of them together."

He held up the small yellow box that Tony had given him.

"I checked the film. There's no doubt it's McShane and Mrs. Aymes," he said. "Gennaro also listed the amount of money he paid the private detective, and his name."

"It looks like we just inherited quite an insurance policy," I said.

Johnny kicked off his shoes and sprawled out on the bed.

"Minnotti was part of the insurance policy. He and Gennaro came from the same village in Sicily. They are real Goombas. There are a few letters that indicate Gennaro told Minnotti all about the Patrone and every dollar he paid him. I bet when I get the list of toll calls from Minnotti's place and compare them with the times Gennaro was down there, I'll find McShane's unlisted number."

"Why would he call McShane from down there?"

"He would make the call with Minnotti standing alongside him. The way I see it, Gennaro wanted a living witness if he had to pressure McShane."

"Perhaps that's why he was killed," I said. "Maybe McShane decided he didn't like pressure."

"The old Dons had Gennaro knocked off," Johnny said shortly. "He was getting in deeper and deeper in Harlem real estate through Sugar Hill. After the riot the mob must have known that the heat would be on. Real estate can be a wonderful villain. The politicians can scream all day long at real-estate syndicates. It's popular. Like in the old days when they used banks as villains. Still, it means attention, and that the mob can't stand. I guess Gennaro felt he didn't want to kill such a good thing, protected as it was by a powerful politician, and refused the mob's orders to dispose of his holdings. It's happened before. The old Dons listen, drink some wine, and say nothing. But then one makes a phone call. The next night there's a big murder. In a few days it all dies down. The cops don't even bother to try to solve it; they know it's almost impossible—"

"And all this is made possible by McShane."

"McShane—and someone else who is more important, Duke."

"Ryder?"

"Mr. Colton Ryder," he mused. He closed his eyes, and for a moment I thought he was asleep.

"Tomorrow we're going to call on a lady, Duke," he said slowly. "And we're going to tell her that if she doesn't help us get James Xavier McShane, she will regret it for the rest of her life."

We slept a few hours, then had breakfast. Back in the room Johnny read excerpts from the diary while I took notes on the typewriter. It was a fascinating and evil document that Gennaro had begun some time after World War II when he started his rise in the underworld. Murders were described, motives explained, accounts of meetings of the Cosa Nostra hierarchy were outlined and what decisions were made; racket setups in the nation's principal cities were exposed; and running all through the book was Gennaro's relationship with the Patrone, whom he had first met through a long-dead racketeer. In the back of the account book was listed a series of contributions to both parties and the fictitious names under which they had been listed.

As Johnny said, Gennaro believed in running on both sides of the street.

The other documents pertained to Sugar Hill Financing Company. Payments were listed by initials to crooked Building Department and Fire Department inspectors. The older Minnotti's role in Gennaro's racket setup was also made clear; his yearly visits to Europe were to a Swiss bank where Gennaro had a numbered account, and also to business contacts in Belgium and France for the shipment of heavy machinery to Cuba through a Dutch national on the West Coast.

"My God, no wonder the Justice boys are so interested in this guy."

"Remember when he was before the committee and they kept asking him about some machine company?" I said. "No one could figure out what they meant."

There was no doubt that the law would get one of its biggest plums when Johnny gave it Gennaro's insurance policy.

[35]

LESS THAN AN hour after our Washington plane had touched down at La Guardia, we were in the elevator going up to the Aymes apartment. It was funny, Johnny said when he came out of the phone booth at La Guardia, she hadn't sounded surprised. She simply said she would expect us within the hour. I was on edge, and as twitchy as a rabbit. Johnny tried to appear nonchalant, but he was tense and apprehensive.

"Well, here goes," he whispered, and pressed the buzzer of the Aymes apartment. We heard footsteps and the door opened. She was stunning in black, her brow high and pale, the hair brushed back into plaits upon her head, streaked with gray at the temples. Her cheeks were stretched tight, and there were deep shadows about her eyes.

She welcomed us with a slight smile. "Won't you come in, gentlemen?"

We entered and took uneasy seats on the sofa. The room was rich in wine-colored wall-to-wall carpeting, white antique furniture, a Chinese tapestry, a gleaming baby grand, and a vase of cut flowers. There were pictures of a fine-looking young boy and a pretty girl, both in mortars and graduation gowns.

"My son, James, and my daughter, Ann," she explained. "These are their high-school graduation pictures; both are out of college now. Jim's going into Foreign Service, and Ann will be married in the fall."

Johnny and I murmured what fine children they seemed to be.

"They mean everything to me," she said. And then added in a quiet voice, "I guess that's why I asked you gentlemen up here."

"Do you have any idea why we are here, Mrs. Aymes?" Johnny said.

"The Gennaro investigation?"

"That's right. I hate to——"

"Don't apologize," she said. "Every day since"—she nodded to me—"Mr. Malloy's newspaper began printing stories about Gennaro and his connections, I knew eventually you would be knocking at my door. I thought for a time of lying to you, but I knew that you would never come here unless you had evidence that I . . ." Her voice trailed off and she bit her lower lip.

I wanted to say it but I just couldn't. I was surprised at the firm, almost harsh way Johnny put it:

". . . that you and Mr. McShane were very close. Is that it?"

"Yes," she said with a stone face.

"I'm afraid that is why we are here, Mrs. Aymes," Johnny said. "Would you tell us?"

She clasped her hands and stared over our heads.

"It's not much, Mr. De Lorenzo, believe me. It's the commonplace story of a woman married to an alcoholic and falling in love with another man. I've known James for twenty years. We have managed for all that time to be very discreet. There were weekends I visited my sister in Long Island and the summers in Darien."

"Did McShane ever mention Gennaro to you?" Johnny asked.

She hesitated, only slightly. "Yes. Once."

"When was that and what were the circumstances?"

"It was a few days after Gennaro was before the Senate Committee," she said. "Jim called me here at the apartment. I was shocked. It was the only time he had ever done that. He said he had to see me. It was very important to him."

"And you saw him?"

"Yes. In the Waldorf Towers. He was alone. He seemed very upset. He explained that in politics he had to meet many kinds of people, some of whom weren't very popular with the authorities. He said Gennaro was one of them. He said he had to do some favors for Gennaro, and now this man——"

Johnny broke in, "Gennaro?"

"Yes. He said Gennaro now wanted a great deal more favors both here and in Washington, and they had some angry meetings."

"Did he say what favors Gennaro wanted, Mrs. Aymes?" I asked.

"No. He just said favors. But I gathered Gennaro did not want to appear before the committee."

"Did McShane say he helped Gennaro?" I asked.

"He didn't say."

Johnny nodded. "Please go on, Mrs. Aymes."

"Jim said the reason he wanted to see me was that Gennaro had told him he knew about us and might make trouble."

"How could a gangster make trouble for you and Mr. McShane?" Johnny asked bluntly.

She flushed. "Jim said he could give that information to his enemies."

"But how did Gennaro know about you and McShane?" Johnny persisted.

She shook her head. "I don't know. Jim said he didn't know either. He only said Gennaro told him he had a friend who had seen us together in Darien."

"And what did McShane want you to do, Mrs. Aymes?" Johnny asked.

Mrs. Aymes studied the well-kept hands clenched in her lap.

"James begged me not to say anything to any investigators who might question me. He explained that politics can be very dirty, and this year more than any other year he might be subject to a great deal of personal abuse."

"And what McShane wanted you to do was deny that any relationship existed between you and him," Johnny said. "Is that correct, Mrs. Aymes?"

"Yes," was the whispered answer.

"And what did you say to that?"

"I said I would."

Johnny now was the prosecutor and he was snapping out the questions in a hard, cruel voice.

"Why did you change your mind?"

"In the beginning I thought it was just a political mess."

"Is that what Mr. McShane told you it was, Mrs. Aymes?"

"He said it was politics. I believed it was too, until after the riots when I began reading the stories that the Russians were using this investigation as a propaganda device. Then I became concerned. One day I decided to call Mr. McShane, but when they connected me with his secretary I hung up."

"Why, Mrs. Aymes? Why couldn't you talk to him?"

"There's a very simple reason, Mr. De Lorenzo," she said evenly. "Because I love him. I didn't want to hurt him."

"But you're talking to us now."

"Only because I am forced to, Mr. De Lorenzo."

"Have you spoken to anyone else about this matter?"

"Yes." She paused. "After I hung up on Mr. McShane's secretary."

The question was asked slowly, deliberately. "To whom did you speak, Mrs. Aymes?"

I could see the muscles in her throat move as she swallowed hard. "To my brother-in-law in Forest Hills."

"His name, please?"

She gave him a pleading look. "Do I have your promise you will never speak to him?"

"If he is not implicated—"

"He is not only my brother-in-law but my attorney."

"Then your conversation is strictly privileged, Mrs. Aymes. I wouldn't call him. Please go on."

Her voice was almost inaudible. "I went to see him and my sister and I told them the whole story. Of course they were shocked, but he advised me not to lie. He pointed out that no official agency would approach me unless they had firm evidence, and if I lied I would probably be brought before the Grand Jury and indicted for perjury." She looked at Johnny. "Is that true, Mr. De Lorenzo?"

The answer was prompt, firm. "Your attorney gave you excellent advice, Mrs. Aymes."

She seemed sincerely shocked.

"And you would indict me?"

"And send you to jail."

Her eyes were hollows of shadows.

"Will you subpoena me, Mr. De Lorenzo?"

"I intend to subpoena you as a people's witness, Mrs. Aymes. And I intend to ask you many questions before the Grand Jury."

Any doubts that Johnny had not been tested by fire vanished.

"You don't leave much for a woman to do, do you, Mr. De Lorenzo?"

She got her answer in a rush of words.

"What do you want me to do, Mrs. Aymes, forget you exist because you have two beautiful kids you certainly never thought twice about when you took up with the biggest grafter in town!"

She was as pale as chalk, but her lips were set and for the first time fire flickered in her eyes.

"If I ever took the witness stand, Mr. De Lorenzo, two innocent lives would be destroyed. My daughter's fiancé's family is very wealthy and very conservative. My son is about to be assigned to his first foreign post. And you know I am married to an alcoholic. This could push him over the edge. . . ."

I deliberately stared down at the carpet and tried to shut out the distant mocking voice of Action Jackson that sleety night in my apartment, a thousand years ago:

. . . something tells me a lot of people are going to be hurt before this is over.

But who would have thought to include the smiling young man and the striking young girl in academic attire on the gleaming piano across this beautiful sunny room.

Johnny was saying in that cold, even voice: "Are you aware, Mrs. Aymes, that a man was murdered in this case, that he was left dying on a meat hook? I don't think he wanted to die any more than your daughter or son want to be tarred with scandal."

"No! No! Jim had nothing to do with that man's murder! I'm sure of it!"

"Perhaps not directly," Johnny said roughly, "but most certainly indirectly. That man was murdered to protect your friend McShane, Mrs. Aymes!"

She closed her eyes and said in a small voice, "Just what do you want, Mr. De Lorenzo?"

Johnny leaned slightly forward. "I want Jim McShane to plead guilty to the indictment."

I clenched my hands as I watched her. She slowly opened her eyes and studied Johnny.

"And if I refuse to cooperate with you, Mr. De Lorenzo?"

"I will bring you before the Grand Jury," Johnny said harshly, "and question you. If you lie I will indict you for perjury. If you refuse to answer my questions, I will indict you for contempt. In either case, Mrs. Aymes, be assured that I will send you to jail." He nodded to me. "And Mr. Malloy will take care of the headlines."

There was only contempt in her face when she turned to me, but somehow I didn't care; I was thinking of the plain woman in the old-fashioned shoes who stood beside me one day in the Long Island cemetery as rifles crashed and the echoes slid out on the frozen air to beyond the big iron gate. . . .

"I'm sure Mr. Malloy will," she said.

"To the best of my ability," I said.

There was a long pause. Then: "You're not giving me much of a choice, Mr. De Lorenzo."

"Don't talk to me about choices, Mrs. Aymes," Johnny said briskly. "I could have brought you before the Grand Jury this afternoon without any notice and smeared you all over the afternoon papers. I'm giving you a break. I'm letting you decide between two beautiful, innocent kids and a thief. You make the decision, Mrs. Aymes."

So there it was, the Lady or the Tiger. All she had to do was open the door of her choice; her children or McShane. I guess from where we sat it was easy to say there wasn't much choice. But actually there was. I could visualize her life, wife of a city official, condemned to wear that phony smile at the phony banquets and meetings, then coming home to the bed of a mumbling drunk. McShane, tough, powerful, earthy, must have been for her many times the difference between sanity and uncontrollable hysteria. At last she lifted her head.

"Please give me the subpoena."

Johnny took out his wallet, selected a paper, scrawled his name, and gave it to her.

"You will testify, Mrs. Aymes?" he asked in a tight voice.

She deliberately looked over his head, unanswering.

"You have a subpoena, Mrs. Aymes!" Johnny said angrily.

"Yes," she said, "but that doesn't mean I will testify against Mr. McShane."

Slowly and firmly Johnny said: "If you ignore this subpoena and fail to appear, I will request a warrant from the court for your arrest."

"I have no doubt you will do just that, Mr. De Lorenzo."

"Then you will not ignore the subpoena?"

"I don't intend to defy the court."

"If you don't intend to defy the court, that means you will appear," Johnny said with an edge of exasperation in his voice, "and you will take the stand."

She stared at Johnny, her eyes bleak.

"I will appear in court to answer to your subpoena," she said in a low, bitter voice. "But that does not mean I will testify against Mr. McShane."

"Well, then, what does—" Johnny began, but Mrs. Aymes stood up—regally, it seemed. Silently she showed us to the door, the long invisible queen's train sweeping behind her.

We were silent in the elevator, but in the sun-splashed lobby I asked Johnny what he thought.

"I'm inclined to believe her."

"That she won't take the stand?"

"I haven't the slightest idea of what she's going to do," he said. "But believe it or not, I'd send her to jail for a year if I thought it would help me get McShane. Christ! I'd even ruin the lives of those two kids." He gestured to a bench across the street against the park wall. "Let's sit down for a few minutes. I'm bushed."

"She must have a hell of a life with that drunk," I said.

He stared out at the passing cars. "Don't go soft, Duke, we can't afford it."

"She's not putting on an act, Johnny."

"Who said she was?" he snapped with a trace of anger.

More to change the subject, I asked him what he would do if by some wild chance McShane pleaded guilty.

"Let him plead."

"To what count?"

"Conspiracy," he said almost defiantly.

"But that's only a misdemeanor!"

He gave me a tired smile. "Do I have to wait until the cock crows three times, Peter?"

"I didn't mean it like that, Johnny," I said quickly. "I just want to point out that in comparison to the felony counts—"

He said patiently, as if explaining for a child, "If we go to bat on the bribery counts, our one strong piece of evidence is Strasser's testimony. Gennaro's diary is wonderful stuff—for a sweeping investigation of the city—but legally I'll have one hell of a job introducing any of it in a trial. It just doesn't link McShane to a damned thing! I've decided that when I'm finished with it I will turn it all over to the Racket section of the Justice Department and let them play with it. It has the basis for an enormous scandal. Now that leaves us with the testimony of a disbarred, crummy little racket lawyer who's probably half crazy now from the time he's spent on that island." He stood up. "Well, we'll have to wait and see. In the meantime I'm going home, take a shower, have a stiff drink, call Connie, and tell her I love her, and sleep until some time tomorrow. How about you, Duke?"

"I'm going to call the office, go home, and then look up the price of that Martini Special to LA."

"Martini Special—" He looked puzzled. "What's that?"

"It's a private joke between me and Gwen."

I watched until he hailed a cab.

"See you Monday morning, Duke."

"I'll be there early, Johnny."

I walked until I found a sidewalk phone. I intended only to give Julian a brief rundown on what had happened in North Carolina, tell him my story was coming down by Western Union, then go home.

But when I reached Betty, she whispered that I had better talk to Turner Elliott; they had been trying to find me all night.

Elliott's hello was heard against the familiar curtain of the sound of typewriters, loud voices, cries of "Boy!"

"This is Duke, Mr. Elliott. I have great news."

"Duke," he said fervently, "where have you been? We've been trying all night—"

"Johnny and I stopped off in Washington. We found the diary and we just finished talking to—"

"Duke!"

I guess out of sheer exhaustion and tension I kept babbling.

"Duke, for God's sake!"

Something in his voice stopped me.

"Duke, listen. Julian was stricken with a massive hemorrhage late yesterday. He's at the New York Hospital."

"Is it serious, Mr. Elliott?"

"I just saw the doctor. He doesn't give much hope. They haven't been able to stop the bleeding."

"Is there anything I can do?"

"Yes. Go up and see him. He's been asking for you, Duke."

"Yes, Mr. Elliott."

"You'd better get up there right away."

I was at the hospital within half an hour. A very efficient busty young blonde took my name, vanished for a moment, came back, and told me what elevator to take. On the seventh floor an elderly starched nurse ushered me into a waiting room. There were fresh flowers, lounging chairs, a television set, and Sam Dolbar, talking to a prim, elderly woman. He was still wearing the same old-fashioned blue suit, and the heavy gold watch chain was stretched across his stomach.

"Hello, Malloy," he said as casually as if we were meeting in a bar. "This is Julian's aunt." He explained to the woman, "This is one of the men from the paper Julian wants to see." He glanced over my shoulder. "Oh, Doctor, how is he?"

The doctor was thin, peevish, and Miami-tanned.

"He's a very sick man, very sick." Then, defensively, "You know I've been begging him to come in for tests."

"Has the bleeding stopped?" I asked.

"There is less bleeding."

I said flatly, "But it hasn't stopped."

The doctor shrugged. "No. But he wasn't strong to begin with."

"He wants to go in and see him," Dolbar said.

The doctor showed interest for the first time. "Oh, are you Mr. Malloy?"

When I said I was, he took my arm and walked me across the hall to another room. His grip was tight and angry.

"He's been asking for you," he said. "Where have you been?"

"Out of town."

He made an angry click of his lips. "He's been sinking all morning.

I kept telling Sam, make him come into the hospital; the tests will only take a day!" He gently turned the knob. "But no—he had to worry about that damned rag with its phony columnists and lousy bridge column. All right, you want to come in?"

The room was surprisingly small. It held only a bed, a shaded lamp. Julian was in an oxygen tent. The doctor bent over and gave a professional grunt.

"He's going," he said. "Maybe in a couple of hours."

"Can I sit here for a few minutes?" I said. "I won't disturb him. Just for a few minutes."

The doctor shrugged. "He's unconscious."

"That's all right. "I'll just sit here."

"No smoking. I'll be outside," the doctor said, and went out.

I sat down in the throbbing quiet of the room. The lamp cast shadows across the face in the crinkly cocoon. Now that the ache of living these past months, filled with their harassments, decisions, frustrations, their doubts, betrayals, and pressures were over, his face seemed to have changed. New serenity was visible, together with dignity and nobility.

I suddenly felt the tears welling, and I got up and walked to the window. Below in the street traffic moved, but no sound entered this hermetically sealed room. There were rooftops, chimneys, walls of glass blinding with the sun. Downtown they were probably taking down the watercolors in his office. Maybe in Ohio they like old European prints in heavy oak frames. But no matter what they put on the walls, it was clear the old building would have to go. One day Dolbar would make the move uptown, and there would be another ghost on Park Row. For men who worked in city rooms all over America, an era was ending. It was a new age, with electronics the enemy. The old giants had been spawned by dreamers, unpractical to the point of magnificence, a swaggering, arrogant breed who bullied, cajoled—but loved their people. Now all they had won would be at the mercy of men like Sam Dolbar and his handpicked publishers, who had never met a deadline, never risked anything, never dared anything. The vitality, the aggressiveness, the arrogance, the individualism would be drained off by Dolbar and his ruthless young men, trained to petty economics, disdainful of the words "crusade," "public service." How's the P&L? The hell with the product . . .

The door opened and a nurse glided in like a shadow, and left. I went back to the bed. The shadows were deeper in Julian's face. I reached under the tent and gently held his hand; it was cold and clammy. Silently I said good-bye, and went out.

"The old man left," the doctor said. "He said for you to go over to his apartment."

Julian's aunt was standing in the room across the hall. She looked as though she had been crying; she clutched a soggy handkerchief in one hand.

"He was a good man," she said. "A very good man."

"He wept for people," I said, then walked down the long corridor, down the empty corridor that was so antiseptic it didn't even have the traditional hospital rubber plant with the sheen of sun-distilled dust on its thick, broad leaves.

Martha, Julian's old Swedish woman, ushered me into the apartment. Her eyes appeared to be red from weeping.

"He is a good, good man . . ."

I patted and consoled her as we passed the old grandfather's clock, the cold and formal living room, and entered a sunny room at the end of the hall. Dolbar was sitting at a folding card table, eating a chicken sandwich and drinking steaming tea in a glass.

"How about a chicken sandwich, Malloy?"

"No, thanks."

"A drink?"

"No, thanks."

He finished the sandwich, wiped his lips with a napkin, then pushed the chair back.

"He's bad."

"He's dying," I said.

He took a sip of tea. "I brought in the best. That little guy is the best stomach man in the world."

"I don't think the best of anything is going to help him now, Mr. Dolbar."

Another sip of tea. "I told him to forget the paper, to take a vacation, but he wouldn't do it."

"Forget what, Mr. Dolbar?" I said.

I was fixed by the cold, flat eyes. "This crazy McShane business." He pushed aside the clouded glass. "That's what I want to talk to you about."

Almost perversely I said, "You want to press harder?"

He wasn't to be goaded; he needed me.

"I want you to start patching things up," he said. "We're in trouble. I was talking to Mr. Colton Ryder last night." He said the name with great respect. "You know who he is?"

"He's a munitions maker, isn't he?"

He gave me a suspicious look. "Munitions maker? Are you joking, Malloy?"

"No. Someone told me he's a munitions maker. Just like the Krupps in Germany."

He studied me, but when I kept a straight face he shook his head.

"No. He's in real estate. He's a big man in this city. He knows a lot of big people in Washington. He gets invited to the White House. He can help us."

"I don't doubt it."

"He told me he wants to meet you. He says you are a hard man to talk to."

"With him I am."

"Well, now it will be different," he said with a wave of his hand. "I told Ryder I want him to fix things with McShane. He said it would take a lot of fixing. I told him you were our chief carpenter. Okay, Malloy?"

"In other words he wants things nice and calm, no more rocking the boat?"

"That's right. Nice and calm. Okay, Malloy?"

So here it was, just as Johnny had spelled it out: the godfathers of the dictators, big and small, the corrupters, the venal, the unmoral. Keep everything nice and easy. Just don't disturb my profits.

"So you want me to be chief carpenter, Mr. Dolbar?"

He cocked his head slightly. "For you it could be a good job."

"You know what you can do with that carpenter's job, Mr. Dolbar?"

The peasant's face never changed. "I think that with every journalism course they should make them take another course—business," he said. "Dollars and cents. How much it costs to get out a newspaper. You know how much this crazy McShane business cost the *Blade-Leader*?"

"The circulation went up ten thousand. The prestige of the paper—"

His look of disgust stopped me.

"What's the matter with you editorial people? Do you know how much it costs just to open those doors every morning?"

"I imagine a small fortune, Mr. Dolbar."

"It costs more money than you'll ever see," he said. "So you go after this guy McShane, and we lose Cummings; then some of the other prime accounts suddenly don't like us. Our advertisers get letters every day."

"That's a phony writing campaign started by McShane's club-house."

"It's readers!" he said loudly. "It's money! You and Julian think a newspaper can clobber advertisers, politicians, prosecutors—even City Hall—"

"You think that was wrong, Mr. Dolbar?"

"Wrong!" he roared. "A newspaper is a business, just like steel, railroads, or the electric-light company. It's got to show a profit or you're out of business! What happens then, Malloy? Will you go to the government and get a couple of million to keep going? How in the hell are we going to pay the unions? Every year they kick the publishers in the ass for another million or two." He got up to face me, a short, angry man in an old-fashioned blue suit. "Do you know what a pressman gets for overtime? Or those guys on the platform? They get money, lots of it, and you want to make enemies with people who can keep this money coming in!"

"In other words you don't think a newspaper should have any enemies?"

"Enemies, all right!" he shouted, his face flushed and angry. "But not enemies who cost money!"

"I don't think you should be in the newspaper business, Mr. Dolbar," I said.

"No?" He peered at me. "What business then, Malloy?"

"The pickle business," I said.

I held my breath. For a moment I thought he would explode, denounce me in a fury; but suddenly the round melon face cracked with a wide smile.

"Maybe in the pickle business I wouldn't have schlemiels like you and my son-in-law to worry about," he said. Then the serious businessman replaced the jolly peasant. "Okay. Let's talk about patching things up, Malloy."

"Perhaps you didn't understand me, Mr. Dolbar. I'm not doing any patching up. All I'm interested in is seeing McShane go to jail."

"I asked Elliott about you, and he recommended I give you a raise. Talk to him once in ten years and it means money."

"I don't want any more money."

His voice was sincerely puzzled.

"What the hell do you want?"

I felt like shouting: Truth, Courage, Integrity, the intangibles you feel in the chalk of your bones—but I didn't.

The phone rang, and he yanked it to his ear in a swift, angry gesture.

"Oh," he said. Then, "Yes . . . yes, Molly, I'll be right over."

He carefully put down the phone and stared out the window. Then he said, "Julian just died."

"He's dead?" I said foolishly.

"Yes," he said. "That was Molly, his aunt." He picked up the phone. "I have to make a call."

I dimly heard him tell the operator he wanted the paper in Ohio; then he was telling somebody named Farber that Julian was dead and he should be in on Monday for a conference.

"That's Lou Farber," he said thoughtfully. "He's our publisher in Ohio. I was going to keep him there but I think I'll bring him here."

I could only stare at him. Is my friend dead? Is Julian Savage gone, that frail, smiling man who was determined his newspaper would hang on the wall in the company of giants?

Is Action Jackson gone, and that plain, sorrowful woman returned to her little truck farm in the backwoods of Missouri? And the Simms family—Adam, the twins, the nephew, the old patriarch with the Indian showing in his face, Vickie, who loves a thief and a coward, and the two dead men—are they in this room that has so much defeat in it I can taste it? So much fear it makes my skin crawl? So much cold-bloodedness it sets me shivering?

I stood up. "You bastard," I said in a voice I didn't recognize. "You lousy pickle maker."

Three times he called me as I walked down his hall.

Monday morning. McShane will plead guilty.

I swear, Julian. I swear.

BOOK TEN

THE DAY OF THE PEOPLE

[36]

I KNOCKED OVER the phone when it rang. The receiver bounced along the floor and I could hear someone saying Hello, hello, hello. Finally there was a click, and silence. All Sunday night the wind was up, and in the early hours of the morning the rain came sweeping in gusts down the street.

I paced the room, ignoring liquor, coffee, even cigarettes. In desperation I turned on the eleven o'clock news, and Bob Trout's free, easy voice was telling me about the opening of McShane's trial in the morning and how contemptuous Moscow was, demanding America show the world the other side of the coin of her justice. Then he came to Julian's death, and I clicked it off.

I pulled a chair to the window, and sat there until dawn began to come up, an even streak of hard light out of the wet darkness, like the cold blade of a poised knife. Sitting by the window I found it hard not to feel betrayed and bitter when I saw, with the sharp, distinct clarity of a fine lens, Julian walking toward me, hand outstretched, a grin of triumph, and behind him, like the backdrop of a play, the cluttered desks, the copyreaders on the rim of the horseshoe, the mounds of pictures, of weary faces—and then it was all gone. Julian was gone. No one left to chase the money changers out of the temple. But we had our hour. We did our best. That was something they could never take away from us.

And Johnny. They would take the ax to him, but at least he now carried his future. Another proud De Lorenzo in a gold frame. Even

Inspector Murphy, his papers in, had his future. And Ricky Strasser, who, Johnny would make sure, received his SS, had Vickie, who was as tough as her mountain scrub oak. They would have a future; it might be filled with terrible shadows, but it was a future. Vickie would see to that, and Adam and all the Simmses in Torytown.

But with me everything had shriveled up in that hospital room. Even the past seemed to have lost its meanings, so that when I tried to put the pictures together they fell apart, and it was impossible to make the images communicate the zest, the triumphs, the ideals. There were only the numbness, bitterness, and desolation.

When the last star had winked out I made up my mind: Gwen and California. Yet, even then, I felt like a deserter. But I pushed it aside, telling myself it had to be left for the next fool to finish.

I'd had it.

There were two more things to do. I suddenly became aware of the unhurried, metallic sound of the ticking clock on the table. Just a few minutes after six. Only a few more hours. Then the business of McShane would be over. For the first time since I had sat down by the window, I felt a wild, almost savage expectancy. Even the thought that this day I would be an observer without portfolio couldn't extinguish it.

Then there was the question of Ryder, who legally had done nothing wrong. More than McShane, he had to be torn down, destroyed. He must not be allowed to continue—like the munitions makers.

But how?

The darkness could not supply the answer, nor did the unfeeling gray dawn that filled the room like an ugly stain.

Foley Square, where Justice sits in New York. The Federal Building. Supreme Court. Criminal Courts Building. The buildings around the square, unlike uptown, were built from the heart—no upended glass coffins constructed by slide rules. After I left the IRT at Brooklyn Bridge, I walked along the quiet paths of City Hall Park, silently saluted the quizzical Horace Greeley in his iron chair, bowed to the wind tunnel of the Municipal Building, and looked out over the square. From there you can see its roof, like a stack of toy blocks shouldering the sky —the New York Criminal Courts Building.

Criminal Courts is not a graceful building; it is bounded on the north by thick gilt letters on dusty windows: BAIL BONDS; on the east by a perpetual stickball game; on the south by the state building and its stream of stoical vehicular inspectors in cars of many vintages and drivers of varied competence; on the west by the majestic, thundering words over its main doors:

EQUAL AND EXACT JUSTICE FOR ALL MEN,
OF WHAT STATE OR PERSUASION

Frankly, I would have liked the old Tombs better, with its bridge of sighs and turreted, medieval courtyard nicked by Red Lawson's bullets when he and his gang broke out in '21, which was somewhere back in the Ice Age, and long before my time.

When I came up, the Associated Press, United Press International, and the World-Telly were on the steps talking to a small, oily-looking man.

AP said, "I'm sorry, Duke; he was a nice guy."

"That he was. You going in?"

UPI gestured to the little man.

"Meet Mr. Rovenko of Tass. This is Duke Malloy of the *Blade-Leader*. I guess he started all this."

Mr. Rovenko gave me a faint smile.

"Oh, yes. I am eager to read his story today."

AP said: "The night desk got a dupe of Duke's story. We have an embargo on it until ten. . . ."

"Oh, could you tell me, please?" The little man took out a notebook, wet a finger, and turned a page.

AP said, "Well—I guess you people get AP. Malloy here says the D.A. has uncovered a sensational document that will have an important bearing on this morning's hearing. Is that right, Duke?"

Rovenko said, brows lifted, "Oh? What is the document?"

"That part of the service you didn't buy," I said. "I'll see you guys inside."

Despite the early hour the press room was filling up: morning papers, evening papers, wire services; the floor writhing with black TV snakes; the night porter cursing in desperation as he cleaned away the coffee containers and cigarettes; telephone men finishing installing the extra phones, metallic katydids of Western Union telegraphers testing their keys.

The dean of the press room, an old wire-service man with whom I covered countless fires, homicides, and suicides when we were both breaking in, came over.

"Ah, Duke Malloy. The last time you were here was to get me to squash a parking ticket."

"Yes. And you never did anything about it, and I paid the ten bucks. How are you, Joe?"

"Fine. Rough news in your place today "

"You'll never know how rough, Joe. Have you seen Johnny De Lorenzo?"

"Not yet. The judge is going to dispose of some sentences first, so the big show won't start until about eleven."

"Fine with me. Who's the judge?"

"Some clubhouse hack. Johnny'd better have something good up his sleeve."

"That he has."

"What's it going to be after this, Duke?" he asked quietly.

I hesitated. The Times, Trib, and AP had come in and overheard. They were waiting. What the hell, it has to come out sometime. . . .

"I'm leaving the *Blade-Leader.*"

The Trib said, "Washington will love that."

"I'll use it in my story tomorrow," the Times said.

"Forget it," I said. "It's not worth a tinker's damn to what's going to happen here this morning."

The room was crowded now with reporters, photographers, TV crews, curious lawyers, court attendants, Western Union messengers, and a man selling shoelaces and razor blades. I decided to get a cup of coffee in the lobby restaurant, and was pushing through the crowd when I saw Johnny and Connie come through the revolving doors.

Johnny gripped my hand. "Duke! I heard about Julian last night on the late news. God, I'm sorry!"

Connie leaned over and kissed me on the cheek. She smelled cool and divine.

"Is there anything . . ." she whispered.

"There's nothing, Connie."

"I tried to call you but the line was busy for hours," Johnny said. "I guess you were asleep."

"I knocked over the phone," I said. "I saw him yesterday just before he died. Then I saw his father-in-law. You'd better know the old man is pulling out."

"Where does that leave you, Duke?" he asked quietly.

"Unemployed."

A young fellow with a headset pulled over his ears came up.

"Mr. De Lorenzo?"

"That's me."

"I'm from the 'Housewives' Roundup.' You know, we give 'em household stuff, news reports, interviews, and so on. Could you give us a statement before court opens?"

Johnny just looked at him.

"Sure he will," I said.

"Who are you?" he asked suspiciously.

"William Fallon, counsel for the defense."

"Oh," he said. "Well, thanks. I'll look you up when our announcer gets here."

"Not at all," I said.

"Let's get a cup of coffee across the street," Johnny said.

"Who's William Fallon?" Connie asked.

"A hotshot lawyer who was around even before I was born," I said. "You'll find him in paperbacks, ninety-five cents."

Nedick's was two deep, so we got our coffee and stood in a corner.

"I met with Flaherty and Hoff yesterday," Johnny said. "I told them I was going to ask for an immediate trial."

"Did you tell them about the diary or Mrs. Aymes?"

"I told them I had a witness who was vital to the investigation. Flaherty asked me if I would tell him who it was. I told him I couldn't. Hoff said I was running true to form. I didn't want to get in any arguments, so I just got up and left."

"He took me out for a drive," Connie said. "We drove for hours. I don't think he said four words. Finally I made him stop somewhere for dinner. The only thing he said was 'Pass the butter.' " She put her head on his shoulder. "Darling, I can't wait until this is over."

"You're kidding about being out, Duke," Johnny said.

"I called the owner a lousy pickle maker. You don't do that to publishers unless you're prepared to resign."

"He must realize the tremendous job you've done, Duke."

"He couldn't care less, Johnny. Dolbar claims the paper has been hurt financially. He wants me to meet with"—I hesitated—"Connie's father and mend fences with McShane and the boys in Washington."

"Don't try to protect me, Duke," Connie said. "He's my father, but I have no use for his methods and I told him so last night."

Johnny said, "Dolbar called Connie's father last night. Connie happened to overhear what he said."

"My father was making it very evident that he could fix things with McShane through his connections in Washington, but he demanded that Mr. Dolbar 'go back to covering fires,' as he put it," Connie said. "From the conversation I guess Mr. Dolbar was only too happy to oblige. When my father got off the phone, I told him exactly what I thought of him and his despicable conniving." Her lips quivered. "I love my father, Duke, but not his world."

Johnny slipped his arm about her waist. "After this morning, honey, I'll be in the same boat as Duke."

"But you should be just beginning, Johnny," I said.

"I agree. But you don't think Flaherty will keep me on after today, do you? And if he does, what good is one man fighting a whole office?

And I wouldn't even have you—or Julian." Johnny sighed. "That's one of the troubles of our society. Too few people care. Well, let's get back."

I looked at him. "What do you think, Johnny?"

"She'll show," he said shortly. "After that, it's anybody's guess."

"If she doesn't appear, Johnny—" Connie started to say, but Johnny cut her off abruptly.

"I said she'll show."

"She must love him very much," Connie said softly.

Johnny pulled her to him. "Would you do that much for me, honey?" he asked jokingly.

"You will never know how much I've done for you, darling."

Then she gave me an enigmatic smile.

Johnny pushed aside his cold coffee. "Let's go back to the courthouse."

We had stopped at the newsstand in the lobby for cigarettes when I heard a bail bondsman alongside me whistling quietly, "Not bad for an old chick."

Mrs. Aymes had passed through the revolving doors and was crossing the lobby. Without doubt she was the smartest-dressed woman in the entire Criminal Courts Building. Under the furs thrown across her shoulders, she was dressed in a smart and expensive blue knit suit with tasteful accessories. She had the figure of a young woman. She looked unconcerned and her walk was leisurely. She looked straight ahead and disappeared into a bank of elevators.

"Who was that?" Connie asked.

"Mrs. Aymes," Johnny said.

"She's a striking woman."

"So are you," Johnny said. "Duke, coming up?"

"I have to make a last call to the office. I'll see you upstairs."

As I entered the busy press room, the AP man shouted to call my office.

It was Turner Elliott, and for the first time in years he sounded furious.

"I tried you all last night!"

"I just didn't feel like talking to anyone, sir, so I took the phone off the hook. I'm sorry."

"I have some things I want to talk to you about," he said in a vexed voice, "but first the Personnel man is here with your resignation. He says he had a note from Mr. Dolbar that you are off the payroll. What's this all about?"

"I guess when you call the owner a lousy pickle maker you're out, Mr. Elliott."

"Let's start from the beginning, Duke." His voice dropped a note, and in my mind's eye I could see him lean back in his chair and stretch out, a familiar gesture that always indicated that he was about to engage in a serious conversation.

I told him everything that happened. "For your own information," I concluded, "your new publisher is named Farber."

"Lou Farber from our Ohio paper?"

"He's coming in Monday."

"A bookkeeper. He took the doors off the booths in the can so the staff wouldn't read."

"Well, happy days, Mr. Elliott."

"This is ridiculous," he said. "I'll talk to the old man right away."

"Please don't," I said. "I'm even beginning to like it."

"Duke, I just don't know what to say. . . ."

"It was nice working with you, Mr. Elliott," I said. "Please tell the boy on the city desk to send on anything he thinks might be personal."

"Do you have any plans?"

"Nothing. Besides reserving a seat on the Martini Special."

"Well, wherever it's going have one on me."

And that was the end of twenty years.

Someone shouted that the judge was ready to reconvene, and I made my way upstairs to join the other lords of the press waiting outside the courtroom in the packed corridor. A court attendant swung open the brass-studded door with a flourish and intently examined each police card. Inside, we filed past the spectators' benches, with the lofty disdain the cavalry has for the foot soldier, to take our places in the crowded press box.

Johnny winked at me from behind a mound of lawbooks that had an impressive number of slips of paper in the pages for the proper precedents. It was all playacting, he later said, for he had never cracked a book or had time to ask Appeals to give him the references for the arguments he might face before the bench.

But I had eyes only for Mrs. Aymes. She sat in the first row, directly behind the rail. She stared straight ahead like a statue. I kept staring at her, mentally urging her to look at me, to give me some hint of what she would do. But she remained impassive, unmoved by the whispering and shuffling about her. Johnny, behind his pile of lawbooks, desperately tried to adopt a casual air, but I knew he, too, was boiling with impatience. Twice he turned as if studying the courtroom, but I knew whose face he was searching.

Then McShane walked in, followed by his attorney, a hotshot from Washington, whose fee, it was said, ran into telephone numbers. He was a slender, arrogant type who dismissed us all in one sweeping, condescending glance.

Johnny turned and with me watched McShane come down the aisle. I saw Mrs. Aymes slowly turn her head. McShane saw her and stopped in his tracks, one hand frozen at the gate. As their eyes met, Mrs. Aymes opened her purse, took out the subpoena, and held it up. The old English script was unmistakable. McShane stood there so long his lawyer, who had leaned out to shake hands with someone, impatiently tugged at his sleeve. Grudgingly McShane opened the gate. He was pale, and licked his lips when he sat down at the defense table.

His attorney turned to him with an annoyed, then anxious look. He said something. McShane lowered his head and replied. The attorney, now worried, rose and told the judge that his client had just had a dizzy spell and requested they be allowed to use his chambers for a moment.

The judge almost fell over himself in ordering the attendants to assist the defense.

I looked over at Johnny. There was a tight, savage smile on his face.

Mrs. Aymes continued to stare straight ahead.

In less than an hour they returned to the buzzing courtroom. I was surprised to note that McShane, while still pale, was composed, almost calm. When the judge asked if they were ready to continue, the attorney rose and informed the bench that despite his advice his client had insisted he change his plea of innocent to guilty on the first, fourth, and sixth counts of the eight-count indictment. He went on to present a rather involved argument that in simple language said that the guilty plea to these counts involving conspiracy to receive money from Vito Gennaro would take care of the other counts which pertained to the actual payments of monthly bribe money.

For a moment there was stunned silence, then a rising burst of sound. The judge tried to act in a dignified judicial manner, as he vainly banged away with a gavel and shouted the usual threats of clearing out the courtroom.

"What do the People say?" he shouted.

Johnny rose and faced the bench.

"The People move to accept the guilty plea, Your Honor, on the proviso that the defendant admit on the record he asked for a certain amount to be paid him every week for protecting the policy-racket activities of Vito Gennaro."

McShane's attorney started to bluster, but changed his mind when Johnny said, with the finest bluff I have ever seen, that the People were ready to start selecting a jury and to call their first witness.

That did it. The nervous judge asked the question, and McShane stood up and admitted his crime.

"Your Honor," Johnny said quietly, "I move that the People accept the defendant's guilty plea."

But it wasn't over. The judge by now had gathered his thoughts, and with a crafty look banged his gavel again and again. When some order of silence returned, he peered down at Johnny.

"Very well, Mr. De Lorenzo. I'll allow the guilty plea to be accepted." He sniffed, and reached down in his robes for a handkerchief.

"However, in view of the speed with which the People apparently wish to dispose of this case, I think it only fitting that I should sentence the defendant immediately. Will the defendant rise?"

So the fix had been in all the time! If McShane had not pleaded guilty, it would have been a toss-out. I had to pinch out that last grudging flicker of admiration I had felt for McShane in pleading guilty to spare the woman he loved. Sure, he took a plea, a slap on the wrist, because he knew that tomorrow it would be business as usual in the Tamayanka Club.

The Associated Press whispered in my ear: "You act surprised. I thought this bum's name on the bench would be a tipoff."

Johnny was now on his feet, and livid.

"Your Honor! You can't sentence without a probation report on the defendant! It will take at least two weeks—"

"You handle your case, Mr. Prosecutor, and I will handle the sentencing in this court," was the blunt answer.

Johnny slammed down his fist so hard the water cooler on the table jumped.

"Your Honor! I insist that a probation report be made on this defendant and his activities in this city! Your Honor, this is vital—"

The gavel crashed down.

"One more word, Mr. De Lorenzo, and I will hold you in contempt of court. Defendant rise!"

I sat frozen in my chair. So they had won after all.

The judge rambled on about the duty of men in high office and the abhorrence the city felt for the policy racket, and then went on to discuss McShane's past performance in city and national politics.

"For Christ's sake, he's going to give him a medal," the Times said in disgust.

Then suddenly it was all over, and the judge, in a flurry of robes, was disappearing inside his room.

The Associated Press said, studying his notes, "He sentenced him to a year's probation, but nowhere did he order him to refrain from any political activity." He looked up and said with an air of disbelief, "I just don't believe it."

The Trib shrugged. "Don't you know this character is running for the Supreme Court bench in the fall? Do you think he's going to hurt McShane?"

"I'm going to do a job on this guy in my Saturday column," the City Hall man for the *Telegram* said.

But the AP said wearily, "And do you think anybody will care?"

They pushed and squirmed their way out of the courtroom, sheafs of notes held high as they exchanged comments. Photographers' bulbs flashed through the small porthole windows of the courtroom. Mrs. Aymes rose, looked at Johnny, then me. There was a slight curve to her lips as she joined the flood swirling toward the door. Her blue hat bobbed up and down, then vanished. McShane said something to his attorney, and walked rapidly after her. Men slapped him on the back, reached out to touch him, shouted at him, waved to him. McShane nodded and gave them vacant smiles. He pushed his way forward; then he too vanished.

Well, I thought, we tried to change an order, and found that to change anything, everything has to be transformed.

I walked over to Johnny. Connie was with him now.

"My friend," he said bitterly, "you have just seen the People get a real you-know-what."

I felt a tug at my arm. One of the court attendants was holding out a folded piece of copy paper.

"The AP reporter in the phone booth said to give this to you, Duke," he said.

It was a brief scrawl:

Duke: Washington just announced McShane removed as National Chairman.

I handed it to Johnny. "They didn't even wait for the verdict."

He read the message and crumpled it into a small tight ball.

"Remember what I told you? The most ruthless people on earth are politicians who either want something or who are running scared."

"Well, that's some kind of victory, Johnny," Connie said. "At least now his power is gone."

Johnny gave her a bitter look. "Are you kidding, darling? Who do you think will be pulling the strings at that convention? This is only for public consumption. Even with a number, McShane will whistle and they'll dance. Wasn't Curley elected from a jail cell? Didn't the President of the United States ride with Frank Hague when he was deporting labor leaders out of his city? And what about that state senator in Sing

Sing a few years ago? Didn't he have the boys ride up the Hudson to get his orders?" He slammed his attaché case shut. "No, darling. McShane is still the Number One boy around here in politics until we get someone powerful enough to really clip his wings. In fact, I'll bet that within a year he'll have a presidential pardon. The Mayor will give him a medal on the steps of City Hall. Come on, Duke," he said. "Connie and I will buy you a drink. In fact, let's get drunk."

A hoarse impatient whisper came across the room. The judge's secretary was beckoning frantically.

"Mr. De Lorenzo! There's a phone call."

"The hell with it; it's probably some newspaper," Johnny said, and started toward the gate.

"It's Albany, Mr. De Lorenzo."

Johnny looked startled. Slowly he put his attaché case back on the table and went up to the clerk, who took him into the judge's chambers.

"Who can that be, Duke?" Connie asked.

"Probably his state income tax," I said, but it fell flat.

As the long minutes passed, Connie searched for my hand, found it, held it. We waited like that together.

When Johnny came out, he appeared dazed. The judge's secretary stood in the doorway, looking after him. He was joined by the judge, who appeared worried.

"It was the Governor," Johnny said. "He's ordering an Extraordinary Grand Jury Investigation of Crime and Corruption in New York County. I'm to be Special Prosecutor."

"That's wonderful!" I almost shouted.

"I guess that means we won after all, Duke," he said as Connie hugged him.

"It wasn't us who got the royal you-know-what," I said.

"That means we can go into the whole thing, Duke: Sugar Hill, the rotten housing, the rats, the payoffs, the tinhorns, the cops, and—everything."

"And my father," Connie said firmly.

"When is the Governor going to announce it?" I asked quickly.

"He has a call in for Flaherty right now. Then he's calling an immediate press conference. Look, you'd better help me get up a statement."

"You don't need any help, Johnny. Just tell them the truth. Tell them you're going to take off the lid and cut out what smells. We'd better go down to the press room."

The judge's clerk, who had put two and two together, had set the courthouse grapevine working. Johnny was greeted with stares and nudges; total strangers came up to congratulate him.

We reached the lobby, and I steered Johnny to the press room. It was filled with voices barking into telephones, typewriters, and the hot lights of television. A TV interview was just finishing. The announcer stepped from around a camera, wiping his face with a carefully folded handkerchief.

"You're next, Counselor," he said.

I picked up the *Blade-Leader* phone and asked for the city desk. Joe Bowers got on and started asking me some foolish questions, but I told him to give me a rewriteman fast; I had a bulletin that was good for a replate. Bowers was a boor but a newspaperman. He gave me the rewriteman, and I dictated a fast bulletin on the Governor's call to Johnny.

The *Trib* man overheard me and came running over.

"Where did you get this?" he shouted.

I pointed to Johnny. "He just got a call from the Governor."

In a moment Johnny was surrounded by shouting reporters and photographers and TV announcers who kept poking their mikes and waving notebooks, bellowing pleading questions.

I leaned over and kissed Connie on the cheek.

"Good-bye, Connie, and lots of luck," I whispered in her ear. "Take care of him; he's a great guy."

She gave me a startled look. "Duke! Where are you going?"

"On the Martini Special. Tell Johnny I'll be in touch."

She tried to push through the crowd, but a sweating TV crew dragging a lamp blocked her.

"Duke! You're coming back?" she cried above the tumult.

"Maybe," I said. "Maybe."

It seemed as if half the courthouse was trying to crowd into the press room. I had lost a button and a good shine by the time I reached the lobby. I was heading for the revolving doors when a big hand pulled me back.

"Just where do you think you're going?" Johnny asked.

"I want out, Johnny. My job is finished. Yours has just begun."

"*Our* job," he said with emphasis. "I told the Governor I wasn't interested unless I could pick my staff with no interference. He told me no politics. I pick who I want." He stabbed me with a finger. "And I want you."

"Look, Johnny, I can't. I wired Gwen I would be on that plane tonight. We're going to be married, and I'm going to write—"

"Okay, get married," he said. "We'll make it a double ceremony. The writing waited this long; it can wait a little longer. No investigation lasts forever."

He ignored my protests and pushed me through the revolving door.

"I'm not asking you, Duke," he said softly, "I'm telling you. And I'm the spokesman for a lot of people. Action Jackson, for one. How about Tom Murphy? And Jackson's sister. And don't forget Strasser. Sure he's a creep, but he stuck with us, didn't he? And Vickie? Did she have guts that night in Jersey?" He asked fiercely, "And what about Julian? What about him, Duke?"

"He's gone, Johnny," I said. "Our part is over."

"The hell it is," he said roughly. "It won't be over until McShane is in jail and Ryder destroyed so there can't be any more McShanes."

His voice lowered. "I checked last night with some old buddies in Washington. I was on that damned phone until almost three o'clock. Ryder's on a spot—a big spot. He's been pulling wires like hell since you hit him with that conflict-of-interests story in the penthouse. But maybe it's too late. That jughead senator has managed to shift the Federal appropriation for Ryder's project over to his committee. Now Ryder's frantic. He's leaving for Washington tonight and told Connie not to expect him for several days. She said he never looked more worried. Their phone has been ringing constantly."

He took a deep breath. "This is your baby, Duke. You gave it to me on a gold platter—from your little girl friend Anonymous." He clutched my arm. "I won't take no, Duke."

Then he was gone in a whirl of revolving glass doors.

I started down that long marble canyon toward the street, my heart bursting, my mind tormented with questions and doubts, when suddenly Connie was at my side.

"Duke, you have to help him."

"My God, how much can I do?"

"I know how much you've done, Duke," she whispered.

"Frankly, Connie, I don't think you do," I said. "I know you love Johnny. I know you would do anything for him."

"I may never know how much."

The way she said it made me stop.

"Did you ever hear of an Anonymous Friend?" she whispered.

I froze.

"I was the one who called you that night, Duke," she said in a small voice. "At first I was going to tell Johnny, but I felt that would be putting him in a horrible position."

"Then you—"

She looked at me, her eyes glistening. "—informed on my own father? Yes, Duke."

"You know Johnny has been working on that information?"

"He told me he was on the phone all night with Washington."

"Connie." I held her hand tightly. "This could ruin your father, maybe send him to jail for years."

"He's destroying innocent people, Duke," she said. "I could hear him on the phone. He was like a"—she groped for the word—"a Nazi. Yes, a Nazi! Anyone could be sacrificed. And would be. He even told the senator that. He's ruthless. I'm afraid of his world, Duke; we must not let it exist any more. It must be destroyed, his kind of people— McShane . . . Here come the reporters," she said, and raised up on tiptoe to kiss my cheek as the small pack of reporters and photographers descended on me.

"Hey, Duke," the AP said, "my office said the Governor has announced De Lorenzo's appointment."

"So what?"

"So Johnny said he just appointed you Special Assistant to the Prosecutor. What do you say?"

The Journal-American said impatiently, "I can just make the Starlight, Duke."

I started back to the lobby.

"What are you going to do?" AP asked.

"Well, I'll tell you the first thing . . ."

"What's that?" they asked.

"Call the Coast," I said. "I have to make arrangements for a wedding."

Across the lobby, Johnny, with Connie, was surrounded by a circle of admirers. One, an Assistant D.A. who had avoided him for weeks, was patting him on the back. A tall, distinguished man came by and shook his hand. He was head of the County Bar Association.

That lonely, barren road we had faced less than an hour ago certainly was becoming a populated highway!

Where had they been when the paper was blank? I wondered, and then headed for the nearest phone booth.

HORAN'S BOONDOCKS,
March, 1965

Horan, James.   The seat of power

bW